Nadia's Song

Forge Books by Soheir Khashoggi

Mirage
Mosaic
Nadia's Song

Nadia's Song

Soheir Khashoggi

A TOM DOHERTY ASSOCIATES BOOK
NEW YORK

NADIA'S SONG

Copyright © 1999 by Soheir Khashoggi

Originally published in 2000 in Great Britain by Bantam Books/Transworld Publishers,
a division of The Random House Group Ltd.

This book is printed on acid-free paper.

A Forge Book
Published by Tom Doherty Associates, LLC
175 Fifth Avenue
New York, NY 10010

www.tor.com

Forge® is a registered trademark of Tom Doherty Associates, LLC.

Library of Congress Cataloging-in-Publication Data

Khashoggi, Soheir.
    Nadia's song / Soheir Khashoggi.—1st ed.
        p. cm.
    "A Tom Doherty Associates book."
    ISBN 0-765-31236-0 (acid-free paper)
    EAN 978-0765-31236-5
    1. Mothers and daughters—Fiction. 2. Illegitimate children—Fiction. 3. Missing
children—Fiction. 4. Plantation life—Fiction. 5. Single mothers—Fiction. 6.
Women singers—Fiction. 7. Egypt—Fiction.

PS3561.H29 N33 2005
813'.54—dc22

                                                                    2004066418

First Forge Edition: July 2005

Printed in the United States of America

0 9 8 7 6 5 4 3 2 1

This book is dedicated to
the memory of my dear nephew,
Dodi al Fayed.
From the day you were born,
I loved you as a precious baby brother.
And you, as a gentle caring adult,
always treated me with love and kindness.
Although you are gone,
in my heart you will live forever.

ACKNOWLEDGMENTS

I am indebted to Lillian Africano for her great work, her wonderful motivation, and interest in making this book possible. I am deeply grateful for all the help she has given me to relive the fascination of Alexandria, the great, mysterious, exciting, and beautiful city in which I grew up. I always longed to write a story that relates to the wonders of Egypt. Lillian, as always it has been a pleasure working with you. Thank you.

To my dearest sister Assia, thank you for your love and care, and always being there for me. What a great and unforgettable life we had in Alexandria.

To all the wonderful people who lived and knew the beauty of Egypt, thank you for all your support, and especially to Minnie, thank you for all your love, warmth, and friendship during all these years.

Finally, I want to pay tribute to my wonderful daughters, Samiha, Naela, Farida, and Hana. They have supported me through some dark days and their love and care means the world to me.

And lest I forget, to the one who stood by me through my ups and downs, my dear and faithful friend, Bob.

.

The Nightingale's Daughter

Alexandria, Egypt, 1983

The keening of the women was deafening, painful, the high-pitched mourning ululation of the Middle East rising from a half-million throats. The corniche was a river of black, hiding the blue sea beyond.

Walking behind the coffin, Gabrielle tried to shut out the sound. The primeval grief that it expressed seemed to have nothing to do with her own. It was real, but it belonged to some other world, a world outside her heart.

For the second time in her life, Gabrielle Misry was attending her mother's funeral.

Ahead, a pocket of the crowd surged toward the coffin. Soldiers pushed them back, not gently: Karima Ahmad had been legendary for her performances for the troops at Egypt's war-fronts and revered for her charity toward wounded veterans when the fighting was over; no one was going to disrupt her final journey. The pallbearers them-selves were decorated combat heroes from each of the nation's armed services. Gaby could see that some of them were weeping. According to the newspapers, men had fought each other for the privilege of carrying Karima to her rest.

Individual voices separated themselves from the roar: "Good-bye, Karima, we love you," or "Why did you leave us, *Karawan?*" *Karawan.* Nightingale. The nickname reflected the pure, heartbreaking beauty of Karima's voice and the natural, unadorned virtuosity with which she sang.

The professional in Gaby could not help comparing the scene around her with the only similar one she had ever witnessed. Six years earlier, as part of a feature piece for NBC, she had covered the funeral procession in Cairo of Um Kalthum, Egypt's greatest singer and Karima's heroine, mentor, and friend.

The crowds had been larger then, far larger, but that funeral had been in Cairo. And Um Kalthum had been more than a legend. Business, traffic, talk—everything—stopped all over the Arab world when her voice came on the radio. It was said that President Nasser himself would never schedule a speech, no matter how important, at the hour of an Um Kalthum broadcast.

A middle-aged woman rushed forward, wailing. "The lost daughter! God be merciful to you, poor girl." Someone pulled her away.

The lost daughter, thought Gaby. *Nadia.* Me.

Suddenly it all seemed too much—the crowd, the noise, the Alexandrine sun, the bobbing black coffin. Her mother was dead at fifty-three. Why?

A strong hand gripped her elbow.

"You're all right?" General Farid Hamza, looming up like a battle tank, looked at her with concern.

"Yes, it's nothing," she told him. For an instant she thought of her father, wishing he were here. But of course, given the circumstances, he had made the right choice.

Hamza stayed at her side, a supporting strength—much, Gaby realized, as he must have been for Karima, until the thing happened from which he could not protect her.

When Gaby first met the general, years earlier, she had assumed that he and Karima were lovers. That assumption had turned out to be wrong. What the two had was something very different: a perfect friendship grounded on the granite of Farid's unshakable devotion.

Hamza's face was a bronze mask of sorrow, but he shed no tears. On Gaby's left her uncle, Karima's brother Omar, had no such control over his grief, crying like a child and calling on the beneficent and merciful God to take him with his sister to paradise.

"It's all right, Uncle," Gaby tried to soothe him, but he shook his head wildly, unconsolable.

The authorities evidently had learned a lesson from the funeral of Um Kalthum, where the crowd had grown so overwrought that the coffin had to be placed in an ambulance to protect it from the mourners. The procession on foot today was merely a concession to tradition, covering less than a mile. A line of soldiers kept the crowds at bay while the pallbearers in their dress uniforms slid the coffin into a hearse for the final journey to the cemetery where Karima would be buried beside her husband.

In a break from tradition Hamza had arranged for a military car for Karima's family, so that Gaby could have a few moments' respite from the thousands of hungry eyes. He opened the door for her. Omar, still weeping, climbed in the other side. As Gaby slipped gratefully into the shelter of the car, she saw a camera lens pointed directly at her from the crowd. There were photographers everywhere. In some Muslim countries they would have had their Nikons ripped from their necks, but this was Egypt.

Something made Gaby watch as the man took his shot and lowered the camera. His eyes reached out and locked with hers; it was Sean McCourt, a world-famous photojournalist who chased conflict as others hunted for treasure. Sean had been a hero of hers once, and, for a short time, perhaps something more. And then he had slipped in and out of her life, like a beautiful dream that disappeared by morning.

In Sean's eyes was the same concern Gaby had seen in Farid Hamza's. Then a sad little smile played on his lips and he raised his hand—a hello across the years. Hail and farewell. Tomorrow he might be in Afghanistan or Argentina. That was the life of Sean McCourt.

General Hamza closed the door.

It was over.

Gaby lingered at her uncle's villa, still trying to piece things together, to make sense of the senseless death that had stolen her mother. Omar was speaking to her of legal details, explaining that Karima had never made a will. Under Egyptian law, two-thirds of her estate went to her brother, one-third to her daughter. It was a great deal of money. "You must take half," he told Gaby, his voice hoarse from weeping. "The law is unfair."

"No. I don't need it, and I'd rather not have the complications. Lawyers."

"Well," said Omar distractedly, "it will all be yours someday, I imagine." He had never married, never had children of his own. The gossips said it was because of his devotion to his sister and to his many charities.

From time to time friends of Omar's stopped in to offer condolences. They seemed mostly to be men like him, men with many business and political connections. Some spoke briefly with him about this or that venture in the marketplace or shift of power in the Government. Some seemed worried. Things had changed greatly with the assassination of Anwar Sadat. Suddenly the ground was not so firm.

In a moment when she was alone with her uncle, Gaby finally raised the question she had been asking herself ever since she heard the news of Karima's death.

"Uncle, why? I can't believe she died the . . . the way they say. Can you?"

Karima had died in her hotel room in Damascus while on a concert tour. Out of respect for an icon adored by the entire Arab world, the Syrian authorities had been deliberately vague about the circumstances, but soon news reports were saying that it had been an overdose: barbiturates and alcohol, the latter more shocking to good Muslims than the former. With the word out, the Damascus police confirmed that, from all evidence, the great singer had indeed died in such a manner.

"I don't believe it," Omar now said flatly. But then he waved a helpless hand. "Ah, but who knows? The world she lived in—all that adoration—it was so different from ours. Of course, you know something of fame yourself. But Karima . . . she was beyond fame. And who knows what that does to a person."

He sank wearily into a chair. "We'll always wonder, you and I, my dearest niece. But please, please, let's talk of something else. This hurts too much."

The sorrow etched in her uncle's face persuaded Gaby to drop the subject. Not long afterward, she bade him good-bye. Before leaving Alexandria she paid a visit to Henry and Catherine Austen, the elderly couple who had employed Karima's father. Only a few people—one fewer, with Karima gone—knew that the Austens were Gabrielle's grandparents. Omar was one of those who knew, but he despised the Austens: Henry because he was English and Catherine because she had denied her Egyptian heritage.

Farid Hamza was with the old couple, who seemed shattered by the loss of Karima. Gaby comforted them as best she could. As Hamza was leaving, she managed a moment alone with him.

"Thank you for all your kindness, General. But please, I have to ask . . . You knew my mother as well as anyone. How can this have happened?"

Hamza shook his head. "I don't know, child. It makes no sense. But when I went to Damascus to bring . . . your mother back, I spoke with the head of Syrian internal security, an old friend. He assured me that there was no mistake."

"She was so young," Gaby said softly, her voice breaking. "It just isn't fair. I thought we'd have time together, time to make up for what we lost. Years and years."

"I, too." Once again the strong hand touched her arm. "Be brave, Gabrielle. Your mother loved you with all her soul. Allah wills many things that we cannot understand, and can hardly bear, but we must accept them all the same."

No, Gaby thought, I can't. I can't accept losing her again, not this way. I can't accept that my mother was a drug addict, an alcoholic. The Nightingale had been more than just a performer; she had been her country's voice, its storyteller. Karima had sung of Egypt's glories, of its sorrows and its triumphs—and Egypt had loved her for it. And now, to end like this, in such a sordid way . . . no, it was not to be accepted.

She did not argue with the general's fatalism. Though Hamza carried his sorrow more stoically than Omar did, he, too, seemed pained by any discussion of Karima's sad and wretched death. Promising that she would stay in touch—she could see very clearly how much this would mean to her mother's old friend—Gaby impulsively kissed the general and returned to her hotel.

There she found countless telegrams and letters of condolence. One was from Sean McCourt—no message, just a photograph of a field of wild flowers with his signature.

She packed and rang for a cab. Her father would be waiting to comfort her. But of course he wasn't her father—not by blood, anyway.

In the airport people stared at her. Everyone in Egypt knew—or thought they knew—the story of the Nightingale's daughter.

Gabrielle had never felt more alone.

Book One

I

The Cotton Pasha

Alexandria, 1940

Each spring when Cairo began to grow oppressively hot, King Farouk abandoned his two magnificent palaces there and retreated to the caressing sea breezes of Alexandria, where he also maintained two palaces. The older of these, Ras-el-Tin, was the official residence and, as such, the setting for formal state functions heavy with protocol and the oratory of diplomats. For serious pleasure, Farouk preferred Muntaza Palace, a few miles east on the corniche that curved sensuously along the Mediterranean. A five-story fantasy of Florentine architecture with a ten-story bell-tower incongruously attached, Muntaza lounged amid swaying palm trees, its long white balconies smiling out over seventy acres of meticulously groomed gardens and the finest beach in Egypt.

It was a seducer's dream, an oasis of exotic flowers, flights of bright-plumed birds imported from the Sudan, and gazelles wandering free, tame enough to drink from the hidden pools where, in later years, the king would indulge in erotic water games with whichever of his uncounted mistresses was currently most favored. By moonlight, accord-

ing to visitors well qualified to judge such matters, the palace may have been the most romantic place on earth.

In short, Muntaza was fun, and in the spring of 1940, Farouk badly needed fun. He was just twenty, a ruler for only three years, a husband for two, yet already his world seemed to be collapsing. His wife, Farida, had recently given birth to their second child, but, like the first, it was a girl. Just as no Arab male was fully a man until he had a son, no monarch was fully a king until he had a male heir. In the aftermath of the bitter disappointment an estrangement had developed between husband and wife, and now Farouk had reason to believe that Farida was having, or at least contemplating, an affair with a dashing young air-force pilot who, unfortunately, happened to be a distant relation of his.

And then there was the war that was destroying Europe. Egypt remained neutral, but for how long? Two hundred thousand Italian troops stood massed on the Libyan border, and Alexandria was under nightly blackout. As for the Germans, no one knew when or where they might strike, but few doubted that the blow would come. Meanwhile the British were pouring in by the thousand to protect the Suez Canal, the lifeline of their empire. Nor were they appreciative of Farouk's efforts to keep his country out of the conflict. It was quite possible, he knew, that they would depose him. They could accomplish the task at any time with a few tanks—and there were more than a few British tanks in Egypt.

Worst of all, at least from the young monarch's viewpoint, his good looks had begun to suffer from the strain. His hairline was receding and he added weight daily—if he wasn't careful, he would soon turn down-right chubby.

But if there was anything Farouk was not, it was a worrier, and his cure for this multitude of ills was the one he would adopt in every crisis to the end of his life.

He threw a party.

"Oh, it's perfect!" said Catherine Austen to her husband as their carriage, in a train of a hundred others, rolled between Muntaza's high gates.

"Lovely indeed," commented Henry Austen in his most agreeable tone. He and his wife had been at odds all morning, as they seemed to be so often these days, and he wanted peace, especially in front of their ten-year-old son, Charles.

"Perfect!" Catherine repeated. "It's just how I picture Tara." She had read *Gone with the Wind* long before the invitation arrived announcing the epic as the theme of a gathering at Muntaza Palace, and had studied it like a catechism in preparing for the party. She had desperately hoped that the cinema version would reach Alexandria before the grand event, but it had not.

Henry had not managed to slog through the novel and possessed only the vaguest mental image of Tara. But he had visited plantations in the American South and he owned plantations in Egypt, and neither greatly resembled the scene before him. It appeared that half of Nubia had been imported to Muntaza's gardens, decked out in costume, and set to pretending to do various rustic tasks amid cotton bales strewn beneath the crape myrtles and bougainvillea.

It was ironic. Henry could trace his fortune—a very large one—directly to the American Civil War. When the northern naval blockade had cut off the flow of southern cotton to England, Egypt had filled the gap. What had been a minor local crop became the country's largest export. Not long after, Henry's grandfather came out, began buying cotton acreage, and steadily grew rich.

Henry's father, like many second-generation millionaires, almost lost it all by spending his time and money in London while hired managers in Egypt robbed him blind. Only the First World War, with its insatiable demand for cotton for everything from uniforms and tents to the fabric skins of airplane wings, saved him from losing the lands. His luck did not last. Two years after the Armistice, he died of a heart attack brought on by drink and overexercise in a London bordello.

His elder son, Henry's brother, inherited the money, the title, albeit a minor one, and the estate in England. Henry got the cotton fields—in the middle of a worldwide crash in cotton prices. No matter. Just past his teens he went out to Egypt himself, fired the managers, built the business step by step into a paying one, became wealthy himself. And now another war was making him richer than he ever dreamed of being or wanted to be.

"Are those black people slaves, Father?" asked Charles. It was his first visit to Muntaza, and he seemed excited. He was wearing what his mother conceived to be the uniform of a Confederate drummer boy.

"They're servants," Henry told him, hoping it was true—God knew, the line between the two categories could be thin in the Middle East.

"But they're pretending to be slaves," Catherine added helpfully. "Why?"

"For money," answered Henry at the same moment as his wife said, "For fun." A brief, uncomfortable silence ensued before Charles laughed at their contretemps.

"I'm told," said Henry to restore the conversation, "that Farouk keeps three hundred full-time gardeners on staff here."

"Really—three hundred?" Any detail of palace life fascinated Catherine. "Can he actually need so many?"

"Oh, I imagine so. Most of them do nothing but water, of course." Henry gazed around bemusedly. "I could cultivate another ten thousand acres with less help than that." Catherine did not respond, and he winced inwardly. Clumsy to have plumped a practical note into what she obviously saw as a fairy tale come to life.

He stole a glance at her. She was, he realized with longing and frustration, as beautiful as ever, her sea-blue eyes picking up a hint of the deep green of her gown—meant to imitate, so she had told him, a dress that Scarlett O'Hara made from a set of curtains. A matching parasol shielded her from the hard noon sun; her creamy skin—the legacy of her English mother, a missionary's daughter—was her pride, zealously protected.

Indeed, except for the jet-black hair inherited from her Egyptian father, Catherine looked like an *Ingliziya*. Yet it was odd, thought Henry: if she had been purely English, he might never have seen her as anything more than a beautiful woman. It was the Egypt in her that lured and fascinated him, that commanded his love, as the land itself commanded it.

His mood darkened as it always did when he skirted the truth of his and Catherine's troubles. They were moving apart—ships passing in the night, that sort of thing—and, as best he could understand it, the reason was that he loved Egypt and the life he had built there, whereas she appeared increasingly to despise both. While he had steadily and happily gone native (as his English friends were all too fond of putting it), she had just as steadily turned her back on the land of her birth and become a raging Anglophile. It seemed to mean nothing to her that he was universally called *pasha,* the highest term of respect that a man could earn in Egypt; in all likelihood she would trade the title in a flash for the poorest baronetcy in Dorset.

They were nearing the palace, and the sound of an orchestra rich with strings welled from the lawn. There would be, Henry knew, another orchestra or two inside; the king was not one to stint on his entertainments.

Henry's string tie had unraveled down the front of his ruffled shirt, and he fumbled at fixing it. According to Catherine, he was costumed as Ashley Wilkes. From what little he had read of the fellow in the book, Henry was uncertain whether to be flattered or appalled.

Catherine watched her husband struggling with his tie. "Here," she finally said. "Let me." His quick grateful smile depressed her. The phrase "wifely duty" flicked through her mind. His teeth were very white against his deep tan—he was as brown from the sun as any Nile peasant. Unavoidable, to be sure, for a planter; still, at any moment the man might start wearing a *galabiyya* and haunting the mosques.

"What's that air they're playing?" he asked.

"The theme from the motion picture," she said. Very like him not to recognize it. She had heard it a hundred times on the wireless.

But Catherine could not sustain her irritability. After all, this was the royal palace. Give that to Henry. He was practically a regular at Muntaza—at Ras-el-Tin as well. The king quite simply liked him—at least, so the wife of an embassy attaché had said. The artfully hidden message, however, was that Henry was perhaps a bit more respectful of the king than befitted an Englishman. The British ambassador himself, Miles Lampson, often and openly referred to Farouk as "the boy."

The carriage halted, and a towering Nubian in the Nile-green silk of the palace livery hurried to hand them down. A splash of greetings met them. Catherine saw with pleasure that the guests were mostly foreigners—mainly British, but liberally sprinkled with Alexandrine Greeks or Syrians, along with the occasional Frenchman or American. Servants hovered with trays of hors-d'oeuvres and drinks. Catherine selected champagne—Château Lafitte-Rothschild '29 for most of the guests, while sweetened fruit juices were available for observant Muslims and the few children.

"Catherine Austen! Miss O'Hara. And Mr. Wilkes, I presume?"

"Jackie! How good to see you," said Catherine, meaning it. Jackie Lampson, the ambassador's absurdly young wife, barely in her twenties, was a lively, lovely little bird of a woman who, despite her notorious flirtatiousness and even despite her doll-like prettiness, had not an enemy in the world.

"I," said Jackie, indicating her own costume, "am the golden-hearted Melanie. Casting against type, I believe it's called."

Miles Lampson loomed up, all six-foot-five and 280 pounds of him, and snapped a salute to Charles. "Military discipline," he said to Henry. "A thing devoutly to be desired these days, but sadly lacking in certain quarters. I suppose I'll have to have a word with our boy."

"With Farouk?" Henry asked. "What's the difficulty?"

"The blackout," said Miles. He had not dressed in costume, but his customary frock suit and bow-tie hardly seemed out of place. He towered over his tiny wife and was nearly forty years older. No one, least of all Catherine, could understand what Jackie was doing married to him.

"One of our ship's captains made an interesting report," Miles went on. "Said he spotted Alex from thirty miles out Saturday night last. What do you suppose the source of the light was?"

"No idea," said Henry.

"We're standing at it. Muntaza Palace. Glowing like a lighthouse." Miles sighed elaborately. "Not saying it was deliberate, of course. But who knows with this lot? Half of them waiting with bated breath for Muhammad Haidar to come goose-stepping in and run us out."

They all smiled, if a little ruefully, at the reference. In a brilliant propaganda ploy, the Germans had planted the rumor that Adolf Hitler was a Muslim, born Muhammad Haidar in a village in Egypt. It was all that the *fellahin* toiling in the fields needed in order to choose sides in the war. Educated Egyptians knew better, of course, but even among them there was a widespread feeling that the Germans could hardly be worse than the British.

"Surely, darling," said Jackie, "we're not going to stand here talking dreariness all day. People are going in. Come along, Catherine. I'll bring this handsome husband of yours. I'm going to exercise all my wiles to bewitch him into dancing with me."

"Your funeral," said Catherine. Henry famously hated to dance and was excruciatingly awkward when forced into it.

Jackie held out her arm for Henry. "Ashley is mah cousin," she said in an attempt at a southern drawl. "And what's a little dance between cousins?"

Inside, Muntaza glittered. Inlaid in gold and jade and topaz, the images of dancing girls in various stages of undress undulated on walls of marble and precious woods. Chandeliers blazed. A menu posted at the entrance to the grand salon promised a feast of twenty courses, quail in sherry, sautéed. Mediterranean prawns, grilled rabbit, figs and soft cheese, a bouillabaisse—Catherine stopped reading. Food was food. What pleased her more was the people: all these lovely women and handsome men costumed as characters from a novel set in a distant era in a land few of them had ever seen. The fact that most of them were English made it perfect.

The salon was crowded. A forty-piece orchestra, silent for the moment, sat at the far end. Jackie was chirping at Henry, who seemed to be at a loss as to how to proceed. Miles had disappeared somewhere along the way, as had Charles with a few other young-sters who had no desire to participate in this dull grown-up ritual.

Catherine felt a light impact on her shoulder. She glanced down to see a pea-sized ball of bread bouncing to the floor. She looked up just in time to see another one arch over Jackie's head and strike Henry in the eye. Henry did not seem surprised. "Your Majesty," he said.

Catherine turned to see the king approaching. Vaguely she recalled Henry telling her about the childish pleasure the young man derived from such pursuits as throwing bread balls at people he regarded as stuffy.

Farouk was laughing. "Henry Pasha, you see what English mili-tary schools did for me—spoiled my aim. I'll never be an artillery-man." He turned to Catherine. He was taller than she remembered. "Endless apologies, madam. Please say you forgive me. Say you'll dance with me to demonstrate your forgiveness."

It happened that quickly. As if by magic the musicians struck up a Strauss waltz and he swept her across the floor. He danced wonder-fully.

"You are the most beautiful woman here," he told her. It sounded like a practiced line—very well practiced. But she reveled in it.

"How is your father?" he asked. It was the last thing she expected. Surely he did not know her father, a modest schoolteacher?

"He was a friend of my father's," Farouk explained as if sensing her doubt. Surely that was a lie too.

"He's well, thank you," she said.

"Why don't you leave your husband and come stay with me?"

Her smile felt frozen. "Your Majesty is in a humorous mood to-night."

"Not at all. It would do wonders for us both." He smiled. There was an almost babyish softness about him but he was very handsome.

He was joking. He had to be. But what if he weren't? The man's reputation! And he was the king—the absolute ruler. There were stories . . .

Catherine smiled back. She didn't know what else to do. One thing was certain, she told herself: she wasn't going to tell the king of Egypt she was nearly old enough to be his mother while waltzing with him.

Farouk frowned sadly. "Alas, alas. It would never work out. I'm a married man." Then he winked and grinned. "But isn't everyone?"

Catherine laughed. It was funny. It was fun. Wasn't it? She wondered if she had drunk too much champagne. What if she had? The whole world had gone mad. Bombs were falling. She was Catherine Kemal, the bourgeois Cairene daughter of an English mother and an Egyptian father. She was married to the richest Englishman in Alexandria. And she was dancing with a charming boy in apparently permanent rut who happened to be a king.

She laughed again and floated on the music.

Henry sipped a pink gin, congratulating himself on having got through his waltz with Jackie without permanent damage to either of them. Catherine was going another round, a foxtrot, with Farouk. On such occasions as this the king did not normally dance twice in succession with the same woman, and Henry might easily have felt alarm. He didn't. He knew Farouk—at least he thought he did. As for Catherine, the obvious fact that she was enjoying herself was all to the good, as far as Henry was concerned. Perhaps it would break her out of the ruddy funk into which she had fallen.

"He's something, isn't he? Our Mr. Farouk?"

An American accent. Henry turned to see a brown-haired, brown-eyed man no older than thirty.

"Jake Farallon," said the American, extending his hand. There was little choice except to shake it.

"Henry Austen."

"I thought I recognized you. The cotton pasha. Pleased to make your acquaintance."

"Likewise I'm sure." Henry found some Americans entirely too forward.

"I really shouldn't be here," said the young man pleasantly. "Wasn't invited. My boss brought me along. I'm with the embassy."

Henry assumed that the fellow was some sort of intelligence agent.

Farallon nodded toward the dance floor. "Yeah, Farouk. Funny. When I first came out here, I met this Egyptian fellow whose wife was having a fling with His Highness. Best thing that ever happened to this fellow. Not only did it make him rich, but after the smoke cleared, the wife was crazy for him. Thought he was a hell of a man." He lowered his voice confidingly. "You've heard about the royal equipment, right? Not exactly fit for a king, if you know what I mean."

Henry had heard some tales about "the royal equipment," but he was fond of Farouk and he was not fond of gossip. The royal equipment, he believed, was no one's business—except the king's. He drained his drink. "Excuse me," he said to the American and walked away.

He wandered aimlessly among knots of chatting, laughing men and women, decided on another pink gin, found one. His mood had turned morose again. Regardless of his own opinion of the matter, if the king danced a third time with Catherine, rumors would be all over Alexandria tomorrow.

The sparkling, playful opulence of Muntaza seemed heavy and monotonous. The party was scarcely half an hour old, yet Henry longed for it to end. He wanted to sit at ease on the balcony of his villa, looking out over the city and its harbor, conversing with someone, laughing with someone. Laughing with Catherine as they had done when Charles was a baby.

Ahead Henry saw Ahmed Hassanein, Egypt's most respected scholar and in his younger days a great explorer, who had also served as the king's childhood tutor. Henry was mildly surprised by his presence: gossip had it that Hassanein was immersed in an affair with Queen Nazli, Farouk's widowed mother, and that Farouk deeply resented it.

A young man who looked vaguely familiar was speaking to Hassanein with evident enthusiasm. At his side a young woman so stylish that she could only be French hung on his every word. Newlyweds, guessed Henry, or soon to be.

"Look at one disease alone," the young man was saying. "Bilharzia. Caused—as I'm sure you know, Ahmed Pasha—by a parasite found in the water, attacking the liver, bladder, lungs and central nervous system, eventually killing its victims. There are villages, hundreds of them, where more than half the people are stricken before they reach middle age. No country can go anywhere carrying such a burden. And that's just one disease."

"You're a doctor," said Hassanein simply. "Find a cure."

"Medical research takes money," said the young man. "But money in Egypt goes to other pursuits." He waved a hand to indicate the palace around him.

"I understand," said Hassanein, "but others might not. Some might even find your ideas revolutionary." The word was a warning, not a compliment.

"No doubt they would," muttered the young man.

Henry stepped into the little group and greeted Hassanein. The young man brightened: "Henry Pasha! How good to see you." Realizing that Henry was at a loss, he quickly added, "Tarik Misry— Hassan Misry's son."

"Of course," said Henry. Hassan Misry was an acquaintance, a bureaucrat in the Ministry of Agriculture. "How is your father?"

"Well, thanks be to Allah."

"Forgive my not recognizing you. The last time I saw you, you were just a lad."

"I've been in Paris for several years. At college."

"Taking a medical degree," the young woman amplified proudly.

"My wife, Celine," said Tarik with equal pride.

"Madame. You're newly arrived from France?" he asked them both.

"Two weeks," said Tarik. "And just in time, at that. The Germans won't be stopped."

"That's sad news."

"They're pigs," said Celine with sudden venom.

"It impresses me," said Henry to Tarik, "that at such a time you still think of Egypt. I overheard a bit of what you were saying. I'm of course aware of bilharzia, but I'm hardly a physician. How much money would be needed to make progress?"

Tarik shrugged. "Who knows? Probably millions."

"I can't spare millions, but perhaps I could be of some little help. Stop by my villa at your convenience and we'll talk it over."

"You're too kind." The young doctor seemed genuinely moved. "I'm not a specialist, but I'll try to put together some facts for you. Some work has been done already. Not much, unfortunately."

"Call on me, too, if you'd like," said Hassanein. "I'm not as wealthy as Henry Pasha, but perhaps I can help in other ways."

"I simply don't know what to say. Thank you."

"There you are, darling!" It was Catherine, glowing with pleasure. "What a lovely party!"

"What's become of your dance partner?"

"Oh, he's taken up with Jackie for the moment. I think he means to dance with every woman in the room."

"Ah. All's right with the world then."

Henry made introductions, and Tarik gallantly asked Catherine for the next dance, leaving Henry little recourse except to ask Celine.

The poor girl, he thought as he escorted her to the floor. First the Nazis, and now this.

The sun was setting, but for many of the guests the party was only beginning. Festivities at Muntaza often ran on until dawn. The Austens, however, had Charles to think of, and Henry was adamant on reaching home before the blackout took effect.

Catherine assented grumpily. She had eaten too much and drunk too much and was irritable. She felt like a sleepy child who nevertheless wants to stay awake with the grown-ups. Why couldn't Henry take the boy and let her get a lift home with someone else? Well, of course, that was nonsense. Why was she so tired? There was a time when she could dance for hours. Was she getting old? The thought did nothing to improve her mood.

They found Charles playing Saracens and crusaders in the gardens with a small pack of boys. He was dirty and Catherine scolded him. Then, at a turn in the path, they came upon Farouk and Miles Lampson. The king looked like a scolded child himself; Catherine assumed that Lampson had been lecturing him about the palace's blackout violations.

Farouk looked at them like a drowning man seeing a lifeline. "Henry! You're not leaving, are you? Not yet? There's something I want to show you. You like motor cars, don't you? What about you, young man?"

Charles shyly admitted that he did indeed like motor cars.

The king led the way, collecting other guests as he went—it was obvious that he had no intention of being left alone with Lampson again.

The Muntaza garage was a converted stable nearly as large as the Austens' home, which was far from small. A servant ushered the group in. The place was lighted like a museum. It *was* a museum. Catherine cared little about motor cars, but this collection was breathtaking. Farouk was naming them off: Duesenberg, Bugatti, Rolls-Royce, Packard, Cadillac, on and on. All were bright red—by royal decree, the only red automobiles in all of Egypt.

"And this one," said Farouk, stopping at a beautiful Mercedes coupe. "A wedding gift. Guess who gave it to me." He made a dramatic pause. "Hitler!"

The Englishmen in the group had stopped smiling. Catherine hoped they weren't going to start on politics. She had developed a throbbing headache.

"I also received wonderful gifts from His Majesty King George," Farouk went on, clearly enjoying himself. "A pair of Purdey shotguns, the finest in the world, and—" another pause—"a set of golf clubs!" He took a mock golf swing so comically awkward that even the Englishmen laughed—except for Lampson, who looked as if he were contemplating assassination.

"What do you think, Henry?" the king asked. "Do you see me winning the Open?"

"I think, Your Majesty," said Henry evenly, "that you should hold onto that Mercedes. One day soon, with any luck, it may be the last one on earth."

"Hear, hear," said several voices, and for a moment Farouk looked nonplussed. Then he laughed uproariously. "Spoken like a true Englishman!"

Catherine was astonished—and filled with pride. Henry hated the Germans, of course, and hoped for British victory in the war, but rarely did he make any display of his feelings; Egypt was neutral, and he apparently thought of himself as Egyptian. And now to have said such a patriotic thing—to King Farouk's face in front of a dozen people! Maybe there was hope after all. Maybe he would see his duty clear and take her and Charles home—home to England. She imagined the palatial estate they would have in the green countryside. Henry would take an officer's commission—he wasn't too old, only forty-two. She pictured him in uniform. A war hero. A knighthood, possibly a lordship. Definitely a lordship. Lady Catherine.

The fantasy might have stopped but didn't. There would come a tragic day, soldiers in dress uniform arriving at her door. Addressing Charles as Your Lordship. Even a million pounds would be no consolation—at first. But after a respectable period of mourning . . .

She almost blushed with shame. No decent person would have such thoughts. She hadn't had them. They had happened on their own. God, her head hurt. She needed a drink. She would have one as soon as they got home. Not champagne. Something with medicinal strength.

The king was bidding them good-bye. So was Miles Lampson. The party was moving on.

As she walked back through the gardens, the fantasy flicked through her thoughts again. All on its own.

———

Mustafa Ismail glanced in the rearview mirror. Madam looked under the weather. The pasha was sitting in back, not in front with Mustafa as he usually did. Mustafa knew why. It was because Madam was under the weather and the pasha didn't want to annoy her. It annoyed her for the pasha to sit up front. Mustafa had overheard her berating him about it once. Why, she demanded to know, did he embarrass her in this way, treating the driver, a servant, like his dearest friend? He was an Englishman. He ought to act like one. The English were the masters. The Egyptians were the servants. That was the way it was. Why did he wish to act like a servant?

Mustafa would not have allowed his wife to speak to him like that. On the other hand, it seemed to him that Madam was right. If he were in the pasha's place, he certainly wouldn't sit with the servants.

Mustafa considered himself a lucky man. He had been one of the *fellahin*, a common peasant when the pasha came to Egypt. But he worked hard and honestly, and one day the pasha called him out of the fields and sent him to learn to drive. He had been the pasha's driver ever since. His house in the servants' section was made of brick and had three rooms, each one larger than the mud hut in which he had grown up. He had a wife and children who also worked for the pasha. All of this put Mustafa as far above the *fellahin* as the pasha was above Mustafa, and he had no desire to pretend otherwise. So, yes, in this respect it seemed to him that Madam was right.

But on the other hand again, despite the pasha's occasional undignified ways, he was an excellent master. A fair one. Which was very good, because at the moment there was a crisis at the villa that a harsher master might blame on Mustafa, a senior man expected to keep order among the other servants.

"Mustafa, slow down!"

He eased the accelerator slightly. "A thousand apologies, madam."

"I have a splitting headache, and the man drives fifty miles an hour," Madam said to the pasha.

Feeling a need to justify himself, Mustafa decided to break the bad news now. "A thousand apologies, Pasha. I was going fast because there is a little problem that I thought you would want to know of."

"What problem?"

"One of the girls—Fariza—is sick." Fariza was more than sick. She was almost certainly dying, if not already dead.

"What's wrong with her?"

"I . . . I don't know, Pasha." Mustafa could not bring himself, in front of Madam, to say that the girl, who was unmarried, had tried to abort herself and that now no one could stop the bleeding.

"Hmm. I'll have a look at her directly once we're there."

The villa was only minutes away, just off the corniche. Madam and Master Charles went into the house. The pasha accompanied Mustafa to the servants' quarters. On the way, Mustafa told him all he knew.

The pasha took one look at Fariza, who was ashen and whimpering that she was cold. "Get some blankets. The girl's in shock. Mustafa, go back to the palace. Ask for Dr. Tarik Misry. Use my name and say it's an emergency—a matter of life or death."

Mustafa hesitated. "It's nearly dark, Pasha. The blackout."

"Damn the blackout! Use the headlamps. If someone stops you, tell them what I said. Go!"

Mustafa went.

Charles had taken a bath and it was past his bedtime, but he was curious about what was happening in the servants' quarters. All he knew was that Fariza was sick and a doctor was there, along with his father. He decided to see for himself.

Slipping out the back door, he was for once glad of the blackout. With the thick curtains in place, there was no chance his mother would look out and see where he was going. She didn't like for him to play with the servants—especially not with his friend Karima. She could get very angry about it when she was drinking.

He didn't understand it. He had played with Karima as long as he could remember. Not when there were other boys around, of course: Karima was a girl and a year younger than he was. But he liked her. They talked about all kinds of things. He even thought that she was pretty—although he kept that a very dark secret.

His mother said he was too old to play with Karima. But his mother didn't know what Karima was like. She wasn't silly like some little girls. She knew things. All the servants, maybe all Egyptians, did. Things about babies, and about men and women. Things his parents didn't know, or at least didn't talk about. These things Karima talked about quite naturally.

He found her in the darkness near the house where Fariza was.

"Hello, Charles."

"Hello, Karima. What's the matter with Fariza?"

"She's bleeding."

"Do you think she's going to die?"

"I heard the doctor say that she might not. It doesn't really matter, though."

Charles was shocked. "What do you mean?"

"Her life is over anyway. She'll probably kill herself from the shame. Or maybe her brothers will kill her."

"What are you talking about? Why kill her? What shame?"

"She was going to have a baby and she has no husband."

Charles began to understand, although he still couldn't see the point of killing anyone.

"They might throw her down a well," said Karima matter-of-factly. "They do that sometimes in the country, where my parents are from."

"But why?"

"I told you. The shame. But don't let's talk about it. It's bad luck. Tell me what it was like today—at the palace."

He told her the high points as he remembered them. The gardens. The food. The king's motor-car collection.

Her eyes went wide. "You saw the king? He talked to you?"

"Yes."

"And the queen?"

"I didn't see her."

"Oh, it sounds so . . . beautiful! I wish . . ."

"What?"

"Nothing."

They had wandered near Karima's house. Suddenly, from the shadows, came an angry voice: "Karima! What do you think you're doing?"

It was her older brother, Omar.

"I was only talking with Charles."

"Only talking with Charles! Only talking with a boy in the dark! Go inside. Now!"

Karima bowed her head but didn't move. Omar grabbed her roughly by the arm.

"What's the matter, Omar?" said Charles. He wasn't afraid of the older boy. Omar might be twelve, but he was still a servant.

"Nothing that you would understand," Omar answered with a growl, "you, or anyone like you." With that he dragged Karima into the house.

Charles stood in the darkness. It made no sense. He and Omar had been friends once. But lately it seemed that Omar was angry with everyone. Why? He wondered if this was something he ought to mention to his father. No, better not. He didn't want to get Karima into more trouble than she was in already.

He walked slowly back to the villa.

"You'll learn to listen to me, *ya bint*."

Karima was afraid to answer her brother or even to look at him. She didn't think she had done anything wrong, but the way Omar was acting, it was as if she had disgraced herself. She wished her mother and father were at home. They must be with Fariza. And now she was alone with her very angry brother.

"Do you know what happens to girls who dishonor their families? Look at Fariza. Just a dirty whore."

She knew that he was right. She said nothing.

"But do you know what else can happen to girls who run wild? Do you?"

She did know—something at least—but she shook her head.

"They cut you—here." He pressed a knuckle into her groin and she cried out.

"Yes, it hurts, doesn't it? They cut you. Not like Fariza. They cut part of you away."

She had heard the stories, stories told in whispers among the women.

"Do you want me to talk with Father?" pressed Omar.

Again she shook her head.

"Then always obey me and never dishonor your family."

He walked out, slamming the door behind him.

Karima stood without moving until she was sure he was gone. She had been afraid in her life, but she had never felt as if she would *always* be afraid. That was how she felt now. "Allah the all-merciful, our only protector," she began, but the words of the prayer seemed only words.

One thing always helped. One thing always pleased others, even grown-ups, as well as herself.

Softly, she began to sing.

2

Waiting for Muhammad Haidar

Egypt, 1942

Despite clinging to official neutrality in the war that was engulfing the planet, Egypt in 1942 resembled a military base. In Cairo the British encampment, surrounded by a high wall and barbed wire, stretched from Tahrir Square all the way to the Nile. British officers were every-where: riding in horse-drawn carriages, visiting friends living in the lux-urious apartments along the Nile, dining at Shepheard's Hotel, the Ritz, or the Cecil, sampling pastries at Groppi's, enjoying the lavish entertain-ments at the Cairo Opera House. For those who had money—and even the enlisted men were well paid by Egyptian standards—there were no shortages. Liquor, cigarettes, toiletries, custom-made uniforms, imported foods—all these were abundant. For soldiers accustomed to hardship and privation, this corner of the war often seemed unreal, and occasionally even glamorous.

Neutrality made for surreal associations. German spies mingled in the best circles, also enjoying the elegant clubs and restaurants and all the European luxuries that Egypt had to offer, but at one-third the prices of Berlin or Paris.

In Alexandria, base to a British fleet, the military presence was more nautical but the spies no less active. At the Automobile Club war gossip was served up in abundance along with the house specialty, lobster-tail-sized grilled Mediterranean shrimp.

For most British civilians in Egypt, word from home, where German bombers were pounding London nightly, was far more compelling than events occurring in the desert just hours to their west. Indeed, for a time, the fighting on the local front provided the only good news that Britons heard. Striking in December 1940 from Mersa Matruh, where Antony and Cleopatra once frolicked on the snow-white beaches by the glass-clear sea, a British force of only 31,000 took 38,000 Italian prisoners in four days. By February the tally of enemy casualties and captives exceeded 150,000; the Italian army in North Africa had simply ceased to exist.

For many Egyptians the stunning victory engendered mixed feelings at best, confirming as it did a gloomy belief that the English were somehow invincible. How would Egypt ever rid herself of them?

The answer to that question seemed to arrive in the spring of 1941, when a German panzer commander named Rommel landed in Tripolitania and launched a lightning campaign that swept across Libya to Tobruk and beyond. Rommel's Afrika Korps was forced to mark time while Germany devoted its resources to the monumental—and ultimately fatal—invasion of Russia, but with the coming of another spring the Desert Fox sent his tanks eastward again. By June he was at El Alamein, just sixty-five miles from Alexandria; on quiet nights the sounds of distant shelling could be heard in the city's western suburbs.

Although Rommel again halted to await supplies and reinforcements, it appeared that nothing could stop him from rolling up the British all the way to the Suez Canal. In Cairo jubilant students chanted "Long live Rommel." All along the Nile, peasants in their mud huts eagerly awaited the coming of "Muhammad Haidar"—Hitler.

It was easy, as always.

Omar spotted the two officers among the shops just off the corniche. They were laboring with awkward armfuls of purchases. Both men were sweating freely, as the British always did, even on balmy late-spring mornings such as this one.

He approached smiling and bowing. "Colonel sirs," he said, "a thousand pardons. I carry for you, colonel sirs?"

The men, who wore the insignia of lieutenants in His Majesty's artillery, exchanged a glance.

"Why not?" said one. "What's a couple of shillings in this bloody heat?"

They loaded Omar with their packages. "I good carry, sirs," he smiled. "You see." Practice had in fact made him quite proficient at the task, for which he skipped school at least twice a week.

The lieutenants visited a few more shops. In one, run by a Greek, they vanished into a back room and reappeared smelling of liquor and bearing packages that obviously held bottles. In the course of their outing, the two—like most of their countrymen—paid Omar little more attention than they would a pack animal. He knew that to them he was merely an ignorant, impoverished native mouthing broken English. The thought that he might speak their language nearly as well as they did simply would never occur to them. Thus he was able to learn the name of their colonel, that they expected to be at El Alamein within the fortnight, and that one of their sergeants had been complaining about possible damage to their ammunition, some sort of corrosion that had taken place at sea.

It wasn't much, but it was something.

At the end of the young officers' shopping jaunt, Omar loaded their purchases into a horse cab and accepted a few coins with a grinning show of gratitude. God willing, the two men would soon be corpses in the desert.

Now came the part of the job that was sometimes distasteful. Skirting through narrow back streets, he arrived at a nondescript building near Alexandria's old quarter. Here lived a man known to him only as Herr Hans. The German was perhaps thirty, blond, very pale, with a softness of muscle that Omar assumed resulted from lack of exercise. His Arabic was gibberish, but he spoke passable English.

Omar made his report and, meager though it was, received considerably more for it than the Englishmen had paid him for carrying thirty pounds of packages. Then Hans offered a cigarette, and Omar knew that this was one of the days when more than information was required. When the cigarette was finished Hans crooned a few words in German, lifted Omar's *galabiyya,* and began fondling him, at the same time unbuttoning his trousers and stroking himself. The whole business made Omar faintly queasy—he could feel himself shrivel at the man's soft, insistent touch. That hardly seemed to matter to Hans, who after a short time made little moans of pleasure and spurted onto the floor.

As usual after these episodes, the German became curt, unpocketing a bit more change and waving a hand in dismissal. Just another dirty Gyppo after all, thought Omar, but he hid his anger. Hans was his only weapon—for now—with which to strike at the British; and of course there was the money, no point in denying that.

On the street the pleasant idea came to him that even if, God forbid, the British won the war, he could turn Hans over to them. Undoubtedly there would be a reward.

Classes were out at the British Boys' School, and Charles found himself with little to do. Many of his friends were gone, to Cairo or further, their families fleeing at the approach of Rommel. One boy in his form had returned to England the year before, when the Germans were still at Tripoli; two months later the boy and his mother were killed by a Luftwaffe bomb in London. The boy had not been especially popular but now everyone spoke as if he had been a close friend.

The villa was empty. Charles assumed that his father was at one of his clubs, or perhaps doing business with his banker or cotton factor. Mother would be shopping or indulging her latest interest, volunteer work for the Red Crescent. The latter seemed out of character to Charles, if only because the organization was specifically Islamic. But Mum was a demon on the war effort.

In his room he idly toed a soccer ball. Summer had arrived full force. Maybe he should go to the beach and cool off with a swim. But you couldn't swim forever and the beach was hot and no one he knew would be there. He decided to settle for a cold drink. Since even the servants seemed not to be around, he went to the kitchen himself. There he encountered Karima.

"Oh! Hello, Charles," she smiled before turning her eyes demurely downward.

"Hello, Karima. What brings you here?"

"I came to see if anything is needed. Um-Rashid's back hurts, and she's resting. I thought . . ."

"Oh. Well, I was looking for something to drink."

"What would you like? Milk? Lemonade?"

"Lemonade."

"I'll make it."

Charles watched as Karima sliced and squeezed lemons. He realized that he had not been alone with her since—when? The night of the palace party. The thought made him acutely self-conscious. "How have you been?" he asked. "Well, I hope."

"Oh yes. Very well."

"Good."

A quick glance from the dark eyes. "I suppose—I mean I've heard it said—that you'll be leaving soon."

"I?" said Charles. "Leaving for where?"

"For England. You and the mistress. Maybe not the pasha."

"Who says this?"

"It's common talk." Karima didn't want to say that the speculation was her father's. "Because of the Germans."

"Rommel? Don't count on it. Our side have only begun to fight." Charles heard the bravado in his own words. They were the same ones his schoolmates used. But did anyone really believe them? Only days earlier Rommel had been driving everything before him and there had been near-panic among the British in Alexandria. Why the Afrika Korps had not advanced beyond El Alamein was a mystery, but no one expected the respite to last.

"I hope the English win," said Karima. "For your sake. And for the pasha and the mistress, of course."

Charles was pleased. So many Egyptians, as far as he could tell, were tacitly or even openly pro-German. He was glad that Karima was not among them.

She chipped ice with a pick. An abundance of ice, even in full summer, was one proof of the Austens' wealth.

The lemonade was cold and sweet. "Have some," invited Charles.

Karima smiled shyly. "Oh no," she said, "I couldn't." Sharing a refreshment with a member of the pasha's family, that just wasn't done.

"Please."

She considered for a moment. Well, if Charles insisted, she should oblige him. "Thank you." She poured a tiny amount without ice, drank it quickly, and washed the glass.

There was a moment when neither had anything to say. It was odd, thought Charles: he was older than Karima—his body was changing in noticeable and disturbing ways—yet he could not think of her as a little girl; if anything, she seemed to be the older.

"I've missed you," he said suddenly, and immediately blushed. "Our talks, I mean. The old days."

"I too."

A voice came from outside: "Karima, where are you?" It was her mother.

"Here, *Ummi*. Master Charles wanted lemonade." She turned to him and whispered quickly, "You know my brother. It's hard for me to leave the house at night. But if you hear me singing, I don't know, any song in English, it means I have a little while—for us to talk."

By the time Charles managed to stammer, "I'll be listening," she was out the door.

Putting one's affairs in order. The very words wore a shroud of gloom, fitting Henry Austen's mood. He had spent much of the morning with his solicitor reviewing his will, particularly as it pertained to Charles. Henry had not the slightest fear that, should something happen that put him out of the picture, Catherine would not do the very best for their son—their love of the boy was the one thing between them of which he had no doubt. Still, it did no harm to take careful measures. And Catherine . . . the truth was that Henry could no longer say what it was that she wanted.

When the lawyer had tidied up the last comma and codicil, a meeting had followed with a very different kind of man: a crusty New Zealander who ran a two-aircraft commercial flying operation. Henry had kept him on a distinctly stiff retainer since the first days of Rommel's June blitz. It was now August, and it was clear that a major battle was in the offing in the desert just to the west. If the Germans won they could be in Alex in a day or two. The trains would be mobbed and the roads choked with refugees. The pilot was paid to be on four hours' call.

"One change in our arrangement, if it comes to it," Henry told him. "You'll have only two passengers. I'll be staying on."

The New Zealander glanced sharply at him, then shrugged. "Like the Yanks say, the customer's always right."

Henry had made the decision only that morning, although he had mulled it over for weeks. He supposed he had known in his heart all along that he would stay, and it was a relief to have made it more or less official. Even so, his decision was why he was lunching at the Automobile Club. At home he would sooner or later have to discuss the matter with Catherine—and that would touch off a miniature war all its own.

The club did little to lift his spirits. Virtually the only English faces were those of army or navy officers. So many of the regulars were absent: the young men and some of the older ones gone to war, the rest simply gone. Henry had an excellent trout amandine—that at least had not changed—then retreated to the bar for a gin and tonic. On his second round he found himself in conversation with a retired brigadier named Mullins, who had first served in the Boer

War, and a middle-aged Italian count with beautiful manners, beautiful clothes, a beautiful old name, and—so far as Henry could tell—nothing else whatsoever.

After the obligatory polite chat about the weather, the inevitable topic arose: Rommel.

"I ask myself one thing," said the count. "Why does he stop? Why does he wait?" He had a northern Italian accent that made "ask" come out as *ashk* and "stop" as *shtop*.

"He stops and he waits," said Mullins authoritatively, "because Hitler is obsessed with Russia. The madman simply will not heed the lessons of history. Napoleon's Grand Army froze in the Russian snows. His own *Wehrmacht* did the same this winter past. Mark me well: if the Jerries fail to take Moscow before the snow flies this year, the Reich is finished."

"Hear, hear," said Henry obligingly. The general's argument, bombastic though it might be, seemed sound enough. But Henry had heard many unfulfilled predictions since the war began, and winter, even in Russia, was far away.

"And this new general," said the Italian. "He is a good one?" He was referring to Bernard Law Montgomery, freshly assigned as field commander of the British forces in North Africa.

"Sir Bernard," said Mullins dryly, "will never be the most popular chap in an officers' mess, but he's a tiger in a fight, and that's the main thing, what?"

"Ah," nodded the count. Henry recalled hearing that the fellow was a spy, but such accusations were everywhere these days, leveled against almost any European not in uniform; probably Henry himself had been called a spy behind his back.

"But you have a point," the general was saying. "Rommel should move soon if he means to move at all. We're far stronger now than we were two months ago."

It was true. Henry had never seen such military activity in his life as was taking place now in Alex.

"I fought for my country in the last war," said the Italian. "But in this one, I would only be fighting for that pig Hitler."

"Quite," said the general.

The count's remark seemed off the subject to Henry. Perhaps the man was feeling the effects of the camparinetes he was sipping. In any case Henry did not want to discuss military service. A hundred times, lying wakeful in the night or seeing the Union Jack flying over a man of war in the harbor, he had considered enlisting. A hundred times he had told himself that Egypt was his country now, and Egypt was not at war. But it was not a pleasant debate for a born Englishman to have with himself.

As if reading his thoughts, the general said, "By the way, Austen, you might not see me around these digs much longer. I've asked to resume my commission."

Mullins was in his seventies and as fat as a man that age was ever likely to be. Henry's surprise at the announcement must have showed because the general quickly went on, "Oh, I don't flatter myself that they'll give me a field command. Be jockeying a desk somewhere no doubt. Still, one wants to do one's bit. Should have done earlier, of course. Suppose it took this Rommel person to make me see the light."

Was the old man speaking especially to Henry? Shaming him? Or simply talking out his own thoughts, reminding himself how he had arrived at his remarkable decision to go back to war at an age when retired brigadiers were supposed to be writing their memoirs?

Henry took no chances. "Quite," he said. "Good show, Mullins." And he ordered another round.

Der Bischof—the Bishop—a smallish, bespectacled, prematurely gray man just beyond forty, did not think of himself as a spymaster, or even as a spy. He was an intellectual, a scholar with an abiding interest in ancient Egypt. This business of meeting with vulgar and trivial men such as Herr Hans, of gleaning and analyzing such information as they were able to bring him, was merely a sideline. A necessary evil. When the man from the German embassy in Cairo had suggested the work to him, the Bishop had at first protested that he had no time. He was far along with a monograph on the oasis of El Natrun, from the dry lake beds of which the Egyptians had once extracted salts crucial to mummification.

It had been a moment of stupidity. The man from the embassy, who did not need a business card to announce him as SS, pointed out that there were far worse places than Alexandria for a German to do his duty to the Führer—for example, in the mountains of Norway, where psychopathic guerrillas were bitterly resisting the Third Reich's humanitarian mission to protect them from invasion by the British.

The Bishop had quickly decided that his research was sufficiently near completion to allow him to take on other tasks. And that was how he came to be sitting, on this steaming August day, in a very French bistro, sipping excellent coffee and listening to Herr Hans report his latest findings. The man kept stumbling, going back to things he had forgotten the first time through. The Bishop did not permit anything to be written down—he had a photographic memory himself—but he had no doubt that Hans had pored over notes to prepare for the meeting; probably the fool had also neglected to burn them.

"The corrosion of the artillery shells is important, *nein*?" Hans was asking.

"Perhaps." In fact it almost certainly meant nothing—just normal tarnishing of the brass casings of a few antiaircraft shells by the salt air.

"Rommel will attack soon, I believe," said Hans. "Do you agree?"

"I don't concern myself with such matters. Neither should you." According to the Bishop's sources, Rommel would attack by the end of the month at the latest. There was no need to share this knowledge with the likes of Hans.

The Bishop noticed an Egyptian at a back table. A businessman by his look. Had he arrived just before or just after Hans? It was unusual for an Egyptian to dine alone.

To hell with it. This game could start you seeing phantoms. It was the pressure of dealing with idiots like Hans. What good were brains when you were surrounded by fools?

"Day after tomorrow, same time, the other location," he said.

Hans rose, recognizing that he had been dismissed. "I'll be there, Herr Bischof." It was obvious that he was trying to recall what the other location was.

When the young sexual deviate—the Bishop knew that from his sources as well—had gone, the spymaster found himself, for no particular reason, thinking about El Natrun. In Byzantine times Christian monks had established nearly fifty monasteries there. A half-dozen still existed. If he ever needed to disappear, it was something to keep in mind.

He nodded to the waiter, put down money, and left.

At the back table, Jake Farallon watched him go. Except for worrying that someone would see through his Egyptian disguise—Farallon himself thought he looked more Turkish—the surveillance had been strictly routine, a matter of connecting a pair of dots. He knew that Hans was a spy and suspected that Martin Bischof—"Bishop" was simply the man's name, or at least the name he used—was running Hans and others. But this was the first time that he had put them together.

So connect more dots. Plenty of them out there. Liaise with the Brits—that was how his job description read.

Farallon paid his check. Funny how everybody raved about French coffee; in his opinion, you could get better in Hoboken.

He was trying to drive her mad, that was the only answer that Catherine could see. Just when everything had been planned and settled, right down to a house waiting in Surrey, now there was this stupid idea that she and Charles should go, while Henry stayed. Not to fight, of course—oh no! To play the blue-eyed pasha, nothing else.

It *was* maddening. In the last months—with the Germans scratching at the door like wolves—Catherine had shared with Henry a daily awareness of danger and a deep concern for their son, and in doing so she had rediscovered something like her old feeling for him. But now this.

"And what will Charles and I do when the Germans drag you out and shoot you?" she asked bitterly.

"I doubt it will come to that," said Henry, with the dry smile that she had once admired but now found insufferably irritating. "The Germans aren't here by any means, and even if they were, I have resources. But in any event, you and Charles will want for nothing."

"We might want for you. Don't you think of that? Don't you think you belong with your son—and your wife?"

"Of course I do," said Henry placatingly. "But you're jumping the gun, old girl. No one's gone anywhere yet. And you have to understand that I have business to mind here—business of importance to all of us."

"Sell the damned plantations!" shouted Catherine suddenly. "Sell them all!" She heard Um-Rashid shuffling further away—but not out of earshot—beyond the door.

Henry sighed and looked so weary that Catherine almost regretted her outburst. "Do you seriously think," he said, "that anyone wants to buy fifty thousand acres that might be in German hands next week?"

"Oh, they might be in German hands next week, but I'm jumping the gun!"

Henry sighed. "I'm sorry. No decision can be perfect in the circumstances. I've done what I think best."

"You don't love me," said Catherine with cold finality.

Henry hesitated for the slightest instant. In her heart Catherine knew that it was out of sheer surprise: the word *love* had not been spoken in the villa for a very long time. But it was a hesitation still.

"I do love you," said her husband. "I've loved you from the moment I first saw you."

"Then act like it!"

"Catherine—"

"You don't love me! You don't! All you love is yourself and—" she waved her arm to encompass everything—"and stinking Egypt!"

"You don't mean that."

"Don't tell me what I mean!"

"Catherine." He moved toward her.

"No! Don't touch me! Don't come near me! You—you fool!"

Catherine stormed from the room. The warm tears on her face felt almost comforting, old friends in a time of need.

In the hallway Charles came toward her. "Mother, what's wrong?"

"Nothing. Ask your father."

She went to her bedroom and closed the door hard. After a time she stopped crying.

I do love you. I've loved you from the moment I first saw you.

Ten minutes later there was a tap at the door and Um-Rashid, smiling and cooing in her toothless old woman's way, brought in a tray with sandwiches, tea, and—though she must have abhorred touching it—a large glass of brandy. In a house without daughters, it was good to have women servants. Catherine sipped the brandy in bed under the cool caress of the overhead fan and drifted to sleep dreaming of how to move her life from where it was to where she wanted it to be.

On the last day of August 1942, Rommel attacked. From El Alamein the battle quickly spread along a front that stretched forty miles, from the Mediterranean to the Qattara Depression in the brutal heat of the deep desert. The British, heavily supplied by the Americans, put up steely resistance—far stronger than Rommel had anticipated. The Desert Fox had never lost a battle, but he was a realist; on 3 September he gave up the attack and went on the defensive.

Montgomery continued to build his strength. In late October he struck. Rommel, in Austria on sick leave, rushed back to the front at Hitler's personal order. He was too late. The Afrika Korps was already being overwhelmed. Within three weeks what was left of its tanks had retreated seven hundred miles; foot-soldiers, who could not match that pace, were left to surrender or die.

With Rommel crushed, and with American armies swarming into Morocco and Algiers, Hitler's dream of North African conquest was over.

In Cairo, Miles Lampson had his own battles to fight that long summer and fall. One was the perpetual struggle with "the boy"—King
Farouk, now twenty-two.

The problem this time was simple. Lampson wanted Farouk to
form a coalition government with the nationalist Wafd Party because
the Wafd was at least nominally pro-British in the matter of the war.
Farouk preferred a faction that contained many who were openly
pro-German.

The usual fatherly talk had little effect. The king seemed to be
feeling his oats. He was evasive, comical, stubborn, and arrogant all
in the same conversation.

Stronger measures were called for. The next morning Lampson
brought in his military attaché. "Gather some tanks—a squadron or
whatever you call it. Send them to Abdine Palace. Tell the commander to crash the gates and park right on the grounds. His guns
should not be aimed directly at the palace—but should not be aimed
away from it, either. Might as well send some infantry as well, in case
the palace guards are in a starchy mood."

It was done. Farouk got the message, and the ambassador got his
government.

The other headache was of a different order. General Montgomery was a man of many original ideas—Lampson found him
insufferably conceited about his intelligence—one of which was to
offer an amnesty to German spies in Egypt. All in free, no penalty,
just come in and admit to spying—and start naming names. A surprising number of spies accepted the offer, especially after things
turned sour for Rommel in the desert. And among the names they
named were those of several young Egyptian army men who
belonged to a group that called itself the Free Officers.

The man at the door identified himself as "British security." Behind
him stood several armed soldiers. The young Egyptian captain

objected strenuously to the intrusion. He was an Egyptian officer in his own home. They had no right to interfere with him in any way.

The man's answer to this was an order to stand aside. The soldiers trampled in. Within minutes they had found the German-made radio transmitter and the young captain was under arrest.

His trial became something of a *cause célèbre*. Throughout it, the young officer protested not only against British high-handedness but against their very presence in his homeland. Before it was over his name, which was Anwar as-Sadat, was known throughout Egypt. That did not, of course, prevent his conviction.

Sadat would spend two years in prison. Incarcerated with him were several of his fellow Free Officers. One of them, a lieutenant named Farid Hamza, became his closest friend. Sadat was emotional, his moods ranging from ebullience to outrage, whereas Hamza was quiet, observant, and tough. Sadat thought of him as a pillar of strength.

Years later, Farid Hamza would become a pillar of strength for Karima Ismail.

3
Changes

Egypt

*Poor Farouk. Just a few short years ago, it seemed as if Allah had blessed
him with everything a mortal man could hope for: youth, beauty, a
lovely young bride, and the adoration of his people. In some quarters, it
had even been whispered that Farouk might be The One to assume the
mantle of Caliph and Commander of the Faithful—a position no man
had held since Ataturk had secularized Turkey and sent the last Ottoman
sultan into exile.*

*The rumors gained weight and substance because it seemed as if
Farouk alone, of all the rulers in the Middle East, could gather support
outside his own borders. He had married off his sister Fawzia to the
young Shah of Iran. He had hopes of marrying Faiza to the Jordanian
crown prince—and perhaps even of forging a union between his sister
Fathia and the child king of Iraq.*

And now it all seemed to be falling apart.

*Though Farouk was always ready with a joke, even in times of crisis,
he knew very well that the damnable Miles Lampson had not given up
trying to remove him from the throne—and to replace him with his*

uncle, the pro-British Prince Mohammed Ali. But unlike many of his subjects who prayed that the Germans would free them from the stranglehold of the British, Farouk had no such hopes. Though his position with the British was tenuous, a German victory would certainly cost him his throne.

Meanwhile his boyish figure was disappearing under layers of fat, a reality even the skill of his tailors could not disguise. Even worse, his fairy-tale marriage had produced only two daughters, which meant that while he might be a king, he was not, in the eyes of his countrymen, quite a man.

He would have to keep trying. But that was easier said than done. Farouk sampled all the known love potions and aphrodisiacs: pigeons, mutton, mangoes, hashish. Nothing helped. His queen didn't seem to care one way or the other; she was too busy carrying on a flirtation with the dashing and athletic Wahid Yussri, the son of his father's first wife. What was he to do?

Even his revered mother, Nazli, the woman who had professed to adore him, persisted in her disgraceful liaison—with Ahmed Hassanein, the tutor Farouk had idolized!

Poor young king. He had magnificent palaces, toys that mere mortals only dreamed of, and, thanks to his father's penurious ways, he had inherited enormous wealth. But he had no real friends, only servants and hangers-on, and a few playmates—among them, the gaggle of Italian courtiers that Lampson constantly pressured him to deport.

The Italians were enemies of the British Empire, Lampson reminded him, and Farouk had signed a friendship treaty with Britain. These particular Italians might be buffoons—or they might not. But their leader, Mussolini, had boasted often and loudly that the Italians and Egyptians were one people separated by an ocean.

Deport them, Lampson insisted, as was his way. Deport them—or else.

Farouk responded: he made the Italians Egyptian citizens. But there was scarcely time for a collective sigh of relief among the new citizens. In order to be true Muslims, Farouk announced, the Italians would have to be circumcised. Immediately. He made arrangements for a surgeon.

No doubt some of the Italians would have preferred deportation. But *at the final moment Farouk withdrew the knife, chuckling over his little joke, enjoying his little victory over the British.*

Lampson was not amused. Nor were many Egyptians, not when the king seemed to be spending more time entertaining himself than on serious affairs of state. Early in his reign he had given land to the poor, he had built schools and hospitals—and he had spoken with passion about his dream for an independent Egypt. But now, his critics grumbled, he was too preoccupied with his own problems and his own pleasures to attend to his less fortunate countrymen. Why, he was not even Egyptian, they said scornfully, and he rarely spoke Arabic, preferring instead the languages of the colonial oppressors, English and French.

In the souks, in the coffeehouses, in the secret meetings of the Muslim Brotherhood, voices spoke against him: Farouk is no friend of the poor. And the British are friend to no one. Both would have to go.

"Close your eyes, Mother, I have a surprise for you."

"But what . . . ?" Shams glanced at the basket of mending that was filled with items from the pasha's house: a tablecloth that had several tiny holes, a sheet that needed to be rehemmed, a delicate square of embroidery that had begun to unravel. These would all have to be repaired before she could prepare her own family's evening meal. There was no time for games.

"Please, Mother," Omar coaxed. "It will just take a moment."

Shams laughed and patted her son's cheek. "As you wish, *ya* Omar. But if I don't finish this work . . ."

Omar's mouth tightened, the smile left his eyes. He hated the idea that his blessed mother must serve the infidel *Inglizi* and his bitch of a wife. Not now, he reminded himself, this was not the time to indulge his own feelings, it was a moment for bringing some pleasure into Shams's hard and work-filled life. He took her by the hand and sat her down on the lumpy divan that lined the wall of their tiny living area. "Now close your eyes." She did so.

Omar stepped outside and returned a moment later, carrying a large, heavily gilded chair with blue brocade upholstery. "This one is fit for a pharaoh," the cabinetmaker in Bab al-Luq had declared. "Luwis Khamastashar," he had explained, giving the local name of the mock-Louis XV furniture that had become so popular under the Ottoman rulers. "It is *exactly* like the chairs in Shepheard's Hotel."

That had been enough for Omar. As much as he hated the foreigners who polluted Cairo, it was well known that they demanded the best of everything. And everything in Shepheard's was the best that Cairo had to offer. Omar had bargained hard, but not as hard as he might have, for he was imagining how Shams's eyes would shine when she saw this magnificent gift.

Now he took his mother's hand. "Open your eyes," he commanded.

She stared at the object that loomed before her, taking up most of the room's free space. "But what?" she asked. "What is this?"

"It's for you," Omar said proudly. "So you can sit down and relax properly when you're not slaving for those wretched *Ingliz*."

"Hush, hush, my son," she pleaded, fearing that Omar's evergrowing disdain for the pasha might cause them to lose everything. For once he did not argue, but simply patted her hand reassuringly.

"But I don't understand," she went on, turning her attention back to the chair. "How did you come to have this? It must be very costly?"

"I bought it, Mother," he said expansively. "I told you about my excellent position in Abu Hakim's shop. He pays me very well because I am a better worker than any he has had before. Why, only yesterday he told me he wished that his own son worked as hard as I did." Omar lied fluently. His "place of employment" was on the outskirts of the city, in a neighborhood his family never visited; the owner was an old man who, for a few coins, had promised to support Omar's lies whenever necessary.

Shams shook her head. This chair must have cost more than a young man could earn honestly in six months. No one she knew had anything like it. She wanted to ask again where he got the money, she wanted to ask if it had anything to do with those times when he left his bed during the night and didn't return till the morning light. Yet somehow she was afraid to put her fears into words, and so she said nothing.

"Try it, Mother," Omar coaxed. "Sit down and tell me how you like it."

Shams rose slowly. Steadying herself on the chair's golden arms, she lowered herself gingerly, as if the seat might somehow expel her.

"There." Omar smiled with satisfaction. "Is it not comfortable as well as beautiful?"

Shams nodded slowly. The chair, though beautiful, was not as comfortable as the lumpy divan. But she would rather cut out her tongue than mar her son's obvious pleasure. She got up and kissed him, stroking his hair, and murmuring how Allah had blessed her with the best of all sons. Then she went to a tiny cupboard, took out a worn white sheet, and covered the chair with it.

Omar frowned. "Why did you do that?"

"I'm protecting the beautiful chair, my son, so that it will stay clean and beautiful."

"No," he said, sweeping the sheet away. "I want you to use it every day. No one else, just you—so that you will know what a great woman you are and how much your son loves you."

Shams felt a swelling in her chest, the tell-tale trace of moisture on her cheeks. She had been truly blessed by Allah. How she loved this son the Almighty had sent her!

And yet with love comes worry, and what was she to do about those long and fear-filled nights?

Charles stepped closer to the mirror that hung over the heavy Empire dresser his mother had recently moved into his room. He dabbed some soap over the barely noticeable hairs that had begun to sprout on his cheek, then lightly ran his new razor over the lather. After wiping his face with a clean towel, he examined his face once more. There, he thought, that's better. Though Henry told him there was no need to shave just yet, Charles saw no reason to wait. Now he went into the bathroom and cleaned the razor, as he had seen his father do, thrilling to the sight of the tiny hairs that ran down the side of the sink.

His father had spoken to him about "becoming a man" with obvious embarrassment, making Charles feel embarrassed, too, about the way his body had begun to change and the way his voice had begun to crack and disconcert him at the most inopportune times. Like when he was around Karima.

He had always enjoyed her company, he had always loved her rich, melodic voice, but now he was responding to her in new and forbidden ways—and the change was as unsettling as it was pleasurable.

"You must speak to him, Henry," Catherine insisted. "You really must have a word with Charles. I won't have him speaking Arabic whenever he pleases. And I don't want him fraternizing with the people who work for you, Henry, I just won't have it! You've set such a terrible example, going about in that *galabiyya* like a peasant, speaking to servants as if they were your equals, setting up that *school*. For servants! Why, you've made us ridiculous. Mrs. Chalmers at the club even hinted that you had Red leanings. Imagine!"

Though the "Red leanings" was a new permutation, this was an old conversation, part of a battle that could not be won. He could say that Catherine was the one who made herself ridiculous, pretending that her English mother was the only part of her heritage that counted. But he would not speak such cruelties. He had loved her passionately once. And he had believed they would grow old together in the warm shelter of that love.

Catherine's parents, both dead now, had been good people. Her mother, the headmistress of the English School for Girls, indulged only one form of snobbery: she had no use for anyone who was stupid or willfully ignorant. She had been devoted to Catherine's father, Shafick, a dedicated teacher in a boys' school, a man whose love of learning had matched her own. Why then, Henry had asked himself time and time again, why had Catherine become such a snob?

Perhaps he should have been forewarned during their first trip to

England. When he had taken Catherine to meet his parents—with her aunt as chaperon, of course—she had been dazzled by the Austens' gracious London flat, their genteel but shabby country home, by the very Englishness of everything she saw. After saying she wished she never had to go home again, Catherine had insisted on a London wedding—even though that meant only her parents, of all her relations, could attend.

The Austens, while not pleased that Henry had chosen a half-breed wife, took some small comfort in the fact that she was half English. And that Henry was a second son, with no hope of inheriting either the family home or the title that would go to his brother.

In those early days, Henry had seen nothing that might mar his future happiness. Perhaps, he thought, like all those who love, he had been blind.

"Henry! Are you listening to me? Have you heard a single word I've said?"

"Yes, of course, my dear."

"Well, what are you going to do about it?"

"About . . ."

"About Charles, damn you! Our only son is going native. Just like his father. If you had taught him what it meant to be a gentleman, but no . . ."

He could have stopped her in midrant, he could have said that being a gentleman could scarcely be taught—and that Charles was every inch the gentleman in spite of his growing fondness for everything Egyptian. But these things, too, could not be said. "It's only natural that he loves Egypt," Henry said mildly. "He was born here. He's grown up here. It's what he knows."

"Exactly!" Catherine declared triumphantly, as if it were game, set, match.

Henry shook his head, not understanding.

"Egypt is *all* he knows," she paraphrased, ignoring the regular visits Charles made to his English grandparents. "That's why you must send him to school in England. So he can learn his true heritage."

"Oh, surely that's not necessary, my dear. When he leaves the

Arthur Academy he can get a perfectly good English education at Victoria College. Why, some of the best minds in England have taught there. They have uniforms, gymnastics—even corporal punishment," he joked.

Catherine did not smile. Her lips tightened, her shoulders squared—and Henry knew that in this, she would win.

Karima rose in darkness. It was only three o'clock on this fourth day of Ramadan. There was work to be done and it had best be done early. After washing her face and hands, she set out the family's breakfast: bread, cheese, olives and *foul muddamas*. After she made the tea that her father had come to enjoy—just like the English—she woke her parents and her brother, so that the family could eat before there was enough light to distinguish a white thread from a black one. After that, there could be nothing to eat or drink until the darkness came again.

There was little conversation around the breakfast table; it was as if they were all conserving their strength for the long day ahead.

When the family finished, Karima washed and dried the few plates and bowls they owned, then stacked them neatly on a shelf that Omar had put up for their mother. Soon her parents would go to the Austen villa, Mustafa to await the pasha's pleasure, Shams to collect the family's laundry.

Karima hummed as she brushed her hair and prepared herself for school. Today the lessons would be easy because the teacher observed the fast. Perhaps they would read some verses from the Quran or tell stories of the Prophet's youth.

A short time later, only Shams and Omar remained in the house. It was the moment Shams had waited for. "My son, what is this paper?" she asked quietly, holding up one of the pamphlets that had been tucked away in his Quran. She had not meant to look through his things. She had simply been cleaning and the papers had fallen out of the holy book.

Omar stiffened, as if for battle, then relaxed. "Nothing, *ya ummi,* nothing to worry yourself about." He reached out to take the pamphlet, but Shams held on.

Though she'd never learned to read properly, she did know a few words. Infidels. Death. King. Silently she pointed, here and there and there, her dark eyes pleading for Omar to say it was somehow a mistake, that these papers belonged to someone else. But even as she waited, she knew there was no mistake. Her only son, her heart, had put himself in danger.

Omar hung his head for a moment. Not because he was ashamed of anything he was doing, but because he did not want to give his mother pain or worry. He could have lied to ease her mind. But a man did not lie to his mother.

"Mother, dear mother," he said, his voice uncharacteristically gentle and soothing, "I don't want you to worry. I'm doing Allah's work. I'm spreading the faith, as He commands us to do. I'm helping the poor, those that no one else will help . . ."

"But if they catch you, my son, they will put you in prison. They might even kill you." She began to weep, softly, as if afraid that someone might hear.

Omar had few tender feelings, but he could not bear his mother's tears. He wrapped his arm around her and drew her close. "I promise you," he said fiercely, "I swear to you upon my very soul that they will not catch me. And I promise you," he added, "that one day, when things are better in Egypt, when men like the pasha are gone, that you will have the things you deserve, beloved mother. I swear to you."

Omar's words failed to console his mother. Indeed they simply confirmed the worst of her fears. Though he promised and promised, could he prevail against the might of soldiers and police? She squeezed her eyes shut, her shoulders still heaving. "I beg you," she said hoarsely, "I beg you at least to be careful."

"I will," he said fervently, glad to bring the matter to a close.

Shams shook her head fatalistically, knowing that now it was in the hands of Allah, who decided all things. If it was written her son would live, then these things he was doing would not matter. And if written otherwise—no, she could not, she would not allow herself to imagine that. In the name of Allah, the Almighty, she began to pray.

It was late afternoon, and Karima was taking the last of the laundry off the clothesline when Charles came upon her as if by chance, though only he knew it was not. Sweat streamed freely down her face, her lips were parched and dry.

"Let me help," he offered, reaching for a large and cumbersome sheet.

"Oh, no, you can't," she protested, knowing what would happen if anyone saw the pasha's son doing a servant's work.

Charles stepped back, reluctantly. He admired Karima's fortitude, but he wished he could somehow make her day easier. He knew better than to offer a drink—he had done that once, before he understood the rules of the fast, and been soundly rebuffed. "Not even a sip," she had told him emphatically. Nor a taste of her favorite sweet, no matter how hungry she was. He knew how hard she worked, how hungry and how thirsty she must be. "I say, you're awfully strong."

She cast her eyes down, felt a flush on her cheeks that did not come from the hot sun. "It's nothing," she said modestly. "My father gives up his cigarettes, and I think that after Allah and his family, he loves those best. And he and my mother do not make *jig-a-jig* till Ramadan is over."

"*Jig-a-jig?*" Charles asked, never having heard the term.

"Don't you know anything?" she replied in that superior way that made Charles smile. "It's when a man and a woman come together. You know . . ."

Now it was Charles's turn to blush. "Oh, yes, I see." Though he was beginning to feel the stirring of a strange new attraction to Karima, he still did not believe that giving up *jig-a-jig* compared with going hungry all day. He watched quietly, admiring her grace as she folded the clean linens with quick, deft motions and placed them neatly in her basket.

"At least sit down and rest for a minute," he said when she had finished. She looked around, and seeing no one to observe them, she found a shady spot and sat. Charles walked to one of the plantation's lovely fountains, dipped his handkerchief into the water and offered it to Karima. She accepted it gratefully, dabbing her face with its cooling dampness. "Thank you," she said. "I'll wash it for you with the day's laundry."

Charles nodded. He did not like being constantly reminded that Karima was here to serve him and his family. "What did you do in school today?" he asked, reaching for a topic of conversation.

"Oh, we talked about Aisha, the Prophet's wife. She fought with him in battle, you know, side by side with the men. She was a great heroine."

Charles smiled at her enthusiasm. "She sounds like a remarkable woman."

"Egypt has had many remarkable women," she went on. "Have you ever heard of Huda el-Sharawi?"

"No, I don't believe I have."

"She opened the first school for girls. She started a magazine for women. *And*, she removed her veil. In public! People attacked her for it—that was in 1929, you know, a long time ago. But she said that it was not the Prophet who ordered women to wear the veil, that it was only the Turks who invented it, so they could keep their women hidden away."

Encouraged by Charles's smile, she went on to tell of Sharawi's fight against polygamy and child marriages.

"But these things still happen," said Charles, who had heard his parents talk about men who had married ten-year-old girls, and others who had three or four wives.

"I know," Karima agreed solemnly. "But still, Huda wanted to make life better for other women—and that was an important thing to do."

"Tell me more."

"I feel like Scheherazade," she laughed. "You always want another story."

"And you always leave me wanting another story," he replied boldly.

She looked at him with something like worship in her eyes. If only her skin were fairer, she thought, her eyes blue instead of brown, her body taller and plumper. But perhaps Charles shared the English preference for women who were scrawny. So many of the grand ladies who called on Mrs. Henry Pasha were terribly thin, even though their husbands were surely wealthy enough to feed them well. "Huda fought against arranged marriages, too," Karima said softly. "She believed that a woman should follow her own heart and choose for herself the man she wants to live with for the rest of her life."

"Is that what you believe, Karima?" he asked, half-teasing.

"Yes," she said fervently. "I believe that if a woman can marry the man she wants, then she would do anything for him. Even fight beside him, as the Prophet's wife did."

He nodded gravely, as if he agreed. Yet he could not help but wonder: did his mother choose his father? And if she had done so, then why was she so cross all the time?

They waited together for the sun to set. Karima had finished her chores and slipped out of the house. Charles had evaded his mother's questions by pretending to go to bed. At last it came: the cannons fired, the lights around the minarets began to flicker, announcing the time of *iftar,* the breaking of the fast. Karima jumped up and down, as if it were all somehow unexpected. Though Charles had eaten his fill at the Austen table, he felt Karima's excitement and shared it.

"Now you'll see," she said enthusiastically, "now you'll see how wonderful food can be." She took his hand and led him to the street vendors who awaited the fasting public with all kinds of fragrant, flavorful delights.

"Let me treat," Charles said. "Please."

"I have my own pocket money. Mother gave it to me, for Ramadan." Proudly displaying her few coins, she bought *foul* and *falafel* and *amar el-din,* the sweet drink made from syrup of apricots.

She ate quickly, for she was well and truly hungry. But when she saw Charles smiling at her, she slowed.

"What's wrong?"

"Nothing. I'm just enjoying watching you eat."

"You're laughing at me! Because I eat like a greedy goat."

"No, never, Karima. Honestly. I was just enjoying your pleasure, secondhand, that's all."

She looked at him skeptically, then finished her food more slowly.

To make up for his gaffe, Charles bought dessert for both of them: *qataif* pastry stuffed with pistachios, almonds and raisins and drenched with sugar syrup flavored with lemon—and a large portion of *kanafa,* the angel-hair pastry topped with raisins, nuts, and cream.

"I can't eat another mouthful," Charles soon declared.

"I can. Come with me."

And he did, braving the fury that would follow if his mother caught him. They went from house to humble house, knocking on doors. *"Ramadan karim,"* they sang out in unison—Ramadan is kind. And everywhere they went they were given a treat—a few pistachio nuts, a nougat, a Turkish delight.

Though there was no shortage of sweets—or anything else for that matter—in the Austen home, Charles shared Karima's obvious pleasure in the bits of candy and in the gathering of it. She's like a little child, he thought, yet feeling more tender than superior. She appreciates such small things—and everything she feels is written on her face.

All too soon, Karima announced she would have to go home. "I have to rest now. Father said that this year I could go with him and Omar to the square tonight, for the reading of the Quran."

As they walked back to the plantation, Charles offered Karima his share of the Ramadan bounty. "My mother doesn't like me to keep sweets in my room."

Your mother doesn't like anything or anyone, Karima thought, then rebuked herself for being unkind, especially during Ramadan.

But it was true. Mrs. Henry was as hard as the pasha was kind. Everyone who worked for the pasha knew that his wife wanted him to be the proper British milord. But Karima accepted the sweets; she would share them with her mother.

> *"Oh my Lord! So order me*
> *That I may be grateful*
> *For Thy favors, which Thou*
> *Hast bestowed on me and*
> *On my parents, and that*
> *I may work the righteousness*
> *That will please Thee*
> *And admit me, by Thy Grace,*
> *To the ranks of Thy*
> *Righteous Servants."*

The sheikh's voice was rich, his intonation melodic, and Karima thrilled to the words of the sura, drawing comfort from the certainty of Allah's grace and mercy. The reading would go on all night, almost to the breaking of the new dawn, but of course Karima and her family could not stay that long, not with another workday ahead.

Between the readings dancers performed, among them the dervishes that Karima loved, whirling and spinning so long and so fast that it made her dizzy to watch. And there was singing, too. Now one of the village women stepped forward and began the familiar Um Kalthum song *"Khuf Allah"*—the fear of Allah. Without thinking Karima closed her eyes and joined in, her clear, sweet voice harmonizing with the older woman's darker, deeper sound. The crowd was very quiet, and even when the song was finished there was yet another long moment of silence.

Karima looked up at her father. There were tears in his eyes as he patted her on the head. "You have truly been given a gift from Allah, my daughter. I hope you will always use it for His Glory."

She squeezed Mustafa's hand, as if to say I will, Father. Compliments rarely came Karima's way—she was, after all, only a girl—

and she took this one straight into her heart. But her moment was brief. A few steps away, Omar was glowering at her. She knew very well what *he* thought, no matter what their father said. Singing in public was wrong, making a show of any kind was wrong, almost everything she did was wrong. She met his gaze boldly, as if to say how could it be wrong to sing for the Glory of Allah? But he stared even harder, as if he were looking deep into her very soul, and she was afraid.

A moment later, an older man came up to her brother and whispered something in his ear. Omar nodded a few times, allowed himself a last scowl at Karima and walked away.

She knew where Omar was going, where he so often went at night. Half their neighbors knew, also. The Muslim Brotherhood was a secret society—membership was banned—but Egypt was like a collection of small villages where everyone knew what his neighbors were up to. Though Karima feared her brother she admired his courage in doing good works, even if they were forbidden. Her own family was more fortunate than so many of their neighbors, who, if they fell sick, could afford neither doctors nor medicine. The Brotherhood took care of such people. And she knew that the Brotherhood taught people Islamic history, so that instead of being ashamed of their poverty they might know of a time when the Caliph of Islam ruled most of the civilized world.

Eid al-Saghir marked the end of Ramadan. The fasting was over, and now heavy eating was all but mandatory. In celebration of the holiday, Henry had given all his employees generous bonuses. Mustafa had bought gifts for his entire family—Karima proudly displayed her new dress, making a point of letting Charles see her in it. And since charity was one of the Five Pillars of Islam, Karima's family would share their Ramadan bounty with those who had much less.

It was Shams's custom to buy bread for the poor every Friday—bread was cheap, and, Allah be praised, they had a generous employer. For this holiday, Shams doubled her bread purchase. At home she and Karima made up small packages, adding a bit of cheese and a few olives to each.

As they set out with their gifts of food, Charles appeared. Running ahead, he tried to take the basket from Karima. "Here," he offered. "Let me carry that. Let me help. Where are you going?"

Shams shook her head, as if she didn't hear. She walked quickly, knowing all too well what the mistress of the house would say if she saw Charles carrying packages for the servants.

Karima shook her head, too. "I'm sorry, Charles, I don't think you should come. The people we're going to see . . . it's hard for them to accept charity. They wouldn't like an *Inglizi* to see them."

"Oh. Well, of course . . ."

"You're not cross with me, are you?"

"Certainly not. I think what you're doing is awfully good." And he did.

But this was the first time either of them openly acknowledged the vast gap that separated them. It would not be the last.

4

A Death in the Breezes

Alexandria, 1944

The fighting was over in North Africa. The Afrika Korps, crushed between the British striking from Egypt and the Americans pouring in from Algiers and Morocco, was gone, killed or captured almost to the last man. But even though artillery no longer flashed like heat lightning on the night horizon, the war still loomed over Alexandria. The city and its great double harbor were like a bustling backstage for the vast drama of the invasions of Italy and southern France. Everywhere were soldiers, sailors, ships, machines of battle. Spies still frequented the clubs and coffeehouses, although those on the German side found their work increasingly irrelevant, the brave among them planning a return to the Fatherland to defend it in its crisis, the rest considering the charms of Argentina or Paraguay.

The Allies were winning, a fact that, however clear it might be, left mixed impressions on Egyptians. Many, especially the poor, still clung to a faith that Muhammad Haidar would somehow work a miracle; there were rumors of invincible secret weapons soon to be unsheathed. The better-informed accepted the obvious—and despaired of ever being free *of the British. Only a few looked further and saw that the war's end would bring a changed world, in which Egypt's role might change as well.*

But for a day or two as the winter of 1944 made its final retreat, none of this mattered greatly. Far more important was the quintessentially Egyptian holiday of Shamm el-Nessim— literally, the "smelling of the breeze." Celebrated by Christians and Muslims alike, it dates from the time of the pharaohs and falls on the first day of spring, the Monday following the Coptic Christian Easter. It is a time for neither war nor politics nor even the past, but for simple pleasure in the new green leaf, the eternal and ever-turning renewal of life.

"I don't understand it, I simply don't," said Catherine. "Why must we ... *mingle* with them, as if we were all one great family. It's grotesque."

"We've always done *Shamm el-Nessim* for the workers," Henry replied evenly. They were in her bedroom, supposedly no servants nearby, but one never knew.

"Not like this. A mob of *fellahin* at the seashore. Really!"

Henry almost sighed but caught himself; it would be like pulling the pin of a grenade. And to a certain extent she was right. Before, the celebration had always been held at one of the plantations, where the lines were clearly drawn and Catherine needed to do little more than make a star turn on the lawn. But this year, with the war danger finally over and Henry's wealth at an all-time high, he had felt a need to do something special. And so he had arranged to truck all of his workers and their families who so desired—which was all of them—to the beach for *Shamm el-Nessim,* and to treat them to a holiday feast on a section of the oceanfront that he had paid a modest bribe to keep clear.

"Perhaps I was overly ... enthusiastic," he said soothingly. "But we can hardly call it off, can we?"

"Hardly," said Catherine with a bitter curl of her mouth.

Henry went to the window, looked out. The sight of the villa's wings and grounds never failed to please him. He had made a place here in which a good life might be enjoyed. "My dear, there might come a time when we shall be glad of treating well those who work for us." It was something he had thought about a great deal. Things had changed, and would change even more. Look at what was happening in India. How long could Britain hold on there, once the war was over? And in Egypt, war or no, there was a steadily rising cry for redistribution of the land. Where would his great plantations be ten years from now, or even five?

There were those who thought that the demand for oil would fall after the war. Henry looked at the black market in gas-ration stamps and saw a dam waiting to break. He had already begun to divert some of his liquidity into the stocks of British and American companies that held drilling rights in Saudi and the Emirates.

"We have never treated them in any other way," said Catherine stubbornly. "If anything, we've coddled them." But for once she was looking at him as a wife might look at a husband on whose decisions her future depended.

It was strange, thought Henry. For a few weeks—or perhaps it had been only a few days—when the German threat was greatest, he and Catherine had shared at least an echo of the old days, when the only real thing on earth was their love for each other. Only an echo, and perhaps driven mainly by their concern for Charles. But it was something. And then, when the danger was over, the estrangement, the thing that had somehow crept up on their marriage unawares, had returned.

"Catherine," he said, touching her hair, letting a finger stray to brush her cheek.

There was a moment, and then it vanished.

"I think not, Henry," she said, looking straight ahead.

He did not close the door on leaving. It would have seemed redundant.

"*Abi*," said Charles—*Abi* was what he called his father; Mother, though, was most definitely Mother, not *Ummi*—"*Abi,* when do you think the war will be over?"

Henry looked up from his book. It seemed to Charles that he read all the time these days.

"Can't find a game, eh?"

Charles nodded. Why did adults always answer a question with another, usually one to which the answer was obvious? If he'd found a game, what would he be doing standing here with the soccer ball still under his arm?

"Most people seem to think that the Germans will be finished by the end of the year," said Henry. "I'm not so optimistic, but I really don't see how they can hold out much longer than that—provided the invasion comes off, of course. Why do you ask?"

"I don't know. Just thinking about it."

Henry closed the book. "Fear you're missing it, son?"

"No. I don't know. It's just . . ." He couldn't explain it. Lately he kept having these feelings, this hopeless restlessness, as if the future was a million miles away and yet at the same time everything was passing him by in a blur.

"It must be hard at your age," said his father gently. "But you'll be a man sooner than you know, and when you are, my fervent hope is that no war is waiting for you—and certainly not this one."

Seeing no reply to that, Charles said, "What are you reading?"

"Trying to read is more like it. Can't seem to get the hang of this Greek. Xenophon's *Anabasis*. It's about some Greek mercenaries who find themselves on the losing side in a civil war in ancient Persia. They have to retreat hundreds of miles through enemy territory. Rough going, for them and me both."

Charles managed a smile. There was no understanding his father. War all around him that he tried to ignore, then sat reading about some war that had happened God knew how many eons ago.

The boy started to excuse himself and then suddenly asked, for no reason at all that even he could see, *"Abi,* how did you and Mother meet?"

For an instant Charles wondered if he had overstepped some-how—his father looked positively alarmed. But then Henry said blandly, "Well, it was at a polo match. Right in Alex. I scarcely got

a glimpse of her, of course, that first time. Things were very different in those days. Very strict rules. And you're very inquisitive
today."

"Sorry."

"Bored, I imagine."

Charles shrugged.

"Well, if you want the gory details, you need to ask your mother.
Take my word for it, women's memories for this sort of thing are
much better than men's."

"All right." In fact Charles was uncomfortable with the whole
subject, had no idea why he'd brought it up.

Henry seemed to remember something. "Not this moment, perhaps. She's having one of her . . . temperamental days."

Charles made his escape and went to dribble the soccer ball on the
back lawn. *Temperamental.* It was a code word his father had used
many times, but today it angered him. He didn't want secret codes.
What he wanted was to know *why* his mother—and his father, too,
for that matter—had so very many "temperamental days." Why were
they always at each other, why couldn't they simply get on? He
swore to himself that he'd never behave like that when he was an
adult—he'd kill himself first.

He was good at soccer—his parents would have preferred that he
play the more gentlemanly cricket more often—and kept the ball in
the air until he had worked up a good sweat, then thumped it
through an imaginary goal. At least tomorrow was the holiday, at
least there would be something to do.

Perhaps it was her very stillness that caught his eye. She was standing under an orange tree watching him, nothing else.

At that moment he realized that he had been hoping all along for
this, but feeling an inexplicable need to look busy, he retrieved the
ball before trotting over to her.

"Hello."

"Hello."

She looked different these days. Softer. It came to him in a rush
that her body was undergoing the changes that would lead to wom-

anhood. The insight flustered his thinking, as if he had been caught in a lie, or asked an impossibly difficult question by a schoolmaster.

"You'll be at the celebration tomorrow?" he finally managed to say. What an incredibly inane question, he thought.

"Of course. And you?"

"Oh yes. I'll be there."

"Do you have your onion?"

"What?"

"Your onion. To sleep with."

"I'm afraid I—"

"Wait!"

She ran to her house and returned with an onion. "You put it under your pillow tonight, so that it will prepare your nose to smell the breezes tomorrow. Have you never heard of this?"

"Actually, I think I have." Of course he knew of the custom. But somehow he had forgotten it temporarily.

It would not do simply to stare at her. He looked around at the house, the servants' quarters. Was anyone watching from the windows? "I haven't seen Omar lately," he said lamely.

"My brother," said Karima with a little moue of distaste, "has become very religious. There is a group. He is always with them. Most nights he comes home after I am asleep, and then in the morning he is gone when I wake up."

"Well, that's all to the good, one supposes." Religion had never been much of a force in Charles's life, what with his father having long since abandoned the Church of England and his mother doing her best to ignore the fact that she was a Muslim. The whole subject interested him only insofar as it might apply to Karima.

"I can only stay for a minute," she said. "I was doing a chore for my mother when I . . . happened to see you. She doesn't like it when we talk."

"Mine either."

There was just a flick of the eyes between them before they both looked away. It was the second time they had acknowledged that, although they stood only a step apart, a vast gulf yawned between them.

"I must go."

"But I'll see you tomorrow."

"Oh yes."

"Until then."

"Until then. Don't forget the onion."

Charles watched her go. And from her high bedroom window, Catherine watched him watching. Sooner or later—preferably sooner—she was going to have to do something about that scrawny little wog.

Monday dawned a perfect first day of spring. By midmorning the celebrants were rolling in, the children and parents wearing their best clothes. A score of lambs were roasting on spits, but there was no need for the hungry to wait for the main course. Mounds of every imaginable food were spread in a vast buffet manned by outsiders hired by Henry so that his own workers might all be at leisure.

Some of the foods specifically symbolized spring: hard-boiled eggs colored with vegetable dye, lettuce and other greenery, onions (for the breezes!) and *fiskh*—pungent salted fish that had been buried in the sand to ripen. Vendors sold strings of fragrant jasmine. The holiday atmosphere was infectious. Charles, scanning the crowd for Karima, saw Omar first and noted with relief that even he was smiling and laughing.

And there was Karima, with a group of women and girls. He could hardly go up and speak with her, not in front of all these witnesses, but he could look as much as he liked, couldn't he? And perhaps later he could get in a few quick words. No one could complain about that.

Henry was slower to get into the mood of the festival. There had been a scene with Catherine. She had absolutely refused to go to the beach before noon, and kept Um-Rashid to wait on her. Perhaps the old woman didn't mind, but it went against Henry's grain. Even so, talking with his foremen and top hands, remembering the names of their children, congratulating them on recent additions in that line, he was soon as deep into the party as a campaigning politician.

At noon the lambs came off the coals and the serious feasting began. An hour later people were groaning happily and holding their stomachs in mock anguish. Some drifted off to sleep on the warm sand. One group of men brought out musical instruments and began to play. One or two men sang, and then there was a call for Karima—with her father's permission, naturally. Mustafa, smiling broadly, wagged his head in vehement approval: most of these people knew of his daughter's talent; now let the rest hear for themselves.

Charles had heard Karima sing, of course, but only during Ramadan or for a handful of the villa's staff. Now, as with genuine shyness but also undeniable pleasure she protested her inability and then allowed herself to be led to the musicians, to the cheers of scores of men and women, he was stunned to see that his childhood friend, the little girl from the servants' quarters, was a figure of glamor. And when she began to sing, there was something far larger than glamor. He realized that except for her voice and the music, there was not another sound on the crowded beach.

Arabic sung sounds different from spoken Arabic, and Charles could catch only the simplest verses. It was one of the old songs of love and longing:

Where are you tonight, my love, where?
Do you sleep after battle? Dream of me?
The sky is big but crowded with stars;
In my heart, as small as my hand, only loneliness.

Karima's voice was clear and pure and haunting. As she stood on the sand, silhouetted against the azure sky and the glittering sea, her dark eyes seemed as deep and as bright as the starry night sky in the song. Charles had never seen anything so lovely.

The song ended—prematurely, Charles thought, for his and

everyone else's taste—with the arrival of his mother, making her usual grand entrance. Yet there remained a kind of afterglow from the performance. Charles sensed it but could not have explained it. Henry, more experienced, thought he could. He saw sun-browned *fellahin* exchange glances and nods with new pride, as if to say *This girl is the real thing. And she is one of us.* Henry himself did not presume to judge: his love of Egypt had never extended to its music; he suspected he was a little tone-deaf. But he was happy for his people, especially Mustafa.

After Catherine had ensconced herself in the shade of a pavilion and received the obeisances of the most important wives, the celebration resumed. The musicians played and a few hardy souls dragged themselves yet again to the food tables. A few voices called again for Karima, but they were ignored. The general opinion seemed to be that there was no need to tamper with perfection.

Charles worked his way to the Ismail family group and, after greeting Mustafa and the other males, said to Karima, "You sang beautifully. Thank you."

"Thank you. I am honored."

Not even Omar could protest at this bit of formal courtesy on the part of the pasha's son. But Shams saw the look that accompanied the words and resolved to talk with her husband at the first opportunity. This had to be stopped before it became truly dangerous.

As Charles wandered back toward the Austen pavilion, the music tinkled to a stop. People were looking out to sea. Above the harbor an airplane was towing something at the end of a long cable. Suddenly the antiaircraft guns of a British destroyer erupted.

A man—one of the foremen—near Charles said, "Are they fighting?" Of course the pasha's son would know.

Like many teenaged boys, Charles had made a fetish of warplanes, warships, and much else about war and knew exactly what was happening.

"It's practice," he explained. "Target practice. That thing behind the airplane is a target drone. They're shooting at it. The bullets are hollow. They're filled with paint, so they know when they've made a hit. Different colors for different guns. And the hollow bullets won't down the plane, in case a shot goes wild."

The foreman nodded sagely, as if his own opinion had been confirmed.

The plane took a long turn and made another pass, and the anti-aircraft guns boomed again.

In the pavilion Catherine had been planning to make an early exit, but the shooting in the harbor stopped her. Like everyone else, she wanted to watch this show. The only trouble was the glare on the water. It hurt her eyes. At that moment she noticed Shams nearby.

"Shams—" using her given name, not the courteous Um-Omar— "please find Um-Rashid and fetch my sunglasses from her. I've left them with her and can't see a thing without them."

Shams hesitated for the merest instant before saying, "Yes, mistress."

The tow plane pulled the drone once more above the harbor. There was an odd instant in which Charles noticed that one of the destroyer's guns sounded louder than before, and then heard, from near the pavilion, a wet smack, as if someone had dropped a melon on a pavement. And then women's screams.

A Royal Navy board of inquiry firmly established the chain of carelessness, stupidity, and plain bad luck by which a gun aimed toward shore had come to be loaded and then fired. A seaman went to the brig, a crew chief was reduced in rank, and an ensign was allowed to resign his commission.

It was pointed out that the accident could have been far worse: an explosive shell might have killed and maimed dozens. The paint-filled target round caused only one casualty. A few steps from the pavilion on her search for Um-Rashid, Shams was struck squarely in the forehead. She was dead as she fell.

———

"My son, please," said Mustafa wearily. "This subject is painful to me. And Henry Pasha is not to blame for what happened. Nor is the mistress."

"She died in their service!" insisted Omar fiercely. "That stupid woman's laziness—that, and a British bullet—killed my mother."

"An accident," said Mustafa. "The shell could have struck anyone, even the mistress herself."

"God willing it had! The earth would be better off without her."

Listening from her room in the little house that now seemed so terribly empty, Karima expected her father to draw the line. Never before had Omar dared to attack the pasha or the mistress openly in his presence. But ever since the accident Mustafa had seemed a different man—older, smaller—and now he merely said, "Henry Pasha paid for the funeral, and for much else. What more do you expect?"

"Nothing more. It is exactly what I expect—for the British to buy their way out of everything."

"My son, let me remind you that the pasha has even provided money for your schooling."

"And I will take it. But only to use my education against him and his kind."

Karima listened in silence. She was a girl and this was talk between men. Even so, it was unfair for her brother to blame the pasha and the mistress for everything. But it was also unfair that her mother was dead. It was all confusing. At least, in his anger at the adult Austens, Omar had somehow overlooked Charles—another reason for her to stay out of it.

"Meanwhile," Omar was saying, "there are decisions to be made. For one thing, someone will have to cook and clean for you. Karima will have to leave school."

Karima held her breath. She had never much liked school—it was mainly about the Quran and how to be a good wife—but her father had always wanted for her to be educated. Surely he would tell Omar so.

To her astonishment she heard him sigh, "I suppose you are right.

But let her finish this term. It's only a couple of months. Perhaps my cousin Nihal can help till then."

"Very well," said Omar.

And with that—although it took months for Karima to see it fully—her brother not only ended her schooling but usurped their father's role as head of the family.

The man called Alexei Tartakov shrugged, exhaled, and pushed his knight to Queen Five.

Jake Farallon looked and looked again. Maybe the vodka had caught up with the Russian. Jake could take the knight with a pawn, and all Alexei could do was recapture with his other knight. A pawn for a knight was a hell of an investment.

Jake reached toward the board then stopped. He thought of himself as a student of the game—not in a class with the Russian, no question there, but he had read a book or two, and he remembered a story about the old world champion, Lasker. In a similar situation Lasker had ignored the tempting sacrifice and made a simple defensive move. Asked why later, he had explained: "When a strong master thinks for half an hour and puts a piece where I can take it, I think that it will not be healthy to take it, and I leave it alone."

Jake made a simple defensive move.

Alexei laughed out loud. "Do you think you are Lasker?" Jake felt goose-pimples.

Six moves later he was facing the loss of his queen or immediate checkmate. He tipped his king, ordered another double vodka for the Russian, and allowed himself a beer. Looking back, he realized that he could have taken the knight and probably won. So he had learned something after all: that Alexei was the kind of man who would run a bluff, even in a chess game—and that Alexei saw him as the kind of man who could be bluffed. These were useful things to know.

"To the rats that eat Hitler's corpse," said the Russian amiably, raising his drink. Jake indicated with his beer glass that he joined in the toast.

He wondered how drunk the man was, or if he was drunk at all. Except for the fact that he looked to be in his midforties, it was hard to tell anything about Alexei Tartakov—if that was really his name. Take the way he let his jacket drape over both shoulders: you had to look closely to see that there was no arm under the right sleeve. Lost at Stalingrad, Alexei claimed. That and other wounds supposedly had put him in the diplomatic corps. Supposedly. In truth, Alexei was exactly the kind of diplomat that Jake was.

Farallon liked Alexei, and technically they were on the same side in this war. But this war was as good as over, as far as Jake could see. What he loved about his job was the feeling that he was a commando operating behind the lines in the *next* war. And in that war, in the view of the agency Jake worked for, Alexei was the enemy.

"I saw your small fat friend," said the Russian in his thick accent. "He was going away. Very far."

Jake was mildly surprised. He had mentioned the little Kraut spy Hans to Alexei as a sort of professional courtesy, a gesture of bona fides. Hans's boss—Bischof, wasn't it?—had come over long ago and easily, wanting only to continue to draw breath and to study the damned Pyramids or something. Bischof had given up *his* boss, a true Nazi pig named Gruber in Cairo. Gruber had been uncooperative at first but at a special camp in the desert had discovered the value of human discourse and come across with some very useful goods, including a lot of information on the Free Officers. By contrast, Hans was too small a fish to bother with, at least in Jake's opinion. But evidently no German was too small a fish for Alexei.

"A wife says to her husband," the Russian went right on—Hans obviously worth no further discussion—"'Ivan Ivanovich, if I die, will you marry another woman?' 'Don't say such a thing,' says Ivan. 'But to think of it, after long sorrow, a man alone, who can say? It's possible.' 'If you marry another woman, will she live in our house?' 'God forbid this can happen. But you see that I have no other house.' 'And if you marry another woman and she lives in our house, will she sleep in our bed?' 'This is nonsense. But it's true that we have only that bed, no other.' 'And if you marry another woman and she lives in our house and sleeps in our bed, will she wear my clothes?' 'Of course not! She is half your size!'"

Jake laughed dutifully; in America it was the old wife's golf clubs and the new wife was left-handed. It would have been an incredible gaffe to ask what had happened with Hans, but he couldn't help wondering. Then too, someday he might be called on to try to recruit Alexei—or even, in certain not impossible circumstances, to kill him. It would be nice to know something about the man's techniques. Oh well. It was a pretty far-fetched scenario anyway. The Russky was already old for fieldwork, and there was the missing arm—if nothing else, it made him conspicuous. No, when the war was over Alexei would be behind a desk in Moscow, getting a little exercise now and then interrogating enemies of the people.

"Where do you think you will be a year from now, my young friend?" asked Alexei, and again Jake had the uncomfortable feeling that his thoughts were being read.

He shrugged. "I haven't thought that far ahead in a long time."

Alexei smiled. "Maybe you would like to see Berlin?"

"We might see each other there."

"Who can say? But you know, here, where we are, is not a bad place for . . . those in our business. Beautiful city. Good weather. Interesting people."

Jake took note. Falling in love with a place could be as bad as falling in love with a woman. It made you vulnerable. Look at Bischof.

"And I think," the older man went on, "that there will be much . . . activity here, in this part of the world. Think of history. Always things happen here."

No disputing that, thought Jake. And with the Canal and Palestine and what the slide-rule boys and rockhounds were saying about the pools of oil just waiting to be tapped out in the deserts, things were going to keep on happening here. "I don't know how it works with you people," he said, "but I go where I'm sent."

Alexei laughed ruefully. "Yes. It is the same with us. So who can say." He gestured at the chessboard. "Another game, yes?"

They set up the pieces and Jake lost again. At least, he thought, he was picking up a few words of Russian in the process of getting his clock cleaned.

On the drive along the corniche, Henry took pleasure in feeling the first cool touch of autumn in the air, and equal pleasure in observing how few warships stood in the harbor, just as there were fewer and fewer soldiers in the streets. In June Italy had fallen and Normandy had been invaded, and now the great battles raged in France and Belgium and on the Eastern Front. Alexandria had become a military backwater, which suited Henry to a T.

"Fine weather," he ventured.

"Very fine, Pasha," agreed Mustafa.

And that was all. Henry grieved at the change in his employee, a man he respected and, as far as circumstances allowed, regarded as a friend. Ever since his wife's death, Mustafa had been remote, preoccupied. Gray had appeared in his hair almost overnight. Once voluble, he now communicated tersely and almost mechanically. Henry felt all the worse because, on some level, he held himself responsible for what had happened. Why had he insisted on the celebration at the shore? Pure ostentation? The usual do at one of the plantations would have been sufficient. Even Catherine had told him so.

He wondered if Mustafa had similar thoughts.

"Omar has started at university?"

"Yes, Pasha."

"He'll do well, I'm sure. And Karima?"

"She has finished with school, Pasha. She completed the sixth form. She keeps the house now . . . since . . ."

For a moment Henry thought that Mustafa would cry. And perhaps that would not be so bad a thing.

"But surely someone else could do that. If it's a question of money . . ."

Mustafa steered the Packard to the side of the road and stopped. He had never done such a thing without an order in all the years he had chauffeured for Henry.

"Henry Pasha, I thank you forever for all you have done. But I have thought of this, and it is better as it is. Karima's mother, who is in heaven, never went to school a minute in her life, any more than I did. And Karima, she has no head for it—she is always in the clouds dreaming of music. I doubt if she can recite two suras of the Quran. So it is better this way. In two years, three, it will be time to find a husband for her. For now . . ."

Unconsciously Mustafa took out a pack of cigarettes and matches—another thing he had never done in the Packard—then looked horrified at the transgression.

"Good idea," said Henry quickly, producing his own cigarette holder. "Trouble you for a light?"

The two men sat smoking together on the verge of the corniche.

"Do you know, Pasha," said Mustafa, "Omar is my son, of whom I am very proud. But Karima . . . she is the one who has the chance to . . . You have heard her sing?"

"Yes."

"Then you know. Ever since she was this high—" he tapped the gearshift knob—"she has this talent. You know Um Kalthum? You hear her on the radio?"

"I've heard of her." Henry knew of Um Kalthum only that Egyptians considered her the greatest singer on earth and that when her Thursday-evening broadcast came on the wireless, traffic, commerce, and everything else halted all over the country.

"Everyone listens, of course. But Karima . . . she *studies* Um Kalthum. Like a scholar with the Quran, I swear to you, Pasha. Sometimes she is even angry, 'How does she do that, I wish I could hear it again.'" Mustafa paused. "I don't know why I am troubling you with these small matters, Pasha. It's just that . . . my wife and I had these hopes, and I try to keep them alive."

With that he finished his cigarette and started the car.

"Forget the club," Henry told him. "We're going shopping."

It was a wind-up victrola, used but still usable—Mustafa had absolutely refused to let the pasha buy a new one.

To Karima it was magic. She had heard of such things but had never seen one, had never dreamed that there would be one right there in her home.

Not only could she now have music anytime she wanted, but overnight she was the most popular girl in the servants' quarters.

"One little thing," her father had told her after the men who delivered the machine had left. "You and I know this is a gift from the pasha, but if your brother asks, I bought it myself, for my own pleasure."

Karima understood.

"And one other thing, daughter. There is a teacher to whom you will go one day a week."

"To school, *Abi?*"

"Not that kind of teacher. One who teaches how to sing."

"But I know how to sing."

"You sing like an angel. But do you know everything? Do you know how Um Kalthum can hold a note so long? Aren't you always asking things like that? This teacher knows the answers."

"Is this from the pasha also?"

"No. This is my gift to you."

She ran to him and hugged him with all her might.

5
At Different Schools

Egypt and England, 1945–1949

A week before Adolf Hitler put a pistol in his mouth and pulled the trigger, Egypt finally declared war on Germany. The move was not a case of belated vengeance on a beaten enemy; it was intended solely to make Egypt eligible for charter membership in the newly proclaimed United Nations. One hope, among many, was that the international organization would find a way to force Britain out of the land of the pharaohs.

That hope was in vain. With the war's end the Wafd Party and the Muslim Brotherhood called openly and loudly for the immediate withdrawal of British troops. But, as they had done ever since 1882, the British found compelling reasons to extend their "protection." Egyptians responded with a series of strikes and riots fomented largely by the Muslim Brotherhood under the unyielding leadership of Hassan Al-Banna.

Disturbances, including riots and even revolts, were nothing new: they had erupted often and again during the long decades of British presence. But now there was a feeling that this was different, that change was at last coming—and coming soon.

For the still-young king, the moment was ripe with opportunity for greatness: the chance to lead his nation to independence. Farouk, however, fat and balding despite his youth, remained passive; perhaps he remembered the British tanks chewing up the manicured lawns of Abdine Palace. Whatever the case, he seemed willing to do whatever he was told so long as he was allowed to rule—and to indulge in his customary extravagances.

People talked of the green telephones in the bedrooms of Farouk's palaces—and the royal decree that no one else could use that color (as if telephones were so common that anyone cared what color they were!). Everyone knew of the 2 royal yachts, the 13 airplanes, the 200 cars. Everyone knew that titles and government positions were for sale for land or money. The king's barbers and gardeners, like everyone else close to him, had grown rich. Meanwhile, the fellahin were poorer than ever. "We are like the needle," their fatalistic saying went. "We clothe others but we ourselves are naked."

One day Farouk's minister of finance voiced the opinion that Egypt's relationship with Britain was like a Catholic marriage—in other words, indissoluble. The minister was shot soon afterward by a group of Free Officers led by Anwar Sadat. Once again, Sadat was arrested and tried. "Condemn me again if you like," he shouted from the cage that restrained him in the courtroom, "but stop the public prosecutor from praising British imperialism in the venerable presence of this Egyptian court of law."

He was acquitted.

When Charles leaned to kiss her, Catherine began to cry.

"Now, Mother, don't go on," he said. "I'll be back, never fear."

"I know. It's just . . ." She could not say what it was. Sadness, certainly, but all mixed up with happiness and nostalgia and pride and . . . everything.

All along the quay people were saying good-bye, many of them young men, some of them friends of Charles's. Not one of them, thought Catherine, was as fine-looking a boy as her son. Taller than his father now, he had the easy grace and broadening shoulders of an athlete. His clothes hung as easily on him as his smile. His hair was chestnut brown streaked with gold, and his eyes, though dark blue, held hints of green. His skin was no darker than any Englishman's who had spent time in the sun.

And he was going to England. To school at Harrow. A sterner academic regimen that he had been accustomed to in Alex—and a more exclusive one; it had taken all of Henry's influence to win entrée for his son, and even then a special examination had been required. If all went well, the next step would be Oxford.

"In fact," he was joking now, "you might see me before you want to. They'll probably send me down the first week."

"None of that, now," said Henry with a mock sternness that was not entirely mock.

"Glad enough to be rid of me, I suspect," grinned Charles.

A bell rang. Henry glanced at his watch. People moved toward the gangplank.

Charles shook hands with his father, and Catherine had time for one last hug. Then her son was leaving, shouting something to another young man who, she noticed, called him "Chip."

Harrow had been her idea, one that she had gradually imposed on Charles and then on Henry. This had all come to her when it was clear that the war would soon end. There was no longer any need for Charles to forgo his birthright as an Englishman. Indeed, Catherine saw, the time would never be riper. Another year, another two years in Egypt, and no one could say what direction Charles's life might take. This way might not be totally predictable either—what was, with young men?—but at least it put him on a solid and familiar course.

Charles and his friend ran up the boarding steps and elbowed their way to the ship's rail. Catherine could see her son searching for her, then smiling as he found her. He raised a hand in farewell. Moments later a deep horn sounded and the steamer slipped slowly backward—it almost seemed as if the land, rather than the ship, were moving—then swung broadside and made for the open sea. Catherine and Henry stood waving until they could no longer make out

Charles's form at the railing. To Catherine's surprise, she realized that they were holding hands. She almost blushed. It had been so long. But it was fitting. Whatever had passed between them, whatever their disagreements—even about Charles himself—their son was something unbreakable that they shared, the one undeniably good thing they had done.

And now, she thought, we're like survivors marooned on some desert island, watching the ship sail away.

In the car on the way back to the villa, a little spasm of anxiety struck her. "Do you think," she asked her husband, "that he'll do well there? Fit in and all?"

"Because he's . . . from Egypt?"

At least he had not said *Egyptian* or, worse yet, *half-Egyptian*. "Yes."

Henry gave it more thought than she would have liked. "Young men can be cruel to anyone who's in any way . . . different," he finally said. "It's why I've always encouraged Charles's interest in sports. Once he's on a team, nothing else will count."

"One hopes so," she said, comforted. She still wished that Charles had liked cricket, rather than the plebeian football. Then, quite suddenly, as her gaze passed over Mustafa at the wheel, two words flashed unbidden into her mind: *safely away*. What a strange thing. Lately she had hardly given a thought to Mustafa's daughter, what was her name, Karima, skinny little Karima. The girl hadn't been so much underfoot since her mother's death—housekeeping for her father, Catherine supposed—and Charles seemed to have stopped mooning over her, if that was what it could be called. One of those cases of puppy love that never lasts, obviously. Fortunately. No doubt the girl had seen the light when she learned that Charles was off to England.

Catherine wondered that the matter had ever concerned her at all. Still, it was pleasant to reflect that by the time Charles returned, skinny little Karima would probably be a fat young matron with two or three dark little babies.

———

"The British!" shouted Omar. "Sixty-five years in Egypt—a man's lifetime!—and what have they done for us?"

"Nothing!" rang a satisfying number of voices from the crowd.

"Oh, but they haven't been idle," Omar went on sarcastically. "It's not as if they've done nothing at all. Haven't they spent millions on airports and roads, the better to move their soldiers—the better to keep their feet on our necks? But where is one school built by them, when millions of our brothers cannot even read? Where is a single hospital, when half our country's children die before the age of five? Where is a single well drilled by the British, when 70 percent of Egyptian adults have parasites from drinking water that crawls with disease?"

Omar had them in the palm of his hand. He was good at this, he thought with pleasure. Only his second year at the university and already a name, a minor celebrity. He did a prizefighter's bounce up onto the balls of his feet—it was becoming his trademark gesture—and prepared to ratchet the five hundred students' energy a notch higher.

But just then a chant broke out among a small group at the fringe of the crowd: "Down with Farouk! Down with Farouk!" A red flag waved. The police who had been desultorily watching the demonstration suddenly came alert, and a couple of them moved ominously toward the source of the disturbance.

Damned Communists, thought Omar. Even the University of Alexandria had its coterie of them. But he was damned if he was going to let them ruin his speech.

"Wouldn't the English love that?" he shouted. "Wouldn't they love to see us fighting among ourselves? No, brothers, Egypt's king is a matter for Egyptians. It's the British soldiers who must go—and now! British out now! British out now!"

"British out now!" The crowd took up the chant at full volume. Someone ripped the red flag from its makeshift pole. "British out now!" The police backed off—Omar could swear that some of them were chanting along.

An hour later he sat in Muhammad Nader's coffeehouse with Ibrahim Khairi, who had witnessed the speech and deeply approved.

"You know how to handle yourself, Omar. We need men with the talent to speak before a crowd. God knows I'm nervous enough just in front of our little group."

Omar had never thought of Ibrahim as nervous about anything. He filed the information away. "Well, it's not too difficult to excite a crowd," he said modestly. "But sometimes I feel that it's just so much air. Just words. The *Ingliz* are still here, after all."

Ibrahim thought it over. "Not all words are just words. Some are deeds waiting to be born." He smiled self-consciously at the imagery, then turned businesslike. "The general strike is next week. The students will be ready?"

"Ready and eager. I can place three or four hundred of them wherever they're needed."

"Good. And what can I do?"

He meant money. Omar pretended to think it over. "Well, it would look better if we could carry some signs. We'd need some poster board and paint."

"How much?"

Omar named a sum that was only slightly too high. Ibrahim would not know the difference—any more than he would know that the materials would in any case be stolen from the university's art department—and Omar would have enough for an evening's gambling and a pipe of hashish.

Ibrahim handed him the money. "Do you know, Omar, when you first joined us, I had my doubts about you. I wondered if you were . . . serious. But no one has worked harder than you. You are the Brotherhood's right arm at the university—you and, of course, Khalid Hamra."

"Well, that's going too far . . ." Omar was genuinely moved. Khalid Hamra was the designated leader of the Muslim Brotherhood at the university.

"Khalid will graduate this year," Ibrahim went on, "and, God willing, will carry our cause into the larger world. We'd like for you to take over from him when he leaves."

"I hardly know what to say."

"I hope you'll say yes. This comes not only from our little group—" Ibrahim waved his arm to indicate the coffeehouse—"but from higher up. Even in Cairo there are some who know your name."

"Allah . . . it's too much. I'll have to give it some thought."

"Of course. No rush."

Omar found that he was actually blushing. "Thank you, Ibrahim," he said in all sincerity. "Thank you for your faith in me."

. . . so as you see, parents, even though there have been some bumpy spots, I'm finally getting the hang of how they do things here.

A friend, very good chap named Dunsworth, has invited me to spend Christmas with his family in London. They do the holiday much larger here than we do in Alex, even though there are still shortages and rationing.

By the way, could you wire a little extra to the account—twenty or thirty pounds ought to suffice—for some life-saving garments? I thought winter was cold in Alex, but here it seeps into the bones—one is never warm.

Hope that you are both well. The servants too. Hello to Mustafa. Ask him for me if Karima is still singing. She must stick to it—a marvelous talent. Tell him to tell her I said so.

I promise to write more often in future. It's just that the easiest courses here make the most difficult at British Boys' look like tea biscuits, so one continually has one's nose to the proverbial grindstone.

Your son,
Charles

. . . £50. Your father says that in England one must never cut corners on clothes.

The servants are well. Mustafa thanks you for your regards.

Do write as often as you can. The old villa seems quite empty these days.

With love,
Mother

. . . some clippings that record some of my (ahem!) exploits on the field of battle for dear old Oxford I'm told that it's unusual for a first-year man to be top striker on the varsity. Note the nom de guerre *"Arab Death" Austen. Some "journalist" decided to re-anagramatize the name of the old silent-cinema actress Theda Bara, and now I must endure no end of guff on account of it.*

Did I mention that I'm reading Russian? The language, I mean. My thinking is that a man who knows English, Arabic, and Russian might be a valuable commodity one of these days.

It occurs to me that in my last missive I neglected to inquire after the servants. Best regards, as always, to Mustafa. I imagine Karima must be married by now, although you've sent no news of it.

Speaking of news, what's the poop on the troops pulling out of Alex and the Canal? It's all over the papers here.

Will write soon.

Your loving son,
Charles ("Arab Death") Austen

. . . acquiesced in the "evacuation" of British troops from Alexandria and the Canal Zone. Of course it was all the work of the Wafd rabble and the so-called Muslim Brotherhood, both of whom are stupid enough to bite the hand that has protected them all these years. Naturally, your father is less inclined than I to see it as a disaster. He is more concerned about what the Zionists are doing in Palestine. He believes it means war.

I confess that the whole business bores me to tears.

We are both very proud of your achievements in your studies, and miss you.

I was thinking just the other day that you must have met a nice English girl by now but are too secretive to mention it. (Mustn't pry, I know!)

Do write soon.

With love,
Mother

. . . gigantic loads of European and "Middle Eastern" history, eighteenth century through what is now the "First" World War, and thinking of reading law—possibly preliminary work here and finish back home. Because it seems to me that old Egypt might someday be the fulcrum for what is fast becoming a monstrous East-West teeter-totter, and that I might have a role to play in all that. All rot, probably, but one does wish to accomplish something in this vale of tears etc. etc.

Spring here resembles winter in Alex. Had a wonderful jaunt, though, with my friend George Abendroth (have I mentioned him?) at the ancestral estate at, of all places, Nottingham. His father (Sir Harold) is no end of an industrialist—Abi, you'd get on with him. Touring and boating etc. with George and his old local flame Cynthia and his sister Elizabeth—quite an amazing young woman, intelligent, witty.

The Times *is rife with rumors of war over Palestine. What do you hear there? I feel as if there had been war all my life and hope that a new one can be avoided.*

Must dash. Will write again soon—promise.

Your son,
Charles

. . . has asked me to add a note about the war as she has no interest in it—calls it a medieval jihad. Unfortunately your news there is

probably more accurate than ours, which is a continual litany of victories and glory. It takes but little reflection to make one wonder why, in view of all this military success, the war is not yet won.

My own opinion is that we have more to fear from victory than from defeat. The "Israelis," as they now call themselves, fight well and fiercely—like cornered animals—but even if they succeed in defending their territory, they are no threat to conquer Egypt. What, though, might America do if suddenly we were seen to be threatening to crush them?.

In any case, the next few months will certainly tell the tale. Neither we nor our so-called allies have the resources or, I think, the will for a long war.

Mother inquires after the Abendroths. Says they sound like lovely people.

Business remains better than one might have expected. The current war has had little effect on cotton.

With all good wishes,
Father

Karima had three loves, but they touched and blended in such a way that sometimes they were more like one. There was Charles, of course, and although she no longer cried herself to sleep at night thinking of him, in his absence he had come to play an even larger part in her secret dreams than when he had been right there, in her eyes and ears almost every day.

There was her music. She had not sung in public since her mother's death, but she kept up her lessons, studied the voices on the victrola as if they were telling her the way to Paradise, and sang to herself for hours each day—not as a pastime, as a man might idly whittle a stick, but as a master carver might work a piece of wood to refine his skills even though he did not intend to sell the carving.

And there was Um Kalthum, every Thursday night on the radio and every day in records that Karima had been able to buy only through hours of sewing or cleaning or marketing done for someone

else. Somehow Um Kalthum brought together Karima's other two
loves. In her consummate skill was everything to which Karima
aspired; in her songs of love forbidden, love doomed, was everything
Karima felt for Charles—and every emotion she tried to put into her
own singing, sometimes holding back tears because that made the
emotion even stronger.

In this way, in music and dreams, Karima drifted through her
hours of cooking and keeping the house immaculate for her father
and brother (although Omar came home less and less often these
days). She knew that it could not last. Sooner or later her father
would find a husband for her—she knew much younger girls who
were already married. But so far he seemed happier to have her there,
and although Omar had once or twice mentioned that it was time for
her to think of marriage, he had not insisted on it.

From her father she had been able to glean only the most general
information about Charles—he was doing well in his studies and
sports, the pasha was very proud of him. There was so much more
she wanted to know. What was his life like in England (which to her
might as well have been the moon)? Had he changed? Did he think
of her? Remember her at all?

The questions were like the painful words of a song.

When he told her he was leaving, his face had shown such excitement and pride that she had forced herself to smile and share his happiness. When he said that he might be gone for four or five years, it
had passed right over her: a span of time that long simply had no
meaning. Now that two years had gone by, she understood how long
it truly was.

She would love him forever, she told herself—more song lyrics—
but she should have the wisdom to see that those sweet moments of
childhood were over. She should put them away in a secret hiding-
place in her heart, and think of her own life. Her life. What would it
be? What could it be? She loved her father, but someday she would
no longer be living here, taking care of him. She would have a husband, children. Yes, of course. But was that all? Somehow she

thought that there would be, *should* be, more—that something was waiting for her, something of which she was aware but had not yet identified, like a mysterious sound in the dark.

She was mooning in just such a mood over kitchen chores one morning when Amina, Um-Rashid's granddaughter, popped in.

"May I play the victrola?"

"Go ahead. But if you scratch a record . . ."

"Don't get so excited." Amina was just Karima's age, plumply pretty and engaged to a goldsmith's apprentice, and ever ready to tease or joke. She put on a record and came to help with the chickpeas. "I suppose you'll be going?"

"Going? Where?"

"To see her, of course."

"Who?"

"You haven't heard? I'm surprised. It's all over the radio."

"*What* is?"

"You really should listen, you know. Then you wouldn't be so ignorant about the war news . . ."

"The war news is depressing."

". . . and you'd know that Um Kalthum is coming to Alex."

"*What!* Are you serious? When?"

"Next month? Something like that."

"To sing?"

"What else? A benefit for the wounded veterans or something."

Karima wiped her hands and rushed to the radio. If this was some kind of joke . . .

But for once Amina wasn't joking.

. . . as for the war, your father says that the Arabs are losing and will have to recognize the Zionists. Well, why not? They do exist. The whole affair has been utter foolishness from the beginning.

Have you visited with the Abendroths again? I notice that your recent letters make no mention of them.

Catherine had fantasized about Elizabeth Abendroth for months. Picturing a typical English rose of a girl, she went on to build images of the family estate, the cathedral wedding, long visits to bouncing English grandchildren—two boys and two girls.

. . . do not see so much of George Abendroth as I once did. Each of us going in his own direction, as it were.

It was the most, and the last, Charles would ever say pertaining to his brief infatuation with Elizabeth Abendroth. He had been a fool, he knew. Loneliness had made him foolish. He had been lonely ever since leaving Egypt. Sports and studies and even friendships might ease the ache but never cured it. Then Elizabeth had appeared in his life, and for a few shining months the loneliness did not exist—until she dismissed him as lightly and laughingly as she might a dance partner. A remark he had heard her make to a girlfriend—he was eavesdropping, might as well admit it—told him all he needed to know about where a person of his particular background stood in the estimation of a certain type of young Englishwoman.

The Sayyid Darwish Theatre was lighted like an ocean liner in the night. Across the street, Karima shivered in the winter evening; she had stood there for hours. Now it was nearly time for the performance to begin, and she had not yet caught a glimpse of Um Kalthum—undoubtedly the singer had used another entrance.

A glimpse was all Karima had hoped for; she certainly could not afford a ticket, and in any case there were no tickets to be had. Like all of Um Kalthum's concerts, this one had been sold out for weeks. Wealthy Arabs from all over the Middle East flew in for them: merchant tycoons from Lebanon, royal princes from Saudi Arabia and the Trucial States. Karima had watched them arrive in their limousines, the women sparkling with jewels.

Soon the great singer would take the stage. A few latecomers hurried into the theater. Karima was heartbroken. Not even to have seen her! Perhaps afterward? But no, it was too cold to wait that long. She crossed the street. The lights looked warm, and perhaps she could hear at least a faint note or two from inside. An usher at the door glanced at her as if expecting a ticket, then looked more closely and waved her away.

"Please," she said, "may I stand here a minute?"

"No, girl. It's not permitted. Go home before you freeze."

"Only a minute, I promise."

"I told you it's not permitted. Now—" The usher paused. "What's your name, girl?"

"Karima."

"Aren't you Mustafa Ismail's daughter? The one who sings?"

"Yes, sir." She recognized the man as an acquaintance of her father's. She hadn't known him in his fancy usher's uniform.

"Does your father know you're here?"

"Yes—he knows I love Um Kalthum." It was only partly a lie, she told herself.

The man glanced around. "Look, do you see that stair? Go up it and turn left. There's a little space there where you can stand."

"Allah! Do you mean it?"

"Go now while no one is watching. And for God's sake, don't make a sound!"

"Yes, sir! Thank you! Not a sound." As if anyone would dream of making noise while Um Kalthum was singing.

She found the place and pushed back into the shadows. Almost immediately the buzzing theater went silent, and she thought for an instant that she had been detected. Then thunderous applause welled up and, peeking out as much as she dared, she saw Um Kalthum.

The performer was not a beauty, or even very pretty. But she had something greater than beauty—Karima felt it, though she could not have put it in words—a powerful and personal connection to the very heart and soul of the audience.

Um Kalthum sang only three songs that night—but each lasted nearly an hour. Over and over she reshaped the same refrain, changing the nuance very slightly with each repetition. At every pause, the adoring crowd called out her nickname: *"Ya Souma! Ya Souma!"*

When it was over, Karima walked home as if in a dream. She knew she would be beaten if Omar happened to be there, and at least scolded if her father were still awake. It didn't matter. She felt as if she had glimpsed paradise—and now all that was needed was to find her way there for herself.

She knew what she wanted to be.

. . . the analysis by the newspaper pundits is that our side lost because they were poorly organized, at each other's throats half the time, and engaged in all manner of corruption the other half, whereas the Israelis were just the opposite. How much of this is merely English prejudice is impossible to say—some of it, surely. And of course the American connection didn't do Israel any harm.

It's difficult to believe that I'm well into my third year here. More and more I find myself missing home—including both of you, of course—and longing for the day when I'll be there again.

Ah well, back to the mines.

Your loving son,
Charles

. . . difficult for me to write about it, or even to think about it. You know Egyptian pride, so you can imagine how hard this defeat— no-one calls it an "armistice"—has struck. Or perhaps you need to be here, to see it in people's faces.

As it happens, your newspaper pundits are right. In a word, we were beaten by efficiency—a quality notably lacking in ourselves and our so-called allies.

Of course, simply admitting that would be too painful. So the cry now is of treason: generals and politicians in the pay of the Americans or of international Jewry—the kind of Twaddle the late Führer used to peddle. Shameful. I would not be surprised to see some sort of military coup.

In short, be thankful you are not here just now. It is not a good time for Egypt.

Fondly—we miss you very much—
Father

Farid Hamza was used to it now, and it no longer irritated him; in fact it amused him. It occurred even with fellow soldiers: they could never decide whether to look into his good eye or at the other one, covered with a black patch and framed in scar tissue.

He nodded at the dozen officers who were trying to make this decision. There were one or two older men, including General Naguib. The rest were young, but several were already colonels. Hamza himself, the youngest man there, was a lieutenant colonel. The black patch had something to do with that.

Hamza had no illusions about heroism. He had been a soldier doing his job on the July day when an Israeli shell blasted one of his tanks and a piece of jagged metal ripped into his face. But because his unit was leading an attack that up until then had been succeeding, and because Egypt desperately needed heroes, he now had a drawer full of medals and a rank beyond his years.

Most of the other men in the room were realists too. Most had seen combat, and all knew from bitter experience how the war had been lost. They had waited in vain for ammunition or reinforcements, had been ordered to attack when attack was impossible or to hold fast when retreat was mandatory, had been sent on idiotic missions dreamed up by someone in Cairo who had no idea what it was like to fight in the Sinai with insufficient air cover.

Because they knew these things, they were here to consider something that would not have occurred to them a year ago: revolution.

There were two factions among them: the firebrands and the cautious.

Hamza's friend Sadat was among those who argued that the time to strike was now. The people were angry and ashamed. They would back anyone who offered something besides the national disgrace that the politicians and the high generals had brought them.

General Naguib was the senior officer among those who counseled patience, but it was Gamal Abdel Nasser who did most of the talking. Nasser pointed out that revolutions were political as well as military events. The world had seen plenty of barrack-room coups that ended up as shabby little dictatorships because proper politics were neglected. What was needed was time—time to build contacts with the political parties, with organizations such as the Muslim Brotherhood, with interest groups of all stripes.

As the junior man, Hamza remained silent until Naguib at last asked his opinion. He smiled inwardly as the glances flicked from eye to black patch. "I think," he said, "that we are all familiar with the results of impatience and hasty planning. I think we should build our strength and wait and watch. When the true time comes, there will be no need for debate. We will all know it."

Even Sadat nodded.

...from France down through Italy, gaining more "culture" every inch of the way. Shall embark, I imagine, from Naples, probably in August. Will of course wire details.

I hope you are not disappointed that I'm not finishing out a "degree" here. That's a mere formality that can be completed anywhere. Oxford, God love her, is not about degrees but about an education. And so farewell to England. I wouldn't have missed it for the world—but how good it will feel to be home again!

Your son,
Charles

6

Layla and Majnoon

Alexandria, 1950

It was a new decade, a new half-century.

Over much of the world people had emerged from the rubble of the murderous 1940s, had ridden out the war-created shortages, had gone back to work.

There were new governments, new boundaries, new inventions, new thoughts.

There were also new weapons. But though these threatened to make the dawning decade even more fearful than the long dark one just past, many people understood better than before the difference between threat and fact.

All in all it was a time for the young, a time to dress in the bright clothes of hope for the future and pleasure in the present.

At this international party, Egypt was like the eccentric uncle who appears in the familiar old suit, telling the familiar jokes, bearing the familiar gifts. Truly, the more things changed in Egypt, the more they remained the same.

Farouk had changed, but only for the worse. His excesses and appetites had gone to the point of caricature, and then beyond. Not one of his hundreds of carefully sculpted Savile Row suits could hide the blubbery ruin of his body. His principal activities in the world at large were night-clubbing, gambling, and the piling up of ever-higher mountains of jewels and gold.

He had one of the world's finest collections of rare books because they were worth money, but his personal reading consisted mainly of comics. The rumor, which happened to be true, had long since seeped out that he was addicted to the form of oral stimulation that one of his mistresses, an American, had taught him—rather late in the game, it was dryly noted. It was said that his private time was devoted almost entirely to indulgence in this pleasure, or waiting to be ready to indulge in it again.

The British had not changed, or at least could not bring themselves to admit it. They were still in Egypt, still watching over their precious Canal as if expecting to see their vanished empire come steaming back through it one day.

The Nile of course had not changed—nor the desert—nor anything else about the land or the lives of the people on it. In other Arab states foreign engineers were tapping the first small pools of what they would learn was a hidden ocean of oil, but although hopeful oilmen swarmed over Egypt as well, they left as empty-handed as the fellahin *themselves.*

Politics were much the same. True, there was a new enemy, Israel, to despise as much or more than the British, but the Wafd still waved the flag of nationalism, the Muslim Brotherhood still went their semi-conspiratorial way while winning the hearts of the poor with acts of charity, and the Free Officers, some of them still in possession of their youthful ideal, still plotted in deep secret.

Egypt itself remained the cultural center of the Arab world, just as Saudi was the center of religion.

Cairo was Cairo, different only in becoming more grotesquely populous with each passing year.

Alexandria had not changed, at least not much, not yet. A little seedier, perhaps, now that the war money and war glamor had gone, but still a city almost as European as it was Egyptian.

Charles had been home for a week and felt as if he had scarcely had a waking hour to himself. Informally, there were a dozen old acquaintances to renew. Formally, there was a round of parties engineered by Catherine and other mothers with a view to reintroducing Charles to local society—specifically, to the part of local society which had eligible daughters to parade before a very eligible bachelor.

For Catherine, all this required some tricky footwork. For one thing, there was the painful reality that for some in Alex's British community her son would never be "eligible." For another, she had a favorite among the young women, Ariel Wyatt, the daughter of Constance Wyatt, who was perhaps Catherine's best friend. Sir Lawrence Wyatt, who had retired to Alex in the hope that the climate would alleviate the lingering effects of his being gassed in the First World War, was a man without prejudices. Constance, an artist and self-proclaimed existentialist—whatever that was—filled their house with abstract paintings including her own, that Catherine could only pretend to appreciate. Ariel combined her father's cool level-headedness with her mother's striking beauty.

Unfortunately, when Charles and Ariel met, it was obvious that the possibility of romantic attraction between them existed only in their mothers' dreams. It wasn't a matter of dislike, but of the immediate, intuitive recognition by a young man and woman that they aren't meant for each other.

"Mother, please!" Charles protested by way of explanation. "I'm in no desperate hurry to settle down. Haven't I just spent a small eternity cloistered in darkest Oxford? Aren't I entitled to a bit of fun?"

Although Catherine would spend long pleasurable hours commiserating with Constance over the matter, her disappointment was less than total; in truth she did not really look forward to sharing her only child with any woman.

These subtleties were far from Charles's mind as he strolled the grounds with his father one morning. He was merely thankful that the string of social engagements seemed at last to be winding down.

"It's pleasant enough, I suppose—up to a point. Still, one does begin to feel rather like a prize beef being shifted from one village fair to the next."

Henry chuckled sympathetically. "Well, soon enough life will be back to normal, and you'll be at loose ends and bored stiff." They both knew what was coming next. "Any thoughts as to what you'd like to do now that you're a certified adult?"

"I should like to muck about till all hours in evil dens full of loose women, frittering away your money. Unfortunately, that doesn't seem to be on the cards."

They both smiled.

"In point of fact I *have* given it some thought," Charles went on. "You remember my letters, all about Egypt's role in the world—etc. etc. Idealistic rubbish, much of it, I daresay. But I still believe we can be something—not a world power, but a broker to the powers. I'd like to have something to do with that, perhaps in diplomatic service. Of course," he hurried to add, "I'd still want to help out where I can with our . . . your business concerns."

Henry felt gratified. Like most men who have built empires, he had always harbored hope that his son would take over someday. And in Egypt there certainly was no impediment to mixing a public career with private pursuits; far more difficult to mix such a career with youthful ideals. But it was not as simple as all that.

"You need to know," he said, "that our interests are more diverse than they once were. There's been a great deal of agitation for so-called land redistribution. Outright Communism to my way of thinking. Nothing may ever come of it, of course, but if it does, you may be sure our lands will be among the first confiscated. So I've hedged our bets. While you were away I sold Karnak and Sake-lardis." These were the names of plantations. "Karnak fetched a good price, Sakelardis not so good—buyers becoming wary. I put the money, the bulk of it anyway, into oil shares. American companies prospecting in Saudi."

Charles looked at him in surprise.

"I know," said Henry. "I'm a planter, not a capitalist. But it's not such a risk, really. Reliable people tell me the oil is there, and God knows Europe will soon be as thirsty for it as the Americans—which is to say as thirsty as an Irishman for his Guinness. I've even put a little into some ventures here in Egypt, not that I have much hope of their paying out. Patriotic duty, as it were. But you'll need to learn about such matters, you see."

"I see," said Charles thoughtfully.

"By the way—another matter entirely—I must apologize. I'd arranged a little gift for you, celebrate your return, but its delivery has been delayed. Be here soon, I should think."

"Very well, *Abi*, you've got me curious. What is it?"

"Top secret, old chap."

Their walk had brought them within a hundred yards of the servants' quarters. At Mustafa's cottage a young woman was hanging laundry. A breeze billowed the shirts and sheets and tugged the woman's loose garments close against her body. It was a well-remembered scene from the past, familiar and yet somehow different.

"My word, is that Karima?" said Charles.

"I believe it is," said Henry.

"Well, I must say, she certainly has grown."

Henry lifted an eyebrow.

Karima finished her task and went into the house without looking their way. Charles stared after her.

Henry cleared his throat. "Nearly eleven," he said, checking the sun—he rarely troubled with his watch in daylight. "Best be starting back. Your mother has scheduled a luncheon in your honor, has she not?"

Charles broke out of his trance and into a wry grin. "The condemned man ate a hearty meal," he said. "But about those oil ventures on which you've mortgaged my inheritance . . ."

It was a 1950 Jaguar XK-100. A two-seat convertible with 190 horsepower under its long, sleek bonnet. Painted the deep forest color that would become known as "British racing green."

Henry had contrived to be sipping a gin and tonic on the lawn with Charles when the car was delivered. "What's this, then?" he frowned as the agent eased it up the drive. "Someone lost, no doubt."

"Will you look at that," murmured Charles with the instant infatuation of a young man for a fast, flashy machine.

To Henry, who had ridden in Packards most of his adult life, the Jaguar seemed to be missing several important parts. But then, it was not his. He made a show of putting on his glasses. "Oh! Now I see. Do you remember my mentioning a belated welcome-home gift?"

Charles stared at his father, at the car, back at his father. "*Abi!* You're having me on!"

"Welcome home, son."

"Well, really, *Abi*! Really. One doesn't know what to say." He was on his feet, drawn to the car as if to a magnet.

Henry had never lavished gifts on his son and could hardly say what had impelled him to do so now. The Jaguar had cost the world, not to mention the shipping charges. But the boy had done them proud at Oxford and had come home a fine-looking young man. And . . . well, Henry had missed him. Why dissect motives? The light in Charles's eyes was reason enough.

Catherine came sweeping out to hug her son. Mustafa materialized magically and listened as the agent explained various knobs and levers. Servants and their children formed a small crowd. Karima was among them.

"Anyone for a spin?" Charles asked.

Several children shamelessly cried. "Me, Mr. Charles, me!"

Charles laughed. "Well, first I must learn to manage the thing myself. Come on, Jenkins old man—" this to the young agent—"show me the ropes." He climbed behind the wheel beside Jenkins and, after a stall or two and some grinding of gears, pulled away to cheers.

Out of the corner of his eye Henry saw Karima's eyes following his son, her expression much the same as Charles's when he had spied her across the lawn the day before. He shrugged off a tingle of worry. These things had a way of working themselves out—and in any case, Catherine had not seemed to notice.

There was no signal, no arrangement. For no particular reason
Charles strolled to the lemon tree one soft, warm night and moments
later saw her walking alone in the light of a high half-moon.

"Karima."

"Mr. Charles?"

She came close.

"How have you been, Karima?"

"Well, Mr. Charles. And you?"

"Very well. It's good to see you."

"And you."

This is ridiculous, he thought. They hadn't spoken in four
years, and here he stood mouthing polite nothings like a shy
schoolboy.

It's wrong to be here, she thought. But she drank in his voice and
his scent and the intensity in his eyes, and knew that she could be
nowhere else.

"You're still living with—" he began at the same moment that she
said, "Tell me about Eng—" Then both said "Sorry" at the same
instant.

"—still living with your father?" Charles finished. The superficial
answer was obvious, but the question went much deeper.

"Yes."

The moonlight made her skin ivory and her dark eyes endlessly
deep.

"He must be fighting off the suitors with a club," Charles could
not stop himself from saying.

"Not really." She too disliked this topic.

"What? None at all? You can't be serious."

"One man has been calling on my father lately," Karima admitted.
"A businessman," she added with a touch of pride.

Charles had overheard servants' gossip about two of his father's
young male employees who had been smitten by Karima. But this
businessman was news. Of course, he thought with a pang of petty

jealousy, in Egypt even the operator of a fruit-drink stand called himself a businessman.

"I haven't seen Omar," he said to change the subject.

"He has his own place now. With some other young men . . . friends of his."

"Still so religious?"

"Maybe not so much. I don't know. It's always been hard to know what Omar is thinking." The truth was that Omar seemed less involved with the Muslim Brotherhood—he had told her recently that it represented the way of the past—but more anti-British than ever. He also talked a great deal about socialist ideals, whatever those might be.

This subject was going nowhere either. Charles and Karima studied the moon as if suddenly absorbed in astronomy.

"I've missed Egypt," he said, breaking the silence. "I didn't realize how badly I'd missed it till I was standing on the ship watching old Alex creep up on the horizon. I started crying like a baby."

Karima smiled at the image, but the concept of missing Egypt was hard to grasp. She had never even been to Cairo. She turned to see his face. In the moonlight he was the romantic hero of the songs she loved.

"Only a minute more," she said. "I told my father I was just going for a breath of air."

"Well—yes, of course."

"It's so good to see you again, Mr. Charles."

"So good to see you." They were back to small talk. "And please, just Charles."

"All right . . . Charles." Of course she could never address him in that way in front of others.

She turned to go.

"Karima!"

"Yes?"

"Meet me here tomorrow night?"

She hesitated. The strangest feeling of stepping into thin air. "All right. If I can."

"Of course you can! I . . . I'll tell you about England."

Walking home she could not control her thoughts. It was a dream. It was all the songs, only real.

She hushed the small voice warning that there was danger in the songs, too.

He did not tell her about England the next night. That meeting was even more hurried than the first: Mustafa had come down with a feverish cold and might need Karima at any moment. The night after that Charles was expected at one of his mother's social engagements. And the following night, although Mustafa was much better, they again had only a few self-conscious moments.

As she was turning to go, Karima said, "If we met later, I could stay longer." She felt herself blush furiously. What kind of woman would make such a suggestion? She wished that Charles had thought of it himself. But of course how could he know when her father went to sleep?

They made their plans.

The next night Charles pleaded exhaustion and trudged off to bed. An hour later he slipped from the house. The lights were still on in his father's study and his mother's room, but no one would expect to see him until breakfast. At the same moment Karima, listening to Mustafa's contented snores, tiptoed from the cottage.

With the luxury of hours before them, they could afford to laugh about their own delicious folly while the moon, nearly full now, did magic tricks with the sculpted landscape and ten thousand insects whirred a symphony in the electric shadows. And then Charles talked about England, and somehow that led to Egypt, and to his dreams for his homeland and himself and the world.

"And you, Karima? What do you want?"

"Nothing, really. Nothing special."

"Come now. I've been babbling forever. The truth."

She could not tell him all the truth, so she told a part of it. "I want to sing."

He was quiet for so long that she thought he found her ambition ridiculous. Then he said, "You must sing. You have the most beautiful voice I've ever heard.

"Thank you for thinking so." She wanted to tell him that she was so much better now than he remembered, but it was vanity and bad luck to say such things.

He could still see, still hear her on the beach that day, before the terrible accident. He had thought of her as beautiful then, but he realized now that he had held only a young boy's notion of a young girl's beauty. The beauty of the woman beside him tonight was of a different magnitude, a different kind; he could feel her beauty in his blood.

He touched her face, drew her to him, kissed her. It was not a kiss of passion, not yet. It was a kiss like the touch of the wind on a sail at the beginning of a long voyage of discovery.

There were more kisses, soft words, soft laughter, until the stars told them that dawn was near. They parted drunk with each other, happier than they had ever in their young lives dreamed they could be.

"There's something we need to discuss."

"What is it, my dear?" said Henry pleasantly, although he recognized all too well the tone of his wife's voice.

"Charles."

"What about Charles?"

"It cannot have escaped your attention that he's developed some sort of attachment to that . . . that servant girl."

So she'd noticed after all. Hardly surprising. "Servant girl?" he said mildly. "You mean Karima?"

"Yes. Of course. Karima."

"But, my dear, they've known each other since they were children."

"Don't be dense, Henry. I believe he's been . . . seeing her. At night."

"Oh, really, Catherine—"

"Perhaps you've been too concerned with other matters. But *I'm* concerned about our son. I want you to have a word with him."

"Oh, come now. Surely it's not as serious as all that."

"Henry." She assumed her no-compromise air. It reminded him of an iron statue that had somehow suffered injury. "I have endured a great deal. I will not endure whispers behind my back that our son is going about with a servant. I will not endure it, do you hear?"

He knew when retreat was the better part of valor. "Very well. If you're persuaded it's necessary, I'll have a chat with him."

"Good." She seemed mollified but added, "The sooner the better, I should think. Before something . . . untoward happens."

"Soon," agreed Henry. "I'll need to give some thought to it."

"Of course. Thank you." Her purpose achieved, she turned and left.

It had been, thought Henry sadly, what passed for a conversation between them these days. And what on earth was he going to say to Charles?"

They kissed now before they spoke, and their hours together were filled with aching sweetness and longing.

Often their talk turned to the implacable fact that faced them: that theirs was a love that could not be. At first, at least to Charles, that fact had seemed less than substantial; if anything, it had lent a thrill of the forbidden to what he was doing. But now, as he and Karima met only in darkness and spoke only in whispers, its reality was beginning to sink in.

"We're like Romeo and Juliet," he said one night.

"Who are they?"

"Like Layla and Majnoon," he explained, remembering the story she had told him years ago of the star-crossed couple whose love had brought them only madness and death.

She shivered. It was frightening but also delicious. Her life was turning into a story, a song.

The next night he said, "I think my father is suspicious of us."

"Allah!" Her eyes widened. "What will we do?" She imagined Henry Pasha firing her father, casting them out of their home.

"Don't worry, it's not as bad as all that." Charles had never really wanted for anything; it was difficult for him to believe that he would not ultimately have his way. How to go about it was the question. "I'll think of something," he said, more to himself than to her.

He took her silence for belief, and leaned to kiss away her tears.

The moon was past full now, the shadows deeper.

"Your father?" said Karima after the first kiss.

"Nothing," said Charles. "Perhaps I'm imagining things."

Neither, however, imagined that their basic problem was solved. The next kiss was like an affirmation that they would face it together. And the next kiss was something more.

Charles took her hand. "Let's walk," he said huskily.

It was the first time they had left the shelter of the lemon tree. Karima knew what was happening but told herself that she did not.

There was a little pavilion on a path, a place for small garden parties and afternoon teas.

"Do you remember my telling you about crying on the ship when I saw Alex?" said Charles.

"Yes."

"I've realized since that it wasn't Egypt I'd missed. It was you, all along." He held her only by her shoulders, facing her squarely. "I want you. I want you so much. You're the only woman I've wanted this way. I love you, Karima."

"I love you, Charles. No one else. Never anyone else." There. It was said.

"I'll find a way for us, I swear it."

The words were stronger than fear, stronger than the memory of Fariza nearly dying from a botched abortion, stronger than the stories of village girls killed for dishonoring their families. Lightly she unfastened her clothing and let it fall.

Naked in the dappled moonlight, she was beyond beauty to him. "My God," he said hoarsely. He fumbled at his own clothing.

Then they were together. There was pain for Karima. She bit her lip and listened to Charles's words of passion.

It was over quickly, his pent-up desire too strong. She cradled his head as his breathing slowed. She savored the feel of his body. At the edge of her mind was still the fear. She had gone to a place from which there was no return.

"I love you," Charles said again. "We'll be together. I promise."

Like a swimmer out of sight of land, she clung to his words. She was his now, she told herself. His love of her would save her.

His hands caressed her, his passion warming again. This time it was different. This time there was time, a slowness, a deepness, a melting. This time she felt what she had heard of but had never experienced. Again. And again.

It was the following evening.

"A drink?" gestured Henry. "Whiskey and soda perhaps?"

"Yes, thanks," said Charles. Oh God. When his father started a conversation with drinks, it was generally something serious. He knew what that something must be.

"Cheers."

"Cheers."

After the obligatory small talk, Henry got to the point. "Your mother has asked me to have a word with you. She—we both—are concerned about you and . . . Karima."

"Concerned?"

Henry considered his words carefully. "It isn't fair to her, Charles. You're being very selfish, you know."

"Selfish? How?" Charles realized that he had not denied being somehow involved with Karima.

"Your attention to her, your interest . . . in my day, we'd have said you were trifling with her. Is it fair to lead her on to believe . . . something that can never be? To divert her from other possibilities? To interfere with her chance at making a good marriage with someone of her own class?"

Charles thought of the businessman who was calling on Mustafa. Karima had told him his name: Munir Ahmad. Surely all that was out of the question now. Wasn't it?

"But what if I'm not trifling, *Abi*?" he said. "What if I'm not leading her on? What if I'm . . . quite serious?"

Henry studied his son sadly. "Then, my boy," he sighed, hating the words as he spoke them, "I ask you to consider how you will live—and what kind of life you will have."

Charles could not fathom it. Surely his father was not talking about disowning him or something of that nature. It was all too melodramatic, a piece of bad theater. Feeling like a child unfairly punished, he lashed back with equal unfairness.

"Oh, I see. An Egyptian is good enough for you, but not good enough for me."

"You know that's not it."

"Then what is it?"

Henry put down his drink. "When you're a little older, Charles . . ." No, that was not the way. "Appearances matter, son. Customs matter."

"Do my feelings matter?"

"Of course. Of course they do." Henry was feeling his way in the dark. "I know you believe you love the girl. I didn't know it till just now. Perhaps you even believe that there will never be anyone else. But that simply is not true, Charles. You will find someone more . . . more suitable, as will Karima. Partners who will bring you—and her—happiness."

"Happiness!" said Charles with disgust. "What would you know about that!"

Henry wanted to protest that he had known happiness once, but how would that sound? He kept silent.

"It's sheer hypocrisy," spat Charles, truly angry now.

"Please, son," said Henry. "Think carefully about what I've said."

"Oh, I'll think about it, all right. Have no fear." Charles turned and stalked from the room and the house. He felt a fool even before he had slammed the door, but there was no going back, not now, at least.

He looked down toward the servants' quarters. Karima would be serving dinner to her father.

He went to the garage for the Jaguar. The purr of the engine, the sweet feel of the steering and the meshing gears, soothed him as he descended to the corniche and sped east along the seashore. At a hundred miles an hour he felt like a desperado running in the night. Running from what? When the beach road no longer allowed for such speed, he pulled over and stared at the starlit ocean.

Henry poured a brandy, adding an extra jolt. He took a fortifying swallow and then sat thinking.

The boy was right: he *was* a hypocrite. Yet there were considerations that Charles, in his present state of mind, simply couldn't appreciate.

What a cliché. Henry could hear his own father saying exactly such a thing. Very well then: what exactly were these overweening considerations?

Of course there were Catherine's wishes. But that did not absolve Henry of responsibility. His wife could demand that he confront their son, but the confrontation and its outcome were between him and Charles.

He had made a tactical mistake in appealing for fairness toward Karima—it had allowed Charles to turn the moral tables—but Henry *was* fond of the girl. Mustafa was a fine man and she had been a good daughter to him.

But they were servants. That was the heart of the matter, wasn't it? The card that Henry should have played from the first?

Or was it? Wouldn't Charles have brushed it aside as more hypocrisy? And wouldn't he be right? Henry was rich but although he was well-born, he had never thought of himself as really upper class. And Catherine was distinctly from the middle classes. How much better off, in truth, had her family been when he met her than Karima's family was now? If he were to relent, give the whole thing his blessing and damn the wagging tongues, might not Karima in a few years be as suitable a wife as Catherine?

Catherine.

Happiness! What would you know about that!

That had hurt. But there was truth in it—perhaps, thought Henry, the only truth that mattered in this affair. What he feared for Charles was what had happened to himself.

But there was no possible way to admit that to his son.

Charles drove aimlessly back into the city. He did not want to go home, not even to see Karima. He dreaded telling her what his father had said.

The bar was on the edge of the Mina, the old waterfront district. It was not one of the knife-and-broken-bottle sailors' dives for which—among other things—the deeper regions of the Mina were notorious. The clientele consisted mainly of slumming locals, students out on a lark, even tourists. Enough actual sailors, usually priming themselves for more serious drinking elsewhere, wandered in to create the atmosphere that attracted the other customers.

Charles had gone there once with a few schoolmates in his final year at British Boys'. Everyone had got gloriously drunk and then ignominiously sick. He went there now simply to be someplace and because one or two of his old chums might happen by.

He was in luck and not. Rodney Quinlan and Fatty Ashbury were there. Quinlan was a pleasant enough chap whose family were from Belfast. Ashbury had been a bully at British Boys' and Charles had never liked him. The two were well into their cups. Charles had no intention of trying to catch up with them but ordered a brandy and soda to be sociable.

Quinlan, it turned out, had spent most of the past four years at the Sorbonne, or rather in Paris occasionally attending the Sorbonne.

Ashbury had done a year at university in Cairo before joining his father's shipfitting company. He was no longer chubby but simply very large.

Charles had started a second drink and was feeling marginally better about his troubles when Fatty and Rodney hit on the idea of a visit to Madame Heloise's. Charles had heard of the place, of course: it was said to be the poshest brothel in Alex. He demurred.

"Oh, come along, Austen," urged Rodney. "Do you good. You've been down at the mouth since you got here."

"Some other time perhaps."

"Austen's always been down at the mouth," said Fatty. "All his ruddy life."

That was Fatty. He could turn nasty in a split second. Charles ignored him.

"Frenchwomen," cajoled Rodney. "Swedes, true blondes. None of the dusky local product."

"Maybe Austen prefers the dusky local product," said Fatty. "Got a dusky little bit of your own, have you, Austen?"

Charles felt a flush of anger. Where had Fatty heard this? Or was he simply being Fatty, picking until he hit a sore spot?

"Well, *chacun à son gout,*" said Rodney blithely, trying to smooth things over.

"That's it, isn't it?" pestered Fatty. "Got a little wog you're shagging? Gone all misty-eyed over it, no doubt. Probably the first you've ever had."

"Really, Ashbury," said Rodney.

"Well, why not?" said Fatty. "Man's half a wog himself."

"Shove it along, Fatty," said Charles. Get up and leave, he told himself.

"Listen to the man talk," said Fatty. "You know, Quinlan, I've an inspiration. Remember that scrawny little servant Charlie boy was always so sweet on? I'll wager it's her. What was her name? Creamy? Karima?"

Charles threw his drink in Fatty Ashbury's face and Fatty came at him.

The scuffle lasted only seconds—the alumni of British Boys' were not saloon fighters. After a few clumsy blows, other men were grabbing at the two to separate them. Caught by an elbow, Charles slipped on the wet floor and fell backward. He saw a blinding starburst as his head struck a table. The next he knew, someone was pressing a wet cloth to his forehead. Fatty was nowhere to be seen. Rodney was handing a few bills to the manager.

"Nasty bash, that," said the man holding the cloth. "Best have someone give it a look in the morning."

Charles struggled to his feet. The room was rolling like a ship. Rodney led him out. In the cool night air he felt better, although his head throbbed.

"A right bastard, as ever, Ashbury," said Rodney. "Pure stupidity. Oughtn't to let it trouble you for a moment."

"Right," said Charles. He felt both exhausted and incredibly energetic.

They were at the Jaguar. "You're up to driving?" asked Rodney. "Look a bit shaky." Clearly he hoped for a chance at the wheel of the sports car.

"I'm fine," said Charles. "Give you a lift?"

"Well, yes, thanks. I came in a taxi."

They piled into the car. Charles opened it up a little on the corniche—not as fast as earlier, but enough to show the Jag's legs. Rodney whooped with delight. Charles grinned. Not from the thrill of speed. From freedom. For he knew now what he was going to do.

It was all so simple, really. If he could fight for Karima in some waterfront pub, could he do less in his own home? He was going to go back and confront his father, not as a petulant boy, but as a determined man who knew his own mind. And if his father still refused to see reason—well, other young men had started with nothing. Charles could have shaken Fatty Ashbury's hand for bringing him this clarity of insight.

Rodney was shouting a joke, something about a priest. Decent sort, Quinlan. Wonder if he'd stand as best man for a couple of wogs.

A cloud must have come over the moon. Or was something wrong with the headlamps?

". . . all right?" Rodney was asking.

"Little dizzy." Charles heard his tongue slur the words.

For an instant his head no longer throbbed. Instead a sudden terrible sickness gripped him. Instinctively he tried to brake, but the move was a spasm and his foot jammed hard on the accelerator.

Rodney's panic-lunge for the wheel made matters worse. The convertible mounted the beach walk, smashed the pedestrian railing, and slammed upside down onto the sand below.

Rodney, thrown free, lived for three minutes with a broken neck. Charles lay crushed beneath the wreckage. No one would ever know that he had died of hemorrhage before the Jaguar even left the roadway.

Henry had identified the body, made the most pressing arrangements. When the news went to the servants' quarters, the women's wailing had begun. He imagined that he could still hear Karima's agonized screams.

Catherine had gone mad for a time. He had called in a doctor who gave her something. Henry hoped she would sleep the night. Morning would be better, surely. It had to be. He poured a drink but did not touch it; Charles's glass was still on the sidebar.

There was a rustle of clothing and Catherine was there, bleary, cried-out. The two looked at each other. Their eyes said everything: that they had failed in their one great responsibility; that Charles was gone; that there would be many more nights like this, just the two of them in a private, well-appointed hell.

"I woke up," said Catherine. "The pill must have worn off."

"Do you want another?"

"No. No, I . . . just didn't want to be alone."

He led her upstairs. In her room they undressed mechanically, not a word spoken. In bed they lay together, almost touching yet so far apart. Henry reached out and brushed his wife's hair away from her face. She seemed not to notice. His hand stroked her cheek gently. Nothing. It was as if she were dead, too.

Henry had suffered his wife's rejection stoically for a very long time; he had learned somehow to live alone. But on this night he could not bear to be alone with his grief. He gathered Catherine into his arms. She went rigid. "No," she said, the single word flat, mechanical.

"Please," he whispered hoarsely, his voice thick with unshed tears. "I need you so much, my dear."

Her body relaxed. Perhaps she, too, could not bear the isolation, the sense of being dead, yet alive. Henry kissed his wife tenderly, brushed her face with his lips, tasting the salty residue of her tears. His hands caressed her body, gently at first, then with growing urgency, as if he were seeking refuge in its familiar contours.

Silently, desperately, they made love, two survivors amid the wreckage of their lives.

7
A Good Wife

Alexandria

If only he had shown more understanding when Charles had come to him. If only he had remembered what it was like to be young. If only he had appreciated the depth of the boy's feelings.

Henry began each day with bitter regret—he was alive and Charles was not. Night brought crushing sorrow, dreams of crumpled metal and bloodied car seats that shredded sleep and left him weary and broken.

When Henry looked in the mirror he saw an old man, someone who resembled his own father, yet who was different. His father had managed to live out his days with some semblance of ease and contentment. His father had never sent a son to his death.

If only.

Catherine sipped her morning tea without tasting it. Food, drink, they were as ashes in her mouth. They served no purpose for a woman who no longer cared if she lived or died.

She closed her eyes and sank back into her pillow. If only she had considered Henry's pleas for another baby, perhaps life might still have some meaning. She sighed heavily, remembering her anger at Henry's shortcomings, the countless arguments, the heavy silences. All that seemed so distant and trivial now. Once, her determination not to bear Henry another child seemed like an eminently suitable punishment for a man who had disappointed her in so many ways. Now she could see that she had punished herself as well.

She thought of that long, desolate night after Charles was killed, when she and Henry had come together in a desperate coupling born of pain and loneliness. For a single mad moment, she fantasized that their desperation might somehow produce a child. But Catherine had gone through "the change" two years ago—what pleasure that transition had given her then, knowing that she had prevailed. There would be no more children. If only.

"What's the matter with you, Karima? Have you gone deaf?" Mustafa was rarely this impatient with his daughter, but he had asked the same question not once but three times. And still Karima stood motionless, staring out the window—only Allah knew at what.

She turned slowly, as if in a trance, to face her father. "I'm sorry, *Abi,*" she said, her tone dull and lifeless. "What did you want?"

"I asked if you could make *mouloukhiyeh* for me tonight. Your cooking is almost as good as your mother's, and I . . ."

Karima began to weep, quietly, her shoulders heaving, her eyes leaking tears. "Yes, *Abi,*" she sobbed. "I'll do what you say."

Mustafa was dumbfounded. *Allah,* he thought, what was wrong with his daughter? Weeping at the mere mention of her mother, walking around as if she were one of the poor simpletons, may Allah be merciful to them, who begged coins in the *souk.*

A moment later he was at Karima's side, embracing her, awkwardly stroking her hair. "There, there, child. I understand that you miss your mother. A young woman needs her mother, but Allah has taken my dear wife to paradise, and it is wrong to reproach the

Almighty. Now wash your face, like a good girl . . ." He fumbled awkwardly in his pocket and withdrew a peppermint candy. "Here you are, a sweet for a sweet."

Karima turned red-rimmed eyes on her father, fighting an almost hysterical urge to laugh. A sweet! As if she were still a child whose pain could be cured by a bit of candy. But she understood that her father meant well. How could he know that she was beyond such innocent remedies? *Allah,* if he did, he would kill her! Swallowing hard, she took the candy and tried to smile. "Thank you, *Abi.* I'm all right, truly. You mustn't worry."

Relieved that he could go to work, Mustafa patted his daughter's head and left.

Karima collapsed into the chair that Shams had loved so much simply because Omar had given it to her. How she longed to feel her mother's comforting arms around her. "*Ya ummi, ya ummi,* I wish you were here," she murmured. No doubt Shams would be just as angry, just as disappointed as Mustafa. Yet perhaps her mother's heart would have prevailed over anger, and Karima would not be facing ruination all alone. If only Shams were here.

Karima shook her head. Shams wasn't here and Charles wasn't here and she was all alone. Lost. Even before the missed period, even before the morning sickness, she had known. This was what happened when you went with a man outside of marriage. She wanted to tell herself that she wasn't sorry. That she was glad she had known Charles's love, if only for a little while. Wasn't that the way it was in so many of the songs she adored? But in the solitary stillness of her father's house, Karima wasn't glad.

While Charles was alive, she could make herself forget the terrible risks she was taking. When he was killed, she wished she had been with him in that beautiful, deadly car. A few moments of pain, perhaps, and it all would have been over. Now she was trapped in a nightmare, and there was no one to help her. No one who would care that she had given away her virtue, her family's honor, out of love. Her story was an old one, worn with the telling, and it always ended with death and disgrace.

She wrapped her arms around her waist—was it thicker than it had been a few days ago?—and began to rock gently, crooning a lullaby that Shams used to sing to her when she was a little girl. Back and forth, back and forth. Suddenly, a fragment of memory. Was it a whispered conversation she had overheard? Between Shams and one of her friends? Yes, that was it, they had been talking about a *zar* the woman had attended.

"My husband would be very angry if he knew I'd gone," Shams's friend had said. "He told me it was for weak-minded women who had nothing better to do. He said the *shaikh* of our mosque had condemned it as superstition more than once."

"And you went anyway?" Shams had said, incredulous at her friend's disobedience.

"Yes. What do men know of women's troubles? Every month, the fullness in my belly increased. I was not pregnant, so what else was there? The thing that killed *Um-Mansour,* that's what. So I went to the *zar,* and I danced and danced until I didn't know where I was anymore. And do you know, the thing—whatever it was—went away!"

"*Allah!*"

Allah, Karima thought. It was a small hope but it was the only one she had.

Dressed all in white, as was the custom, Karima trudged the streets of Backouz, clutching the tiny purse that held all the coins she had managed to save. She did not know much about the *zar,* only what she had managed to glean here and there, with innocent-sounding questions that hinted, she hoped, at mere curiosity rather than desperate need. "The *zar*—the visit," she was told, "is to drive out the djinn that made you ill. Or caused your husband to be unfaithful. And if the djinn will not go away, then you must try to appease him, so that he will no longer bring you sickness and misfortune."

Karima wasn't sure she believed in djinn, but so many people still did. Perhaps they were right and she was simply ignorant. She paused in front of a darkened shop, checked the address she had scribbled on a scrap of paper, and opened the door.

It was dark inside, too, but she could see five other women sitting cross-legged on the floor. There was a small table near the door, and Karima could make out a hand-lettered sign that said "Offerings." Karima added her money to the small pile of bills and coins. As her eyes adjusted to the darkness, she saw that all the other women were wearing white, too. They called out greetings; Karima returned a salaam. A heavyset woman of about thirty-five beckoned Karima to sit beside her. Karima complied.

"Your first time, child?" the woman asked. Karima nodded.

"Well, don't worry. We'll all look after you. There's nothing to fear. My name is Salwa, by the way. And you are . . . ?"

"Karima." The windows were shut, and the heat was stifling. The place smelled of cinnamon and cardamom and allspice and cumin—no doubt spices had been sold here—but Karima saw very little by way of merchandise. Feeling a little faint, she patted her face with a handkerchief and hoped she wouldn't be sick.

"All you all right, child?"

"It's just the heat," Karima said, swallowing hard.

"The heat is good, Karima. If you perspire freely, the djinn will jump from your body."

"What . . . ? I mean, how . . ."

"Just wait for the *shaikh* to arrive, child. Then you will tell him your problem and he will create a special spell that speaks to your djinn. I have very bad hemorrhages every month. They make me weak and I cannot care for my family. But after today all will be well. Just watch and do as we all do."

"Why are we all wearing white?"

Salwa looked surprised by Karima's ignorance. "Why, it's part of becoming a bride to the djinn."

Now Karima was more confused than ever. Marry the evil spirit and then drive him out? But she felt too embarrassed to ask any more questions.

Presently the *shaikh,* an old man of at least seventy, appeared.

Salwa rose and spoke to him softly, so only he would hear. He nodded sagely. A moment later the woman at the end of the semicircle began to beat a small drum. And Salwa began to dance, slowly at first, then gathering momentum and urgency, her hips swaying from side to side, thrusting forward suggestively.

> *"Ya* Sultan Ahmar," *the* shaikh *began,*
> *invoking the red Sultan, the king of blood.*
> *"Red king of kings, you king of djinns,*
> *Recall your spirits, that all of them may attend.*
> *Oh, you little bride,*
> *You are the bride of the Sultan*
> *And your bridegroom is like a lighted candle.*

Faster and faster Salwa whirled, swaying, thrusting, panting hard—until she collapsed, her body drenched in sweat, her eyes unfocused and glassy.

Karima felt she should help the woman, but when no one moved she kept her place, afraid to compromise the spell. Eventually Salwa rose, smiling, brushed herself off, and resumed her place in the semicircle.

One by one, the other women danced while the *shaikh* chanted spells addressed to their djinns. By the time Karima's turn came, she was no longer self-conscious or afraid. She told the *shaikh* she had "womanly problems' and that she had suffered a great tragedy. He nodded as before, as if there were nothing in this world he had not already heard.

The drumming began and then Karima was moving, spinning freely, undulating rhythmically to the beat. Sweat ran into her eyes, clouding her vision, but she kept moving, keeping pace as the drumming quickened. Her legs ached, her arms were heavy, but still she danced. Suddenly the room fell away and the women in it disappeared—and all she saw before her was Charles. Smiling at her, his arms held out as if to embrace her. She cried out joyfully. And then he was gone.

Laughing and weeping all at once, Karima hugged Salwa, hugged all the other women. Charles had come back to bless her—and their child. Somehow she would be saved.

She felt a warm breath against her cheek, the touch of a hand on her bare skin. The dream was so vivid she could feel Charles beside her, stroking her shoulder, murmuring her name. She sighed and stretched, clinging to that last remnant of sleep, that last sense of Charles.

Then she opened her eyes—and there was Omar, his face just inches from hers, his dark eyes glittering, his lips half-open. Karima recoiled, wrapping the sheet tight around her. "Brother! What are you doing here? What do you want?"

He frowned at her tone, anger replacing whatever had been before. "A fine way to greet your brother, Karima! I'm a busy man, you know. Yet when our father mentioned that he was concerned about you, I took time from my own affairs to come. And you behave as if I were a thief come to rob you! Or worse!"

Karima was stunned by the diatribe. It was true that she had been startled by Omar's appearance. And there had been something in his expression that frightened her for a moment. But why was he so angry?

"I'm sorry, brother. I just . . . I was just having a bad dream, that's all."

Omar was not appeased.

"I'll make you some coffee," she offered. She sat up quickly, using the sheet to cover her nightgown. But as she started to get out of bed, she felt suddenly lightheaded. Steadying herself against the bedpost, she willed herself not to faint. A wave of nausea sent her running out to the privy, where she vomited the remains of last night's dinner.

Omar was waiting for her. "What's wrong with you, Karima? Tell me!"

"It's nothing, brother. Nothing."

He tore the sheet away and stared, raking her face, her body with his gaze. "Tell me what is wrong or I will kill you where you stand."

Karima bowed her head, saying nothing. The gesture was as good as a confession.

Omar slapped her so hard she almost fell. "You're pregnant, aren't you?"

"No, brother, no . . ." She began to cry.

"Aren't you? It was the *Inglizi,* wasn't it? Wasn't it!"

Her sobs intensified, drowning out her feeble denials. Omar struck her again. And again. Blood streamed from her nose, from the cut on her cheek that Omar had opened with his ring.

"Get dressed, whore. We're going to Um-Ali's. Then we'll find out if you're a liar as well as a slut."

Karima ran into the house, terrified of what the midwife, Um-Ali, would say. She wiped her face and got into her clothes. Protest would be useless.

Omar dragged his sister along the street as if she were a recalcitrant dog. She whimpered at first and then she was silent, knowing that there was worse to come.

Um-Ali lived alone in a small mud hut. It was said she told fortunes in addition to delivering babies, so Karima was doubly afraid of the old woman.

"Examine her," Omar said without preamble. "I want to know if she's pregnant."

Um-Ali held out her hand. Omar gave her some money.

The old woman studied Karima, then nudged her toward a tiny curtained area. "Wait outside," she told Omar.

The midwife was not gentle. Her chapped hands were rough as she poked and probed Karima's body. Karima understood. She was of no consequence now. If her brother suspected pregnancy she was presumed to be a worthless slut, undeserving of care or respect.

When Um-Ali finished her examination she gave a satisfied grunt, as if to say it was as she expected. For the first time, she looked into Karima's eyes. Then she took her hand and studied it. "You will have great sorrow in your life, and loss," she said. "But you will also have great triumph and joy. And only Allah knows in what measure." Before Karima could ask the meaning of Um-Ali's words, the old woman stepped outside. "The girl is pregnant," she said to Omar. "About two months, I believe."

He said not a word. His eyes were hard and dead as he gripped Karima's arm so tightly she feared she would faint. But she was afraid to scream, afraid to release the terrible anger she saw in his face.

They returned home in silence. When they reached the house, he slammed the door and shoved her inside. The first blow to her stomach came with lightning speed, knocking Karima to the ground. It was followed by a kick, and when she tried to get up an open-handed slap felled her again. "Whore! Slut! Bitch! It would be better if you were dead!"

As blows and curses hailed down on her, Karima tried to protect her belly with her arms. The gesture enraged Omar even more, and he renewed his attack—as if he would kill the child that lived within her, as if he could destroy the very memory of the Englishman. When the savage beating finally stopped, Omar was panting and breathless. He spat at Karima and left the house.

Karima huddled under the covers, her body a throbbing mass of aches and bruises. She could not remember how or when she had dragged herself to bed, she did not know how long she had lain there.

When Mustafa had come home looking for his supper, Karima told him she was not feeling well and begged his forgiveness.

"Ma'alesh," he said. "There is bread and cheese. That will be enough."

Alone in the darkness, Karima prayed for Allah's protection. She prayed that Omar's anger was spent and that he would leave her alone. But most of all she prayed for deliverance.

Omar did return. But there were no more beatings. He seemed to simply be watching her, always watching, and Karima began to feel like an animal being stalked. Waiting for the moment when her life would end.

A few days after he had dragged her to Um-Ali's, Omar arrived at the house shortly after Mustafa had left for work. "I want you to prepare lunch today," he said. "A good meal. Chicken and rice. And salad. Some yogurt. Go to the *souk* now and buy what you need." He flung some money at her. She took it quickly and fled.

Mustafa had said he would not be home today—he would be driving the pasha to Cairo—so why did Omar want lunch? Were the two of them going to sit down and break bread together? Was she to be forgiven? She could not imagine that, and yet what else could Omar's demand mean?

Karima shopped quickly and returned home. Omar was seated on a chair outside the house, reading a newspaper and smoking one of the French cigarettes he occasionally favored. He glanced at her and went back to his newspaper.

The meal would be a simple one, but Karima took special care with it. She marinated the cut-up chicken in olive oil and *zatar* and garlic, then baked it in the small oven that Mustafa had given Shams on her last birthday. Next, she sautéed fine noodles in clarified butter and added rice, to make a tasty *pilaf*. Finally she cut up the fresh greens she'd bought in the market and dressed them with lemon and olive oil, garlic and fresh mint. The bread was left to warm atop the oven while Karima set the table. It was just before noon when she heard voices outside. Omar—and another man.

"Welcome," Omar was saying. "Welcome to my father's house, my good friend."

The man was Munir Ahmad, the businessman who had called on Mustafa from time to time—and who had seemed more than a little interested in her. But why was he here now, when Mustafa had expressly said he would not be home for lunch?

"You remember my sister, Karima?" Omar said.

Munir did remember Karima. Her sweet singing voice. Her sunny disposition. Her beauty.

But today, as she served the meal, Munir noticed not her beauty but her red-rimmed eyes. He sensed the anger that Omar was trying very hard to conceal beneath a forced air of joviality.

Munir politely joined in Omar's small talk. How was Munir's

business? It was fine. And how were Omar's various enterprises? Very successful.

After Karima went into the bedroom, as she had been told to do, Munir asked quietly, "Is there something wrong, my friend? Perhaps I can help . . ."

"What could be wrong?" Omar protested.

Munir persisted, for he sensed that he had been invited today for a purpose. Gently, persuasively, he pried the story from Omar—though it was a story much altered from the truth. An English swine had forced himself on Karima in spite of Omar's best efforts to protect her. And now the swine had gotten himself killed before Omar could avenge his family's honor.

"I see," said Munir, his expression sadder than usual. "I see."

Munir's beloved wife, Nadwa, and his young son had died in the great cholera epidemic that swept Egypt in 1947. He had never hoped to marry again, not until he saw Omar's sister, experienced her sweetness and kindness. And now Karima was disgraced.

Munir thought long and hard. So this was why he was here. He had not asked for Karima's hand before because he had seen no answering interest on her part. After the happiness he had shared with his first wife, he did not want a woman who was not fond of him. Now Karima was available to anyone who would have her. Damaged, yet so sadly vulnerable.

Omar watched him, shrewdly understanding the struggle going on within the older man's heart—and calculating what he might gain if he gave his sister to Munir. Honor was one thing, but perhaps there was a more profitable course. There was the bride price, of course. And then there were Munir's various business enterprises—all legitimate, in contrast to Omar's shady schemes. "You could save Karima's life," he said, bluntly. "Otherwise I don't know what will happen to her."

In the end the bargain was concluded. Munir would marry Karima and they would pretend the child was his. One way or another, people would gossip—it took no great skill to count to nine.

But if Munir, a respected and prosperous businessman, claimed paternity, who could say otherwise?

Extracting the bridal price took some doing under such circumstances. But Omar managed.

No one was more surprised than Mustafa when Omar announced that he had found a husband for his sister. Munir was wealthy, a man of good reputation. His dead wife's family sang his praises to the heavens.

"Do you accept this man?" Mustafa asked his daughter.

"Of course she accepts him," Omar snapped. "Munir Ahmad is better than *she* deserves."

Mustafa turned on his son. "Never speak of your sister in such terms," he thundered, "do you hear me?"

Omar flushed—this was the first time his father had spoken to him so harshly—but he kept his own temper in check. "Yes, *Abi*. And I beg your pardon. What I meant was that any young woman would be blessed by such a marriage."

"What you say is true. But what I want to know is if Karima accepts him. I am not one of those fathers who would force a daughter into marriage."

"Yes, *Abi,*" Karima said softly, "I do accept."

Mustafa was again surprised, this time by his daughter's reply. But perhaps this was the answer to Karima's moods and spells. Perhaps what she needed was a home and a family of her own. "Very well. I will speak to Munir. And we will set a date for the wedding."

"This is better than you deserve," Omar told his sister on the day Munir gave her a ring. "I have gone to a great deal of trouble on your behalf. Remember that. Never speak of the *Inglizi* again, never disgrace your husband in any way—or I will kill you with this hand, I promise you."

Karima would have preferred a quiet ceremony, and then the chance to hide herself away. But Munir had done nothing to be ashamed of, and there was no reason for him to hide. A hasty wedding, uncele-brated, for a man of his stature would generate the very kind of gos-sip they wished to avoid. An older man, a young bride, this was nothing new. A baby born a bit early, well, some tongues would be set wagging, but that would pass in time.

With Henry Pasha's permission, Mustafa married his daughter off on the grounds of the plantation. A canopy was set out in front of Mustafa's small house, and food was prepared for a hundred guests. All the plantation workers knew and loved Karima, so there was joy on her behalf and heartfelt congratulations.

The celebration was at a considerable distance from the pasha's house but when the singing and dancing started, the sound of joyful music carried, causing Henry more pain than he could have imag-ined. A wedding. A new life for the young girl Charles had loved.

He held Catherine's hand, knowing they shared the same thoughts. Would it really have been so terrible if they had let Charles do what he wanted? Social standing, education, wealth—what would those things have mattered if their son were still alive and this were his wedding day?

The wedding night was not what Karima had once imagined in the full flower of her passion for Charles. But Munir was a kind and gentle man, and he took her tenderly, whispering endearments against her ear and promising to love her until his dying day. Karima gave herself willingly, with gratitude. He had saved her life, and he would make a good home for the baby she had come to love. It was more than she had any right to expect.

Six and a half months later, Nadia was born. She was tiny, all the better to promote the fiction that she was "early." A porcelain doll with creamy skin, lapis-colored eyes—Charles's eyes—and dark, dark hair—Allah be praised for that! If Karima fell in love, totally and completely, with her baby, Munir was almost cartoonish in his pride. "I swear to you," he told his wife, "I swear to you that already I love her as my own." He gave little gifts to all his employees, and a party to celebrate "his" daughter's birth. "Such a fuss for a girl," one of his assistants marveled. "I've never seen a man carry on this way over a daughter. Especially when he has no son!"

Day by day, with every kindness, with every gesture of concern, a bond was forged between Karima and Munir. She was now mistress of a spacious and comfortable villa in Roushdy, one of the city's best neighborhoods. And she had servants of her own. From time to time she thought of Um-Ali's prediction. Great sorrow and loss, she had experienced those. Was this, then, the joy and triumph?

She tried to be a good wife in every way she knew, but not out of fear of her brother. No one had ever been so generous, so good to her as Munir had been, no one. She had known passion once, and once would have to be enough. To Munir she gave her gratitude, her respect, and her affection. On most days it could pass for love.

Now she sang to Nadia every day, of Allah's blessings, of love, of redemption. She listened faithfully to Um Kalthum's records on the splendid walnut Philco phonograph Munir had given her; it had been imported from America!

Almost daily, she assured Munir that she was happy. But he heard the sadness in her songs, and to him they seemed so much more convincing than the happy melodies.

He thought—and he thought. And then he invited his friend Spyros to dinner. Spyros worked in the entertainment business. He managed singers, dancers, and some of Egypt's finest musicians. Munir said nothing to Karima of his intentions, only that he hadn't seen Spyros in a long time.

If Karima was surprised by the feast he ordered their cook to prepare, she said nothing. There was a *mezze* of Greek and Cypriot dishes, a succulent lamb roast, heaped platters of rice and vegetables, cheeses and olives, two bottles of excellent ouzo, and trays of pastries and *baklava* from the finest pastry shop in Alexandria.

When Karima met Spyros, she understood the Faroukish proportions of the dinner: he was a mountain of a man, with a florid complexion, a splendid mustache, and a laugh that could surely be heard in all the neighboring houses. He ate with gusto, showering Karima with compliments, on her beauty, on her housekeeping—and on the obvious contentment of his old friend, Munir.

After they finished a second round of thick, dark coffee with cardamom, Spyros said, "Well, my dear, Munir tells me you can sing like an angel. Will you honor me with a song?"

Karima protested. Munir coaxed. Spyros insisted.

She sang—the same song of love and longing she had sung on the day her mother had been killed:

> *"Where are you tonight, my love, where?*
> *Do you sleep after battle? Dream of me?*
> *The sky is big but crowded with stars;*
> *In my heart, as small as my hand, only loneliness."*

When she was finished, Spyros spoke one word: "Sublime."

Three months later, Karima stood backstage—in the same theater where she had once watched Um Kalthum perform—deep in the throes of stage fright.

"Just sing to them as you sing to me and our sweet Nadia," Munir said, rubbing his wife's icy cold hands in his own. "Look at me when you sing. I'll be in the front row. I promise you, all will be well." Munir had seen to it. He had hired three dozen people to cheer and applaud, not because he didn't believe in Karima's talent, but because he wanted her to believe in it.

Now it was time. "Alexandria's own songbird," the announcer shouted, "Karima Ahmad!"

The claque immediately burst into raucous whistles and cheers. Their noise was infectious and soon others joined in. Munir smiled contentedly and took his seat.

Karima began with a song about a young man who pines away and dies because the girl he loves is forbidden to him. She sang with her eyes closed, as if she were feeling the young boy's pain. And when tears slipped from her eyes, many in the audience wept with her.

Next came a song of homesickness, of sadness and loss:

"Do not lament your life's work that has failed,
your schemes that have proved illusions.
But like a man prepared, like a brave man,
bid farewell to her, to Alexandria who is departing."

She sang the refrain over and over, just as Um Kalthum did, drawing out the melody, improvising. And when the last note was sounded, the crowd roared. "Karima! Karima! Karima! *Karawan!*" Nightingale, they called her that night when all of Alexandria fell in love. It didn't hurt that Karima was beautiful. But it was the heart she had shown them that had won their own hearts.

Perhaps there was one in the crowd who did not rejoice in Karima's beauty or her voice. But he was feeling other powerful emotions. His sister had betrayed him. She had turned away from him and soiled herself with an Englishman. And for that, he could almost hate her.

Karima's career moved quickly upward. Spyros arranged concert after concert, and soon a record. Though the radio airwaves belonged to Um Kalthum on Thursday nights, the Nightingale's music was played often as well. She was seen not as a rival to Um Kalthum, but as a kind of younger sister whose turn would come.

About a year after Karima's first concert, she was cast in a small film, a Romeo-and-Juliet story in modern dress. The movie was a modest success, and the critic from *Al-Ahram* used Spyros's word—"sublime"—to describe her performance. "She is," the critic continued, "a gifted actress who can make us feel what it is like to be torn from the one you love and to suffer forever after."

The morning the review appeared, so did Omar. Karima welcomed him warmly, for by now she had accepted the fiction that he had been her benefactor.

Omar glanced around the villa. His own flat, which had until this moment seemed quite comfortable, now seemed like a hovel. Another reason to resent his sister. But because it suited his purpose, he made the appropriate noises when Karima showed him his bastard niece. And he managed to choke out congratulations on Karima's success.

After serving him coffee and pastries, she asked, "Is there anything I can do for you, brother?"

"Not for me, *nushkorallah,*" he replied with an air of piety. "But for our father . . ."

"What?" she asked. "What's wrong with our father? I saw him just yesterday and he didn't say a word to me . . ."

"He doesn't want you to worry," Omar cut in. "He knows you have your own family now, your career. You're a busy woman . . ."

"But never too busy for our father," she protested. "Tell me, Omar, please."

"It's his health. He needs to see the English doctor. It will be expensive. And he will need medicine . . ."

Before he could finish, Karima ran into her bedroom and came back with her purse. She emptied out its contents on the table, not bothering to count. "Take it, brother, and tell our father . . ."

"No," Omar said firmly. "If I tell him the money came from you, he will be very angry. He doesn't want you to know he isn't feeling well."

"I understand. I will not say a word. Just make sure Father has everything he needs."

Yes, of course he would. But for the moment, he had need of this money himself.

The more Karima prospered, the more often Omar's hand was out. Sometimes he wanted money, sometimes favors from Munir. Karima gave. And gave. She believed, after all, that without his intervention she might well have perished.

8
Black Saturday

Cairo, 26 January 1952

Cairo was burning.

Smoke rose into the cold gray winter sky from every quarter of the city, even the Gezira, the island in the Nile where the British congregated at their posh and ultraexclusive Sporting Club and where many of Cairo's wealthier Europeans resided.

Mobs roamed the streets, cursing the English, their own politicians, and anything else that came to mind. There were even shouts against the once-beloved King Farouk.

The day before, a contingent of British soldiers had massacred scores of unarmed Egyptian police in a confrontation at the Suez Canal. Now Cairo was taking its revenge. But on whom?

"Wogs burning their own city."

The speaker was a ruddy-cheeked, waistcoated Englishman sipping a gin sling in the Long Bar at Shepheard's Hotel. The Long Bar, like the hotel itself, was an institution, a true crossroads of the

Middle East. Shepheard's had come through many storms since its founding in the late 1800s by a former pastry chef for a British steamship line. This was not the first time that throngs of Cairenes had stood before it shaking their fists and screaming "English go home." Yet obviously a rather sticky situation had arisen, and, in the time-honored manner, the barman had declared drinks on the house until the crisis abated—as every Englishman in the room appeared certain it would.

Munir Ahmad wished he could be as certain. He knew how deeply the sorry affair at the Canal had cut into his countrymen's pride.

All in all, he wished he were somewhere else. More important, he wished that his wife and child were somewhere else.

There had been no hint of trouble that morning as they had driven in from Alex. Karima was quiet, slightly edgy, as she always was before a performance, while little Nadia squirmed excitedly, a handful for the patient old servant woman, Um-Ibrahim. Nadia had begged to come; it would be the first time she had heard her mother sing professionally.

The occasion was a large private party in the hotel's grand ballroom. It was going on even now, the wealthy and influential guests apparently unconcerned with the growing riot outside. It did not trouble Munir that he was not invited. He was not given to pride, except where Karima was concerned, and although he had achieved considerable success in business he was by no means a grand pasha; enough that such men desired to listen to Karima. Of course, so did a great many other people. Oh, she wasn't Um Kalthum quite yet—traffic didn't stop all over the Arab world when she came on the radio. But her day was coming—no-one could deny that voice. And she was so young.

Munir glanced nervously toward the front of the building as the noise from the street swelled momentarily. It was nearly time for Karima's performance to be over. He finished his iced lemonade and went to wait outside the ballroom. Through its thick doors he could hear her well enough to make out the refrain of a popular song:

"Ah, ya Masr ya hooby, al waakt ghiar, al asefa fee albak magnoon zay el hawa. Shoufna wagaa, shoufna saada . . ." (Oh, Egypt my love, you have changed as the seasons. The storm in you is as wild as the wind. We have seen pain, we have seen happiness . . .).

Munir could picture the emotion on his wife's face as she embroidered the refrain over and over, making subtle changes each time, deepening the song's meaning with each iteration. A waiter stood near the door, listening like Munir; there were tears in the man's eyes as the song ended.

"There you are! Could you hear me? Was I good? What's going on outside?"

Munir wished that he could take Karima in his arms, right here and now, and tell her how beautiful she was, how much he loved her.

"You were wonderful. Did Nadia enjoy herself?"

"Oh yes. They put her right behind the stage with Um-Ibrahim. Listen, they want me to sing another song after the meal. Do you think that will be all right? Or should we leave now? My God, it sounds like a war out there."

Munir considered it. "No. Go ahead and sing. I'm sure we're safe here. In fact, we might want to stay here until order is restored." He told himself that it was probably true. Like many Egyptians, he had a near-mystical faith in the ability of the English to protect their interests and their own.

Shepheard's was almost as much a corner of the Empire as the British embassy. Men like Stanley and Livingstone, even Lawrence of Arabia, had sojourned here. Probably, Munir told himself, there was no safer place in all of Cairo.

Karima beamed. "Good! They're a good audience. Will you get me something cold, husband? I'm just going to freshen up. Then I'll go and visit with Nadia."

She smiled and spun away. For a moment Munir forgot the trouble outside. His wife was beautiful, and as happy as a child. She was a child, really—only twenty. Less than half his age. He neither dwelt on the thought nor tried to suppress it. It was simply a fact, as inescapable as his love, a love that had begun the moment he first saw Karima and that had grown ever deeper in their two and a half years of marriage. He would do anything for her.

Easy words. But hadn't he done for her what not one Egyptian man in a thousand would have done?

That thought Munir did smother. He made his way back to the bar to buy Karima's cold fruit drink. As he waited to order, the shouting in the street suddenly rose to a new level. At the same instant he heard a window breaking. Every face in the Long Bar turned toward the sound.

In a small, dim corner backstage, Nadia had fallen asleep in Um-Ibrahim's lap almost as soon as the buzz of conversation replaced the familiar loveliness of her mother's voice. The old servant herself was drifting off, even though the hard chair made her bones ache. Then, through her drowsiness, Um-Ibrahim became aware that something was wrong. There were shouts, the hubbub of movement, a crash of dishes and silverware.

What were the foreigners doing? Um-Ibrahim understood not a word of English. Well, it was not her place to question. God willing, someone would explain to her later.

Nadia stirred and sleepily mumbled, "Mama?"

"Shh. She'll be here any second, child," soothed the old woman. Then she smelled the smoke. Fearfully she stood and carried Nadia toward the light that spilled onto the stage.

Peeking out, she was astonished to see that the ballroom was empty. The smell of smoke was quite sharp.

A man in the gold-embroidered crimson jacket of a Shepheard's waiter rushed across the stage and pulled a fire extinguisher from the wall. Turning, he saw Um-Ibrahim and Nadia.

"You must get out of here, Mother," he shouted. "The building's on fire."

"God protect us!"

"Go that way," said the man, pointing. "You came in by the service entrance?"

"Yes, sir. Of course, sir."

"Go out the same way and you'll be safe. Go quickly." He hurried away with the fire extinguisher.

Um-Ibrahim moved faster than she had been able to do for twenty years. There was a hallway that seemed familiar and, at the end of it, a stairwell. She remembered coming upstairs. How many flights? Two, at least, she decided; it had been a long climb.

At the bottom of the second flight, she realized that she had miscalculated. The door opened into something that looked like a basement. She turned and climbed, breathing hard. Three steps from the landing her knee gave way. She screamed as she fell, sheltering the child in her arms.

A terrible knife pierced her hip, her leg. She tried to rise but the pain took her breath away. Nadia was howling in terror.

"Are you all right, child?"

"I want my mother!"

"Listen, Nadia, I'm hurt. You must get out of here. Outside. Go up that stair and run."

But the little girl only clung tighter.

Grimly, Um-Ibrahim began the effort to drag them both up the endless steps.

Karima had seen wealth—after all, her father had worked as chauffeur to one of the richest English families in Egypt—but she had never been in a bathroom as resplendent as the ladies' room of Shepheard's Hotel. Shining marble, big crystal-bright mirrors, gold-plated fixtures, a matronly attendant hovering to pamper her. It was like something in a palace—although if the stories were true, the bathrooms in King Farouk's palaces made this one look like a *fellah*'s outhouse.

Karima dawdled to luxuriate in it all, repairing the dark kohl around her eyes even though it was nearly flawless. A middle-aged Englishwoman came in and glanced at her with surprise. "Aren't you the singer?"

"Yes, ma'am."

"You have a lovely voice. But isn't there a dressing-room for the entertainers?"

"No," Karima lied.

"Hmm," said the woman and began renewing her lipstick. It had always fascinated Karima: why did Europeans paint their lips as red as blood but leave a woman's most alluring feature, her eyes, looking like little glass buttons?

From outside came a muffled tinkle of breaking glass, then another, followed a moment later by a loud pounding on the door. The attendant scurried to it and returned in an instant. "Please, ladies, you must leave. There is a fire."

"Naturally," said the Englishwoman acidly, and shot Karima a glare as if this news were her fault. Karima scarcely noticed. She pushed the attendant aside and ran to find Nadia.

It took only seconds to see that the rioters were attacking Shepheard's after all. Rocks smashed through the windows, and as the panes broke, the howls from outside became louder. Ten yards in front of Karima a bottle with a burning rag in its neck crashed through a window and skittered across the floor. With a sudden whoosh it exploded. A man ripped a Persian rug from beneath a table and threw it over the flames.

Karima fought her way toward the private ballroom against a crush of frightened guests. Smoke was beginning to trail along the ceilings. The ballroom stood empty. She raced backstage shouting for Nadia and Um-Ibrahim. No one!

"Karima!"

It was Munir, ashen, panting as if he had swum the Nile.

"Munir, I can't find Nadia!"

"She's safe, thank God," he gasped. "They're both safe." He caught his breath. "A waiter told me. He said they got out."

"Are you sure?"

"He saw them go himself. We need to join them, my love. This building is going to burn."

With a last look and a last cry for Nadia, Karima allowed her husband to lead her from the ballroom. The smoke was choking now, stinging her eyes. She saw no flames but could hear their crackling from above and toward the front of the building.

An Englishman in the uniform of a military officer blocked them. "Not that way! The side entrance. Follow me."

A moment later Karima was outside, gulping the cool, crisp winter air.

But the scene was hellish. Behind them, the great hotel was dying, flames leaping from its upper windows, billows of cottony smoke climbing the sky. A wrought-iron balcony broke free and hurtled down the building's florid Italianate façade. On the street, hundreds of young men and teenaged boys milled in ragged, yelling groups, some still heaving rocks at the doomed building. Karima saw two Englishmen, drenched with blood, being beaten and kicked on the ground amid shards of glass. One of them was trying to shield his head with his arms. The other simply flopped like a broken doll. There were no police, no firemen.

Heedlessly Karima pushed into the mob, calling Nadia's name, searching frantically for a glimpse of her daughter's red dress or the familiar hunched figure of Um-Ibrahim. Munir followed.

They circled the burning hotel once, then again. Then Munir clutched at her arm.

"You go on, Karima. I've got to sit down. I think I breathed too much smoke." He sank weakly to the curb and leaned back against a lamppost. He was sweating despite the cold.

Karima hesitated. "You'll be all right? You're certain?"

"Yes. Yes, it's nothing. I'll be right here. Who knows, they may be going in circles too."

"All right." She pressed on alone, questioning anyone who would stop to listen. But although some thought they might have seen the child or the old servant or both, no one could say where they might be now.

Badr al-Khoury, ensconced in a broom closet, waited his chance. The busboy knew that timing was crucial. Everyone out of the way—that was the key. Wait too long, though, and—well, the old building was finished for sure. But his job was burning with it, after only two months, and he was a poor man. He needed to salvage something from the disaster.

How long since he had heard anyone in the hall? A minute? Two? Badr opened the closet door and knew immediately that he had been too patient. The smoke was as thick as water. Gagging, he covered his face with his apron and ran as low to the floor as he could toward the private ballroom.

The smoke was a little less dense there, and things were as Badr had hoped: the silverware everywhere, unguarded—real silver, the headwaiter had boasted, worth a fortune. Badr raked pounds of knives, forks, and spoons into the apron, rolled it up, and stuffed it under his jacket.

It was clear that the only way out now was the service entrance— but since Badr had never used any other, that had been his planned escape route all along. God willing, if any of the waiters or other hotel staff were outside, they wouldn't notice his sudden gain in bulk. Or maybe they had all taken their share too.

Along the hallway, light-headed, suffocating. Down the stairs. Just a few steps more.

Timbers crashed on an upper floor. Then Badr heard something else. A cry. A child.

There. The stair to the hotel's lowest level.

Move along, he told himself. If you linger here, you could die.

Ah, well, whatever Allah wills.

He scrambled down the dark stairway and almost tripped over the wailing child and an old woman who was wheezing with pain.

"For the love of God, save the girl," begged the woman.

"And you, Grandmother? Can you move?"

"I'm nothing. For the love of God, leave me and save her."

Badr pulled the child from the old woman and clutched her against the bundled silver on his belly. "I'll be right back, Granny," he said.

At that moment there was a thunder of collapsing structure and the top of the stair became a wall of flame.

Badr stared wildly. My God, how had that happened? Well, no help for it and no time to waste—the only refuge now was downward.

He left the old woman praying and groped along some sort of passageway. The smoke was less suffocating down here, but everything was blind dark—black as a djinn's cave. The child clung to him like a whimpering monkey.

"Hush, little one. There must be a door here somewhere."

He blundered against one, felt for the knob. Locked. He kicked. Solid as bedrock.

He retraced his steps, running his hand along the wall. Another door. Open. Light! Praise Allah.

Badr recognized the linen room. Piles of immaculate laundered tablecloths, napkins, even chef's hats.

The window was high up. He stacked packets of linen and climbed. Cursed be the builder of this place! It was just a ventilation slit. He was looking out at ground level.

A man reputed to be a burglar had once told Badr that if he could fit his head through an opening, the rest of him could squeeze through too. Badr pressed his face against the slit. No good. Too tight by far.

But the child?

He pushed her head into the slit. Tight. The little girl screamed as the window-frame scraped her flesh, cut her ears. The bundle of silverware fell to the floor. Silver be damned! There! Her head was through. Now the shoulders. Allah, it was working! Her little behind. Done!

"Run, little one," shouted Badr. But she had already moved beyond his field of view.

A rush of combustion. He jumped down and slammed the door against the flames, then climbed to the ventilation slit again, sucked precious air, and called on man and God for help until a sharp crack and a wash of radiant heat told him that even Allah could aid him no more in the living world.

Nothing in Nadia's two years of life had prepared her for what was happening now. Nothing around her was like anything she had ever known.

Where was Mama? Papa? Why didn't they come get her? What had happened to Um-Ibrahim? Why had that man hurt her?

She had run from the fire and the pain, only to find herself in a crowd of angry, shouting men with terrible looks on their faces. She was pushed, knocked down sometimes, stepped on. No one paid any attention to her cries. No one would tell her where her mother was.

Finally a man noticed her. He wasn't shouting. He picked her up and asked questions, but she couldn't understand them. He carried her for a while. She hoped he would buy her something cold to drink. She was so thirsty.

Then there was more shouting, and loud pops. The man turned the corner of a building and crouched. Nadia could tell he was afraid. Another man swung around the corner. "Let's go, Ahmad. They're coming."

"I hear, my friend," said the man who had been carrying Nadia. He pushed her toward a pile of smelly garbage. "Hide behind that. They won't hurt you. Wait till you see a lady, and go to her."

He pulled off his jacket and wrapped her in it. Then he was gone.

Nadia slipped behind the garbage pile and huddled there shivering. She didn't know what to do. She wished Mama and Papa would come. Or a lady. She wished she were in her bed. She hurt.

She curled up in the ragged jacket and slept.

————

Night. The stench of smoldering ashes was everywhere, but most of the flames had long since died. More than 750 buildings had burned that day, including the legendary Groppi's, the Rivoli cinema, the TWA building, Barclay's bank, the Ford showroom, the Cicurel department store. All had some foreign association, primarily British. By one count, twenty-six foreigners had been beaten or burned to death, but there were many counts, and no one would ever be sure how many Egyptians had died, either.

But now Cairo was quiet—unusually so, as if the great city were hiding its face in shame after its paroxysm of rage. The normally teeming streets lay nearly empty. Even the police, called out too late, had drifted off to warmer places to spend their long night's watch.

Down the Desert Road came a black Chevrolet, moving slowly, driven by a distinguished-looking middle-aged man: it was the physician, Tarik Misry. He had been visiting his hometown of Cairo, though he had resided for some years now in Paris. With him was his French wife, Celine. They were driving to Alexandria, where they would take a boat for Marseilles. The doctor had many friends in Cairo but his only family now was Celine. He wanted her out of the city. The giant was sleeping, but who knew what might happen when it awoke tomorrow.

Despite the cold, the doctor drove with his window down, so that anyone who might be looking would know he was Egyptian. It was bad enough that the car marked him as wealthy; he certainly didn't want to be taken for an Englishman, or even an American.

"Damn it," he said suddenly.

"What is it?"

"I've missed the turn for the bridge. You'd think I was a tourist. Everything's so different."

He could go up and around—no, he'd just use that little alley up ahead for a U-turn. He was in a hurry to put Cairo behind them so he could raise the window.

As the doctor shifted into reverse, something in the alley caught his headlights.

"Look at that little boy," said Celine. "Is he hurt?" Without waiting for an answer, she got out of the car. The child stood like a frightened animal in the glare. Celine picked her up and brought her back to the car. "A little girl!" she corrected herself. "She's cold. And there's blood here, see?"

"Just some scrapes, I think. This isn't the place to conduct a proper examination."

"Close the window, Tarik, she's like ice." Celine reached for the bottled water that she was never without in Egypt.

"Thirsty as a camel," observed the doctor. "That's enough; not too much."

"Look at her," said Celine, taking in the creamy skin, the lapis-colored eyes, as she wiped dried blood from the girl's face. "She's not all Egyptian, you can tell."

They both had seen many children like that in Cairo, one side of the equation that added thousands of lonely British soldiers and an equal legion of poor Egyptian whores.

"I suppose we should take her to the police," said Tarik.

Celine said nothing. She simply hugged the child closer.

Tarik sat quietly for a moment, then backed the car out of the alley. Slowly at first, then with gathering speed, the Chevrolet rolled up Kasr el Nil Street and turned the corner toward the Nile bridge and Alexandria.

Nadia closed her eyes, leaned into the arms that enveloped her and went to sleep.

9
The Last Pharaoh

Cairo, 1952, 1953

The fires were extinguished, the rubble cleared. Throughout the night-mare of Black Saturday and its aftermath, Farouk still believed he was in control. While others struggled to rebuild and replace what had been destroyed, the king lived life as usual. He dismissed one cabinet; three others resigned. One of his new appointees was Hussein Sirry Amer, a man who knew the identity of the Free Officers.

Three days after Amer's appointment, Omar met with the Officers in a small house in one of Cairo's seedier neighborhoods. The temperature outside was hot, the atmosphere inside tense. In the background an old wind-up Victrola played Rimsky-Korsakov's *Scheherazade*, the melody that would become the Free Officers' theme song.

"The king will go," Omar said authoritatively. "And he will go quietly. My source—someone very well-placed in the court—has assured me that Farouk is so frightened, he jumps at the slightest noise."

The Officers exchanged glances among themselves but said nothing. "And who is your source this time?" demanded a young captain who made no secret of his dislike for Omar. "The king's barber? His valet?"

Omar ignored the sarcasm. "I must, of course, protect my sources," he said piously. "But I can assure you, they are in the king's confidence. He knows he is finished. It only takes a push—" he made a sweeping motion with his hand—"and he will go."

Omar waited for a reaction, a hint of the Officers' plans. He knew that a military coup was at hand. But when? That information would help him implement plans for his future—a future when he would trade handsomely on his connections to the new regime. And, of course, he could also sell the same information to those who would need to leave the country—because they were undeniably linked to the throne.

But no reaction came. Omar realized but did not like the implications of the silence: a man who traded in other people's secrets could be useful, but he was not to be trusted. Gamal abdel-Nasser inclined his head toward the door. Omar understood; it was time to leave.

He rose, making polite farewells. He paused for a moment in the doorway. Sometimes Omar was paid for his bits of information, sometimes not. Today, no one followed to offer money. Ah, well. He was short of cash, as he always seemed to be these days. The cards seemed set against him. And the roulette wheel as well. But his payment would come in richer forms—and in the not-too-distant future, *inshallah*.

As soon as Omar left, discussion among the Officers resumed. "I say we keep to our original plans," insisted the young captain. "If we rush into this, we could lose everything. How can we be sure the king will offer no resistance? How do we know that Omar isn't simply telling us what he thinks we want to hear?"

Nasser smiled thinly. "I wouldn't trust that one to give me the correct time—if he believed there was an advantage to lying. But in this instance, it is very much to his advantage to be honest—or as honest as he knows how to be. He believes we will prevail, I'm certain of that. Therefore, he understands very well what will happen to him if he feeds us false information. I say we must act soon—or we run the risk that Amer will betray us."

There were murmurs of assent. And more discussion. In the end, Nasser prevailed: the coup the Officers had planned for 1955 was moved up to November 1953.

When the gathering broke up, Nasser took his friend and colleague Anwar Sadat aside. "We will have to eat Amer for lunch before he eats us for dinner," he said. Sadat nodded.

The clock was ticking.

Good-humored as always, even in time of crisis, the king found time for the usual card games with his Italian cronies. During one hand his favorite playmate, Antonio Pulli, threw down what appeared to be a winning hand: "Four queens," Pulli declared with a broad smile. The king's returning smile was even broader. "Yes," said Farouk, "but I have three kings—and I am a fourth—so I win."

And so it was. What Farouk did not like, he ignored. And what he did not like were whispers that his regime was in trouble. He had his throne—and he was certain the army was behind him. He had, after all, done so much for them. He had worked hard to secure American arms, worked equally hard to get Egyptian officers into West Point. He was like a benevolent father to his military. Could he not then expect loyalty in return? He certainly believed so—in spite of the warning signs that all was not well.

In early January, Farouk had put up the much-hated General Sirry Amer as his candidate for the presidency of the Cairo Officers Club in Zemalek. The Free Officers accused the general of plotting to sell Egyptian war *matériel* to Jewish smugglers—who in turn were selling the goods to Israel. They launched a vigorous leaflet campaign against Amer and put up a candidate of their own: the venerable war hero, General Mohammed Naguib.

Expressing his opinion of Amer in a more direct way, Nasser led an assassination squad that fired more than a dozen shots at him.

None reached their mark. Though Naguib won the election by a landslide, though the pro-Naguib leaflets declared: "The Army Say NO to Farouk," the king still did not seem to understand that sentiment was running against him.

He not only declared the election invalid, he banished General Naguib to a post in the desert outside Cairo.

He would do his own house-cleaning, Farouk decided, reasoning that if he could mitigate his regime's worst excesses, the British and Americans would support him. He appointed Naguib el-Hilaly, a prominent lawyer with an impeccable reputation, to clean house. And he chose Colonel Isma'il Shirin, Princess Fawzia's second husband, to be Minister of War. A relative, he believed, could be trusted to keep an eye on the Free Officers and make whatever arrests were necessary.

It was too little and much too late.

The July temperatures in Cairo were hot, 117 degrees and higher, a sleepy time when no one expected anything to happen. A good time for a revolution.

The Free Officers moved swiftly, efficiently. On 23 July at 7:30 a.m. the reading of the Quran on the radio was interrupted. The voice of Anwar Sadat rang out: "Egypt has gone through a difficult period in its recent history, which was plagued by bribery, graft and corruption . . . That is why we have carried out a purge. The army is now in the hands of men in whose ability, integrity and patriotism you can have complete confidence."

Soon the streets of downtown Cairo were filled with tanks and soldiers. The monarchy had come to an end. And so had 1,400 years of foreign occupation and rule—the Hyksos, the Persians, Greeks, Romans, the Arabs, the Fatimids, the Ayyubids, the Ottomans, the French, and, at the end, the British. For the first time in centuries, Egypt would be governed by real Egyptians.

Many among the Free Officers favored a bloodbath to wash away all traces of the monarchy and the corruption that had plagued and crippled Egypt. Above all, many argued, the king must die. In the end, Farouk's life was spared by one vote: Nasser's. "History will sentence him to death," he pronounced.

The king made a list of demands. Nasser refused them all. It was enough that he would be allowed to live. And he would get a 21-gun salute as he sailed out of Alexandria to Naples. Nasser had insisted on this gesture: it would show the world that Egypt, unlike other Middle Eastern countries, was capable of making a civilized transition.

Humbled, beaten, the king signed the document of abdication on 23 July: "We, Farouk the First, whereas We have always sought the happiness and welfare of our people, and sincerely wish to spare them the difficulties which have arisen in this critical time, We therefore conform to the will of the people . . ."

The royal yacht *Mahroussa* was loaded with 566 pieces of luggage— for Farouk, his wife Narriman, the royal children, and the staff of bodyguards, nurses, and governesses. Under the watchful eyes of the military, Farouk packed only two suits—he had more than a thousand—and six shirts; Narriman took seven outfits, leaving behind her dazzling collection of European couture and designer furs. The nurse did a bit better: in a suitcase full of diapers she managed to conceal four of Prince Fuad's finest gold and jewel-encrusted ceremonial gowns.

As if to further humiliate Farouk—and inflict pain on his well-known appetite—provisions for the three-day trip to Naples were strictly limited. Instead of caviar and succulent game, stores of bread and cheese and cottonseed oil filled the yacht's galley. Grilled cheese sandwiches would dominate the menu of a man who was known to eat one or two dozen eggs at a sitting.

But the Free Officers did allow Farouk to take many crates of champagne and Scotch on this last official journey. It pleased and amused them that his much-publicized abstinence had turned out to be yet another royal hypocrisy. Here Farouk had the last laugh: the bottles contained not liquor, but jewelry, gold ingots, and other priceless objects.

And when the packing was done, Farouk stood on the bridge of the *Mahroussa* for a last look at the city, just as his grandfather had done some seventy-five years before—on his way to exile.

Crowds gathered along the shore to watch the royal family's departure. The 21-gun salute was given. The *Mahroussa* left the shore. Some cheered, others wept quietly, remembering Farouk's golden days, his love for his people, the good he had tried to do when he believed he would be allowed to make his own choices. The yacht passed the point where the Pharos Lighthouse, the Seventh Wonder of the Ancient World, had once stood, and then disappeared from sight, leaving behind the city of Alexander and Ptolemy and Cleopatra. The last pharaoh was gone.

But the new regime was not yet finished with Farouk. One day out of Alexandria, the *Mahroussa*'s captain, who was loyal to the king, got word that a gunboat was in pursuit. One of the Free Officers, Gamal Salem, took it upon himself to defy Nasser's order that the king should live. He had planned to shoot Farouk during the 21-gun salute at Ras-el-Tin, but that scheme had been thwarted by the presence of an American contingent. Now he would try again—and fail. The *Mahroussa* zigzagged across the Mediterranean and eluded Salem's assassins.

Failing to destroy the king, the Officers contented themselves with assassinating his memory and punishing all his associates. Farouk's cousin Prince Abbas Halim was given a twenty-five-year sentence for selling defective weapons during the war with Israel. The sentence was suspended in return for Halim's testimony that Farouk cheated at cards, that he gambled with Jews—and that his playboy image was simply a mask for his impotence.

The Officers took foreign journalists on tours of the royal palaces, pointing out Farouk's framed photos of Hitler (Farouk supporters claimed these were plants), his dozens of gold-and-diamond-studded walking-sticks, his thousands of silk shirts, his $27 million stamp collection—and his extensive pornography collection. After the propaganda value of Farouk's possessions waned, the Revolutionary Council commissioned Sothebys to auction off the entire lot.

In time scholars and political scientists would be kinder to Farouk, noting that it was he who kept alive Egypt's dreams of independence and that it was he who, by standing up to the British, set an example to other vassal states in the Middle East.

Farouk tried to burnish his own tarnished image by publishing his memoirs, which began to appear in weekly installments in Europe. General Naguib, now prime minister and commander-in-chief, sent a warning to Farouk: if he persisted in his troublemaking, he could still be brought back to stand trial for high crimes and misdemeanors.

Farouk complained about the financial condition of his son, whom he compared to "any unfortunate Neapolitan orphan." The Revolutionary Council officially deposed King Fuad, aged eighteen months, and brought the dynasty of Mohammed Ali to an end.

Also ended was a way of life. The glamor and luster of the royal court gave way to a different kind of culture, dictated by the sons of civil-service workers and *fellahin*. The monarchy's property was confiscated; 100,000 acres were distributed among the *fellahin*. The titles of *pasha* and *bey* were abolished.

Unlike some of his compatriots, Henry Austen had seen changes coming. He had sold much of his plantation land and made new investments, particularly in oil exploration. But his servants still called him "pasha"—even Mustafa, whose son, Omar, was apparently part of the new regime.

Still, Henry viewed the king's departure with mixed feelings. He loved Egypt enough to wish it well, regardless of who was in charge. But he was enough of a student of history to understand what many in the Foreign Office had failed to grasp: that the era of Western influence in Egypt was likely to end, too. Over gin and tonics with his friends, he said: "England—and America, as well—have bet against the king. I fear that time may prove them wrong."

Karima, too, had mixed feelings. Her own loss was so deep, so all-encompassing, that the loss of a king, a throne, seemed trivial. Yet as she had stood on the shore and watched Farouk leave, she could not help but remember the lyrics to one of her old songs:

> *"When at the hour of midnight*
> *an invisible choir is suddenly heard passing*
> *with exquisite music, with voices—*
> *Do not lament your fortune that at last subsides,*
> *your life's work that has failed, your schemes that have proved illusions,*
> *but like a man prepared, like a brave man,*
> *bid farewell to her, to Alexandria who is departing."*

Omar, on the other hand, felt only triumph and jubilation. Before the *Mahroussa* had even reached Naples, he had opened his new office. In addition to his various enterprises, both legitimate and otherwise, Omar was now officially a middleman, a broker, a conciliator. The Middle East was full of them—business would grind to a halt without them. Their success depended entirely on the people they knew and the influence they could sell. Omar believed he was very well situated indeed.

10

The Sorrowing Star

Alexandria

Great sorrow and great triumph—the midwife's prediction kept repeating in Karima's head. She looked at her husband, who had suffered a heart attack during the fire that had stolen her daughter. Now, months later, he looked pale and shrunken against the white bank of pillows; his breathing was labored, his eyes closed.

The doctors had collectively shaken their heads about Munir's prospects of survival, but Karima refused to accept their verdict. "No," she cried, "no, no, no! I've lost my child, I will not lose my husband!"

During the long, dreary weeks at the hospital, she had remained at his side most of every day and throughout the nights. Holding his hand, murmuring words of love and encouragement, Karima willed Munir to survive. And slowly, slowly, he appeared to respond.

Karima's joy at his apparent recovery was soon tempered by reality. Munir had not died, but the doctors could not say how long he would live—or even in what state.

Now he was a veritable invalid, shuffling between his chair on the veranda and his bed. Karima prepared his favorite foods and fed them to him, morsel by morsel. Since he could no longer go to his office, she entertained him with bits of gossip. "Did I tell you what the Sothebys appraiser found when he went to the Kubbah Palace?"

Munir shook his head.

"The keys to fifty Cairo apartments! Each with a different young woman's name on the tag. What do you think of that, Munir?"

Munir smiled. He knew exactly what his wife was up to. Though Karima had little taste for gossip or small talk, she now made a point of gathering bits of news—nothing too serious or sad—to amuse him.

"And do you know there is talk that Narriman may leave the king? Can you imagine that?"

Munir shook his head, as if to say, "What has our world come to?"

"Well," Karima continued, "a good friend of Narriman's told me that she's very unhappy about leaving behind all her beautiful things—the Dior gowns, the sable, lynx, ermine, mink. I'm sure she needs all those furs in Italy's arctic climate."

Munir's smile broadened. He wanted to thank Karima for trying to entertain him when her heart was broken. But instead he matched her effort with his own. "The royal family has had a bad time of it, eh?" he said in a raspy whisper.

"You might say that. When Spyros called yesterday, he told me that Farouk's sister Fawzia lost all her jewels, even the ones she got from her first husband, the Shah."

"Spyros?" Munir was suddenly alert. "What did he want?"

"Nothing. Nothing at all." Karima regretted the slip. This was a subject she did not want to reopen. "Spyros simply asked how you were feeling. If you might welcome a visit one day this week."

"Karima." Munir's gaze was reproachful. His wife's white lie was so transparent it could not even deceive a sick man. "He wants you to sing."

"What Spyros wants is of no consequence," she said firmly. "I am exactly where I want to be. Doing what I want to do."

Munir shook his head. "This is not a life," he said, waving a hand as if to define the shrunken boundaries of their existence. "You are a singer, Karima, a great singer. You love what you do. I don't want you to sacrifice yourself in a sickroom."

She frowned. "This is not a sickroom, it's our home. I love it and I love you. We don't need money to live, so why should I leave my husband to be among strangers?"

"Karima." Munir's expression was sad. "Have we come to this? Must you speak to me as if to a child? You need to sing, my love—as much as all of Egypt wants to hear you."

But the more Munir—or Spyros—entreated her, the firmer Karima was in her resolve. At a time when her life might otherwise have been over, Munir had been her friend, her protector, her champion. The least she could do now was to repay his love and generosity.

Spyros had sworn she was more in demand than ever. In the eyes of her fans, Karima's sorrow made her even greater. Before, they had heard pain in her songs, but without knowing its source. Now something they could share and understand had been revealed. The loss of a child, even a girl, that was a tragedy—and Egypt loved tragic stories even more than it loved stories of great love.

But there was another reason why Karima kept refusing Spyros, one she had not shared with Munir because he might dismiss it as mere superstition. She did love her singing, perhaps more than even he could imagine. But the midwife had spoken of triumph and sorrow in the same breath. So, she reasoned, if she gave it all up—the music, the triumphs—perhaps Allah would allow Munir to live in spite of the doctor's bleak expression. And perhaps He would return Nadia to her. It was a trade she made gladly.

She had hired detectives to look for her daughter, she had paid bribes. The detectives reported nothing but dead ends; the bribes elicited a wealth of worthless information. Nadia had been seen in Cairo in the company of a sinister-looking man. She had been spotted in Luxor with a foreign-looking woman. And so on. Follow every lead, Karima told her detectives, no matter how slim.

Meanwhile, her voice was stilled. And the loss she and Munir shared brought them even closer. In every true sense, Nadia was their child. When Karima cried in her sleep—during the day she tried to keep up a brave front—Munir wept with her. When she was disconsolate, he consoled her. "She will be found, dearest," he promised, as if he knew. They compared dreams and their meanings, for Nadia appeared regularly in sleep to both of them. "I know she's alive," Karima would say, her eyes pleading for confirmation.

"She is," Munir would declare fervently.

The day began like any other. Karima had brought Munir the pomegranate drink he liked so much and a plate of *foul* with pita bread. He ate lightly, then leaned back on his pillow.

"Can I get you something else?" she asked. "Perhaps a piece of fruit? Or ..."

"No, nothing else. But sit down beside me for a moment, won't you?"

"Of course."

"I want you to make me a promise, Karima. This is very important to me."

"Anything. Just ask."

"I want you to sing again."

"But ..."

"Hush." He put a finger to her lips. "I've heard everything you have to say. More than once. But I am telling you now that I cannot die in peace ..."

"Munir, no!"

"All right, then, I cannot live in peace until I know that you will use your beautiful voice as Allah intended. You must promise me, Karima ... it's all I ask of you."

She couldn't refuse. "If that's what you wish, then I promise. But you must promise to get better. It's only fair, Munir. Promise me."

Munir smiled at his wife and patted her hand. And in his eyes she saw love and tenderness and, yes, even happiness.

He slipped away during the long dark hours between midnight and dawn. One moment he was breathing, and then he was not. Karima felt the difference at once. She bolted upright, patted his hand, then his cheek. "Munir," she called out, "wake up, Munir, you must wake up."

She ran from the bed and called the doctor. And while she waited she rubbed his hands, begging Munir to return yet one more time. "Don't leave me," she pleaded. "You're the best man I've ever known. Please don't go."

The doctor came quickly, examined Munir, then shook his head. "I'm sorry," he said. "There's nothing to be done. He is with Allah. Shall I call the ambulance?"

She nodded. Soon Munir would be taken to the hospital, there to be prepared for burial. And then she would not see him again until they were both in paradise. Numb, exhausted, almost beyond grief, Karima dressed in the stage costume that had been Munir's favorite, a jet-black silk gown richly embroidered in silver. Returning to Munir's side, she whispered, "All right, my dearest, I will do what you asked." And she began to sing, not one of her familiar standards, but a new song, the melody from her heart, the words coming to her as if from the heavens. Or from the departed soul of a man who had truly loved her.

> *"Where are you, my darling child?*
> *I miss you so much, so much.*
> *When I close my eyes, I see you before me.*
> *No rose can brighten my home, no candle can light it,*
> *As long as you are far away from me . . ."*

Later it would become part of Karima's legend that this song of lamentation was heard throughout Roushdy, that it rang out in the stillness of the afternoon—and that all who heard it wept. In her heart Karima called it "Nadia's Song."

———

Black-bordered headlines trumpeted the news: Um Kalthum was ill. A mysterious throat ailment had silenced the great voice, and all of Egypt keened and lamented: "*Ya souma, ya souma,* we beg you not to abandon us. We pray that Allah will let us hear your golden song once more."

It was said that the singer had visited every well-known doctor in Egypt. None would treat her. No one would risk the shame of damaging, perhaps even destroying the famous voice.

Spyros convinced Karima that Um Kalthum's illness was a sign from Allah; that, and Munir's dying wish, must surely mean the Almighty intended Karima to return to the stage. Immediately. He did not feel the need to mention that the revenues from a concert now would be tremendous.

Though Karima knew that Spyros's motives were often less than pure, she felt that what he said might be true. She *had* promised Munir. And indeed in singing her songs she did lose herself, if only for a little while. During that little while, she could almost forget the crushing sorrow that was her constant companion.

Spyros had blanketed Alexandria—and all the major cities of Egypt—with posters and advertisements. Karima Ahmad, the *Karawan,* was back, in her first appearance since the tragedy of Black Saturday.

The concert had sold out within days. According to rumor, members of the Saudi royal family would be flying in by private jet for the occasion. Wealthy Alexandrines planned postconcert parties to celebrate the return of their native daughter to the spotlight; those less fortunate looked forward to hearing Karima on the loudspeakers that would carry her voice outside the concert hall. This was a concession she had insisted on whenever she sang in her hometown: the music must be free to those who had no money to pay.

In the past Karima had always suffered some stage fright before a concert. Munir had always reassured her, with soothing words and his faithful presence, that all would be well. Yet now, as she prepared to sing once again, Karima was not at all nervous. Perhaps she no longer cared if the audience liked her or not. Perhaps she was simply beyond such everyday feelings as nervousness or anxiety.

As she stepped onto the stage the crowd roared. She waited quietly for the tumult to subside, then began her set with a medley of old favorites. Just as she was sounding the final notes, there was a stir in the audience, an audible buzz. In the rear of the auditorium appeared a figure in black, someone important judging from the entourage surrounding her. A brightly colored scarf was wrapped around her neck. It was Um Kalthum.

The crowd exploded with whistles and cheers, for the singer onstage and for the one in their midst. It took a quarter of an hour to calm the audience. When the ovation was over—and from that night forward—it was known throughout the Arab world that Karima Ahmad and no one else was the chosen successor to Egypt's greatest singer.

In time, doctors at the US Naval Center in Bethesda successfully performed a surgical procedure that removed a growth from Um Kalthum's larynx. It was probably this single gesture that held American-Egyptian relations together during the presidency of Gamal abdel-Nasser.

As he stood on the threshold of the Austen house, Omar noted with some small satisfaction that it no longer seemed like a palace to him. But that wasn't enough. The old pasha was still here. Not ruined as some *Ingliz* had been; not driven back to where he came from. But still here, as if he belonged, as if he had every right to Egypt.

The pasha's presence, his continued prosperity, was like a gnawing canker that disturbed Omar's pleasure in his own elevation. It didn't matter that the revolution had brought him new and abundant sources of income. Or that his sister had turned Munir's business over to him. For Omar's peace of mind, it was necessary that the *Inglizi* should suffer.

He had tried to use his new friends to accomplish this. Could not the pasha's land be taken under some pretext or other? Given to some high-ranking officer, some worthy sponsor of the revolution? But no, the cursed Austen seemed to have friends at least as powerful as Omar's. He had even won the gratitude of his workers, because he had sold to them most of his plantation holdings, offering cheap, long-term credit. Couldn't the fools see that this so-called generosity was just a scheme? That Austen would have lost the lands he sold? But no, his workers were like sheep; even his own father still talked about the pasha this and the pasha that. Omar had a mind to inform about the liberal use of the honorific "pasha," but that might have caused his own father some difficulty. Never mind. There were other ways to inflict damage and cause pain.

And that was why Omar was here today.

He lifted the heavy knocker and rapped three times. A young maid appeared. When he asked to see "Henry Austen" she sniffed audibly, as if he weren't of the quality that usually came to the house. The impertinence!

His clothes were as elegant as those of any Englishman: a linen suit made in Italy, shoes from England, a shirt cut from the best Egyptian cotton. His hair had been freshly barbered and slicked back with brilliantine. He cut a fine figure, damn it, and let anyone try to make him feel otherwise!

A few minutes later the little maid showed him into Henry's study. Omar was pleased to see that the Englishman's hair had gone completely gray, and that his shoulders were almost as stooped as Mustafa's. He greeted Omar in a manner appropriate to one of his present standing. Good. The pasha understood he was no longer just the son of a servant. Henry offered a drink. Omar made a show of refusing.

"Perhaps some coffee then? Or tea?"

They agreed on tea.

"We haven't seen you in a long time, Omar," Henry said. "Though, of course, we always inquire of your father."

"Very kind of you, I'm sure," Omar said, his voice edged with sarcasm.

Henry took no notice.

"I've been quite busy," Omar continued, with an air of self-importance. "Things are changing rapidly in Egypt. And we who are part of that change have a great deal of work to do."

"There have been changes," Henry agreed. "I hope they will be for the better."

"Oh, yes, they will be. The days of Egypt's oppression by foreigners is over. In fact, the days of all foreigners will be numbered. Even people like you, Henry Pasha," he said with obvious malice. "One day Egypt will be only for Egyptians."

"Yes," Henry agreed solemnly. "And *inshallah,* it will be for Egyptians who love their country more than they love power or money." He stared pointedly at his visitor, so there could be no mistaking his meaning. Though he had not seen Omar for a time, he had heard about his business dealings, his influence-peddling, and, above all, his readiness to sell a neighbor for a few piasters.

"Money?" Omar sneered. "Who are you to talk when you care more for money and position than you ever did about family? And," he added, his eyes glittering with spite, "Allah has punished you for it."

"What are you talking about?"

"You have lost your son, have you not, Henry Pasha? And you have lost your grandchild, the only one you will ever have. She was a beautiful child. I held her in my arms often, played with her. Now she is gone—and you will never see her again!"

Henry stood frozen. Not knowing what Omar meant, yet somehow knowing. He wanted to call the man a liar, but even before Omar began, spitefully, to spit out his story, Henry knew that it was the truth.

It had been Omar's intention to break Henry's heart. He succeeded.

When Henry heard the story of Karima's daughter, of her disappearance on Black Saturday, he slumped into his chair and began to sob, not caring that Omar saw—or that the bastard was smiling.

Catherine found him an hour later, hunched over with his face in his hands, staring blankly at the wall. The brandy decanter was in front of him, and it was clear he had taken more than one drink.

"What is it, Henry? What's happened?"

"Omar was here. Mustafa's son."

"That dreadful man? What did he want?"

Henry took a long shuddering breath. "He wanted to tell me about our grandchild. About Charles's daughter. With Karima."

Catherine gripped the desk, swayed as if she might fall. Her lips moved soundlessly as she tried to take in what Henry was saying. A grandchild? Charles's daughter? Dear God, could it be true? But with Karima? All right, the girl had become quite famous. But she had been a servant, the daughter of a servant. Catherine sat down heavily, still gripping the desk. "A child, she murmured. "Charles's child." She closed her eyes, imagining a little girl with beautiful eyes and a smiling face. Charles's face. A tear slid down her cheek and her heart yearned to embrace this unknown child. And suddenly it didn't matter so much that Karima had not been well-born. Charles's daughter was part of him, and Catherine knew she would love her until the day she died. Her eyes flew open. "We must go to her, Henry. Now. Oh, just think of it—Charles's baby!"

But Henry shook his head. "She's gone," he said hoarsely, "that's what Omar came to tell me. She vanished during the fires. Omar wanted me to know that we would never see her, never know her."

Catherine reeled back as if she had been struck. Oh, this was too cruel, this could not be endured. A precious gift proffered and then snatched so quickly away! "Never . . . Oh God, Henry." Now she was weeping, and though he had no comfort to give, Henry rose and put his arms around his wife. They stood together for a time, crying and remembering, each wondering if they were being punished yet again for failing their only son.

"We must go to Karima," Henry said finally.

"Do you think she'll see us? After all . . ."

"Yes, I know." Bitter memories surfaced. A conversation about an unsuitable match. The dismissal of love as somehow unimportant. A terrible accident. And a young girl who must have faced the agonizing discovery of an unplanned pregnancy alone.

"What if she slams the door in our faces?" Catherine asked.

"Perhaps she'll give better than we deserve."

Karima did not slam the door in their faces. When her maid announced the Austens' arrival, Karima was sitting alone on the veranda in Munir's chair, humming the song: "Nadia's Song."

She rose to greet them, almost as if she had been waiting. She didn't ask why they had come or what they wanted.

Catherine stared at the young woman she had scorned and rejected. Karima was not only beautiful, she had an aura of dignity. Like a queen. She was so different from the girl who had served them that Catherine felt somewhat intimidated. Shyly she reached out her hand. Karima took it, and a moment later the two women were in each other's arms, weeping once more for the man they had both loved. The past was lost to them, but Charles had loved Karima and their love had made a child. They were family now, and that was all that mattered.

Book Two

I

Little Girl Found

Paris, 1959

"See that orangy stuff, Gaby? That's the fat. Ignorant people wash it off, but it's the tastiest part."

Celine was instructing Gaby in the art of shelling langoustine. The heads and shells were going into the stockpot. Gaby did not need to be told that any proper fish or meat dish began with a good stock; she had known that since she was six.

Tarik folded his *Le Monde*—nothing in it but more trouble in Algeria anyway—and regarded his wife and daughter. The Misrys had a social life that took them to mansions and even palaces, but Celine never seemed happier than at moments like this, just the three of them together in the apartment off the Boulevard de Courcelles. The four of them, actually, counting Mickey the toy poodle (named for the celebrated American mouse), who now tiptoed eagerly back and forth behind Celine and Gaby, hoping for a dropped morsel.

The big country-style kitchen, a rarity in Paris, was the main reason they had taken the apartment despite the formidable rent. Celine was from Provence and considered the kitchen the center of any decent home. She would never have dreamed of hiring a cook, even though they could easily afford it these days, and thanks to her labors of love, the apartment was always filled with the aroma of simmering tomatoes and onions and garlic and spices.

The neighborhood had really been Gaby's choice. On a Saturday picnic she had fallen in love with the elegant little Parc Monceau. Tarik had decided then and there to look for something nearby.

Tarik savored these family moments as much as Celine did, all the more so because they came too infrequently. Though he loved his family above all else, his work often took him away from them. His superb skills and his reputation as a diagnostician had brought him a successful local practice, but it represented only a small fraction of his income.

With his knowledge of Arabic and his familiarity with Arab customs, he was greatly in demand among wealthy men, including royalty, throughout the Middle East. It was not unusual in any given year for him to spend a month in Saudi, a week in Bahrain, a few weeks in Jordan. Whenever possible he took Celine and Gaby with him; Gaby, especially, loved these extended house calls in exotic settings. But of course it was often necessary to go alone. On these occasions Tarik missed his wife and daughter terribly. When he was in Paris he spent as much time with them as possible, enjoying one of Celine's Provençal masterpieces, dining *en famille* at a favorite bistro, perhaps taking in a movie.

"Did you know that it's possible to cook fish without fire?" Celine asked.

Gaby wrinkled her nose skeptically. "How?"

"With lemon juice. Or lime juice. You marinate the fish in it and the acid cooks it."

"Oooh, let's do it," said Gaby, indicating the glistening gray langoustine.

"No, *chéri*," laughed Celine. "We don't want them cooked just yet. But someday soon we'll make ceviche and you'll see."

"Good."

Most nine-year-olds, even French ones, Tarik reflected, would object to the idea of raw fish soaked in lime juice. For Gaby, it was just another adventure. She was turning into a classic Parisian *gamine,* deep blue eyes flashing with mischief, intelligence, and humor beneath her mop of dark hair.

Nine years old (or just possibly ten, Tarik thought—that dark little cloud that was always there). It seemed impossible. In his mind's eye he could see so clearly the tiny, trembling, defenseless little thing they had brought home from Egypt.

There had been no problem at customs. The child was asleep and, as usual, the DM on Tarik's passport cut questions short. Then, for several fearful days, they all but hid out in a hotel while concocting a story to tell others. The little girl knew only Arabic, and only as much as a child of eighteen months or so would know. They learned that her name was Nadia, but by tacit, guilty agreement they pried no deeper. She had nightmares the first month and often seemed sad or listless. But those spells ended surprisingly quickly; a time came when Tarik wondered if she remembered anything at all of her former life.

Celine named her Gabrielle, Gaby for short. It was the name she had always wanted for a daughter in the years when children had been her fondest hope—a hope that became an obsession toward the end, before the examinations and tests revealed that she would never have children of her own. Then Gabrielle became a name she used when talking about the daughter they might someday adopt. And then came Cairo.

The child took to French like an otter to a stream, although for more than a year she exhibited a certain confusion about her new name, referring to herself as "Gaby and me," as in "Is there chocolate for Gaby and me?"

They officially adopted her as soon as they could muster the courage. Their story: she was the illegitimate child of a servant in Egypt who had died in a fire. The bureaucrat who processed the case was highly sympathetic, but unfortunately the lack of proper papers, although certainly not unheard-of in such circumstances, might create difficulties ... Tarik said that he understood. He was more than willing to pay for any extra work that might be required. He named a sum. Would cash be acceptable? It would indeed.

At first they planned to tell Gaby the fire story when she was old enough to understand. For one thing, it was very possibly quite close to the truth. But as the years passed Celine demurred: Gaby was *their* daughter; why tell her anything else? For Celine the notion that the girl's mother was a prostitute had become incontrovertible gospel. Even if the woman had not died in the riot, she had assuredly come to some other bad end.

Celine held the French certainty that her native language was the glory of the world, so what was the point of laboring to learn any other? She knew enough Arabic to order in a Middle Eastern restaurant, no more. And Tarik had never told her that in Gaby's early days with them she cried not only for a mother, but also for a father.

Years ago, troubled by conscience, he had suggested that they ought to do something, perhaps place notices in the Cairo newspapers. The look in Celine's eyes was that of a tigress whose cub is threatened, and he had never brought up the subject again.

Partly to ease his guilt, but also because he felt that it was important and, to be honest, enjoyed it, he had always tried to impart to Gaby bits and pieces of her Egyptian heritage. He made sure that she kept up her Arabic, though she now spoke it with a thick French accent. From the first, when the little girl learned some new French word, *chat* for example, Tarik would interject, "We call it *quttah*." Even now, encountering some new term in one of her schoolbooks, Gaby would ask, "What do we call it, Papa?"

She had been to Egypt only twice, even though Tarik went there regularly to visit his relatives. Both times Tarik and Celine had expected every woman passing on the street to cry out, "Nadia!" Now Celine always found a reason why she and Gaby could not accompany Tarik to his homeland.

Instead, they made pilgrimages to the Obelisk of Luxor in the Place de la Concorde, then strolled in the Tuileries, where a sorbet accompanied history lessons disguised artfully (Tarik hoped) as tales of heroes. And of heroines: he had no desire that she hear only of good Muslim wives living in their husbands' shadows, so he made room for Egypt's famous poetess el-Khansa, and for the courageous early feminist Huda el-Sharawi, who had opened the first general education school for girls in 1910. Gaby was amazed to learn that there had been—and still were—places where girls did not go to school. And she was fascinated by the story of el-Sharawi's publicly removing her veil in 1923, denouncing it as a symbol of male domination and an invention borrowed from the Turks at that.

Sitting at the kitchen table, Tarik realized that either his strategy had worked or, as seemed more likely, he need never have worried about his daughter's self-confidence. Only yesterday she had told him seriously that she wanted to be a doctor, like him. Tarik had been deeply moved, although of course he expected her to change her mind a hundred times in the years ahead.

The years ahead. That dark little cloud again. What if there had been no years at all? What if one day Gaby had disappeared, never to be seen again? How could he and Celine have endured it? Was there, somewhere in Egypt, a parent, or two parents, enduring it now? In his fine warm kitchen, in the company of the two human beings he most loved, Tarik Misry, a man of science, not of religion, prayed for his soul.

2

A Voice from the Past

Beirut and Alexandria, 1962

In 1962 Beirut was still a sparkling jewel on the rim of the Mediter-
ranean. The banker and financier, the shipper and importer, the middle-
man and broker—not only for Lebanon but for the oil nations and
kingdoms and emirates clustered around it; the city was still called the
Switzerland of the Middle East. The name testified to the country's lively
banking trade—and to its majestic mountains.

Like many of the world's great cities, Beirut was a true cosmopolis,
home to people from scores of nations and hundreds of ethnic groups. In
a region where religions had warred on each other from time immemo-
rial, in this one place Muslims and Christians—Sunni, Shiite, Druse,
Maronite, Eastern Orthodox, Greek Orthodox, Armenian Orthodox and
Armenian Catholic, and countless other sects and denominations—man-
aged for the most part to coexist in at least a semblance of tolerance and
cooperation.

True, only four years earlier President Eisenhower had sent in US
Marines in order to ensure that the government of the Maronite Christ-
ian president Camille Chamoun would not be overthrown by a Muslim-

based revolt. It wasn't much of an invasion: the Marines in their battle
gear waded ashore amid astonished sunbathers on Beirut's beaches. The
revolt soon faded, compromises were made, and the political fires were
banked. One day they would burn again, hotly enough to turn beautiful,
worldly-wise Beirut into a blackened symbol of human folly and hatred.
But in 1962 few would have dreamed that such a day could ever come.

"So this," smiled the big, balding man, "is the famous Gaby!"

"Famous?" said Gaby with the acute self-consciousness of a
twelve-year-old.

"Notorious then," the man laughed. "Your father has told me all
about you."

Gaby rolled her eyes.

"Our host, Antun Karalyan," Tarik explained to Gaby and
Celine.

"Just Antun," said Karalyan. "A pleasure to meet you both."

"What a magnificent place," said Celine, knowing at once that her
compliment was inadequate. Karalyan's Beirut apartment included
the top two floors of a new high-rise overlooking the Mediterranean
on one side and the glittering lights of the Hamra district on the
other.

"Consider it yours," said Antun. "Seriously, you are the guests of
honor tonight. I doubt that this overpriced pill-dispenser mentioned
it, but without him, I might not be here to enjoy your company."

Now it was Tarik's turn to feel self-conscious. "I did nothing," he
said. "Antun's was a case of patient, heal thyself." It was, as far as he
could tell, true.

There were more than a hundred banks in Beirut. The one that
Antun Karalyan owned was neither the largest nor the smallest, but
it was one of the most solidly profitable. Over the long years of making and keeping it that way, Antun had acquired another trophy:
bleeding ulcers. The renowned Dr. Misry, summoned from Paris,
had prescribed the usual medicines and dietary regimen. He had also
spent hours simply talking with his patient: about the pleasures of

life; about how much money was enough; about the value of still more money balanced against the very real possibility of death.

A few months later the ulcers were gone. How or why, Tarik had no idea. It could not have been the medicines or diet, both of which Antun neglected. Perhaps it was the talk. Why not? Tarik was convinced that ulcers were just another of the many ancient miseries about which he and other twentieth-century physicians remained profoundly ignorant.

"Everyone's upstairs," Antun was saying. It transpired that "upstairs" meant the roof, which the banker had turned into a beach, complete with sand. Small palm trees hung with tiny, starlike white lights waved gently in a breeze from the Lebanon Mountains just to the east. Hidden speakers piped music out into the balmy night.

Fifty guests dined on food that would have gratified any gourmet in Paris. Antun was everywhere, laughing, joking, enjoying the pain-free existence that—in his mind, at least—Dr. Tarik Misry had given him. As an incredibly delicate cheesecake with fresh raspberries was served, he announced another special treat—the latest recording from the great Egyptian artist Karima Ahmad.

Tarik told himself that he must be getting old. Fed and contented, he wanted only to go back to the hotel and curl up in bed with a good book and Celine. Certainly he had no interest in an Egyptian songstress. Like many expatriates he had lost touch with the music of his youth. It seemed too sentimental, melodramatic, unsophisticated. He preferred jazz.

The opening bars of the song did nothing to change his mind. Although the voice was undeniably beautiful, the lyrics—*Where are you tonight, my love, where?*—were precisely the kind of maudlin stuff he had long outgrown.

Silver clattered on china as Gaby dropped her fork. Tarik turned to see his daughter pitch forward—he caught her just in time. Her eyes rolled back in their sockets. "My God, what is it?" gasped Celine.

Tarik checked quickly for throat blockage. No—the child was breathing freely. Pulse rapid but steady and strong. Someone had shut off the music. Antun was urging everyone to move back and give the girl room to breathe. Celine held her daughter's head. "It's all right," said Tarik and, thanking God, he saw that it was. Gaby was coming around already.

"What happened?" she said.

"You got a little dizzy. Probably just a stress reaction, maybe a little dehydration as well." Mentally he ticked off other possibilities. Some sort of sugar reaction—not likely, but it wouldn't hurt to test once they were home. A virus, possibly, or maybe a touch of dysentery, common enough while traveling.

Antun, so concerned that Tarik feared he would have a relapse of his ulcers, ordered up a car. By the time it arrived Gaby was her old self and begging to stay, but Celine wouldn't hear of it. On the ride to the hotel, Tarik asked some routine questions that led nowhere. Then Gaby said, "All I remember is that song starting, that voice. Just that quick, I felt like I was in a tunnel. The next thing, I was lying in the sand with you two pinching and pulling at me."

Late into the night, long after Celine had checked on Gaby for the last time and finally surrendered to sleep, Tarik lay wakeful. A woman's voice. An Egyptian woman's. Surely it meant nothing. What was the name? Karima something. Ahmad. What did it matter? The woman was a famous singer. What did she have to do with anything? What?

Forget it.

But in the morning he still remembered the name.

His hometown saddened Tarik. Something was missing. Energy. Variety.

Great things were happening in Egypt. The Aswan High Dam was actually being built—imagine taming the Nile! New alliances were afoot—in Cairo Tarik had met several Russians, most of whom claimed to be engineers. And Nasser's agrarian reforms were in full swing, the great landholdings cut down to less than a hundred acres, the excess distributed—in theory, at least—to the *fellahin*.

Foreigners were hit especially hard. And that was what was wrong in Alexandria, Tarik decided. So many people had gone "home" to the Greece or Italy or England that they might, in fact, never have seen. Shops, restaurants, whole neighborhoods—all changed.

Incredibly, Alexandria was becoming dull.

Tarik's purported reason for this return to Alex was simply to see old friends and a few very distant relatives. A visit was overdue, and Celine, as always, had no objection to his going. But then, she had never given a second thought to the name of the singer that night in Beirut. And he had never forgotten it.

He was no detective. He had made small talk with his relatives about the famous Karima Ahmad, but they were elderly and hard of hearing, and he learned only that she was just that—famous. He was wondering whether to make more diligent inquiries when, one afternoon, he saw two young women entering a record shop. It seemed as good a place as any to look. He followed them in.

Astonishingly, the first voice he heard was that of Karima Ahmad. Apparently the store was featuring her latest album. The two young women stood admiring the album sleeve. Tarik edged close enough to see: an austere black-and-white photograph of a hauntingly beautiful woman—her eyes seemed to engulf the camera.

One of the young women shook her head. "Listen to that voice. Like an angel. But what a tragic life."

The other woman nodded. "First her child, then her husband. I don't know how she survived it."

Tarik mustered his courage. "Forgive me, ladies. I couldn't help overhearing, but I'm ignorant of all this. What happened to the child—and the husband?"

The women stared at him as if he had dropped from the moon. Surely everyone knew the terribly sad story of Karima Ahmad.

"I've lived out of the country for years," said Tarik apologetically.

"Well," said the first woman, "her husband died—of grief, they say—after the child disappeared."

"Disappeared?"

"On Black Saturday, in Cairo. During the fires, or whatever it was. She was never found. A beautiful little girl only two years old. Nadia, her name was."

Tarik's blood froze. "You're right," he said. "That's very tragic. Thank you."

Shaken, he left the store, feeling the women's eyes on his back. It had to be Gaby. What other possibility was there? But wait. Think rationally. Coincidence is the exception, not the rule. There are a dozen other possibilities. A hundred.

A few doors down was a bookstore. He went in.

"Do you have anything on Karima Ahmad, the singer?"

The clerk indicated a shelf loaded with copies of what looked to be a fan magazine. On the first page Tarik found a surprising sentence: "She was born the daughter of Mustafa Ismail, a poor man who later achieved a comfortable life as the chauffeur of the well-known cotton pasha, the Englishman Henry Austen." Henry Austen. Tarik remembered the night he treated one of the Austens' servants for hemorrhage. Karima would have been there, a little girl, one of half a dozen watching fearfully at the edge of the light. He had no recollection of her.

He bought the magazine and read it over a mint tea at a sidewalk café. The author was shorter on facts than on gushing adulation, but the essential story of the daughter's disappearance was there, and to his relief Tarik discovered that he could actually take hope from it. Karima's little girl had been with her at Shepheard's Hotel. He had found *his* Nadia miles from there. How could a toddler have gone so far, especially in a riot?

Nothing was conclusive. Everything could mean anything.

Tarik decided that it was time to renew an old acquaintance.

The Austen villa was less imposing than Tarik remembered, a faint aura of disrepair about it. He had seen neither the house nor its owners since shortly after the world war.

Henry Austen rose from reading a book to greet him. He had

aged considerably, Tarik thought, yet there was something serene, rather sad and philosophical, about him; he might have been a retired Oxford don who spent much time out of doors. Catherine, on the other hand, Tarik would scarcely have recognized—gray-haired, plainly dressed, soft-spoken, and obviously a devoted companion to her husband. After some pleasantries she excused herself to see to matters in the kitchen.

Henry and Tarik talked of many things. Yes, Alexandria had changed. Egypt had changed. The former cotton pasha no longer had his plantations, only this place, with a handful of servants too old to go elsewhere. Fortunately he had invested well in other areas; he and Catherine were comfortably fixed.

"What happened to the girl I treated that night?" wondered Tarik.

Henry shook his head. "She left one night early in the war. Perhaps she found herself a soldier. One hopes so, at any rate."

"And where is Charles?"

"He died in an auto accident in 1950."

"My God. I'm so sorry to hear it. How terrible for you and Catherine."

Henry gave a small nod and was silent for a time. Then, as if coming back from a distance: "And your wife? Celine, was it?"

"Celine. She's well, thank you." Tarik hesitated but added, "We have a daughter, Gabrielle."

"Ah. Congratulations."

"Thank you." Tarik felt as if he were manipulating this old friend, a man who had known such grief. But the subject needed changing in any case. "I understand one of your own has become a celebrity."

"Karima? Yes, we're very proud of her."

"They say she's quite rich."

"Oh yes." Again Henry seemed to retreat into some remote, interior place. "Do you know," he said at length, "there was more to the story of my son's death than I've ever told anyone—except of course Catherine. I should like for someone to know—Catherine and I won't live forever. I think I should like to tell you. Perhaps it's just that I know you'll hold it in confidence, to yourself only."

"Of course, Henry Pasha." Tarik didn't really care for this return to the subject of Charles; he had hoped to learn more about Karima.

"A drink? It's a tale that takes some telling."

"A small brandy, please."

Henry made drinks for the two of them and told it all.

At the end Tarik found himself at a loss for words. "I—I don't think I've ever heard anything so sad," he blurted at last. His compassion was genuine, but his feelings were confused. He had learned so much—yet what had he learned? The part of the story that concerned him still ended with the disappearance of a little girl from Shepheard's Hotel.

Then Henry went to a drawer and took out a small, silver-framed black-and-white photo. "From her mother," he said. "You can't tell it from this, of course, but her hair was dark and her eyes deep blue. Or so one's told."

The child in the picture was little more than an infant, but Tarik had his final answer. It was Gaby. No one else.

He fought back an almost overwhelming impulse to tell Henry then and there; otherwise, what was he but a common criminal? Even more, he wanted to tell Gaby. But could he? *How* could he? He needed time to think, time to sort this out.

As soon as he civilly could, he bid the Austens good-bye, promising to visit the next time he was in Alex. He left feeling like Judas.

The next days were hell. The question was always on his mind. He slept little, and his relatives joked about his absentmindedness. From one moment to the next, impulse pushed him toward a different decision. And the decision was his alone: only he held all the pieces to the puzzle, and he could pass them to no one else.

Not until he was on the plane to Paris did he make up his mind. It might be wrong—it *was* wrong—but he could not rob his wife of the daughter she loved so entirely. The Austens and Karima had their grief, but they had also accepted their loss and gone on. With Celine, it was no exaggeration to think that the blow might kill her. No, whatever it might cost him, he would keep the secret.

3
An Estrangement

Egypt, 1956–1957

In the summer of 1956, as an assertion of Egypt's sovereignty after cen-
turies of subservience to foreigners, Nasser closed the Suez Canal. In
October, English and French warplanes bombed Cairo while Israeli
ground troops invaded and occupied the Sinai. Before the UN eventually
stepped in to halt the fighting, Egypt had suffered what amounted to
another defeat. Yet, if anything, Nasser emerged from the war stronger
than before. He had thrown down the gauntlet to the great European
powers that had dominated his nation since the time of Napoleon. It was
bitter, certainly, that Israel was once again victorious. But this was not
the debacle of 1948. Egyptian soldiers had fought hard and courageously
in the face of what, to the man in the streets of Cairo or Alexandria or in
the fields along the Nile, were insuperable odds. Egypt had shown that it
was no longer a doorsill upon which others might wipe their feet with
impunity.

Nasser emerged stronger than ever. Using the war as an excuse to sup-
press all opposition—including the Wafd and the Muslim Brother-
hood—he sent thousands to prison.

The makeshift medical ward was in a schoolhouse in a desert town near the Canal. It was not exactly at the battlefront, but close enough for the sounds of artillery fire and exploding bombs to agitate the dapperly uniformed young captain who had escorted Karima from Cairo.

"This is a hellish place," he said as the battered jeep ground to a stop. "Don't take too long, madam."

From an armored vehicle nearby, wounded men were being carried into the schoolhouse. One of them cried out to Allah as he was lifted. Karima saw that his legs ended in wads of bloody bandages at the knees. She fought off a surge of nausea. She had seen many wounded soldiers, but that had been in regular hospitals. Here the suffering was raw, brutal.

The visit to the front had been her idea. Her country was at war and she wanted to do what she could. She had given and would continue to give concerts to benefit the wounded, but it didn't seem enough. Intuitively she felt that her presence, even just for a few hours, would mean more to the men doing the fighting, would remind them of all the women at home who were hoping and fearing and praying for them.

Spyros had vacillated wildly on the matter, all for it one minute, dead set against it the next. Finally he had consented and made the arrangements.

"Well, I'm going in," Karima said to the captain. He and his driver accompanied her.

Inside was a vision of hell. The single room had been cleared of furnishings. A few men lay on camp cots, others on their prayer rugs or simply on the floor. Some writhed in pain. Some were deathly still. Less badly wounded soldiers sat or stood leaning against the walls. There were agonized moans, curses, calls to Mother or to Allah. A civilian doctor and a young army paramedic were examining the men who had just been brought in.

As Karima stood in the doorway, the curses and even most of the

sounds of pain dropped to murmurs of amazement: "A woman";
"What? Who?"; "It's her—the songbird, Karima"; "Who's that?";
"You know, idiot—Karima. *Karawan*." Nightingale. She had been
called by her nickname at concerts, but she had not expected to find
it here.

She knelt by the soldier who had lost his legs. His face was a mask
of suffering; he trembled with the pain. The doctor merely looked at
the dressings on his wounds.

"Can't you give him something?" asked Karima.

The doctor shrugged. "There's nothing left to give."

"There's a first-aid kit in the jeep," Karima said to the captain.
"Doesn't it have some kind of painkiller in it?"

The captain nodded to the driver, who went to fetch the kit.
"You'll come through, by the will of Allah," Karima told the
wounded man. "You're strong. I can see it." He looked at her as if at
a ministering angel. It was all she could do not to weep.

Now other soldiers called to her. All had the same request. Are
you going back to Cairo, *Karawan*? Will you pass through the town
of such and such? Do you know the village of so and so? Please tell
my mother, my father, my brother, my wife that I'm alive. The captain had a notebook, and Karima made him write down the places
and names. She had no idea how she could honor all these wishes,
but she meant to try.

A series of explosions rattled the walls. The captain glanced up
nervously. A battle-grimed soldier grinned: "A mile away, at least."

"But getting closer," said another. "You should go now, lady."

The captain nodded as if this were good advice. Karima went on
taking names.

From outside came a clanking rumble.

"Tanks," said a soldier. "Our tanks are pulling out."

"Go now, lady," urged the man who had said this before. "Unless
you want to visit Palestine." Suddenly he stared past her. Around
him some men tried to climb to their feet.

"Stay at ease," came a calm, commanding voice. "We're a long
way from the parade-ground."

Karima turned. She had never seen the man but knew him imme-diately. The black eyepatch, the scarred, hawklike face were famous all over Egypt. He was covered with dust and looked deeply weary, but authority radiated from him.

Farid Hamza studied Karima for a moment, then spoke to the sol-diers. "Trucks are coming up, men. You're going home. It won't be the most pleasant ride, but tonight, *inshallah,* you'll sleep in real beds."

The men visibly relaxed. There were murmured thanks to Allah. "Some of us can still fight for you, General," volunteered one man who looked barely able to stand.

"Another day," said Hamza. "We're pulling back, but we're not giving up. And you men have done enough for now." He regarded Karima again. "Of course," he added with a thin smile, "I didn't realize you had a visitor. No one would be so rude as to abandon a guest—especially such a beautiful one. So I'm afraid I must ask the lady to leave immediately."

It was an order. Karima made her way to the door as the soldiers shouted good-byes. "Don't forget us, *Karawan!*"

The general followed her outside. "You're the singer?" he asked. The captain hastened to make formal introductions.

"What are you doing here, Mrs. Ahmad?"

"I wanted to do something . . . to help."

"I was ordered to escort her to some of the rear positions, Gen-eral," explained the captain. "For morale."

"This isn't the rear."

The captain shrugged helplessly. "It was when we left Cairo, sir."

Again the thin smile. Hamza turned to Karima. "As I told those men, we're retreating. The fighting in the valley—" he gestured toward the east—"is our rearguard. The enemy will be here in a matter of hours."

It was a beautiful desert winter day, hot but not unbearably so. Despite the tanks rumbling in the dirt street, despite the evidence of the wounded she had just seen, Karima found it hard to believe that men were killing one another on such a day. It seemed a sin against God. "What about the trucks?" she asked. "For the wounded men."

"The trucks will be here soon. If they can get through at all."

"And if they can't?"

"We'll take the men out on the tanks." The general glanced grimly skyward. "It won't be good if planes spot us."

Karima thought of the jeep. "We can take two with us now," she said. "Three if they can stand the crowding."

He looked sharply at her. "It's good of you to offer. But unnecessary."

"Don't be silly," Karima astonished herself by saying. "In fact, I won't leave without them."

The hawk's eye pierced her. She lifted her chin.

"You know there's no reason to refuse. It might save lives."

For the first time Hamza grinned broadly. "I surrender. Captain, choose two men who can ride in that vehicle." The captain scurried to obey.

"I must apologize," said Hamza. "I was wrong. When I first saw you in there, I thought it was just a stupid publicity stunt. But you're very brave."

Karima could think of nothing to say to such a compliment.

"I saw what you did for my men," the general continued. "I won't forget. They won't either. The other extreme, in fact. There are three dozen wounded in there. Within six months, every soldier in the Egyptian army will have been one of them."

The captain reappeared, the driver and the medic helping two walking wounded to the jeep.

"Mission accomplished," said Hamza. "You'll consent to go now, Madam General?"

"At your orders, General."

He focused a serious gaze on her. "When this is over, may I call on you? To thank you properly?"

"Of course." She said it lightly, but something passed between them in that moment. She could feel it. A connection. Something that said *This person will be part of your life*.

"I mean nothing untoward, of course."

"Of course."

"God's peace," said Hamza.

"With you too." The ritual words seemed wildly out of place here.

The captain hurried her to the jeep. The driver wasted no time. When Karima looked back, Farid Hamza had vanished behind a cloud of dust.

"Timing," said Omar to the husky man across his desk. "Timing, good or bad, is everything."

The man nodded as if these were words of deep wisdom. Omar had no desire to offend a potential client by lecturing him, but in truth he believed that timing *was* everything. Look at his own life. It had been good timing to break off spying for the Germans when he did—not a moment too soon, in fact. Later, and even more important, he had picked just the right time to leave the Muslim Brotherhood, when they were still supporting the revolution and it seemed natural for him to cultivate Nasserist connections. Now many of his former brothers were in prison, while he was steadily rising under the new regime.

Of course, it had been necessary for him to denounce some of the men with whom he had once worked—Ibrahim Khairi was a painful example. But whose fault was that? Hadn't he warned Ibrahim—all of them—again and again that times were changing, that their inflexible fundamentalism was outdated?

So now Ibrahim was mulling his Quran in some desert prison, while Omar had a fine new house in Roushdy—although hardly as fine as he expected eventually to have—and an office in one of Alexandria's better buildings, with an expensively framed photograph of Nasser on the wall. Someday Omar hoped to have the picture autographed by the great leader. Then potential clients would be even more impressed than this one clearly was.

"I believe that the time is ripe," Omar said crisply. "These projects are going to go forward—and soon. By God's will Egypt isn't like it was just a few years ago. The men at the highest levels—" a tiny hitch of his shoulder indicated the photograph—"aren't content to sit and watch the world go by. They want action."

"Thank God for that," said the man sincerely. He was a contractor working with a few World War II American trucks and any building materials he could beg, steal, or barter for. His specialty was fences. His ambition was to win contracts for fencing some of the new prisons that were being built to hold political dissenters. Even when surrounded by fifty miles of burning sand, a prison needed a fence, if only for psychological reasons. "You and I think alike," the man said with bold hope. "Can I count on your help?"

"You're a friend of Yusef's," said Omar smoothly, referring to the acquaintance who had put them together (and who would have to be suitably rewarded). "Who else would I help?" He assumed a mildly troubled expression. "Of course, I'm only a go-between. I can speak with the right people, but they may have their own . . . priorities."

The contractor was not slow. "Of course," he said. "Business is business. I've set aside a certain amount for such contingencies."

"Very prudent."

"It's not much, only five thousand." The man glanced quickly at Omar, who allowed himself to look embarrassed.

"At the very most I could do seventy-five hundred," the contractor added after a moment.

Omar pursed his lips. "You understand that the men I deal with will have other offers. For fifteen, I could almost promise you the results you want."

"I'm sorry, but that's . . . It's just not possible. Ten, maybe, but no more."

Omar nodded. Clearly the client had reached his limit, perhaps even exceeded it. "I'll do what I can. Don't worry, we may not get every little plum, but you will do well." It was true enough. He could not give the man every prison in Egypt, maybe not even one prison—there were established operators out there with more powerful contacts. But he could get something, more than enough to make up for what Omar preferred to think of as a brokerage fee.

The contractor was thanking him profusely. Omar was equally courteous. Delivery of the money was arranged. Both men spoke highly of Yusef. There were reassurances. Good times to come. God's peace. And with you.

Alone beneath the portrait of Nasser, Omar congratulated himself. A good day's work. He could count on fifteen hundred for himself, maybe even two thousand if all went well. It would go a long way toward easing his financial problems. The tables had been brutal lately. He was sure he was ahead in the long run, but in the short run . . . And the new house was eating him alive. Well, two thousand was two thousand, and the dice might turn this very night.

And if they didn't? In an emergency there was always Karima. God knew she was doing well enough, especially if you counted what that damned Greek was stealing. It was amazing what people paid to hear her sing; there had been plenty of days, around the old house, when he would have paid her to keep quiet. The old house. She still visited their father almost every day. And still lived in that small villa of Munir's when she could afford a castle. With all that money.

It was painful to borrow from her. He'd done it before once. Or a few times. She always had a million questions. In fact it was as much his money as hers. He was the man in the family, in principle at least, now that their father was getting so far along. And hadn't he given her valuable advice on her career? And kept an eye on the Greek? You'd think she would give him a commission on all she earned.

To hell with it. Enough business for one day. Time to relax. Freshen up at home. A few drinks in the usual friendly spots. A pipe or two. Then the matchless excitement of the bouncing dice, the teasing fortune at your fingertips.

Life, as far as Omar could see that day, was very good.

Spyros Pappas's face was a mask of ancient Greek tragedy. "I think we have this concert," he said with deep sadness. "But maybe you won't like it. Maybe I made a mistake."

"What concert?" Karima asked. "What's wrong with it?"

Spyros shrugged regretfully. "For one thing, it's outdoors. Microphone, speakers, all that technology."

It was true that Karima disliked artificial amplification. "Outdoors where?"

"Oh, outdoors. At the Pyramids."

"The Pyramids! What is it, some American tourist group? A political event?"

"No, no. Open to all. Under the stars. Who knows? A hundred thousand, maybe two hundred thousand people."

Karima stared. "What's the joke?" Numbers like that were nonsense.

"And then there's the other thing," said Spyros mournfully. "You get second billing."

"Second billing?" Karima didn't ask out of pride. It was simply that there weren't many singers these days to whom she would be expected to take second billing. Not many at all. "Oh sweet Allah," she said.

Spyros beamed. "Yes, Um Kalthum herself. Unless, of course, you have some objection."

"You madman. Oh, Allah!"

"You don't mind the microphone?"

"I'll suffer through it."

Spyros turned serious again. "You understand there's no money in this—not directly. No way to charge admission. But everyone there will want your records."

"Whatever you say, Spyros. Just tell me when." She felt as giddy as a teenager. "You're not joking, are you? This is real?"

"Very real." He named a date less than two months away.

"So soon!" Suddenly she was nervous. "It's really certain? What if something goes wrong? Um Kalthum—her health. At night, the cool air . . ."

Spyros waved off her questions. "Will you stop worrying? Isn't it the Muslims who say that it's all in God's hands? We should be celebrating." He summoned his secretary and told the young man that an ice bucket and champagne were in order.

It was while they were waiting that Karima had the vision. Spyros was burbling out one plan after another for press releases, film rights, maybe even a live recording, although he said that was technically difficult. Karima was thinking how proud her mother and Munir would be, if there truly were a paradise and they were watching from it.

Just then, although perhaps it was an echo in the room, she heard a child laugh and say, "Sing, *Ummi*!" and at the same time, as fleeting as a butterfly at the edge of her vision, she saw a little girl and knew that it was Nadia. Not Nadia as she had seen her last, but as she must be now, a running, laughing child with sparkling blue eyes and a face like an angel.

"What's the matter?" said Spyros. "Karima? Are you all right?"

"Yes. It's ... I'm fine."

"You look as if you'd seen a ghost."

"No. No, just the opposite. I was ... thinking of my daughter."

"Ah."

"I saw her, Spyros, just now—I swear it. Or felt her—I can't explain it." Karima drew a breath. "I've always known she's alive. Always. It's what keeps me going. But it's hard, too."

"It must be terrible, my dear. I don't know how you bear it." Spyros had no children—Karima had come to understand that he was one of those men who was unlikely ever to have a wife—but it was clear that he understood the loss of a child was the greatest possible sorrow.

At that moment the secretary bounced cheerily in with the champagne.

"A winged angel," said Spyros. "A glass for yourself, Georgios. And you, Lady Karima? Just on this special occasion?"

She hesitated. She had never drunk alcohol in her life.

"I hear," said Spyros mischievously, "that Um Kalthum goes through the stuff like water."

Karima had to laugh. "Liar. But maybe just a sip. To celebrate."

Georgios, obviously ecstatic to be included in his employer's coup, raised his glass: "To the rising star!"

"That, of course," said Spyros quietly. "But let's also drink to good wishes that come true."

Karima almost choked on her first swallow of champagne—she told herself it would also be her last. Eyes watering, she gasped, "It tastes like medicine with bubbles in it!"

The two men laughed as if it were the funniest thing they had ever heard.

"This is it?"

"Yes, General," said the colonel.

Farid Hamza had not expected such a modest villa. It was a pretty place with a lush garden, but it was definitely not the ostentatious dwelling of a star. It pleased him.

He had come in an official staff car with the colonel and a major. He wanted no possible suspicion that this was a clandestine visit, some sort of assignation. Moreover, he was on a perfectly legitimate official mission.

Separate knots of men and women stood across the street from the house. Hamza counted six women, five men. Fans, he assumed. Autograph-seekers.

The major knocked on the door. A female servant answered. Yes, the widow Ahmad was expecting the general. She would only be a moment.

And then she was there, more beautiful somehow than Farid remembered. The color in her cheeks—was it for him, or only the self-consciousness of a young woman whose living room was suddenly full of military brass?

She served the coffee herself. After a suitable interval of polite small talk, Farid came to the point—the official one, at least—of his visit. President Nasser had awarded Karima the nation's highest medal for civilian heroism; the president would present it to her himself at a ceremony in Cairo. Farid was here merely to make the formal notification and to ensure that she could attend.

Karima seemed embarrassed by it all. "It was nothing," she kept saying. "I visited some wounded men and gave a few of them a jeep ride." The colonel and the major were clearly charmed.

Farid finished reading the official citation and set it aside. "It's true that this language is a bit flowery," he said. "But it's not true that you did nothing. You did something when many others were sitting safely at home. If you don't believe it, talk with my men. It was they who asked me to recommend you for this award. A delegation of them, with a written petition. Actually, they wanted you to have a decoration for bravery in battle—none of them knew that there were different awards for civilians. I told them I couldn't recommend you for a soldier's medal, but they more or less demanded that I give you this." He reached in his pocket and produced a bright bit of color. "It's a campaign combat ribbon. It means that you were there."

The colonel and the major exchanged a glance. They had never heard so many words at once from Farid Hamza.

The general cleared his throat and stood. "And now I'm afraid we must leave. But it would be an honor to escort you to the medal ceremony in Cairo."

"Thank you. But I'll be in Cairo before then, for a concert." She said it as if everyone in the Arabic-speaking world had not heard of this particular event. "I'd be honored myself if you—all of you gentlemen—would attend as my guests. I'll see that you have the best seats."

"I'd be delighted," said Hamza. The other two officers made sounds of polite interest. They were beginning to understand that this visit was more than a matter of official duty for their general.

"Well, until then," said Karima.

"Thank you, Madam Ahmad. Good-bye."

In the car the colonel ventured the opinion that Madam Ahmad was a remarkable woman. "Yes," said Hamza. "She is." He knew that, for him, she was much more than that. And he wished with all his heart that they had met a long time ago—before he had married Fadwa. They had been married for less than a year—newlyweds still—when she had been stricken with spinal meningitis, a disease that had spared her life but left her crippled in body and mind. Farid swore then that he would care for Fadwa until the day one of them died. He had kept that promise with honor, and he intended to continue doing so. He loved Fadwa still, but as a father loves a vulnerable and dependent child. The illness was not her fault, nor was it her fault that his life outside the army was a lonely one.

Perhaps that was why he'd been so drawn to Karima Ahmad. There was something about her that was reminiscent of the Christian women, the nuns, who had put aside all possibilities of a personal life. Ah well, it was a mystery. But what he had felt that day in the desert had been reaffirmed and reinforced. Somehow this woman was joined to his soul.

In the quiet of her bedroom, looking at the combat ribbon, remembering the men suffering in the desert schoolhouse, remembering the way Farid Hamza had looked at her then—and again today—Karima was as mystified as the general. That first day he had been simply a presence, a force, the power of which she instinctively recognized. Today it was a different feeling, as if a benevolent older brother had suddenly appeared in her life, a strong friend she knew she could count on. Perhaps it would be different again the next time.

> From the *Akhbar* (Cairo):
>
> . . . Last night in the clear desert sky framing the Pyramids, there arose alongside the brightest star in the firmament of Egyptian song a new star whose future magnitude can scarcely be calculated.
>
> . . . and when it was all over except the cheers of the vast multitude, and the great Um Kalthum insisted on bringing her young protégée once more onto the stage to share the adulation, it was in every mind that although this was by no means a coronation, it was at least the formal recognition of a royal heir.

Karima was ecstatic and terrified. A quarter of a million people— someone had told her there were that many—had turned into a single living thing before her eyes. This screaming, undulating entity seemed to love her so much it wished to devour her.

"Enough, now," said Um Kalthum at her side. "We bow like good wives and go—quickly, without looking back."

Karima did as she was told.

Backstage was pandemonium. Spyros was beyond philosophy or clowning. "A triumph," he shouted. "My God, I've never seen anything like it!"

A professorial-looking man whom Karima recognized as Um Kalthum's principal adviser glanced portentously at his watch. "If we wait for them to leave, we'll be here all night." His manner seemed intended to communicate to Spyros that he himself had seen a number of things not unlike this one.

"I don't mind waiting a little," said Karima.

"For what?" said Um Kalthum. "Where are the cars, Ali?"

The professor gestured unhappily. "Back there. A long walk surrounded by a mob."

"Perhaps you need a military escort."

It was Farid Hamza, resplendent in full dress uniform. He smiled at everyone, but his eye hardly left Karima.

Um Kalthum noticed. "General Hamza, what an honor. I don't think you've ever attended one of my concerts before."

"Military duty has always interfered, unfortunately."

"Then how lucky that you could come to this one."

"Lucky for me, anyway. You were magnificent. Both of you."

When the little entourage—the two singers, the professor, and Spyros—were ready, Hamza led them through the sea of fans. People pressed in dangerously until they recognized him, then made way as if he were one of his tanks.

"Will you be in Cairo long?" he managed to ask Karima over the noise.

"No. I go back to Alex tomorrow."

His face registered disappointment. "Perhaps I can visit you there again sometime. With your permission."

"Of course. You're always welcome."

At that point Um Kalthum stumbled slightly. Farid caught her and offered his arm. Flashbulbs popped.

In the newspapers the next morning, the famous general looked like the devoted consort of Um Kalthum alone, while Karima and the others trailed insignificantly in the background shadows.

Karima saw that there were many tricks to learn in this business besides those that one could play with one's voice.

It was seeing Spyros Pappas that started things. A chance meeting in a place Omar occasionally visited. Cordial at first: they even stood each other reciprocal rounds of *arak*. The liquor warmed Omar all the way to his fingertips, and for a time he considered that it had been good luck to run into Spyros. But then the Greek began to irritate him. It wasn't just that the man puffed himself up as a starmaker, or even his obvious perverted appraisal of some of the younger men in the room. It was a dozen things.

Four months had passed since the Pyramids concert. Karima's name seemed to be on the lips of everyone Omar knew. That had its value, of course. On the other hand, there was nothing pleasant in being introduced for the hundredth time with the words "You know the singer? This is her brother." Nor was it enjoyable to reflect that, almost overnight, his baby sister was becoming far richer than he had managed in years of tricky and dangerous swimming in the shark pools of political influence.

". . . a private concert," Spyros was saying. "This is the Saudi royal family, mind you. Care to know what they're offering?"

It was too patronizing. "No," said Omar abruptly. "All I care to know is that you're taking proper care of my sister."

Spyros stared. "Have I given you any reason to think otherwise?"

The man was stealing, Omar was certain of it. Skimming money. Everybody did it. "Just be sure that you don't give me any reason," he said.

"What are you saying?" Spyros asked very quietly.

Omar caught himself just in time. The man might be a homosexual, but it wasn't wise to call any Greek a thief to his face. There were better—safer—ways to handle the matter. "You've misunderstood me," he said with his best smile. "I just worry about Karima. As a brother should. Let's have another." He signaled the waiter and slid money onto the table.

There was the problem: money. He was living from one deal to the next. Munir's so-called business was foundering—and after Karima had played Lady Bountiful in giving it to him. When Omar had mentioned to her that the earnings had been very poor, she had blamed *him*. "Perhaps if you didn't turn the business over to strangers to run, if you spent a few hours looking at the figures every now and then, you might see why things aren't going well." Just like his sister: to give him something that was going downhill anyway and then lecture him about why he wasn't saving it.

Worse, the dice had run ice-cold for two solid months. Oh, now and then he had a fair night, but he could no longer delude himself that he was anywhere near breaking even. In fact he had no more money to gamble—barely enough to pay for these drinks. Another loan from Karima loomed as a likelihood.

Spyros tacitly accepted Omar's unspoken apology by downing the Johnny Walker and ordering another round, but soon afterward he pleaded another appointment and left, clearly not completely mollified. Omar decided to make the rounds of places where he was well known and immediate payment could be avoided—at least for tonight. But after several more drinks he found himself in a black depression. He wasn't asking for much, he thought—only to be fairly rewarded for his efforts. Others were plucking fortunes like plums from the trees while he scuffled like a ground squirrel for every penny.

The night took an upturn when an acquaintance who shared some of Omar's tastes suggested a pipe of hashish. The biting, resinous smoke drawn from the cooling *nargilah* was immediately soothing. Jokes and anecdotes seemed funny again. Music became enjoyable, not saddening. He indulged in a favorite fantasy: himself immensely rich, ensconced in a mansion and pampered by servants; Henry and Catherine Austen, broken by government policies that Omar had helped to set, labored for him in the most demeaning jobs.

After a time the hashish-loving acquaintance wandered off; his wife, he said, was expecting him. And Omar was on his own again. All alone, he reflected, his fantasy giving way to maudlin self-pity. Why had he never married, started a family of his own? Not for lack of opportunity, certainly; many families would gladly have given him their daughters. But he had never found a woman who could begin to compare with his mother, and what was the point of choosing someone who could not satisfy his high standards. And besides, he had always been too busy improving himself, raising himself up from the life of a servant's son. Perhaps one day he would find a simple country woman, one who was beautiful as well, someone who would devote herself to making him comfortable and to raising his children.

As he continued to sip Scotch, he found he was unsteady on his feet. Perhaps he should go home. But it was early still, and the prospect of a long night alone was unappealing. There was a prostitute he used occasionally—an unsatisfying experience, all in all, but better than a sleeping-pill. But of course she would demand cash. Ah, well. One more drink.

A loan from baby sister. What a humiliating prospect. But it was while he was contemplating it that Omar had an inspiration. He wondered why he hadn't thought of it before: a way to get the Greek and put himself on solid ground at the same time.

Karima was surprised to see him, but she recognized immediately that he was drunk, and she surmised that he would sooner or later ask for money. That was what his visits these days usually meant.

At least he made an effort at brotherly talk—about their father, her latest record; nothing, thank God, about getting her married again. Finally he came to the point.

"Little sister, I'm worried about you. You're at a level now that can actually be dangerous. You need a man to look after your interests."

"I have Spyros. And *Abi*. And of course you." She did not mention

Farid Hamza, who in the course of a few all-too-short hours in her life had become the adviser, the brother, the father, the friend to whom she would turn first in any crisis.

Omar frowned and draped his arm over her shoulder. "Ah, little sister, that's just what I mean. Father spends his days in the coffeehouse trading gossip with other old men. And Spyros—Spyros is robbing you, don't you know that?"

Although Karima was no businesswoman, she had suspected for some time that Spyros was taking more than was due him. "All agents cut corners," she said. "Um Kalthum told me so." Actually, Um Kalthum had said that all agents were thieves, but that a good agent was worth far more than he could steal.

"You see?" said Omar. "You see?" For a moment he stared blankly, and Karima realized that he had lost his train of thought. He was certainly very drunk. "Cut corners," he said at last. "One day all the corners are cut and your money is gone. Gone. Bye-bye."

"I hardly think—"

"That's it! That's it exactly." He tightened his hug and gave her shoulder a slight shake for emphasis. "You don't think. You live in a dream, little sister. Your music, all those things . . . Listen to me. I'm your brother. You're lonely. Confused. You're a woman. You need a man's protection."

"I told you. I have Spyros and Father and you."

"Forget Spyros! Forget Father! I want to help you. Why won't you let me?"

His breath reminded Karima of spoiled grapes. She was beginning to feel like a fool, standing in the middle of the room with him draped over her.

"You do help, brother. But you're tired. You should sleep. We can talk in the morning."

"I'm not tired. Listen. Munir's been dead a long time now. You need a man in your life."

So it was going to be the marriage lecture after all. Karima wanted to cry, scream—something.

Then, suddenly, the unthinkable happened.

"Little sister, you . . ." said Omar, and his hand fumbled downward and touched her in a way that could not be misunderstood.

For the first and only time in her life, Karima slapped a man.

"Get away from me! You bastard! You drunken fool! Get out of here—now!"

Dazed, Omar backed toward the door. "I . . . I only wanted—"

Karima advanced on him. "You're my brother. I can't avoid that. And I'll help you when you need it. But only when you really need it. And if you ever again do what you just did, I'll forget that you're alive—I swear it by my lost daughter."

In the reeling night, Omar tried to piece together what had gone wrong. It hadn't seemed real—it was like watching a movie of himself even as he did it. What a stupid thing. What on earth had possessed him? He couldn't quite fathom it. And he had only wanted to help her.

Now what? How did that happen? Stand up. Pants torn, knee scraped. Walk. He should go back and confront her. No. Go home. Go home. He was proud of this resolve. It showed strength, character. An intersection. A taxi? Money? Some change, enough probably. He fell gratefully into the seat. As the lights wheeled by, one thing was clear: in her usual fashion, Karima had made him the villain. What was so wrong—a little slip that could happen between any brother and sister? "The bitch," he muttered to the driver, who seemed to understand. "The bitch!"

To all appearances—but only to appearances—they might have been a devoted married couple reunited after the husband's business journey, the wife's visit with distant relatives. Karima had made Farid's favorite meal of stuffed vine leaves and cucumber and yogurt salad. And he had brought her a gift— the latest German high-fidelity record-player, which he was struggling manfully to set up. They had touched only in greeting, and then had moved apart with their separate thoughts. They had not seen each other in a month.

Karima poured lemon tea and watched him with amusement. "Any luck?"

Farid waved the instruction manual. It was written in several languages, none of them Arabic. "I thought I could read English," he said, "but I'm not so sure Germans can write it."

"Have some tea."

"In a minute. I've almost got it."

A minute passed. And more.

"What would you do, Farid," said Karima, "if someone were taking money from you that he ... wasn't entitled to?"

"You mean Spyros," he said.

"What makes you think that?"

"Who else could it be?"

"Well ... if it were Spyros—not saying it is—what would you do? I mean, what should I do?"

Farid put down the little screwdriver with which he had been attacking the German enemy. "What's his commission?"

"What it's always been—10 percent."

"Always?"

"Since we started. Maybe I should have—"

"And you're sure he's stealing?"

"Well ... skimming."

Farid thought it over. "If it were one of my quartermaster sergeants ... But it's not. Let me suggest this: raise his pay by half, and at the same time, make it clear that this will have to suffice. No more little tricks."

"I could do the first part," said Karima. "But I don't know how I could tell him the second part. Without making him angry, I mean."

"Let me handle it. I'll call on him before I leave." He smiled at her look of concern. "Don't worry—it won't be a court-martial. I like Spyros. I think we'll understand each other."

And that, as it turned out, was exactly what happened.

4
Family Secrets

Paris and Morocco

"Pack your bags, Celine, we're off to Morocco," Tarik announced as he breezed into the apartment.

Celine gave an exaggerated sigh. "Honestly, Tarik, Gaby and I scarcely have time to unpack before you whisk us off again. You're turning us into gypsies!"

"And what beautiful gypsies you are," he laughed. His frequent trips abroad were a running family joke, but he knew very well that Celine loved the travel as much as he did.

"Morocco!" Gaby clapped her hands with delight. Though she was on the brink of womanhood—"an infuriating stage," Celine's friends had warned—she was still as bright and open and forthright as she had been in early childhood. "Oh, Papa, can we go to Casablanca? My favorite movie was filmed there. And can we go to Egypt? It's not very far from Morocco, and I've always wanted to see the Pyramids. And then . . ."

"*Un moment, ma petite, un moment,*" he teased. "Let's not forget I have a patient to treat. Prince Rashid—the king's favorite son, I'm told—is ill. I'm going to Morocco to make him well, not to play." Seeing Gaby's chastened expression, Tarik relented quickly. "But after the work, of course, we'll play. We'll go to Casablanca, though I suspect your movie was made in Hollywood. And perhaps we'll even visit some places you never heard of. You'd like that, my sweet?" He said nothing about Egypt; he would not risk taking Gaby there if he could possibly help it.

"Oh, yes, Papa!" She seemed not to notice his omission. "I hope your patient gets well very quickly. I mean, for his own sake, of course," she added quickly. "It's not very pleasant to be sick."

"No, it's not, *ma petite choux*." How lovely she is, Tarik thought, this beautiful girl, with her elfin face and big, luminous eyes. She had brought so much joy, so much wonder into his life and Celine's. But as always, however, the pleasure of loving Gaby came with a twinge of guilt—and the gnawing suspicion that someone else had lost the richness he had gained.

Tarik and his family were flown to Rabat in the royal jet, then settled in a sumptuous suite in the palace. After freshening up hastily, Tarik went directly to the nursery, praying silently as he walked: let this be a routine call, *ya Allah,* and make my skills equal to whatever the boy needs. Though he'd been trained always to maintain a professional demeanor and a certain level of detachment, Tarik found this very hard to do where children were concerned.

The symptoms seven-year-old Rashid had exhibited were vague, but somewhat troubling: intermittent low-grade fevers, malaise, a loss of appetite. The royal physician had prescribed various palliatives, but the symptoms had persisted.

At the nursery door, Tarik found the boy's nanny wringing her hands and near tears. "Oh, thanks be to Allah that you've come," she wailed. "I've tried everything I know to bring the color back to my darling's cheeks, but nothing seems to help. He won't play with his toys and he scarcely touches his food, even when I prepare his favorite dishes. All he wants to do is sleep."

Tarik murmured a few words of reassurance, then turned to his patient. Prince Rashid was a handsome lad, but Tarik could see at once that the nurse had cause for concern. The prince's eyes were dull, his thick dark hair was dry and brittle. As he continued the examination, Tarik found that the boy's fingertips were cold, though the room was quite warm.

"You haven't been feeling well for some time, is that right, Your Highness?"

"I'm just tired," the prince answered listlessly. "I want to ride my horse. And I want to go hunting with my brothers. But I get tired so quickly. My father says you will make me better. He says you are much more clever than the court doctor."

"I shall do my best to get you back on your horse," Tarik said with a smile. He'd heard how the king had roared his impatience with the court physician's failure—and then demanded: "By God, if you can't heal my son, then send for Dr. Misry!"

Turning to the nanny, Tarik asked, "What about the boy's bowel movements? Has he been regular?"

She answered without hesitation. "I have to give him laxatives."

"And are his hands always cold like this?"

"Oh, yes," she replied, nodding vigorously, glad to be of service.

If Rashid were an adult, Tarik might have hazarded an educated guess on the spot. But what he had in mind was rare in children, and Tarik had only read about it in medical literature. After exhorting the prince to be brave, he took a blood sample. He knew there was a laboratory in Rabat, but he preferred the reliability of his own laboratory in Paris. No problem at all, said the king's chamberlain. The blood was put on ice, and the royal jet was quickly dispatched.

Less than twenty-four hours later, Tarik was in the king's private quarters, reporting his results: Prince Rashid was suffering from a rare form of pediatric hypothyroidism.

"How serious?" the king asked.

"Very serious if left untreated. But thanks be to Allah, we have excellent treatments available today. Prince Rashid will have to take a tablet every day, a small dose of thyroid extract. And his blood will have to be tested at regular intervals. I'll fly back to examine him in six weeks. If his thyroid levels are stable, then we'll run the tests twice a year." Anticipating the king's next question, he added: "I expect Prince Rashid to have a full recovery—and a normal life in every way, *inshallah*."

The king's gratitude was boundless. The simple payment of a fee, even a princely one, was not enough. There must be something else. Surely Tarik could think of something he desired. A new automobile perhaps? One of the king's Bugattis?

"Well," Tarik said finally, "my daughter did want to see something of Morocco before we return to Paris . . ."

"My pleasure! It would be my great pleasure to show you Morocco." The king was delighted with Tarik's request, for he loved nothing better than to extend his hospitality to esteemed visitors. "But before you go," he said, "you must allow me to give a small party in your honor."

The "small party" turned out to be a lavish desert-style feast, complete with singers, dancers, magicians—and, of course, mountains of food: entire roasted lambs, *tajins* made with lamb and hare, *b'stilla* with chicken, beautiful salads and heaped platters of couscous.

"I like it here, Papa," Gaby said, as a servant refilled her plate. "I feel very comfortable. Not like a tourist." Tarik patted her hand affectionately. Later, as she began to hum along with one of the entertainers—a woman who was singing an old Moroccan folk song—Tarik studied his daughter, taking in her creamy skin, her jet-black hair. Was she feeling something he could not understand? A pull toward a place, a language, a state of mind? Had he and Celine been wrong to send her to the American School in Paris instead of building on what was most likely an Arab heritage? They had discussed the matter and decided that in the twentieth-century world, it was best for Gaby to be fluent in English. But had they subconsciously wished to distance her, in every way, from her origins? He sighed, then patted Gaby's hand again, and tried to enjoy the evening.

The following day, the king's chamberlain informed Tarik that he and his family had been assigned a caravan of luxuriously fitted Land-Rovers and a trio of guides. Everything would be open to them, every corner in the desert kingdom was at their disposal.

"Think of yourself as Marco Polo, old friend," the king said expansively, as he bade them farewell. "My kingdom can't compare with that of Kublai Khan, but every corner of it is open to you and your family."

And so the Misrys visited the walled city of Fez, frolicked on the beaches of Agadir, shopped in the bazaars of Casablanca, sipped mint tea at the famed Mamounia Hotel. Gaby wanted to see a real French Foreign Legion post, so they visited Zagora. Celine loved the medieval city of Taroudant; Gaby adored the movie-set seediness of Tangier and the "Red City" of Marrakesh.

They toured the seventeenth-century imperial city of Meknes, and Gaby listened intently as the guide explained that this had once been the capital of the ruler Moulay Ismail, nicknamed "The Bloodthirsty." They all marveled at the massive ramparts and entrance gates that had been built by 25,000 prisoners of war.

"This is the best trip of my life," Gaby announced. "I'll never have a better one."

"Really?" Tarik teased. "Well then, there's no point in my taking you anywhere else, is there?"

"Oh, Papa," she laughed, "you know you'll take Maman and me *everywhere*." She paused. "Won't you?"

"Yes, yes, of course I will." He laughed and hugged his child. "To the moon and back, if that's what you want."

"Silly Papa."

It might have been the most glorious trip the family had ever taken. It might have ended with a rich legacy of memories. But Talal, the guide, had told Gaby that the views from Morocco's highest mountain, the snow-covered Toubkahl, were magnificent, and she was not one to leave any treasure unexplored.

The excursion began easily enough. Given the palace directive that anything the Misry family wanted should be made available to them, Talal had quickly procured supplies and a small caravan of mules. The day was warm, the sky was a dazzling blue, and the promise of a small adventure made even Tarik agree that Gaby's idea had been a good one.

At first the ascent was fairly simple. Gaby chattered happily about all the stories she would have to tell her classmates; Talal smiled benevolently, amiably answering her questions about this bit of scrub plant or that tiny crawling creature as he expertly led her mule over the winding trail.

After an hour or so, Gaby's questions slowed; after two hours, she began to wriggle in the crude saddle. "Perhaps we could stop for a little while?" Tarik called out.

"Soon," Talal agreed, "soon we will come to a place for stopping." A few hundred meters later the trail widened, and the guide brought the small caravan to a halt. Canteens of water were passed around, along with some dried apricots and figs. "If you are hungry, sir, I can prepare food," Talal offered.

"Oh, no," Gaby protested, "I don't want to eat now. I want to go higher." And so the ascent resumed, the climb steeper now, the trail narrowing. Talal walked in front of Gaby's mule, holding the animal's bridle, carefully navigating round rocks and ruts. "We come to a village soon, one hour more," he said, pointing upward to a cluster of adobe houses. "Then we will rest and have lunch."

Behind Gaby, Celine smiled as she watched her daughter urge the animal forward. Always in a hurry, she thought fondly. But just as the caravan approached the tiny hamlet of Aremd, a brilliantly colored bird soared past them, then circled back, dipping so low it almost brushed Gaby's arm. "Oh, look, look, Maman, Papa!" She lunged to the side as if to touch the bird—and then she fell, screaming for her father.

"Gaby!" The word was torn from his throat. Gripped with terror, ignoring Talal's warnings, Celine and Tarik ran back down the narrow trail, lunging through brambles and weeds, stumbling over rocks without a thought for their own safety. "My baby, my baby," Celine screamed, weeping as she ran.

"*Ya Allah*," Tarik prayed silently, "punish me for what I've done. Not Gaby, I beg you."

They found her on a small ledge about thirty feet down. She was cut and scratched and bleeding freely. Her eyes fluttered weakly and she tried to smile. "I'm sorry, Maman, I didn't mean to . . ."

Celine tried to speak but could not. "Hush, hush, *ma petite*," said Tarik, "there's no reason to be sorry. All that matters is making sure you're all right." Quickly he ripped off his shirt and bound her cuts. He and Talal improvised a litter and carried Gaby down the mountain to a waiting Land-Rover. Celine followed, weeping and praying, "Dear God, don't take her from us, please don't take her."

"It's all right, nothing serious," Tarik reassured her, though he couldn't be sure of Gaby's prognosis. "We'll have her checked at the hospital. And before you know it, we'll be on our way to Paris."

The nearest hospital was many miles away, and the ride was long and bumpy. Tarik and Celine crooned words of comfort to their child, clinging to each other like shipwreck victims. In his mind Tarik kept repeating the same prayer: *Ya allah, ya allah,* I beg you not to punish the child for my wrongdoing. Punish me instead, I beg you.

By the time they reached the small and rather primitive hospital, Gaby was ashen-faced, her pulse weak and thready. Internal bleeding, Tarik was thinking, though he said nothing to his wife.

A short time later, his diagnosis was confirmed, Gaby's spleen was ruptured; it would have to be removed. "She will need blood transfusions, of course," said Dr. Jabbar, the resident physician. "Type AB. It's somewhat rare. And since our blood supply is very limited, it would be best—and safest—if you and her mother gave blood. My technician has already tested your wife. She is type A. I assume then that you are type B."

Tarik blanched. For a long moment he couldn't speak. "No," he said finally. "I'm O Negative. I can't give Gaby blood."

The doctor was quiet. He knew as well as Tarik did that Gaby's father could not possibly be O Negative. "I see," he said finally. "So you are not the girl's father . . ."

"No, dammit!" Tarik cut in with a ferocity that startled the younger doctor. "Not for your purposes. But in every other way . . . It doesn't matter dammit, man! Take my wife's blood. And for God's sake, hurry!"

So intent was Tarik on saving Gaby's life that he did not realize that she was lying on a gurney six or seven feet away, separated from him and Jabbar only by a white cotton curtain.

Not her father? How could that be? Shock gave way to a rising sense of betrayal. They had lied to her, both of them. And Tarik had pretended to be her father. So it must be that Celine had had an affair. But why? Tarik must have done something terribly wrong to drive Celine into another man's arms. And now he had robbed her of the only father she had ever known.

The operation went well, in spite of the primitive conditions. But after Gaby woke from the anesthesia she would not speak to Tarik, nor would she look at him when he spoke to her. And when he gently asked, "Are you in much pain, *ma petite?*" she snapped, "What do you care?"

Celine and Tarik were stunned. Their daughter had never spoken to either of them in that way. It must be the pain talking, they decided, the shock of her injuries. She would be herself soon. After they returned home, all would be well.

But all was not well, not after they returned home, not after Gaby's long but relatively uneventful recovery, not even after she went back to school. She became distant, difficult, often impossible. Conversation with her parents—once a source of such joy to them—all but dried up. Now monosyllables or American slang replaced the give-and-take that had brightened the Misrys' evenings at home.

Gaby took up smoking, though she knew how much Tarik detested the habit. Had she not been present during the months he had coaxed and nagged Celine into stopping? When Tarik tried to persuade Gaby to reconsider, she said, "Oh, man, don't be such a drag," and walked away.

When Tarik brought up Gaby's falling grades, she simply rolled her eyes. "This is important, *ma petite*. If you want to go to medical school, you'll . . ."

"Medical school?" she cut in. "Who said I was going to medical school?"

"But you . . ."

"That was baby talk, when I didn't know any better. When I thought that following in your footsteps would be a great thing . . ."

"Gaby, my . . ." He reached for her hand.

"No, don't!" She recoiled. "I don't want to hear what you have to say. But I'll tell you something—you're the last person in the world I'd ever want to follow!"

Tarik felt physically ill. What had he done to deserve such anger, such contempt? Surely this behavior couldn't be normal, could it? Celine had said they must be patient. "All young girls go through a period of rebellion," she'd said. "And when my parents protested, I thought they were horribly old-fashioned. As I got older, I decided they weren't so bad after all."

Tarik found no comfort in Celine's reminiscence. Surely they should do *something*. Perhaps it was her American classmates who caused this troubling behavior. The newspapers were full of stories about the anarchist tendencies of young Americans. Perhaps they should consider moving Gaby to a French school?

"She would hate it. And she would probably hate us," Celine said simply. "We couldn't give her a single good reason why she should leave her friends behind and start over in a new school."

"But who are her friends these days?" Tarik asked.

"I don't know," Celine admitted. "She doesn't bring anyone home after school anymore. And when I ask questions, well, you know how she's been. It's almost as if she's turned into a stranger."

Indeed it seemed as if their sweet and lovely Gaby had gone, leaving in her place a sullen stranger. She cut her beautiful hair so short she looked almost boyish. She dressed in black, wore black stockings, affected pale makeup that made her fair complexion almost dead white.

When she began staying out late, sometimes with excuses, often without, Celine's worries escalated. These were wild times, Celine knew, especially among American youth. Young people were using drugs, having sex, doing heaven knows what. She still thought of Gaby as a child, but clearly Gaby thought of herself as an adult. And an emancipated one at that.

Celine approached the subject of Gaby's late nights gingerly. Gaby's response was a bitter laugh. "What's the matter, are you afraid I'll be a chip off the old block? Well, don't worry, I'm not at all like you, Maman. I won't have stupid affairs. I wouldn't degrade myself in that way."

What was she talking about? Celine had scarcely dated before she met Tarik. But before she could ask the question, Gaby had slammed the door and left the apartment. Again.

Book Three

1

Gaby

Paris and New York, 1967–1972

It's a club with chapters everywhere.
The club has only one rule: the rules are changing.
There are only two requirements for membership: you have to
know the rules. And it helps to be young.
The club has no name . . .

"What's this? A poor starving writer scribbling in a café? How romantic. How tragic."

Gaby moved to close the notebook but Denise was too quick. No secrets between best friends.

Denise skimmed the page. "For *La Grenouille?*"

Gaby shrugged. "Just the usual *merde.*" *La Grenouille* was the name of the column she wrote for the student newspaper at the American School. A *grenouille* was a frog—the name was meant as a humorous play on the derogatory English term for a French person.

"What's it about?"

"What's going on. What's happening. The whole scene." Gaby's gesture indicated not just the bistro but the larger world that she and Denise shared with millions of others who were in their teens and early twenties—a world that was changing very fast.

"The big picture," said Denise. "Nobel material."

Gaby grimaced. "It's *merde*. I can't find a hook." She was never satisfied with the column. It embarrassed her to read it. What amazed her was that others seemed to love it. It had made her something of a celebrity at the school.

Denise looked at the page again. "Maybe the club needs a name."

"Club 1967. *Club Ici et Maintenant*."

"*Club Merde*. Like Club Med."

Gaby laughed. "Like they'd really let me use that." It wasn't bad at all. Maybe she could sneak it in somehow.

Denise had lost interest in literary pursuits. She was observing a golden-blond boy at a table across the room. His hair hung to his shoulders. He was very handsome. "I want that bod," said Denise. "Tonight. This afternoon. Now."

Gaby was accustomed to her friend's sexual boasts. She was unsure how much reflected fantasy, how much reality. She herself was restricted almost entirely to fantasy in this department. In fact she knew that she had a reputation as a bit of a prude. Which wasn't fair. She wasn't that way—not really. It was just that, with all that crap with her mom . . . "He's American," she said. "From California, or so one's told. He speaks less French than a monkey."

"Cool," said Denise, and in her mercurial fashion switched subjects again. "Why don't you sing with us tomorrow night?"

"Because I sing like a sick goose," Gaby replied truthfully. She had an ear that could pick up inflections of spoken language like a tape recorder, but she was not a great singer.

"Who cares? You don't actually have to sing. Just beat on a tambourine and look good up there. God, I wish I looked so good." Denise was tiny, black-haired, fiercely energetic. She was the lead singer for a barely organized group that called itself *Le Papillon Rouge*. She had terrific stage presence and a singing style that struggled to combine Edith Piaf and the wild new American Janis Joplin.

Gaby was considering the invitation when Nop came bouncing in.

"Ladies, how beautiful," he bubbled. "The hair, Gaby, something new? Nice!" He lowered his voice conspiratorially. "You're invited. *Chez moi* in half an hour? I have it, you know. *Sergeant Pepper*. Want to hear it? Just a few select people."

Nop was a Thai scarcely taller than Denise. In theory he shouldn't have belonged to the scene. For one thing, he was at least twenty-five, maybe even thirty—it was hard to tell. For another, he worked in a bank. But he owned the best sound system in Paris, was always the first to have the latest album, and kept his door, kitchen, and bar open to all comers. He was especially solicitous to pretty young women because where they went, handsome young men soon followed—and that was where Nop's true interest lay.

Which was cool.

The photograph that changed Gaby's life was on the front page of *Le Monde*. She would always remember that she first saw it when she and Denise were walking to Nop's that afternoon.

Gaby had fallen into a mood and Denise was dispensing a pep talk. "I mean, what's the problem, Gab? You aced the SATs. You're golden. You have a ticket to any college. Here or in the States . . ."

But that scenario presumed that the golden girl had some vague idea of what she wanted to do with her life.

"It's just so cut and dried," Gaby said. "You're right, it's like a ticket—like getting on a train, on a track."

Denise shrugged. She herself had not taken the SATs—for the simple reason that she didn't want to.

They were passing a newsstand. Gaby stopped short. "Look at that."

"What? *Le Monde*? Don't tell me you read that establishment rag."

"The photo," said Gaby.

It was obviously from Vietnam. Taken from a high angle, it showed two old men and four young women, all in black, one of the

women carrying a small child, running across a flooded field. A mass
of fountaining splashes intersected with the runners, and a man and
woman were falling. The woman with the child shielded it with her
arms, her face turned in hopeless terror toward the camera. Looming
over the group and almost filling the photograph was the hawklike
shadow of a helicopter. The caption read *"Free Fire Zone.* South
Vietnamese peasants flee a US Army helicopter gunship near Ngoc
Ninh. The American military designates the area a free fire zone
where pilots and gunners may attack any targets at will. American
photographer Sean McCourt, aboard the aircraft, recorded the
action."

Gaby bought the paper.

At Nop's the new Beatles album was played over and over. As
amazing as the music was, the words were hard to follow even for
Gaby. A boy translated the lyrics aloud from the sleeve liner as seriously as if reciting Baudelaire. Now and then a joint circulated.
Gaby took one or two sociable puffs, but marijuana was not her
thing; it was pleasant in its way, but too often it seemed to send people off into their own cocoons.

As the party progressed, her eyes kept drifting back to the newspaper photo. It was haunting—real people frozen in the instant of
real death. Anger burned in her. How was this allowed to happen?
The photographer's name caught her attention. He had taken a great
photograph, give him that. But what kind of man could stand calmly
pressing the shutter release of a camera while a machine-gunner two
feet away mowed down unarmed men and women.

And what about you, Miss Misry? How very fine to sit listening to
songs about girls with kaleidoscope eyes and how love is all you need,
while people hunt down other people like rabbits.

"Hi. Whatcha lookin' at?" It was the California boy, sauntering
up with a lazy smile. He inspected the photo with slightly bloodshot
eyes. "Far freakin' out." He had said the same thing about every track
on the Beatles album.

Gaby raised an eyebrow at Denise and said in French, "Still interested? You have a thing for zombies?"

Denise shrugged. "A little necrophilia now and then might not be completely bad."

"You're hopeless. Seek professional help."

Soon afterward Gaby excused herself on the grounds that she had to hit the books. She couldn't tell if Denise was annoyed at the sudden exit or pleased that the field was now clear to the golden California zombie.

On the Métro Gaby wondered what was wrong with her. Why so angry? So there was a lot of crap in the world and people could be phonies—her parents, for example. That wasn't exactly news, was it? But God, it just seemed as if she were marking time while life rocketed past. Did she even want to go to university? Maybe Denise had the right idea after all.

That evening as she plugged half-heartedly at her column—it seemed as stupid as anything else—the photograph "Free Fire Zone" led off the TV news. The words of a US military spokesman were translated: the area around Ngoc Ninh was so penetrated by the Vietcong that everyone in it was either VC or a VC sympathizer.

To Gaby's surprise Tarik stood up and glared at the television. "Does that include the baby?" he said. "Was the baby a Vietcong? Incredible! The arrogance of these people!"

Tarik opposed the Vietnam War in a philosophical sort of way, supporting neither side, blaming both. Gaby had never seen him show anger about it one way or another. In her mind he was like most of her friends' parents, a typical middle-aged bourgeois. She realized that the photograph had caused his reaction. It came to her almost as a revelation. Think of it: a photographer pressed a button. A few hours later and half a world away, some dots of ink on newsprint showed what he had seen—and had the power to touch people's emotions, perhaps to change their way of thinking. Millions of people.

The idea did not leave her, that night nor in the days and nights that followed.

Sean McCourt could do it with a photograph.

Maybe Gabrielle Misry could do it with words.

———

Gaby made her decision in the winter of her last year at the American School. For some reason she announced it to Tarik first, showing him the acceptance papers.

"Columbia? In New York? The United States?"

"Yes."

"Well . . . but—why? You can go to any university in France."

Gaby started to tell him that America was where it was happening, but realized she'd have to explain what that meant. "I think I want to go into journalism," she said. "Columbia has one of the best journalism programs in the world. Plus I can really polish up my English there."

Tarik looked doubtful, as if thinking that she spoke English quite well already.

"I want to broaden my horizons," she added, wincing inwardly at the cliché. "I've been here all my life—here, if you don't count visits to the Middle East. I want to see more." She couldn't tell him the rest of it: that she yearned to be on her own, to make her own life far from this place where his and her mother's hypocrisy was like a small but ever-present cloud.

"Journalism," said Tarik. He gave a sad little smile. "Remember when you wanted to be a doctor?"

"Oh, Papa—" Gaby caught herself. Another second and she would have broken into tears. She had no wish to hurt Tarik—she had at least gotten past that—but they had covered this ground before. "That was so long ago. I know," she went on briskly, "that it will cost more for me to go to school in New York, but I can help out. They say students can make good money waiting tables, things like that."

"Don't worry about the money. I just want you to be sure of what you're doing."

"I'm sure."

"Well . . ." The man she could not help thinking of as her father wiped his eyes. "It's just that it's so far away."

"It's not so far these days. I can come back for a visit any time you can afford a jet ticket."

"You know what I mean. Your mother . . ."

"Will you help me tell her?"

When Tarik smiled, Gaby saw lines that she had never noticed before. "You mean will I take your side?" he said.

"I guess that's what I mean."

He put an arm around her shoulder and gave her a quick hug. "Gaby, my dearest child, I've been on your side since the moment I first saw you."

That night in bed, Celine let out all the fears that she had held back in giving her blessing to Gaby's decision.

"My God, Tarik. New York."

"Well, it's not the end of the earth. Gaby's right: by jet it takes less time than the train to Marseilles."

"It's not that. You know what America is—they're all like spoiled children. Anything goes, isn't that what they say?"

"You can't believe everything you see in the movies. Manhattan's not that different from Paris." Tarik had been to New York for a UNICEF conference on childhood diseases. It was not his favorite city, but he was not about to voice that opinion now.

"What if she gets sick? They say you can die on the street and people will step right over your body."

"That's just talk. I saw nothing like that. And they have some of the best hospitals in the world."

"Oh, I know. It's just . . . she just seems . . . it's like she's still my little baby."

"She's not a baby anymore, my love," said Tarik softly. "That's what we have to accept, you and I."

Later, with the lights out, he felt her weeping quietly. When he reached to stroke her cheek, she turned and huddled to him. "Just hold me," she begged like a frightened child. "Just hold me."

———

At that moment Karima and Farid sat talking quietly in her little villa in Alexandria. Show-business gossip, army anecdotes, anything to keep the silence at bay.

The city was in one of its not-uncommon power outages and Karima had lighted candles. In other circumstances their soft glow might have encouraged romance. As it was, the subdued light seemed merely somber, almost ceremonial.

They were able to see each other only three or four times a year—not even enough to wag the neighbors' tongues—but they always made sure of being together on this one day and night. Years ago Karima had decided that Farid was the only person she wanted to have with her on Nadia's birthday.

What they did for the occasion depended entirely on Karima. Sometimes, if they could create a cover story that would not generate gossip, they went out on the town, even though that meant crowds of autograph hounds. More often they spent a quiet time like this one.

As usual, Farid tried to keep the conversation light, but somehow he kept coming back to his own troubles. For the first time in his career he was considering retirement—had been considering it for months, in fact, ever since the debacle of the so-called Six-Day War. He was weary—weary of defeat, weary of seeing men die, weary of dealing with politicians and political soldiers whose incompetence all but guaranteed the defeats and the deaths. For days before the fighting broke out he had urgently pressed to have Egypt's armed forces put on full alert. But always the inertia, always the excuses. The Israelis finally struck on 5 June 1967. When they did, they destroyed virtually the entire Egyptian air force in a matter of hours—not in the air, but still on the runways. The war was as good as over from that moment on. Without air cover Farid's ground soldiers in the Sinai were little more than livestock waiting to be slaughtered. And so now, the Sinai was occupied by Israel.

"I don't know," he said. "There's a rumor that they're looking for a new deputy director of intelligence, and that I'm a candidate.

Maybe a change would be good . . . Although I hate the idea of sitting behind a desk. And if I'm their idea of intelligence, the country's
worse off than I thought."

"I know that whatever you do will be right," said Karima vaguely.
"It always is." He knew that her thoughts were elsewhere.

"In fact I'm in the mood to make a change myself," she said after
a moment. "But I don't know what . . ."

"Perhaps you should sell this house. Buy something on the sea.
You know how beneficial the ocean air can be . . ."

"I've thought about that, but . . . I just can't."

Farid was quiet. He had learned that Karima revealed herself
slowly, one layer at a time.

"I don't suppose anybody knows why I've kept it so long," she
went on. "It's just . . . I guess I'm superstitious. I always thought as
long as I was here, maybe somehow she'd . . ."

In an instant she was racked with sobbing. Farid had seen all the
kinds of suffering that war could bring, men and women standing in
rubble with their loved ones and possessions destroyed, but what his
friend endured, this endless open question mark, seemed the worst.
He moved to her and put a hand on her shoulder.

"Just hold me for a minute," she said. "Only for a minute, just
hold me."

Assistant Dean of Students Harmon S. Eastman last night
proclaimed in a press conference that although student ideas will
be given "due weight," all final decisions regarding Columbia's
core curriculum will continue to be made by faculty members.
Student leaders vowed immediately to take action in protest.

At her desk in the newsroom of the Columbia *Spectator,* Gaby smiled
to herself at the paragraph. It was the lead of a story she had written
for one of her first assignments in J-school. It had received a grade of
D. Her professor had dissected it mercilessly: "Where did he hold this
press conference? The Oval Office? The Shamrock Bar? Which student leaders? What action?" The professor, an old-school newsman

whose tough talk was undercut somewhat by his resemblance to Mickey Rooney, had added several criticisms of her word-choices: On *proclaimed*: "Who is this guy, the pope?" On *vowed*: "They swore on their swords, or what?" On *be given* and *be made*: "Passive!"

Ever since, Gaby had kept the paragraph where she would be sure to see it often. It reminded her of where she had started—and of how far she had come. These days she would never begin a straight news story without the four *W*s—*who, what, when*, and *where*— answered clearly and concisely in the first paragraph. (If *how* or *why* fitted in too, that was fine—but the four *W*s were sacred.) As for her vocabulary, it was certainly less stilted. Her imitative ear had served her almost too well. She not only wrote like an American, but she was beginning to talk like a New Yorker. Though she still had the hint of an accent, out-of-towners assumed she was a local. Even natives were forever claiming to hear traces of Sheepshead Bay or Staten Island or Hell's Kitchen in her accent.

"Brenda Girl, star reporter," greeted Stan Abramowicz, the *Spectator*'s sports editor. Except for him and Dave Gleason, the managing editor, the newsroom stood empty—tomorrow was Saturday, no paper to put out.

Stan was sorting busily through a mass of index cards. Gaby saw no need to acknowledge his lame pun, although she felt rather proud of being Americanized enough to catch it. "What're you doing, Stanley? Trying to figure out who's shaving points before you call your bookie?"

"Looking for a lawyer," said Stan, "to sue people who impugn my journalistic integrity."

"You're gonna need more than one, then," said Gaby. It was typical J-school repartee. She deeply enjoyed the cynical humor that journalism seemed to breed. A fix of it was the main reason she had stopped by the office when she really should be studying.

She spread that day's *Spectator* on her desk and immediately spotted a bizarre typo in her story on a feminist demonstration. "Look at this," she complained. "'As a finale to the gathering, a dozen women took part in a bar-burning.'"

"Dumb broads," said Dave Gleason. "What kind of way is that to win the hearts and minds of the people?"

Gaby didn't laugh. It wasn't funny when it was your story, when "bra" became "bar" and left readers scratching their heads in wonderment. No matter how careful you were, you were always at the mercy of some space cadet at a keyboard. She flipped impatiently through the rest of the paper. In the schedule of upcoming events a name caught her eye: Sean McCourt. Rang a bell. Right! The *Free Fire Zone* photographer. He was lecturing at a poli-sci seminar. Today. How had she missed the notice before? Christ, the lecture was for two o'clock and it was nearly three already.

"Hey, Dave, do you know Sean McCourt, the photographer? That picture of the helicopter gunning down the Vietnamese peasants?"

"Everybody knows the picture. Didn't remember the guy's name."

"He's on campus. How about I try to set up an interview?"

Dave shrugged. "Why not? Last I heard, Vietnam was still news."

Gaby grabbed her coat and ran.

The lecture had just ended when she got there. In the dispersing crowd she picked out McCourt even though she had never seen him. Surrounded by pallid New York winter faces, he had a deep, outdoors tan. The surprise was that he was young, not much older than some of the students; she realized that she had always imagined him as being in his forties. He was listening politely to a young woman who seemed to be delivering a strong opinion. Then, with an apologetic gesture and a look at his watch, he broke away. As he passed Gaby he gave her a quick, uncertain smile, as if he thought he might know her, then hurried on. She rushed after him.

"Mr. McCourt?"

"Yes?" He was neither short nor tall, wearing a military-looking olive turtleneck. Wavy dark hair, which grew past his collar in back, tumbled rakishly over his forehead, giving him the look of a dashing brigand. Except for his sea-green eyes, which somehow looked both sad and merry, he was not what she thought of as conventionally handsome. And yet he had what the tabloids would call "star quality."

"I'm Gaby Misry with the *Spectator*—the campus newspaper. I wonder if you could spare time for a few questions."

"The trouble is, I'm late for an appointment. My agent. Sorry." He seemed genuinely regretful but kept walking.

"Sometime tomorrow then?"

"I'm flying out in the morning."

"Oh."

He stopped. "I'll tell you what. How about dinner?" Seeing her expression, he smiled. "No funny stuff. It's just that otherwise I'll have to ask my agent, and believe me, his face is not one to set off a good meal."

Gaby hesitated for only a moment. "Sure."

"It's true, then," said McCourt.

"What is?"

"That Misry loves company."

"Oh, God, how many times have I heard that."

"Deepest apologies."

They made quick plans to meet, and McCourt hurried on his way.

On the subway home, Gaby wondered if Ron would object to this sudden arrangement on a Friday night. Probably not. Her lover was not one for conventions. Not often, anyway. And he would understand that it was work.

At the apartment they shared, she found that the question was moot. A note from Ron said that he had a meeting. Probably with the SDS, Students for a Democratic Society, she thought, or what was left of it. Long, windy discussions of revolutionary strategy. As much as she admired Ron, there were times when she didn't envy him.

The restaurant was on Prince Street in Soho, an Italian place— northern Italian, Sean stressed. The owner greeted him like a long-lost nephew, complimented Gaby on her beauty, led them to the best table, and recommended the veal rollatini.

After they ordered, Gaby asked the routine questions and learned that Sean was twenty-six, born in Ireland but a naturalized US citizen, that he resided in San Francisco but saw his apartment for only a few weeks out of each year, and that his journey tomorrow would take him back to Vietnam.

"How do you feel about that?" she asked noncommittally.

"I'm excited. But at the same time I dread it." He averted his eyes, as he often did when talking about serious things. "It's possible to love a place and hate it too."

Gaby waited, but he seemed disinclined to go any further.

"Actually, it took some arm-twisting to get back in," he said. "I'm not exactly the Pentagon's fair-haired lad."

"Why not?"

"Apparently I'm just not their type." He smiled but the smile faded. "Mainly, though, it's that one shot."

"Free Fire Zone?"

He nodded. "You wouldn't believe how often I'm accused of treason for taking that photograph."

"I first saw it when I was a teenager. It moved me tremendously, it's part of why I went into journalism." Gaby hesitated. "But there's something I've always wondered about it."

A faint flicker of impatience crossed Sean's face, and Gaby realized that he must be very weary of questions about the picture. But he said only, "What?"

"I know this is naïve, don't take it wrong, but I always thought . . . I wondered . . . how it felt to . . ." She couldn't say it.

Sean nodded. "You mean how could I let it happen. Why didn't I do something to stop it. Is that it?"

"Yes."

He studied his wine as if it held the answer. "It never entered my mind," he said bluntly, but glanced at her as if to read her reaction. "Maybe that sounds callous. But remember, I'd already seen a lot of . . . other things." Again the quick glance. "But the truth is, I'd made the decision long before." A pause. "So will you, if you want to be a journalist. Because unless you're going to write for the society pages or something, sooner or later you're going to find yourself in the same position."

She tried to imagine that.

"So what you've got to decide," he went on, "is whether you want to do the job. Because the job is telling the story." Suddenly he grinned. "Sorry. I seem to have gone a bit pompous there. Already given one lecture today, don't want to get in the habit."

She smiled back. "In fact my Journalism 101 professor said exactly the same thing."

"Dear God, I'm not only pompous, but a plagiarist."

Their entrées came. The rollatini was perfection, the thin veal rolled with layers of prosciutto and a Swiss-style cheese she could not identify, the whole dish lightly breaded and herbed and delicately baked. They skipped dessert in favor of strong, dark espresso with little glasses of sweet, licorice-tasting Sambucca on the side.

"You're, uh, involved with someone?" Sean asked suddenly over his second glass of the liqueur.

"Yes."

She told him about Ron. He apologized for not having heard of the famous student activist. "I'm out of touch with so many normal things. But good for you. Sounds like an interesting fellow."

"And you?"

He shrugged. "No one steady. I've tried a couple of times, but who'd put up with the way I live?"

When they left the restaurant it was snowing.

"Want to walk a bit?" asked Sean. "I won't be seeing this stuff for a while."

In Washington Square they were suddenly caught in an impromptu snowball fight among the street musicians, NYU students, marijuana dealers, and assorted citizens of Greenwich Village who frequented the park.

They were still shaking snow from their clothes on the cab ride uptown.

Sean saw her to her door, the cab waiting.

"It was fun," she said, meaning it.

"I enjoyed it too. Listen, this may seem a strange thing to ask, but would you write me now and then? Over there a letter can make the whole day."

"Sure." The request touched her.

"Go through my agency. They can always find me—except at pay time. I'm good about writing back, you know."

She found herself wondering who else shared this kind of correspondence with him. No one steady. What an odd thought. Why should she care? She wrote her address on a page from her notebook and they said good-bye.

Upstairs, Ron was stretched out on the couch with a beer, watching the ten o'clock news. "Missed you, beauty. Where you been?"

She told him. She heard herself making it sound a bit more businesslike than it had been, and felt a twinge of guilt. "And you? How'd the meeting go?"

"Arrgh. I had to split. Pseudorevolutionaries. They're worse than Nixon." He looked at her curiously. "Speaking of the establishment, what's he like? The famous photographer." To Ron, anyone whose work appeared in major newspapers was self-evidently a member of the establishment.

"Well, he's younger than I expected," Gaby said. "Twenty-six. And Irish. From Ireland."

"No kidding. Hope for him yet." Ron regarded the Irish as natural revolutionaries.

"Arrgh," he said to the TV weatherman. "A *foot* of snow? Hard to change the world when you're up to your ass in sooty slush."

"It's a dirty, thankless job, but somebody's gotta do it." It was a catchphrase with them.

Ron gave her a familiar, mischievous smile. "What do you say we go to bed before we get too sleepy?"

"I thought you'd never ask."

They curled to each other with a kiss. Gaby loved the warmth of his body, the assurance of his desire, but she often asked herself if this was "forever" love, the kind of love Tarik and Celine had shared. She and Ron had fun, and their values certainly matched—that was important. But from time to time, when she fantasized the distant future, the picture in her mind was fuzzy and indistinct.

As they walked to their bed, which was in an alcove of this typical New York studio apartment, she clicked the TV off in passing. "No news," she told him, "is good news."

She and Sean McCourt wrote each other for nearly a year, but toward the end the letters were far apart. That was the trouble, Gaby thought: she and Sean were far apart as well. Not just geographically—they lived in different worlds, saw different things, used different words. In time Sean became only a pleasant memory, a fascinating acquaintance across a table in a restaurant and in a snowball fight in Washington Square. What did it matter? She had the man with whom she would probably share the rest of her life.

Gaby would never forget the day she met Ron Gillman, although at the time he was little more than a blur in a swirl of events, like some interesting feature of the landscape glimpsed from a hurtling roller-coaster.

It was a day of anger that grew to rage. President Nixon's invasion of Cambodia had just become known. On college campuses all over the nation young men and women gathered in the hundreds and the thousands to protest what they regarded as a criminal expansion of a war that was criminal to begin with.

Gaby was in the *Spectator* office that spring afternoon. As one of the younger staffers, she was doing a dull, footwork story comparing textbook prices in various bookstores. She wanted to file it so she could go out and join the protesters. She had just finished when the office's old AP teletype gave three rings, signaling that a major story was about to come over the wire.

Elaine Rosenbaum, the editor-in-chief, strolled over to the machine. A standing joke about Elaine was that the only time she got excited was when she ran out of the Camels she chain-smoked. So it

was all the more stunning when she ripped the paper from the teletype and screamed, "Shit! The Nazi bastards! They're killing students now! American students! Us!" Her face contorted in
revulsion.

It was Kent State.

Someone turned on the TV—a sure sign of urgency at the *Spectator,* where broadcast journalists were regarded as lower life-forms. A
famed anchorman repeated the AP bulletin in portentous tones;
obviously there was no film yet. Gaby put fresh paper in her typewriter simply to be doing something. From outside came shouts. A
boy poked his head in the door: "Come on, people, we're taking it to
the streets!"

"Hell, yes!" said Dave Gleason. The newsroom emptied. Only
Gaby thought to bring her notebook.

The campus teemed with pairs and trios and small platoons of
students heading for Low Library. In minutes the plaza was filled,
the steps to the library jammed with protesters. Old chants were
revived: "Hell, no, we won't go," and "Two, four, six eight ten, NLF
is gonna win." One after another, radical leaders rose to denounce the
US government and received fierce cheers. To Gaby, writing down
the sights and sounds, it was exciting but oddly and frustratingly
familiar. She had witnessed many demonstrations. What had they
accomplished?

After a time others seemed to catch her mood. At the edges of the
assembly, people began to drift away. But then a new speaker arose.
Gaby recognized him from other rallies but didn't know his name.
He *looked* like a revolutionary—a taller, New Yorkish version of Che
Guevara. "Who is that guy?" she asked a girl next to her.

"Ron Gillman."

She wrote it down.

Gillman had presence. He stared out over the crowd for a long
moment, letting anticipation build, then shouted, "Is this America?"
It was, as he must have known, a surprisingly difficult question to
answer under the circumstances. He answered it himself: "Hell, yes,
it's America. It's our America—mine and yours. The people's Amer-

ica. But there are places where they don't believe that. They don't believe it in the White House. They don't believe it in Congress. And they sure as hell don't believe it in the Ohio National Guard."

Each line drew a roar.

"What we've gotta do," Gillman shouted, "is *show* them that it's our America. We gotta take it back!"

Great, thought Gaby, taking it all down. Terrific words. But just words all the same.

"Tell me what's happening in Washington," Gillman went on. "Business as usual. What's happening at Kent State? Business as usual. And what's happening at Hamilton Hall?" He pointed in the direction of Columbia's administration building. The crowd answered for him: "Business as usual!"

"Right. Two American boys and two American girls killed by American bullets, and for Columbia University it's business as usual. So what we've gotta do—what we're *gonna* do—what we're gonna do right *now*—is shut it down. Shut it down!"

Immediately it became a chant: "Shut it down! Shut it down!"

Gillman waited just long enough for the frenzy to peak, then waved his arm like a field commander leading a charge. "Let's do it! Now!"

He moved rapidly toward Hamilton Hall, the crowd surging behind him. Gaby fought her way to the front. The few policemen on the fringes of the demonstration did little more than man their radios. The students poured into the building, Gaby with them. In offices, middle-aged typists looked as if Armageddon had arrived. From somewhere the chancellor materialized, ordering the intruders out. Gillman turned on him: "Is this America?" The question seemed to fluster the older man, as it had the crowd. "No offense," Gillman told him, "but we're not going anywhere. Get used to it."

Soon the chancellor and the workers were gone. The demonstrators disconnected phones and office machines. The administration building was out of business.

Gaby got close enough to Gillman to conduct a miniinterview.

First she asked him to spell his name. He did so with an amused grin. "What are you, the census taker?"

"A reporter. Why are you doing this?"

"Somebody had to do something."

"But why this?"

"You do what you can do. I can't shut down the Pentagon. Not yet anyway."

He turned back to his troops.

As night fell the occupation of Hamilton Hall became a party. A radio tuned to the Columbia Station WKCR blared Creedence Clearwater. Pizzas were smuggled in. A television crew arrived just in time to photograph students painting the verdigris Alma Mater statue in bright shades of orange and yellow. Gaby decided that she had seen enough, walked back to the empty *Spectator* newsroom, and wrote a story—not straight news, but an I-was-there feature. It began with Ron Gillman's question: "Is this America?"

She stopped at five hundred words. Not short, but not long either. She had no idea why she had written it. No one had assigned the story to her. But she thought it read well. Maybe the *Spectator* would run it. Maybe not. On the way out she passed the office of her faculty adviser, her old Journalism 101 professor, the Mickey Rooney look-alike. His name was Tenny Carson—Tenny short for Tennyson. She was surprised to see that he was still there. He waved her in. He had a television set, and for the first time Gaby saw the Kent State images, the Guardsmen suddenly firing, the faces of the dead students. It was horrifying.

"Bad stuff strikes Centerville," said the professor. Gaby smelled liquor—the professor was said to keep a bottle in his desk. He was a throwback—not an academic, but an old-time working newspaperman.

"Whatcha got there?" He indicated the small sheaf of typewriter paper that held her story. "Something I can read?"

"I guess. Why not?" It wasn't as if he had never seen her work. She gave it to him. He read it very quickly, then read it again.

"I'm gonna call a fellow," he said. "Give me a minute, will you?"

She waited in the hall, no idea what was going on, until he called her back in. "You know how to phone a story?"

"I've done it a few times."

"Good. Give it to this guy." He handed her the receiver.

"Who is it?"

"Just do it."

She was so nervous that the man on the other end had to ask her twice for the spellings of names, which she should have given automatically.

Carson took the phone. "You got it? Whaddya think? Yeah, me too." He hung up and gave Gaby a Mickey Rooney grin. "No guarantees, but you might want to read the *Times* tomorrow."

"You're kidding."

"Not a bit. Now get outta here. I'm a busy man."

Her feature appeared the next day as a sidebar to the jump of the front-page *New York Times* story on the Kent State killings. The headline read: Is This America? The War Comes to the Campus.

That same morning Columbia announced an indefinite suspension of classes in light of the events at Kent State.

Ron Gillman wandered into the *Spectator* newsroom, exchanged "hi's" with a couple of staffers, and walked over to Gaby's desk. "You said you were a reporter, but I didn't know you meant a *reporter* reporter. Congratulations."

"You do what you can do," she said.

They saw each other almost every day and night for a month before they became lovers. At first it wasn't what Gaby had expected, but soon it became quite pleasurable. Ron prided himself on not being one of those disgusting "Wham, bam, thank you, ma'am" MCPs—male chauvinist pigs—and he made a point of trying to satisfy Gaby in bed.

After another month they decided that paying two New York

rents made no sense. Gaby's apartment was marginally larger and closer to the subway. Ron moved in with her.

The summer before her senior year, Gaby took Ron to Paris to meet her parents. He had wanted to meet them for some time—or at least had said he did. Gaby wondered if anyone in human history had genuinely looked forward to such a thing. God knows she had dreaded the introduction to Ron's family—once it had become unavoidable.

The Gillmans had been pleasant enough. They had invited Ron and Gaby to dinner at Il Mulino in Greenwich Village; the prices on the menu were high, but the décor was understated and the service congenial. "I hope you like this place," Ron's father said. "Your mother and I figured you young people wouldn't be caught dead in one of our uptown 'establishment' spots—right, Grace?" Here he turned and winked conspiratorially at his wife.

"It's very nice," Gaby said dutifully.

"It's fine, Dad," Ron agreed, "more than fine. When we go out to eat on our own, it's usually Moon Palace," he added, naming a cheap neighborhood Chinese restaurant.

It was clear the Gillmans had given some thought to this meeting. It was also clear that they were trying hard to be welcoming to Gaby. Larry Gillman ordered lavishly of wine and food; he made a point of consulting Gaby on the wine selection because "a young lady from Paris must know a lot more about wine than a fellow from New York."

At one point Mrs. Gillman, under cover of professed interest in Gaby's last name, inquired as to her "background."

"My father is from Egypt, my mother is French." Surely, Gaby thought, Ron must already have told her this.

"How interesting! Your father, is he—I hope it's the right term—Islamic?"

"He was brought up as a Muslim, but he's not religious."

"I see. And your mother—being French, I imagine she's Catholic."

"A very lapsed one." Only Gaby, thinking of what she assumed was her mother's infidelity, was conscious of the irony of her words. "I was taught about both faiths, but I don't belong officially to either."

Gaby couldn't tell whether Mrs. Gillman regarded this state of affairs as a good one. She had a hard-to-pin-down but clear impression that, as gracious as the Gillmans might be, she was not exactly what they had in mind for their adored son.

"They didn't like me," she told Ron on the subway back to their apartment.

"Sure they did, babe." He gave her a quick hug. "They just have trouble showing it. It's their whole generation. They all grew up uptight and never had a chance to get over it."

These days Ron sometimes met his mother for lunch at Le Perigord when she ventured into the city on a shopping expedition, and occasionally played handball with his father at the New York Athletic Club. On these occasions the elder Gillmans always sent their regards to Gaby.

Ron himself was at loose ends. A year ahead of Gaby at Columbia, he had graduated that spring. Now he was discovering that a bachelor's degree in history and a reputation as a student activist didn't carry much weight in the world beyond the campus. At least he didn't have to worry about the army. In the Selective Service lottery, his birth date had drawn a number so high that, as he joked, "they wouldn't draft me if the Russians were coming up Fifth Avenue." He was thinking of entering law school—his dad would happily pay for it—with a view to a future in politics. It would be a turn toward the establishment, no question, but wasn't the best way to defeat the enemy from within?

All in all, his "lost summer," as he called it, was a good time to visit Paris.

"Nervous?" Gaby asked him as the jet taxied toward the terminal at Orly.

"Pas du tout." It came out sounding something like "paw doo too." His French was execrable, no matter how hard he worked on it.

Gaby patted his hand.

Tarik and Celine were waiting. Gaby's first impression was that they both looked much older than on her last visit, only a year earlier. Or maybe not. Maybe it was just the strain of meeting the daughter's boyfriend.

At the apartment the aroma of Celine's bouillabaisse was an invitation to sit in the kitchen. Ron tried a compliment in French. Her parents' polite expressions told Gaby that only she had understood. "He says it reminds him of an inn where his parents used to vacation. In the state of Maine. The owners were French."

Tarik and Celine beamed. Gaby wasn't so sure she was pleased. With tall American Ron in it, the whole apartment felt smaller than she remembered. And while it was certainly well appointed by French standards, she had a sense that Ron might be measuring it against his parents' various homes: a Manhattan apartment on Park Avenue, a large country house in Westport, Connecticut, and a "winter getaway place" in Palm Beach.

It was over dinner that Tarik asked the casual question: "So, Ron, do you live in the same part of New York City as Gaby?"

Ron started to speak, reddened, looked to Gaby.

"We live together," she said simply. There. She had known all along that she would have to tell them eventually—just hadn't expected it to come up so soon. She had wondered for weeks how they would take it; she saw it as a test of their faith in her.

There was the briefest pause while they digested the information. Then Celine said, "Ah." It was, thought Gaby dryly, the French equivalent of "How interesting!" Tarik only glanced from his daughter to Ron and back again, then offered Ron more wine. "Gaby tells us that you're thinking of studying law," he said.

And that was all.

Later, when she and Ron had a moment alone, he mimed wiping his brow. "That wasn't too bad. Easier than I thought."

Gaby shrugged. "Me too, I guess." She wasn't really sure what

Celine and Tarik felt. Somehow she had expected—hoped?—that they would show more concern.

"They're cool," Ron went on. "A little older than I expected."

"I was a late baby." She had wondered a thousand times if that was the explanation—if something was wrong with Tarik, and Celine had found another way to have a child. Would that make a difference? She didn't know. She had never told Ron about any of it. She saw no need for anyone else but her to know.

Their three weeks in Paris passed like three days. Gaby showed Ron the sights, took him to some of her old haunts, introduced him to a few friends from the American School days. (Denise wasn't among them; Gaby learned to her amazement that her old pal had married an Australian television producer and moved to Sydney.) There were long afternoons at sidewalk cafés, nights of talk and music in the bistros.

Not until the day before their flight back to New York did Gaby have anything like a serious discussion with her mother. Ron and Tarik were watching a soccer match. Gaby and Celine were in the kitchen. Celine touched Gaby's arm and said, "He seems like a nice young man, darling. You're happy with him? It seems to me that you are."

"So far, so good." Gaby couldn't think of anything more profound to say.

"Good. I only wanted to say that . . ." Celine searched for words, "that it's not always, won't always be easy, you know."

Gaby waited. Was this it? Was Celine going to reveal the secret now, unaware that Gaby already knew? But Celine only broke into tears and said, "Oh, Gaby, I wish you could stay a little longer."

"I know, Maman, but really it's not that long—just till December. Graduation. You and Papa are coming, right? I mean, you said you would."

"But I thought that was in the spring."

"No. Don't you remember? I'm graduating a semester early—all those extra courses I took."

"Yes, of course. I do remember now." Celine brightened noticeably. "December, yes."

"I'll show you the Big Apple. *La Grande Pomme.*"

Celine laughed. And at the airport the next day she cried only a little.

"See you in December, Maman," said Gaby. "Don't forget this time."

Celine looked like a schoolgirl who had missed an answer in class. Then she smiled. "December. I won't forget."

Celine did not attend Gaby's graduation. Tarik came to New York alone.

"I didn't want to upset you," he explained. "Neither did your mother. But she's been a bit under the weather lately, and her doctor doesn't think it's a good idea for her to travel. I concur."

"She's sick? What's wrong?"

"Nothing to worry yourself about, my love. Probably just stress, the time of life—you know."

"You're sure that's all?"

"You know what might be nice? After the graduation, why don't you fly home with me for a little visit. Just a few days. My treat, of course. It would do her good, you know."

Ron was none too happy with the idea when Gaby broached it to him. He had set up a week of skiing in Vermont as a graduation present.

"We can go later."

"I've already put down the deposit. Besides, I'm going to be pretty busy later." He had finally decided on law school and was working on his applications.

"Well, I have to go."

"Then why ask me at all? Go ahead and do it."

They ended up not speaking to each other for a day—the first time that had ever happened to them.

The day after the graduation ceremony, Gaby flew to Paris with Tarik. Ron stayed in New York. Maybe he would go to Vermont alone, he said half jokingly; that way the deposit wouldn't be totally wasted. Gaby thought that was a good idea. She was beginning to feel it had been unfair to spring the Paris journey on him so suddenly—particularly if, as her father said, Celine's illness was nothing urgent.

On the plane Tarik told her otherwise.

"She wouldn't let me tell you, absolutely refused—didn't want anything to spoil your big day. But it's not good, my love."

"What is it then?" Gaby wanted with all her heart not to hear this.

"Lung cancer first. In her spine now. Liver. Everywhere."

"Papa! No!"

"I'm afraid so, my love."

"Can't anything be—"

"We've done everything. Gaby, we're losing her."

There was just enough of Celine left for Gaby to recognize the wasted, shrunken old woman in the oxygen tent as her mother. Tarik had done his best to prepare his daughter for this, but no warning was sufficient. Death wasn't a movie where the pretty star faded away with a touch of pale makeup and every hair in place.

Celine was on strong painkillers. For much of the time she was semiconscious. Now and then she spoke quite normally, asking about the graduation, about Ron, about Gaby's plans for the future. More often she was in her own world, delusional—one afternoon she carefully instructed Gaby to put the yellow flowers in the blue vase. There were no yellow flowers and no blue vase. Then Gaby remembered: yellow flowers bought from a street vendor one day when she was a little girl; the cat had broken the blue vase a few years later.

The end came as dusk fell on a gloomy winter day of cold rain. Celine had been drifting in and out of consciousness, her breath ragged, her pulse growing ever weaker and more fitful. Her brothers and a sister were there. Suddenly she woke and looked at Gaby. For just a moment her face was radiant with joy. "My angel!" she said. "I'm so glad I found you." Then she closed her eyes, made a tiny choking sound, and died.

Gaby managed to reach Ron at the ski lodge. He was shocked and couldn't stop apologizing for not having gone with her. It wasn't his fault, she consoled him—he hadn't known; neither had she. They agreed that there was no point in his coming to Paris. He would wait for her in New York. She would let him know her schedule as soon as she had one.

There was a simple funeral mass. The brothers and sister stayed another day then went their ways. That evening Gaby found Tarik sitting alone at the kitchen table. The familiar room seemed terribly empty.

"I suppose I'll find someplace else," said Tarik. "I've loved this place, but now . . ." He gazed out at the gathering twilight. She put a comforting hand on his shoulder.

"Sit down, my love," he said. "There's something I must tell you. Perhaps now is not the time, but . . . well, it's past time, you see."

Gaby felt an icy apprehension. *Oh, God, he's going to tell me about the affair, how he's not my real father.* She calmed herself. "I don't think it matters anymore," she said quietly. "Do you?"

Tarik looked at her oddly. "Well, of course, that's entirely up to you, dear Gaby—whether it matters or not. But I owe you the truth. I only hope you can forgive me for withholding it so long."

"It's about my real father, isn't it?"

Tarik stared. "Your father?" Clearly he had not been expecting her to know.

"Look, Papa, I know that Maman had an affair. I know that I'm not your daughter—biological daughter. But like I said, it doesn't matter now."

He shook his head. She thought that she had never seen him look so sad, not even at her mother's deathbed.

"It's not just about your father, my love," he said slowly. "It's about your real mother too."

Gaby felt frozen in her chair. This couldn't be right, she must be missing something, misunderstanding something. "What are you talking about?"

"Are you all right? It's a shock, I know. Let me get you some water." He rose.

"Will you tell me what you are talking about?"

Tarik lowered himself into the chair. "Your mother—Celine—and I lied to you, Gaby. All your life, we lied. We tried to tell ourselves it was for your benefit, for your protection. But we were selfish, too. We came to love you so much, we could not bear to give you up."

"What lie?" she said, hardly daring to breathe.

He told her.

It was a nightmare. She wanted to wake up and find that it had vanished.

"Please don't hate us," Tarik was pleading. "And if you must hate, then hate me, for Celine loved you more than life itself. At the last, I think she only willed herself to stay alive so she could see your face once more."

Gaby was not there anymore. She was somewhere else in the room, outside herself, watching another Gaby slap at him, hearing another Gaby scream: "Liar! You say you love me, but look what you did! You stole everything—my identity, my name! You stole my *me*!" The screams turned into harsh, racking sobs. Gaby wept for herself, for the mother she never knew, for the mother who died.

"I'm so sorry," Tarik said, "so sorry, Gaby dear. I know we were wrong, but we never meant to hurt you. Never."

She closed her eyes. Just shut it out. Shut it all out.

"I'll do whatever you want," she heard Tarik say. "Even if you never want to see me again, I'll understand. It's up to you now. I'll do whatever you want."

2
A Second Home

Cairo and Alexandria

As the Air France jet circled Cairo airport, Gaby opened the well-thumbed fan magazine on her lap, turning to the story she had read and reread a dozen times. But who *is* she? Gaby wondered as she scanned the melodramatic account of Karima Ahmad's life. What is she really like? She studied the accompanying photograph: a dark-haired woman with deep, haunted eyes and an expression of stoic resignation. My mother, Gaby thought, trying on the concept once again, still struggling to fit this stranger into her sense of self.

Gaby's feelings were confused, had been since Celine's death. Sorrow, grief, these she understood; she could not imagine a day when she would not mourn Celine. There was shame and guilt, too, for what she had imagined since her accident in Morocco: that Celine had been an adulterous wife, that she had borne the child of an unknown lover. And of course there was anger—at being snatched from the woman who had obviously loved her, at being raised in a lie, at . . . at . . . oh, sometimes she couldn't even sort out at whom or what.

Tarik reached out and touched Gaby's hand. It will be all right, he wanted to say, as much to reassure himself as his daughter. His daughter—he could not stop thinking of Gaby in that way, even though she now knew she was the child of two other people, one of whom had suffered her loss for years. He had begged Karima's pardon when he told her that Gaby was alive and wanted to see her. But she had been too dazed to respond. All she wanted to know was when she would see her child again. Perhaps there would be no forgiveness, but at least he would try to make things right.

When the plane touched down on the runway, Gaby's jaw tightened, her fists clenched. *"Courage, ma petite,"* Tarik murmured. Her response was a half-hearted smile.

Minutes later, as father and daughter stepped out of the plane, they saw a crowd on the tarmac, waiting for them. A swirl of color—and a cluster of military uniforms. *Allah,* Tarik thought, was he to be arrested now for stealing the child of Egypt's beloved *Karawan?*

But no, here she was, Karima Ahmad herself, her lovely face radiant with joy, tears streaming down her face as she rushed forward to embrace Gaby. Her lost child. Tarik stepped aside, feeling like an intruder—worse yet, a villain—in this reunion. "My daughter, my baby," Karima wept, "my darling Nadia."

Gaby's body tensed at the new name, the unfamiliar embrace. Then she looked into the ravaged eyes and felt something—a connection, not just with Karima, but with her own distant past. This woman had given her life, and she wanted to give something back. She wanted to say the word "Mother." But she couldn't, not yet, not so soon after Celine's death. It would have felt somehow disloyal. No matter what Celine and Tarik had done, Gaby knew they had always loved her. She took Karima's hand and squeezed it, as if to say, "I'm here now. For the rest there will be time."

Karima smiled through her tears. Then she turned and nodded toward an older man with a scarred face and a black eyepatch; he was clearly a high-ranking officer and the one in charge of the delegation. "This is my good friend, Farid Hamza," Karima said. "General Hamza. One of Egypt's great war heroes."

"Just a soldier of Egypt, Miss Nadia," Hamza said, with a courtly half-bow.

For a moment Gaby looked blank. The "Nadia" was still unfamiliar to her ears.

Karima noticed. "It's all right, child," she said softly. "All this must seem very strange to you. If you prefer to be called Gabrielle, just tell me so. And if you ever feel uncomfortable with me, please tell me that as well."

Tarik marveled at Karima's restraint. He wondered how he would behave in her place.

Hamza helped the two women into a black staff car. Tarik attempted to follow. Hamza put out an intervening hand. "Why don't you come along with me?" he said. Though his tone was gentle, the suggestion had the force of an order. Tarik complied ungrudgingly. He had arranged to bring mother and daughter together. Now he would step aside and allow them to find one another again. It had been arranged that he would stay at the Cecil Hotel, within easy reach of Karima's house, should Gaby need him.

In the privacy of the staff car, Karima stared worshipfully at her only child. "My daughter," she murmured, "my dearest daughter." There was a world of love in the words.

"I'm used to being Gabrielle," Gaby said softly. "I don't think I can give that up. But you can call me Nadia. And maybe in time . . ."

Karima gathered her daughter to her, kissed the top of her head. "Now I can die happy," she sighed.

The drive to Alexandria took about three hours. On the veranda of Karima's house, a reception committee of one awaited: Karima's father. Wrapped in a blanket and reclining on a wicker chaise, he tried to get up when he heard Gaby and Karima arrive. "No, *Abi,* no," Karima protested, "please don't exert yourself."

"But I want to see her. I want to see our Nadia," he argued, his voice weak and thready.

"And you shall. Here she is, *Abi,* your granddaughter, Nadia." Karima turned to Gaby, in her expression a plea: be kind to this old man.

Gaby took Mustafa's hand and kissed it; it was a gesture of reverence and respect she'd seen during her travels in the Arab world. Mustafa smiled benevolently and patted her head. "Beautiful," he said. Just like your mother." And then he seemed to drift off, his eyes closing gradually, his breathing shallow.

"Is he all right?" Gaby asked.

"He's just tired," Karima explained. "He had a stroke a few months ago. But when he heard you had been found, he wanted to come with me to the airport. I persuaded him to stay at home, but he insisted he would not rest until he saw you with his own eyes."

Gaby gazed at the old man. Her grandfather. She looked from him to Karima, searching for a family resemblance.

Karima laughed. "I was always told I favored my mother. I'll show you her picture later, after you've had something to eat."

When Gaby said she wasn't very hungry, Karima laughed again. "Then consider this your initiation into Egyptian life. Food is more than something to sustain life here. It's a way of saying 'welcome' or 'I love you'—or in some cases, 'see how prosperous we are.' Please allow me to say 'welcome' and 'I love you.' If you don't, my housekeeper will be very upset with us both. But first, let me show you around the house."

Karima walked her daughter through one room and then another, pausing expectantly from time to time. Gaby complimented the simple elegance of the home Karima had created, the graceful lines of the antique inlaid furniture, the warmth of the copper and brass trays and urns, the charm of the crude folk art that adorned the whitewashed walls.

Finally, Karima took Gaby into the room that had once been hers. Karima had redecorated it several times, marking Nadia's transition from toddler to schoolgirl to young woman—always in the superstitious hope that her child would one day occupy it again. Where the crib had once stood, now there was a double bed with a hand-carved headboard and a finely embroidered coverlet of Egyptian cotton. There was a matching dresser and a mirror of inlaid mother-of-pearl, an overstuffed chair covered with brightly colored appliqué-work, a bookshelf filled with English classics and an antique Sarouk rug on the floor.

"It's a beautiful room," Gaby said.

"I'm so glad you like it. Do you . . . do you remember anything of this house? Anything at all?"

Gaby frowned, concentrating. She wanted to think of something, if only to please Karima. "I don't know," she answered finally. "But I feel . . . comfortable here."

Karima nodded, as if that were always her intention. "This was the home I came to as a bride. Munir and I . . . we were so happy here after you were born." She sighed, remembering both happiness and loss. "Later, Spyros kept telling me I should buy something bigger and grander. Omar—my brother—agreed. But I couldn't leave this house, where you had lived with us. So I stayed. Hoping you would come back." The simple declaration was heartbreaking. Gaby took Karima's hand.

"And I did."

"Yes." Karima's smile was dazzling. "I just wish . . ."

"What?"

"I wish Munir could see you . . . he loved you so much. And Charles . . . he would have loved you, I'm sure of that."

A pause. "Perhaps they *can* see us," Gaby said. She had never been very religious, at least not in any formal way. But in the presence of her mother's unwavering faith, Gaby was ready to concede that there might be more to the universe than those things she could see and hear and touch.

After the lavish lunch had been set out, picked at, and put away, Gaby asked the question that was foremost in her mind. "Will you tell me about my father? Tarik—my other father—said he was English."

"Yes, he was . . . well, half-English to be exact. And his parents, your grandparents, want so much to meet you. We'll go there tomorrow, if you're ready. They'll be able to tell you all about Charles, from the time he was a baby."

"Yes, I'd like that. But I want to hear how you remember him."

The story Karima told was one she had revised in her mind as the years passed; in retrospect, she and Charles were like Romeo and Juliet, star-crossed lovers destined for tragedy. But the theme was constant: a young girl, the chauffeur's daughter, had loved a beautiful young man, the son of the cotton pasha. She spoke of their friendship, of watching him grow up, of the miraculous day when she heard the words "I love you."

As Karima spoke about Charles the years seemed to slip away, and Gaby could see in her mother the innocent child who had adored a golden boy beyond her reach. She understood then that she had been conceived in love. And that Karima's dream of a life with Charles had probably been doomed from the start. Poor Karima, Gaby thought, feeling more like the parent than the child.

"Then what happened? When you became pregnant?"

"Charles never knew."

"And his parents? They didn't help you at all?"

Karima began to explain. She was the daughter of a servant, he was the son of a great man. Then she stopped. "It was all such a long time ago. None of that matters now. Munir was kind enough to marry me, and when you were born he rejoiced as a true father would."

Gaby awoke to the sound of her mother's voice; it was joyous and triumphant, though the words she sang were plaintive and sad:

"Where are you, my darling child?
I miss you so much, so much.
When I close my eyes, I see you before me.
No rose can brighten my home, no candle can light it,
As long as you are far away from me . . ."

That's me, Gaby thought, that's me she's singing about. That's "Nadia's Song" . . . she had heard about it. How strange that so many people knew about me, all of Egypt, when I didn't know who I was. She began to feel a stirring of anger and then she remembered Karima's words: "None of that matters now." If she can let go after suffering so much, Gaby thought, then maybe I can, too.

She closed her eyes, luxuriating in the warmth of sunlight on her face, the smell of jasmine outside her window. A far more exotic sensory cocktail than what she'd been accustomed to in Paris, yet very pleasant and not totally unfamiliar.

She'd been here just over a day, but already she liked and admired Karima. As for love, well, Gaby was confident that would come, too.

Tarik had phoned last night to ask how she was managing. He mentioned that he had called on the Austens. Gaby knew he had been dreading the visit, just as she knew he needed to make it. "How did it go?" she asked.

"Henry's a decent man. He understood that I wasn't making excuses for what I did, that I just wanted to tell him how it all happened, what it was like that awful night when all of Cairo seemed to be on fire. How desperately Celine wanted a child. And how we believed, at least for a time, that you were abandoned or orphaned, and that we were probably saving your life. He listened very carefully, and then he said he was in no position to judge anyone. I'm grateful for that. And you, *ma petite,* how are you doing?"

"I'm fine, Papa." She could have said more, but somehow she did not want to share the details of her time with Karima.

After a pause, he asked, "Do you have any idea how long you'll be staying in Egypt?"

She had already asked herself that question, and her answer had been: As long as I need to be here. She did not want to hurt Tarik, but she did not want him to imagine that her life would go on as before. "I'm not sure how long I'll be here, not yet. But it may be a while. So if you need to get back to Paris . . ."

That didn't come out right, Gaby realized at once; it must have sounded like a dismissal. So she added, "I need this time, Papa. I need to be with her. That doesn't mean I don't love you."

"I know, *ma petite,* I know. And I do understand."

When Gaby later had a similar conversation with Ron, he was not so understanding. "What do you mean, you have no idea when you'll be back?" he demanded.

"My whole life has been turned upside down," she said, "and you just seem to be thinking of yourself. Can't you see that I need time and space to sort it all out?"

"And you can't even estimate how much time and space we're talking about . . ."

"I . . . no, I can't," she said softly, refusing to be pressured.

"That tells me you're not really committed to this relationship." He paused, hoping perhaps for a denial.

Gaby's response was evasive. "I told you, Ron, I really need to be with my . . . my mother. And I need to get my own head together before I can think about anything else."

When they hung up, both were hurt and angry and the relationship was left in limbo.

Gaby was prepared to dislike the Austens, at least a little. Though Karima had not criticized them in any way, Gaby understood that in their eyes, the daughter of a chauffeur had not been fit to associate with the son of the house. Yet when Gaby met the Austens she found not the overbearing snobs she'd expected, but two silver-haired people, still quite handsome, even distinguished, with an air of quiet sadness about them.

"My daughter, Nadia," Karima said solemnly, then added, "though she has been raised as Gabrielle."

Catherine yearned to embrace the beautiful young girl who stood before her, if only to feel something of Charles in her arms once more. But a sense of decorum restrained her. She was keenly aware that she had no claim on this young woman's affection, that she was being allowed a second chance only because of Karima's generous heart.

"These are your grandparents, Nadia. Catherine and Henry Austen."

"How do you do, my dear," Henry said, taking Gaby's hand. "I'm so very happy to meet you at last."

"And I as well," said Catherine, grasping the other hand.

Gaby stared openly at these two attractive people. More grandparents. Her father's parents. How strange this all was. A new family and a new history. "I . . . I don't know what to say," she faltered.

"Perfectly understandable," Henry interceded. "It's a great deal to take in all at once. Give yourself time, my dear. Perhaps you'd like to see some photographs of Charles. Family albums, that sort of thing."

Gaby agreed at once, and soon she was immersed in a mass of photos and memorabilia. Karima wandered into the garden, as Gaby began to piece together her past. There were photographs of Charles in his pram, with Catherine and Henry standing by proudly; Charles at six, riding his pony; Charles playing cricket; Charles with his classmates on a soccer field. Charles astride a beautiful white Arabian mare. In some pictures he was serious, in others he was laughing— but the eyes that looked back at her from those images were her own lovely eyes.

"Tell me about my father," she asked, repeating the request she'd made of Karima. The story the Austens told was of a child beloved and indulged from the day he'd been born.

"And my mother? What do you remember about her? I understand she grew up here."

Catherine looked quickly at Henry, then she smiled somewhat unconvincingly. "She was a lovely child."

"And talented," Henry added. "Everyone who worked here loved to hear her sing." The Austens went on in that vein for a while. Then Henry stopped abruptly and said, "I won't lie to you, my dear. We didn't always appreciate your mother. And we were not always kind.

But we have paid dearly for that. I hope we will have a chance to be better with you."

The simple honesty of his words melted Gaby's reserve. "Yes," she said, "I hope we'll all have a second chance."

Karima sniffed the air as she and Gaby were ushered into the salon of Omar's new villa. Yes, it was there—he'd been smoking hashish, and not too long ago. But today was not a day for recriminations. She would say nothing, and hopefully Gaby would not notice.

A moment later Omar appeared, wearing a richly embroidered *galabiyya*, his face wreathed in smiles. "*Ahlan wa sahlan*," he boomed, "welcome to my house."

"Hello, uncle," Gaby said, shyly trying out the word.

"Dear child of my heart, you've brought light and happiness to my home," he declared, embracing her warmly and kissing both cheeks.

Gaby's first impression was that her uncle looked a little like Omar Sharif: dark, handsome, but with a hint of dissipation.

He summoned his houseman and ordered drinks. A selection of imported Scotch whiskeys—Omar's favorites—was brought, along with *arak*, various soft drinks and a chilled bottle of vintage Veuve Cliquot. With great ceremony, he popped the cork on the champagne and filled three glasses. "To celebrate this happy day," he said, raising his own glass. "To my sister's happiness."

Then trays of *mezze* appeared—*hummus bi tahini, baba ghannoush, foul muddamas,* cheeses, olives, flatbreads and pitas, and at least a dozen small dishes that Gaby didn't recognize.

"Don't eat too much *mezze*," Karima warned Gaby. "My brother has an excellent cook, and she will be very upset if we don't do justice to lunch."

Indeed Omar's cook had outdone herself, and the imported marble dining-table was heaped with grilled pigeons, a variety of fish, assorted salads and platters of rice garnished with pine nuts and almonds.

Throughout the meal Omar was ever the attentive host, filling and refilling his sister's plate, then his niece's, urging choice morsels of meat on one, then the other.

He certainly seems devoted to my mother, Gaby thought. I'm glad she's had him to lean on all these years. Just as coffee and a selection of pastries were brought to the table, the houseman appeared. "A telephone call for you, sir. A Mr. Samir. Shall I tell him you will phone him later?"

Omar rose. "No, no, I'll take the call." He stepped into the adjoining foyer and began to speak in a loud voice. "Do not give me excuses, Samir. I brought you into a deal that could produce millions. Now I expect you to fulfill your obligations."

He paused. "Do not insult us both by begging."

Karima stifled a sigh. She knew all about Omar's deals. It seemed to her that the less substance there was to a scheme, the more noise he made about it. Ah, well, if that were the case, he would soon come to her for money. Again. Not for the first time, she wondered how her brother managed always to spend more than he had.

Omar returned to his guests with a self-satisfied air, as if to say: "See what an important man I am." "Business," he sighed, "it's a demanding mistress."

"What kind of work do you do, uncle?" The question was innocent, but it elicited the hint of a scowl, followed by a thin smile that ended at his eyes. "I'm not a star performer like your mother, of course, but I have my little projects."

"Omar has been very successful," Karima chimed in. She knew that her brother's ego always needed massaging, and she wanted so much for this reunion to go well. So when he asked if Gaby would like to see his new house, Karima quickly answered for her: "Yes, of course she would."

The villa, which overlooked Alexandria's harbor, had been built to Omar's specifications in a graceful Italianate style. But it was filled with heavily gilded French reproduction furniture, and the overall effect was garish, even vulgar. Still, Karima knew he was proud of the place, especially since it was bigger and far more elaborate than her home. So she tried to point out the villa's attractive features—like the lush garden and the beautiful view. When they came to Omar's office, she touched a chair that stood in the middle of the room. "This belonged to our mother," she explained. "Omar gave it to her. She was so proud of it . . ."

Omar's expression grew tender with the mention of his mother.

"I wish I'd had the chance to know her," Gaby said.

"She was a wonderful woman. A saint," Omar declared.

"My father's parents seem like good people, too."

Omar's expression changed in an instant.

"It's getting late, brother," Karima said quickly, hoping to avert an outburst. "I know you have a great many things to attend to, so we'll be on our way."

He was breathing heavily when the farewells were made. But the storm did not break. "What's wrong?" Gaby asked when they were outside.

Karima thought for a minute, not wanting to say anything negative about her brother. "Omar was very protective when we were growing up. He felt he should look after me. So . . . there were times when he and your father did not get along."

She was a beautiful young woman. Almost as beautiful as her mother. But she had the *Inglizi*'s eyes, the *Inglizi*'s expression, reminders of his sister's shame. And she was a bastard, even if that old fool Munir had pretended she was his child. Now she had insinuated herself into Karima's life—and, by extension, into his own. In his heart, Omar wished most heartily that she had stayed lost.

The weeks that followed were a continuous round of parties, receptions, luncheons and introductions. All of Egypt rejoiced that the *Karawan*'s daughter had been found; President Nasser himself welcomed her home.

Much as Karima wanted her daughter to herself, she also wanted

Nadia to know the country of her birth, to love it—and, perhaps, to linger awhile.

When Gaby confided that she wanted to be a journalist, Karima whisked her off to Cairo and introduced her to the formidable Amina Said, publisher of Egypt's leading newspaper. "My daughter is a brilliant reporter," Karima boasted shamelessly. "And since you and I are old friends, perhaps she would be willing to write some stories for you."

Amina laughed aloud. "I'm very grateful," she said in a husky near-baritone voice roughened by thousands of cigarettes. She looked Gaby over for a long moment. "Well, if she's intelligent as well as pretty, I may accept the favor." Turning to Gaby, she said, "If I give you an assignment today, can you have a story for me in two weeks?"

"Of course," Gaby replied without hesitation.

"Good. I'm going to give you a controversial story. One that should stir things up a bit."

"I like the sound of that," said Gaby, enjoying the sparkle in the older woman's eyes.

"Even better. I want you to write about the present state of family law in Egypt. There are some of us—we've been called lunatics, heretics, infidels and worse—who feel that women are not chattels and that they should have rights to children and property when a marriage ends. I want you to interview women who have been divorced by their husbands—and to tell their stories in simple, straightforward terms. I'll give you a few contacts to start with—and if you are a good reporter, you'll find the rest."

"I'll do my best."

Gaby traveled throughout Egypt in search of women who would be willing to talk to her. Some felt so shamed by being cast off that they would not discuss their plight, some were afraid of retaliation by the families of their former husbands, many were so accustomed to being hidden that they refused to draw attention to themselves in any way. Gaby persevered. She promised to disguise the identity of her subjects. And, finally, she succeeded in gaining the trust of a half-dozen women.

The story she wrote described women whose lives all but ended when their marriages did: women who lost children, the means to subsist, their very identities. Those whose families were relatively prosperous could look forward to a future of caring for nieces and nephews or aged parents, in return for their daily bread. Others were less fortunate, reduced to begging or worse. Yet among all there was a kind of resignation: this is how things were; this is how they probably always would be.

It was the resignation that fired Gaby's passion—and her story. The piece was serialized and ran for three consecutive days. It was widely read because of Karima's celebrity—and widely discussed because it challenged deeply entrenched and widely accepted social norms.

Spyros, a tireless gossip, dropped in after the first installment to give his reaction. "I don't think this is such a good idea," he said, waving the newspaper. "There are strong conservative elements in Egyptian society these days, and I don't think inflammatory stories like this one will do your career any good."

Karima bristled. "I'm proud of Nadia's work. Whatever she does, I'll support it. If that causes the 'conservative elements' to be unhappy with me," she shrugged, "so be it."

Spyros tried to retreat a little. "Me, I think it is an excellent article. Well-written, indeed. I simply think you should be aware that it might be seen in a bad light. Especially since your daughter is not Egyptian . . ."

"Not Egyptian?" Karima's voice rose. "The child of my blood? Born to me in this very city? How can you say such a thing?"

Spyros surrendered. "I didn't mean . . . I just . . . forgive me if I've offended you, Karima. I was just concerned with your welfare, as I always have been."

"You're forgiven, Spyros. And I appreciate your concern. But I have no intention of telling my daughter what she may or may not write about."

After Spyros left, Karima thought about what he had said. She smiled to herself and decided to put Spyros's criticism to the test. She took the newspaper into her father's room. He was resting quietly, but brightened immediately when he saw Karima. "I want to read something to you, *Abi,*" she said, "an article our Nadia wrote. I want you to tell me what you think of it."

The old man listened intently as Karima read, his eyes flickering from time to time. And when she was finished, he smiled. "She likes to stir the pot a bit, your daughter, eh?"

Karima returned the smile. "Perhaps."

"She's a good girl. Like her mother."

The sweetness of the sentiment pricked Karima's conscience. "*Abi,* I'm not so good. There's something you don't know, something I never told you . . ."

"Hush," he cut in. "There's nothing to tell. I don't want you to say the words. You are a good daughter and a good mother, Karima. Allah will forgive you for the rest, may He always be with you." And with that, he closed his eyes and drifted off to sleep.

Two days later, with Karima and Gaby at his side, Mustafa passed away. Though Karima sensed that he had grown tired of his life and his infirmities, she mourned him deeply. Was it always to be like this? she wondered. A moment of joy followed by a new sorrow?

A good-sized crowd turned out to see her father to his final rest, not just fans of Karima's, but people who had known and cared for Mustafa. Among them was Henry Austen, who kept a careful distance from Omar. "I know your brother dislikes me," he later told Karima, "but I couldn't bear not to say good-bye to my old friend Mustafa. Did I do the wrong thing by coming?"

"No," she replied. "My father would be honored if he knew you were here."

Knowing how much Karima loved her father, Henry tried to offer some comfort. "I think it was Mustafa's love for you that made him linger with us longer than he wanted to. He was very concerned after your husband died—he spoke to me often about the tragedies you'd suffered. But when your daughter was returned to you, well, I believe he felt it would be all right to surrender to Allah's will."

There it was, she thought, Henry was saying what she had feared: a daughter returned, a father lost. Triumph and tragedy, just as the fortune-teller had foretold.

3
Where the Action Is

Egypt, October 1973

Egypt was at war. Again. But this time the unthinkable was happening: Egypt was winning! "Allahu Akbar," the ground troops shouted as they stormed across the Suez Canal. "God is most Great," pilots cried out as they bombarded Israeli positions in the Sinai. The mood in the country was euphoric.

For decades to come, it would be debated who fired the first shot. That issue was of little concern to President Anwar Sadat. He had seen Egypt pay a heavy price for unpreparedness in the Six-Day War of 1967. He had seen his friend Gamal abdel-Nasser die a broken man after that ignominious defeat. And he had promised himself and his country: never again.

Eager to avenge the humiliation of 1967, Egypt's troops fought fiercely. Within twenty-four hours Israeli resistance on the Canal was broken. "We crossed! We crossed!" crowds shouted outside the presidential residence. The myth of Israeli invincibility had been shattered.

In the coffee-shop of the Cairo Sheraton, Jake Farallon was sharing a morning coffee with a man he thought of as "another suit." This one was from the Pentagon, he had a name—Carson or Carlson, something like that—but there was little to distinguish him from the legion of suits that had passed through Jake's long career.

"Two shipments have already gone out," the suit was saying, "tanks, planes, rockets, cluster bombs, all kinds of goodies from the US of A's big hardware store. They should reach el-Arish in a day or so."

"So what do you need from me?" Jake asked. "Against all that firepower, the Egyptians don't stand a chance."

"We need to be sure. Hell, we never thought they'd get this far. We thought the Bar Lev Line on the Canal was impregnable: 110 miles long, 47 feet high, 238 million bucks . . ."

"Yeah," Jake cut in. "One of my Russian pals told me once it would take an atomic bomb to get through . . . he probably told the Egyptians the same thing."

"But they did get through, Farallon. And that's why we're giving away a couple of billion dollars' worth of goodies. Israel has to win. Period. You've been here longer than any other agent. You know the country, the people. We want your thinking on what else we can do to bring this thing to a quick end."

Jake sipped his coffee, stalling for time. He liked Egypt and the Egyptians. He admired the hell out of Anwar Sadat. And he planned to retire here in a couple of years, when his pension kicked in. He hated the idea of playing even a small part in screwing the Egyptians yet again. Finally he said, "As soon as it gets out that America is riding to the rescue, Sadat's going to start thinking cease-fire. He's a real patriot, but he's not a fanatic; he won't send men to be slaughtered in a lost cause."

The suit nodded, wondering if Farallon was as sharp as he used to be. The agent had been banging around the Middle East and Eastern Europe for a long time. A lot of people thought he was already dead; certainly many of his cronies were. "We already figured that. But we want this to end fast. The Arab countries are making noises about an oil embargo if we don't back off. We're not backing off, we can't. So—there are going to be gasoline shortages, skyrocketing prices, long lines at the pump, all those things that get John Q. Public really steamed. Enough to give his congressman an earful. The faster we can get this thing finished, the sooner we can normalize relations in this part of the world."

Asshole, Jake thought, running his fingers through his steel-gray hair. Didn't he realize that he'd be dead and buried and relations still wouldn't be "normalized?" America had made too many mistakes here, had blown its image as the Great White Hope of the world. It would take more than military hardware and suit-type thinking to mend the damage. "Well," he said slowly, "I understand that Egypt has asked Libya for help. They need oil to make up for the shortfall from the fields they had to close. They want Qaddafi to let them use the port of Tobruk, in case Alexandria gets hit; and they want spare parts for their Mirage planes. Word's out that Qaddafi said yes to everything—but he hasn't delivered yet."

"What's your point?"

"Qaddafi's still pissed off at Sadat for not letting him sink the *QE2*. If you use a third party, it wouldn't take much to get him to stall Sadat till it's all over. And you could probably get him to escalate his propaganda campaign against Egypt. He was really burned that Sadat didn't tell him he was going to war, so he had his radio broadcasters preaching that Egypt didn't have a chance, that its soldiers were cowards who'd go down for a fourth time. I'm sure he could really get going with a little encouragement."

The suit laughed and shook his head. "That's good, Farallon, I like that. If you have any more good ideas, I'll be at the Embassy until tomorrow."

No, Jake thought, that's all you get from me.

"Please come home, Gaby," Tarik pleaded.

"I am home," she cut in gently. "This is my second home now. I thought you understood."

"I do, *ma petite,* I do. But you're in the middle of a war, and who knows..."

"Papa, the war is why I especially want to be here. This is my chance to write about something important. Something that people need to read about."

Tarik was silent. When Gaby was like this, he knew he would not be able to change her mind. All he could do was pray for her safety. So he told her he loved her and asked her to please call often, to put his mind at ease.

When she hung up the telephone, Gaby returned to the story she'd been writing:

FIRST LADY ADMINISTERS FIRST AID

Just one day after President Sadat received the devastating news that his young brother, Atif, had been shot down over Israel, the First Lady was back in the military hospitals. Nicknamed *Um al-Abtal,* Mother of the Heroes, Jehan Sadat moved among the sick and wounded, feeding young men who could not feed themselves, comforting those in pain.

Standing at the bedside of one young soldier, grievously wounded but clinging to life, Mrs. Sadat gently stroked his brow, as a mother would. When he opened his eyes and saw the First Lady, he whispered: "Mother, do you know that I was the first one to plant our flag on the east side of the Canal?" Then he took Mrs. Sadat's hand and kissed it.

With tears in her eyes, the First Lady took the soldier's hand and kissed it in return. "Yours is the hand to be kissed, not mine."

Gaby went on in a similar vein, describing the role that Egyptian women—her mother foremost among them—were playing in the war effort. Her stories were somewhat partisan, not the objective kind of reporting she'd been taught at Columbia, but Gaby didn't care. When she trailed the First Lady, when she saw her mother risk her life at the front, something in Gaby stirred. She was coming to love this rediscovered country, just as she had come to love her mother. Objective or not, Gaby's pieces were being picked up and published in Europe as well as in Egypt. And she had even done a few television pieces that had been broadcast in France.

Still, she yearned to go further, beyond the women's-interest pieces she'd been doing. But whenever she asked Amina Said for a hard-news assignment, the publisher would simply smile and take a verbal detour. "Did your mother tell you that I once worked as an assistant to Huda Sharawi?" Or: "Did you know that I had to publish my first articles under a male name—because no one would run a woman's byline?"

But what did these autobiographical tidbits mean? Gaby wondered. That she should use a pen-name if she wanted to do hard news? Or that she should create her own opportunities?

Day after day, Egypt racked up victory after victory. During the first three days of the war, the Israeli air force suffered major losses. Then Syria joined the attack, knocking out much of Israel's airpower in the north. By the fourth day, Egyptian forces had destroyed over 120 tanks in Israel's foremost armored brigade. The foreign press corps reported that Defense Minister Moshe Dayan had broken down and wept. The impossible seemed to be happening: the road to Tel Aviv appeared to be open, should the Egyptians decide to advance.

But suddenly the news from the front shifted. The number of Egyptian casualties began to swell—and the nature of the wounds began to change. New and terrible weapons were being used in ever greater numbers. The United States had intervened, bringing new powerful technology into the conflict.

Now, Gaby decided, if I'm ever going to be a real journalist, now is the time.

"Go where the action is," Sean McCourt had said. She remembered that advice and now she intended to take it. Without telling anyone, even her mother, of her intentions, Gaby hitched a ride to Red Crescent headquarters. Since she was known to all the personnel as the Nightingale's daughter, it was an easy matter to engage one of the ambulance drivers, a great fan of Karima's, in conversation.

"I've been assigned to report from the front," she lied. "My vehicle broke down a few miles back and I need a ride. I hoped I could come along with you when you go to pick up wounded."

The man looked alarmed. "Oh no, miss, you can't do that. It's very dangerous at the front. No civilians are allowed. Especially women."

"But I'm not a civilian," she argued, trying not to lose her temper. "I'm a journalist."

The ambulance driver looked uncertain. Gaby understood his dilemma. He may have believed she was a journalist, he may even have read some of her stories. But she was still a woman—and war was not the business of women. Gaby played a trump card. "I have General Hamza's permission." And for good measure: "He's a very good friend of my mother's."

"Ah." Hamza's name worked its magic, and an hour later Gaby and the ambulance crew were *en route* to the Canal. They had traveled only a short distance when Gaby spotted two Egyptians with a movie camera and sound equipment. They were standing at the side of the road alongside an aged and disabled jeep.

"Stop! Please stop!" Gaby begged the ambulance driver. Then she waved at the stranded Egyptians, two very young men who scarcely looked old enough to shave. They were also on their way to the Canal, they said, to film a five-minute segment for a Cairo television station. But the engine on their jeep had seized up and now they were stranded. "I'll take you," she said boldly, "if you'll shoot some film for me."

"*La, la,*" they answered quickly in the negative. Gaby sighed. The female factor again. So once again she invoked the names of Hamza and her mother—and then pulled out a wad of bills from her pocket. The two men looked at each other, then nodded in unison and loaded their equipment onto the ambulance.

The road they traveled had been pitted and pocked by tanks and mortar shells; the ride grew bumpier by the mile. Soon plumes of smoke appeared on the horizon, and the sky took on a murky coloration.

The scene at the Canal was chaotic. The sound of shelling was thunderous. Clouds of dust and smoke made breathing difficult. All around her Gaby could smell the acrid odor of gunpowder, the ferrous reek of blood. Where a short time before Egypt's army had crossed in triumph, now there was only retreat. "Set up here," Gaby instructed her rented crew, pointing them toward the line of wounded and equipment streaming across a hastily erected pontoon bridge. Then she stopped a young recruit who had limped across the bridge, supported by another, less badly injured, comrade. "Where is the enemy?" she asked.

"Don't worry, they're coming," was his reply.

At that moment an artillery shell exploded in the sand a few hundred yards away. Gaby flinched—but she held steady as a rock when another shell burst even closer, clearly in the frame. "This is battle," she told the camera. "Bullets and blood, bodies maimed, lives cut short. Wives and mothers bereft, children orphaned. A short time ago young men crossed this bridge in triumph. Now they retreat to bury their dead . . ."

"*Yallah, yallah,*" the two Egyptians urged Gaby as the rain of shells accelerated. They were desperate to leave, and she was inclined to agree. Quickly wrapping up her segment, she concluded: "Gabrielle Misry at the Suez Canal."

Suddenly she felt a tap on her shoulder. She whirled round—and there he was, Sean McCourt, six feet tall, sooty, dirty, rumpled, but still devilishly appealing. With his cameras crisscrossed over his body, like a Mexican bandolier, he resembled a hero from an old war movie. Gaby felt herself flush, and not from the heat. "Go home," he said pleasantly and without preamble. "You could get killed here."

"What about you?"

"I'll be OK." He grinned. "I always am. Go on now, go back to Cairo. That's where all the words are anyway."

"But where are you going?"

"Over there. That's where the pictures are. See ya," he said, chucking her under the chin and turning away.

For a long moment, Gaby thought about following him, with or without her makeshift film crew. But then an army jeep roared up to where she was standing. A young captain jumped out. "Gabrielle Misry?"

"Yes."

"Come with me."

"Why? What if I don't want to?"

"Orders from General Hamza. You'll have to come along."

Gaby didn't dare resist. She and the two Egyptians piled into the jeep, which immediately shot forward. She turned back just in time to see Sean trudging across the pontoon bridge toward the sound of the guns.

Egypt's allies rallied to her defense: President Tito of Yugoslavia sent 140 tanks; President Boumédiene of Algeria, 150. The Shah of Iran contributed 50,000 tons of oil.

But these were no match for American cluster bombs and rockets. Faced with the full force of the United States government, Anwar Sadat announced a cease-fire. "I am willing to fight Israel no matter how long," he told his supporters, "but never the United States."

Gaby's brief tenure as a war correspondent was over. But when the Egyptian film reached the outside world, she had job offers from Paris, from London—and from all three major networks in New York.

4
Beginnings and Endings

New York

"An apartment on the West Side, with a view of the park if possible. And a terrace. Two bedrooms," Gaby had instructed the realtor the network had provided. The realtor complied, and now Gaby had a five-room apartment in a splendid prewar building on Central Park West. The place had 18-foot ceilings, beautifully detailed moldings, an old-fashioned kitchen that reminded her of Celine's, and a balcony that overlooked Central Park. The view was breathtaking, and Gaby could imagine watching the change of seasons unfold before her like a brilliant Impressionist painting.

Now at last she had *space,* that most precious Manhattan commodity. Room for the furniture that Tarik had given her, the precious pieces that Celine had collected and loved. Pristine white walls on which to hang her growing collection of family photographs: those she'd begged from Karima and the Austens, and those she'd brought from Paris. Exquisite parquet floors on which to scatter the antique Berber rugs Karima had given her. After the addition of some choice bits and pieces culled from the city's flea markets and antique shops, the result was what New Yorkers called "eclectic"—eye-catching yet inviting and eminently comfortable.

When Tarik had heard that Gaby wanted to buy an apartment in Manhattan, he had offered her money. "Just until you've saved some of those network checks," he said, knowing how much she prized her independence. "Then you can pay me back." Karima had done the same, using almost the same words, emphasizing how much pleasure it would give her to help. In the end Gaby had accepted a small loan from each of her parents, more to make them happy than out of need; New York banks were always ready to offer mortgages to clients with large salaries and excellent prospects.

Now Gaby wanted to show her new home to Karima, to share it with her. Karima had been cheated of so much for so many years, it was time she enjoyed the pleasures of having a daughter.

As soon as the painters were finished, the furniture in place, Gaby called Egypt. "I'm settled now, *Ummi,*" she said, using the Arabic word for mother. It had been her compromise, her way of loving Karima while still treasuring the memory of Maman, Celine. Karima had cried the first time Gaby said it.

"I miss you already," Karima said wistfully. "You're so far away."

"Not really, *Ummi,* not when I can jump on a plane in the evening and be with you the next day. The network has promised me frequent assignments in Europe and the Middle East. In fact, I've been pushing to do a special-interest story in Beirut. You know, the impact of the war on families, especially children."

"*Ya Allah,* no Nadia, Beirut is still very dangerous . . ."

"Don't believe everything you read," Gaby said, though in fact the network brass had resisted her request on the grounds that Beirut *was* "high risk." "From what I hear, the foreign press corps sit in the St. George Hotel and drink martinis all day long."

"But surely there must be other stories, other places?"

Gaby heard the plea in her mother's voice. "Don't worry, *Ummi,* I haven't been given the assignment yet. In fact, everything I'm working on is just routine and very safe. Right now I'm doing a story on a pair of Russian defectors—ballet-dancers with the Kirov, a husband

and wife. It's a good story, lots of human interest, but not in the least risky. And you, what are you doing?"

"Working hard. If it were up to Spyros, I would be singing every night." Karima laughed. "That man even wants me to sing in Israel, can you believe that?"

"Well . . ." Gaby was concerned. A trip to Israel could be dangerous for her mother.

"Don't worry. I told Spyros, when there is peace, I will be happy to go. Until then, I will just pray for peace."

"I'm glad. I haven't asked about Uncle Omar. How is he?"

"Your uncle is . . . the same. Though I wish . . ."

"What's wrong? Isn't he well?"

Karima sighed. "Yes, he's well. It's nothing for you to worry about. Ah, *ya* Nadia, I wish you were here."

"Well, actually, that's why I called. My new apartment has a beautiful guest bedroom with a view of Central Park. I want you to come, *Ummi*. I want to show you New York the way you showed me Egypt. Will you come? After you finish your concert engagements?"

"Oh, yes, my darling girl, I will *inshallah*."

In truth, Gaby's new job was not exactly what she had imagined, though she would not have complained to her mother for the world. Yes, her salary was a very comfortable six figures, with the promise of much more. And yes, even in the short time she'd been in New York, her name and her face were coming to be well known—at least familiar enough so that the clerks at the Zabar's deli counter gave her quick service, often to the consternation of other customers who had been waiting patiently in line.

But the work itself was different from what Gaby had expected. As a newcomer, she was assigned fluffy magazine-type stories that were folded into the early morning news. The Russian ballet-dancers had been the only substantive story she'd been given; for the most part, she talked to women who had lost a hundred pounds, women who had lost their husbands, women who had survived one type of trauma or another. Perhaps that was to be expected; she hadn't for a moment imagined that she'd be given the choice features covered by network veterans. But she had hoped to do stories with some meaning and depth. Moreover, she had always researched and reported her own stories, and here, almost every piece seemed to be a committee project—parsed, edited, discussed *ad nauseam* before Gaby presented it on the air.

She had expected the kind of workplace camaraderie she'd enjoyed at the *Spectator,* or at least a grown-up version of it. But what greeted her were smiles that showed a lot of teeth but little warmth, and "welcome aboards" that lacked sincerity. Gaby tried to be friendly to one and all, but it seemed as if she were intruding on a private club where she was not welcome.

Gaby told herself not to take the cool atmosphere personally. Perhaps, she thought, it was a kind of initiation period. She was, after all, the "new kid."

Instead of focusing on her own feelings, she worked hard at the job: up at 4 a.m., a quick cup of coffee, a cab ride to the studio for makeup, more coffee and a final review of her story. She was generally on-camera at about 7:40; after that came meetings and discussions of pending pieces. Though she tried to maintain the semblance of a normal schedule, her internal clock was so mixed up she'd often stumble into bed around 4 p.m., sleep for a few hours, then wake up hungry and fitful. It was a solitary existence, her "friends" being the commuters who tuned into the *Good Morning* show for traffic reports, quick news bites, weather forecasts—and perhaps the sound of human voices to ease the loneliness of urban life.

When, after a few months on the job, one of Gaby's producers announced his retirement, the network gave a farewell party at the Four Seasons. Gaby hoped this might be a good opportunity to mingle with her coworkers, perhaps even to break the ice.

Wineglass in hand, she wandered through the crowd, looking for a familiar face. When she spotted Carly Bickers, one of the few female gaffers, she walked over to the young woman and introduced herself. "Hi, my name is Gabrielle Misry. We've never been formally introduced, but I . . ."

"I know who you are," Carly said coldly. "Everyone does."

"Oh . . ." Gaby felt as if she'd been slapped.

"You're the one who took Harper Barrett's job."

"I don't understand . . ."

"Some network big shot thought you looked hot on camera. Thought you'd be the flavor *du jour,* so Harper gets the axe. She'd just had a baby. And when she came back, she was still a little heavy. They gave her one month to take it off. One lousy month! Then she was out and you were in. Everyone loved Harper. She was good at her job and she fought to get more women on the crew. I wouldn't have my job if it weren't for her. So if you think you can just come in and . . . well, you have another think coming, girl."

"But I never applied for Harper's job," Gaby tried to defend herself. "I didn't know anything about her being let go. When they called me, there was no mention of replacing anyone else."

Carly rolled her eyes. "Uh-huh."

"Look, I'm sorry about Harper. If what you say is true . . ."

"Damn right, it's true! Are you calling me a liar?" Carly assumed a fighting stance.

"No, of course not. I'm just . . . I'm just saying I had nothing to do with it."

Without another word, Carly turned and walked away. Well, Gaby thought, at least now she understood why she had been so isolated, so . . . unpopular. But knowing made her no less lonely.

She thought suddenly of Ron. She had not called him since her return to New York. His lack of understanding when she was in Egypt, the fact that he had never called again, made her conclude that whatever they'd shared was over. But perhaps she'd been wrong. Certainly there was no harm in finding out.

She made the call. To her surprise, Ron was friendly. More than that, he was warm. "I'm so glad you phoned, kid. I saw you on the tube early one morning while I was getting ready for work. You looked great! I told my secretary to get your number, but the network wouldn't give it. I was planning to do a little digging on my own—but here you are."

"Yes, here I am."

"So do you want to get together for dinner?"

Gaby did. "But it'll have to be an early night. I have to get up in the middle of the night."

Ron had changed. A lot. The student rebel was gone; in his place was a man who might have made the cover of *Gentleman's Quarterly*. His hair was cut short and close to the head, in a style that, like his suit, was European. Where once he had been rough-cut, he was now sleek, well-groomed and obviously prosperous.

He looked around Gaby's apartment, nodding his approval. "Nice. I prefer the East Side, but this place is definitely nice."

"I'm so glad you like it," she said dryly.

He missed the tone. "I've made early reservations for drinks," he said, "and dinner reservations nearby. I'll get you back before your bedtime."

In front of Gaby's building, a Lincoln Town Car and a driver awaited. "This is a long way from a studio apartment on 112th Street," she observed.

"Yeah, well that was a long time ago. We're both different people."

Gaby agreed. But were they now different from each other as well?

Ron took her to the Metropolitan Club on Fifth Avenue for drinks. Though the prestigious old institution wasn't necessarily Gaby's kind of place, she appreciated the grace and elegance of the room, the beautiful wood paneling, the discreet, hushed service. She wished that Ron didn't feel it was necessary to point out how difficult it was to gain membership and what a coup it was for him to be admitted.

After a round of drinks—Pernod for Gaby, sherry for Ron—they strolled to Le Perigord, with Ron's car following discreetly. He ordered dinner with care and precision, and when Gaby teased him about the kind of fast-food meals upon which they'd subsisted at Columbia, he wasn't amused. "Everyone has to grow up, Gaby. Chock Full o' Nuts is fine when you're nineteen. But when you work on Wall Street with clients who invest millions, it's important to know about food and wine and entertaining."

Ron talked about his job at a leading brokerage house; he told Gaby anecdotes about some of his famous clients, but he seemed much more interested in her work.

"I guess it's crazy to complain about a job that pays so much," she said, "but it doesn't feel like journalism at all. I thought I was hired because they thought I was good. Or at least potentially good. Then the first thing they do is tell me to change."

"Change you, Gaby?" He flashed a smile, and for a moment she saw the old Ron, the rebel, the fighter for the good cause.

"The first thing they hit was my name."

"Your name?"

"Yup. I thought maybe it was the old 'Misry loves company' thing, and you know, I could almost see that. But it turned out that they thought it sounded too ethnic. Can you beat that? And before I finished saying no to that, they're saying maybe I should let my hair grow a little longer, make it a little more feminine."

This time Ron nodded sagely. "Well, Gaby, what they're talking about is packaging. In case you haven't noticed, New York television is much more sophisticated than the Middle East. They want everything glossy and . . ."

". . . and homogenized."

Ron didn't smile. "Look, Gaby, you're on a career track. Keep that in mind. I don't mean you should let them step on you when it comes to salary—and speaking of that, I can put you in touch with a good agent if you don't have one. But when it comes to superficial details that make you more interesting and desirable to viewers and the network, well, I think you should . . ."

". . . toe the party line."

"Yeah."

In spite of Ron's new conservative orientation, Gaby still had a reasonably pleasant time. And when she reminded him that she would have to get up at four, he immediately called for the check.

When the Lincoln pulled up at her building, he drew her close for a chaste kiss. He did not press for more. "I'd like to call you again." It was a question.

"I'd like that."

Gaby tried to take Ron's advice. There was no point in being hard-headed if she wanted to make a success of her new job. She grew her hair to chin length, and she bought a few suits with softer, less tailored lines. But cooperation yielded strange results. Instead of being given better assignments, now she was often sent outside the studio to cover a variety of "human interest" stories. Some were reasonable enough, she thought, like the child who had to live in a plastic bubble because his immune system was compromised. But most were silly, if not bizarre: a woman who insisted she'd had personal encounters with extraterrestrials; a counselor who claimed people's homes were the cause of their relationship problems, and so on.

Gaby was discouraged, but Ron was positively enthusiastic. "You're getting face-time kid, lots of it. What could be better?" Gaby could think of any number of better developments in a journalistic career. But how to make them happen? In the end it was her mother who showed the way.

Karima arrived in New York early in December. To say she arrived, was, however, an understatement. She breezed into the city like a gust of fresh air. Everything was wonderful, everything was beautiful, even the everyday sights that Gaby took for granted.

Manhattan often dazzled visitors, but perhaps never more so than in December, when it glittered with lights and holiday decorations and gave off a heightened energy and excitement.

Forgetting fatigue, Gaby spent every free minute showing her mother the wonders of her adopted city, enjoying it as she never had before. Like the crowds of tourists they oohed and aahed at the magnificent Rockefeller Center tree, watched the ice-skaters glide and dance on the landmark rink. Gaby had never bothered to visit Radio City on her own, but she took Karima to see the annual "Christmas Spectacular," featuring the famous Rockettes in their perky fur-trimmed costumes.

Karima and Gaby rubbed elbows with sidewalk Santas and chestnut vendors. They visited department stores—Macy's, Lord & Taylor's, Saks—glittering with lights and decorations and overflowing with merchandise from all over the world. And they dined in Central Park's Tavern-on-the-Green. Karima's face was radiant as she took in the winter wonderland illuminated by tiny fairy lights, right in the middle of the busy, bustling city. "Oh, Nadia, my dearest child," she whispered, "thank you for showing me such beauty."

For a moment Gaby could not speak. Then she squeezed her mother's hand. "You deserve a nice holiday, *Ummi*. And much more."

Karima laughed. "Believe me, it took all my willpower to make this a holiday. When Spyros heard I was coming to New York, he began making phone calls. It turns out there is a big Arabic community in Brooklyn, so he got very excited and told me I must have a concert. 'No,' I said, 'no, no, no.' At first he would not give up, but finally I convinced him. 'This time is for my daughter and no one else,' I told him. I will sing the next time I visit. If Nadia thinks it is a good idea," she added shyly.

"Nadia thinks it's a great idea! I'd be proud to have you perform here, *Ummi,* very, very proud."

In the spirit of the holiday, Gaby showered her mother with gifts: perfume, beautiful silk scarves to wear with her costumes, a large box of delectable Teuscher candy—and a day of beauty at Elizabeth Arden. Though Karima protested—"*ya,* Nadia, no one but me has ever washed my feet"—mother and daughter each indulged in a pedicure, followed by a manicure, facial and massage.

"You're spoiling me," Karima said with a sigh when they returned home. "You've done so much . . ."

"I want to spoil you."

"I wish I could spoil you in return, dearest Nadia. But what can I give that you don't already have?"

"Just yourself. As much as possible. Promise me that."

"With all my heart." Gaby lit the logs in her fireplace, and she and her mother sipped hot chocolate, watching the flames crackle and pop.

"So, my dear child," Karima said, "you are happy, then, in this beautiful city?"

Gaby started to give the easy answer. And then she decided to indulge herself in the luxury of her mother's love. "For the most part," she replied. "I'm lonely a lot of the time. My colleagues resent me—it seems I replaced someone they all loved and admired. And my work . . . well, it's often just . . . stupid."

Karima listened thoughtfully. "Well," she said finally, "if you don't like doing silly stories, why don't you do a story about the two of us?"

"Oh, I couldn't . . ." Gaby began. And then she stopped. Why not? Outside of the Arab communities, Karima wasn't known in the United States. But her story, their story, was certainly as interesting as any that Gaby did day after day.

She took the idea to her executive producer the very next day. She spoke forcefully and persuasively. "It's a good story, Jim. Human interest. Triumph over tragedy. All those things you like."

It turned out that little persuasion was needed, especially after Gaby showed the producer a picture of Karima. Jim Coburn, like many other network executives, recognized the ever-growing popularity of "confessional" television. Gaby's piece would include romance, tragedy, and a happy ending—winning elements, all. After some jockeying back and forth on who would decide what actually aired, it was agreed: Gaby could tape a ten-minute segment, and she would be allowed veto power over the final cut.

As she prepared for the taping, Gaby thought that turning her own mother into a "subject" might have its awkward moments. Yet Karima made it all easy. She was open, unguarded; for her daughter's sake she was prepared to answer any question, to say anything, but with one exception. She would not tell the world that her Nadia was not Munir's child; she could not dishonor his memory by making him an object of pity or scorn. Gaby agreed: there was no need to revisit every detail of her mother's suffering.

On camera, Karima was a natural. She spoke movingly of her love for Nadia, of the terrible fire that claimed both her husband and her child. Her English was heavily accented and not always fluent, yet when she faltered, searching for a word, a phrase to express her innermost feelings, her story was all the more touching. She talked of the years apart, of times she could literally "see" her child, of her certainty that Nadia was alive. And when she spoke of finding her daughter once again, her face was radiant. There was a hush in the studio when she finished, a quiet that wasn't broken even when the director signaled "cut." Gaby knew she had done a real story at last. She reached for her mother's hand and squeezed it. The tears in her eyes made words unnecessary.

Though the segment aired early in the morning, it generated considerable attention. Call volume through the network switchboard increased by more than 30 percent. The reaction was overwhelmingly positive, to the story and to Gaby.

There was one personal call that Gaby took herself.

"Sean McCourt here," said a husky baritone voice.

Gaby was speechless.

"Nice story," he went on. "I don't usually deal with words, but yours made me call my mother."

"Thank you . . . thank you so much. It's good of you to call. I . . ."

"It's OK, Gaby. I remember what it's like when you're just starting out. A pat on the back can mean a lot, and you deserve one."

Gaby pictured the sea-green eyes, the tousled black hair, the devil-may-care grin. "Where are you?" she asked, plucking up her courage to invite him for a drink.

"Kennedy Airport. They just called my flight. So I'll see you when I see you. Stay away from mortar fire." And then he was gone.

Damn, she thought. One of these days I'm going to see him again. And maybe I won't let him get away so quickly.

Around the studio there was a noticeable thaw. Now Gaby was no longer simply the usurper of Harper Barrett's job; she was that frightened little girl who had lost her mother in a tragic fire. "Thank you," she told Karima. "Thank you for knowing just what I needed and for giving it to me."

The *New York Times* picked up Karima's story and did its own interview. The piece included quotes from residents of Brooklyn's Atlantic Avenue and from the shopkeepers who always displayed Karima's records in their store windows. "We are proud of our *Karawan,*" they said. "We love our Nightingale."

Saying good-bye was painful, the sadness alleviated only by mutual promises of another visit. What Gaby hadn't expected was the gap that Karima's departure would leave in her life. Her mother had been in New York for only a few weeks, yet Gaby found herself missing the sound of Karima's voice, the fragrance of the food she prepared in the little-used kitchen, the bunches of flowers she set out in every room, the warm, loving gestures she made every day.

It was probably missing her mother that made Gaby accept Ron's invitation to a weekend in Westport. "My folks are having a little get-together on Saturday night and they asked me to come. With a date," he added.

Though Gaby wasn't keen on parties, she pictured a country setting, people gathered around a fire, an atmosphere of warmth and congeniality. She said yes.

The Gillman home was a converted farmhouse that had been fitted with every modern convenience. It was decorated in a style that bore the imprint of a well-known Manhattan decorator, and though the result was pleasing to the eye, the house did not invite relaxation.

The very perfection of it made Gaby fear that she might mar some surface or damage some delicate antique if she wasn't careful.

Ron's parents welcomed her enthusiastically; apparently her celebrity had smoothed over whatever imperfections they'd once perceived in her. Gaby assumed there would be separate rooms; she had made it clear to Ron that she wasn't ready to resume a sexual relationship; he had said there was no rush. She was given a light and airy third-floor guest-room furnished with nineteenth-century antiques and a wonderful old bathroom with a big clawfoot tub. After the drive from the city, Gaby took her time getting ready for the party, luxuriating for almost an hour in a warm scented bath.

She dressed carefully in black cashmere pants, ankle-high suede boots and a long black cashmere tunic, adding only a heavy silver necklace for adornment. Since this was a "country" party, Gaby simply dusted her face lightly with powder before applying lipstick and her usual dark mascara.

She didn't realize, though she soon found out, that she was one of the party's main attractions. Everyone who came in was introduced to "Gabrielle Misry, from the *Good Morning* show . . . she's a friend of Ron's, you know." Well, she thought, I guess "face-time" not only erases imperfections, it makes you an object of desire. She didn't mind. The fire was warm, the food was good, and the wine was excellent.

"They have a nice lifestyle, don't you think?" Ron asked as he filled her glass. It was odd to hear this observation coming out of Ron's mouth. Had his fervent denunciations of the establishment been completely forgotten?

"A lot of people in the arts and the media live up here," he continued. "Paul Newman and his family are just a few miles down the road. A couple of executives from your network, too. Of course, I think the perfect situation is what my parents have: you remember, a nice apartment in the city, but a real home in the country. And a winter getaway, somewhere warm. They still have the condo in Palm Beach—right on the ocean and not too much upkeep. In fact, they'd be there right now if Dad didn't have some business in the city." He paused. "So what do you think, Gaby?"

The question took her by surprise. "I've never really thought about a lifestyle," she said. "I have my hands full just trying to take care of my apartment."

"Well, of course, the idea is to have good, competent help. I don't understand why you don't have a housekeeper."

"I guess I don't feel I need one. I have a cleaning service once a week, and that seems to be enough." Wait a minute, she thought, why am I explaining myself? She put an end to the discussion by excusing herself to go to the powder-room.

But in Ron's eyes, the interruption was simply an intermission. The following morning after brunch, he once again brought up the joys of country living, the pleasures of multiple homes, the ingredients of the perfect lifestyle. It was as if he were saying: "All this can be yours." It may have been meant as a promise, but to Gaby it seemed like a threat. He was a nice guy she conceded, but not for her. The Ron Gillman she had admired in college had been replaced by an alien in a very good Italian suit.

Before they drove back to the city, Gaby was certain that the only relationship possible here was friendship.

The positive repercussions from Karima's interview continued, and Gaby's stories began to get meatier and higher-profile. When Um Kalthum died, Gaby was sent to Cairo to cover the funeral. She was sure she'd see Sean McCourt there. She had planned a dozen strategies for engaging him in conversation. But when she searched the ranks of the international press corps, Sean was not among them. She asked some of the other photographers where he might be, but no one could say with certainty. "I heard he was in Ireland," one volunteered. "Don't know if it's work or personal."

On the day that Egypt's most brilliant star was laid to rest, all of Cairo grieved. Businesses closed, the government halted, the streets turned into a sea of black and the sound of weeping was heard throughout the city. As the ambulance bearing Um Kalthum's body made its way to the cemetery, thousands pushed forward, straining to see, to touch for one last time.

Behind the government officials and members of the singer's family, Gaby walked with her mother.

"I didn't know her very well," Karima said, "yet somehow I felt she was my dear friend. All of Egypt felt close to her. She was . . ." She broke off, a sob catching in her throat.

"I understand," Gaby said gently, remembering the assassination of John F. Kennedy, the sense that something important had come to an end.

"It seems as if the fortune-teller's prediction has come true once again," Karima said. "Sorrow about my friend's death. Joy that you are here."

"No," Gaby said, "I don't want to hear that. You've had enough sorrow, *Ummi*. You deserve only joy from now on."

"Whatever Allah decides."

When Gaby returned to New York, she was bumped up in the network pecking order. There was a vacancy on the 6 p.m. news magazine. It was offered to Gaby. More money, more exposure.

She became the network's resident Mideast "expert." When an assassination attempt was made on the Shah of Iran's sister in the south of France, Gaby was sent to interview the princess. When Jehan Sadat visited New York, Gaby was given the story. All right, she thought, all right, I'm on my way.

Time went quickly now as she became busier and busier, with a staff and a secretary of her own. She made time for regular visits with her mother and with Tarik, though these were often squeezed in between interviews, calls and appointments. "I have no time for a normal social life," she told her parents by way of apology. "But I will, after I'm really well established. Then I'll find a way to take it easy."

"But what about a home and family?" Tarik asked with growing concern.

"Don't you want a home and family?" Karima asked once again. "Surely you don't want to end up with nothing but your career?"

Gaby fended these inquiries off with jokes or quips. "I thought you believed no mortal man was good enough for your daughter," she teased Tarik. "If you could see the men I've dated lately, you'd understand why I'm still single," she told her mother.

"Keep an open mind, my dearest girl," Karima urged, "so that when your *nasib* comes along, you'll recognize it."

Gaby smiled at the notion that Destiny would one day drop the perfect man on her doorstep. But in truth, she *had* tried to keep an open mind. She had dated an ophthalmologist who dabbled in real estate whom her secretary, Lisa, had described as "a real catch." Gaby fought boredom as the doctor described in detail his collection of martial-arts paraphernalia. She pasted a smile on her face when he launched into a detailed history of the wine they were drinking, making certain to mention the price. At the end of a long and painful evening, she came to the realization that she would rather be alone than spend another moment with this "catch."

She went out with an attorney who had been widowed the year before. He was good-looking and clever, but when he began to talk about marriage after only three dates, Gaby felt that he was desperate to find a substitute for his dead wife—and a stepmother for his three children.

"Doctor, lawyer . . . that leaves only Indian chief," she told Lisa, who seemed intent on matching Gaby up with *someone*.

"Make jokes if you want," Lisa said, "but it's much nicer to be married than single in this city." Lisa spoke with the authority of one who had been married for almost a year—after many years of searching for Mr. Right in singles bars and personal ads.

Wrapped in a comfortable old bathrobe, sipping an oversize mug of *café au lait,* Gaby was watching the early morning news. It was, in fact, her old segment. A story called "The Face of the IRA" was running, and Gaby had to admit that her replacement, Sue Ann

Fenwick, had done a good job. The images that flashed on the screen were powerful and disturbing: exploding bombs, gutted houses, children with dirty faces made homeless, young men with hard, world-weary expressions. Suddenly she heard a familiar name: ". . . photographer Sean McCourt, who contributed many of the pictures you've seen, talks to our reporter about his brother Eamon, who has been imprisoned for the last five years."

And there he was. Quickly Gaby turned up the volume. "My brother was jailed when he was just eighteen years old. He was not a terrorist, though he's likely to be one now. He was not a member of the IRA—or any organized group—though he is very likely to be one now. Eamon was picked up during a demonstration, one that had been peaceful until the military showed up and started clubbing everyone who stood in their way: women, children, young boys . . . you've seen my pictures, so you know that what I say is true . . ." Sean went on in this vein, his words as harsh as his pictures.

Gaby picked up the phone and called the station. "Sue Ann? I just saw the Irish piece. It's really good. Where did you interview Sean McCourt?"

"At the Elysée Hotel on East 54th. He stays there whenever he's in New York. Why?"

"No reason. There's just something I want to ask him. About one of my stories."

"He's quite a hunk, isn't he?" Sue Ann said, fishing for a response.

Gaby gave none. She ended the call, dialed Information, and then the Elysée Hotel. He might be gone already, she thought. He might be out, he might . . .

Sean answered on the fifth ring.

"Nice story," she said when he picked up.

She was thrilled when he recognized her voice. "Gaby? Gaby Misry?"

"Right on the first try."

"Where are you?"

"Not in an airport. In fact I'm just across town." She plucked up her courage. "Can I buy you a drink, since we happen to be in the same place at the same time for once?"

Sean laughed. But there was definitely a hesitation before he answered. "Sure. Come on over. I'll meet you in the bar."

He was almost the same. Perennial tan. A few strands of gray woven through the still unruly hair. Those beautiful eyes and that heartstopping grin. Yes, Sean was just as she remembered him.

He gave her one of those light hugs that pass between acquaintances as well as friends, and then he released her quickly.

They ordered drinks—Pernod for her, Jameson's straight up for him—and played with the bar peanuts as they made a little awkward small talk. "That really was a good story," she said, not knowing quite how to get things rolling.

Sean nodded. He was not going to help much.

"I'm surprised you're still in New York."

"I've been commuting back and forth to Washington," he said. "Seeing some people who might help get my brother out of jail."

"And? Have you had any luck?"

"Don't know," he replied tersely, as if the subject were not one he cared to discuss. At least not with her.

"Well," she said, "if you think there's anything I can do, just let me know."

Now he smiled and touched her hand. "Thanks," he said, his expression softening, "I appreciate the offer."

The smile made her bold. "So," she said, coming to what was really on her mind. "How long will you be here?"

"Not long. Another couple of days."

Now or never, she thought, remembering the lawyer and the ophthalmologist. "I don't suppose there's anything that could persuade you to stay a little longer?"

He reached over and took her hand. "Look, Gaby," he said, his voice soft and gentle. "I like you. Really. And I admire you. And if I were a different kind of guy I wouldn't need any persuasion. But . . .

I'm not a relationship kind of guy. I tried it once a long time ago."
His eyes misted briefly with remembered pain. "It didn't work. And
I was good for nothing for a long time. I'm comfortable the way I
am. I keep moving and that feels right."

I wish I could disappear, she thought. Just close my eyes and disappear. But no, he's rejecting me and I'm stuck here until I can think
of how to get away. "You don't have to explain," she said briskly.
"You're not interested and that's that. Don't make a federal case out
of it."

"Damn, Gaby, don't say that. You're a beautiful woman, you're
smart and gutsy, and I *am* interested—don't you get it? If I
weren't . . . well, I could reach over and kiss your beautiful mouth
until you couldn't breathe . . ."

Suddenly she couldn't breathe.

". . . and I could take you up to my room and make love to you all
night . . ."

Her cheeks flushed; she could feel the heat rising to her scalp.

". . . and then in a day or two, I'd still be gone."

She caught her breath. There was the bitter taste of defeat in her
mouth.

"Gaby . . ."

"It's OK, Sean, drop it." She rose from the table. "I'll see you
when I see you," she said. And she did not look back.

Gaby attacked her stories with renewed fervor and energy. If this
was all there was for now, she would do it well. Better than that, she
would be the best. And to hell with Sean McCourt.

She was getting ready to fly to Jordan for an interview with Queen
Noor when she received the news of her mother's death.

5
A Murder

It was a proud day—the annual celebration of Egypt's triumphant cross-ing of Suez. Tens of thousands turned out to remember the glorious but all-too-brief moment when their army had reclaimed their territory from Israel.

President Sadat had dressed carefully that morning, in a new uniform he had personally designed for the occasion. At the military review that was now unfolding in Nasr City on the outskirts of Cairo, Sadat was seated on the reviewing stand, his vice-president to his right, his Minister of Defense at his left. Nearby were members of the president's family, including his wife Jehan and his five-year-old grandson Sherif, who was also in uniform.

As the parade of Egypt's armed forces began, a formation of Phantom jets flew overhead, performing a series of acrobatic maneuvers and leav-ing brightly colored plumes of smoke in their wake.

Suddenly an army truck pulled out of the line and stopped in front of the reviewing stand. Three uniformed men jumped out and ran toward the stands, machine-guns blazing. After that, it was all confusion: screams

and cries and broken glass, exploding grenades and a hail of bullets. And
when it was all over, Anwar Sadat lay mortally wounded.

Alone in his luxurious villa, Omar slept the sleep of the troubled.
Nightmarish dreams heightened by alcohol and drugs and extreme
worry haunted him. Images of monsters and djinn and people long
dead—those he had loved, those he loathed and those he had
wronged—intermingled. His beloved mother, the Nazi pervert,
Hans, former friends who had died in prison—all visited him night
after night, until the only remedy was more alcohol and more
hashish.

Tonight the nightmares were heightened by a terrible pounding in
his head. Louder and louder it grew, until he sat up abruptly, wide
awake. No, the pounding was coming from outside. Where was that
cursed houseman? Was he deaf that he did not hear such a terrible
racket? Omar threw on a dressing-gown and went to the door.
Opening it cautiously, he saw two men, well-dressed but with a
vaguely foreign look. "In the name of Allah, what is it you want in
the middle of the night?" he demanded.

"We only want what belongs to our employer," the smaller one
replied, with an accent that might have been Russian.

"And we want it now," the heavier fellow added, his tone menac-
ing, his fractured Arabic oddly accented.

Though still fuddled with sleep, Omar understood at once the
purpose of the call. During two drunken days and sleepless nights,
his gambling losses had mounted to astronomical proportions. Now
he was expected to pay money he did not have. Trying to maintain a
semblance of dignity, he wrapped his robe around him and said, "Is
this the way to do business? To disturb the sleep of a very good customer?"

"Did you hear that, Petrovich?" said the heavyset fellow, laughing
heartily. "He calls himself a customer, he pretends to be a customer—
but he's little better than a thief."

"You have no right to say such things," Omar bluffed, knowing he was in no condition to defend himself, especially against men like these. "I am an honorable man, and I have always paid my debts."

"If you are prepared to pay your debts, then of course we will apologize," the one called Petrovich said. "You *are* prepared . . . ?"

Omar shook his head. "Not tonight. I was certainly not expecting anyone to call at such an hour . . ."

"Enough!" Petrovich cut in. "Enough words and enough excuses. If you don't have the full amount, we will take an installment. A show of good faith," he added in a more conciliatory tone.

Omar's misery showed on his face. "What if I . . . what if I can't . . ."

"Then," said Petrovich, hardening again, "something very unpleasant will happen."

"You'll beat me, break my arm or my leg?"

"Not at all," the smaller man smiled, showing very white teeth. "We don't indulge in such primitive business . . . we leave that to Americans. No, we take the position that those who behave in a dishonorable way are not fit to live. And we give them a ticket to paradise."

Omar swallowed hard. "But I don't have the money. I can't wring blood from a stone," he pleaded.

The men looked at him contemptuously. "You have a rich sister, don't you?" the smaller one demanded.

"Yes," he said, eagerly grasping the lifeline. "My sister is as rich as a queen."

"Well, then, all you have to do is tell her that if she wants her brother to continue living on this earthly paradise instead of the other one, she will pay his debts."

"It's just a loan, Karima. I've had some reversals. The new regime . . . I've lost some of my connections, and that has hampered my ability to service my clients. But I am making new contacts, Karima, and as soon as that happens, my business will revive again—and then I will pay you back, I swear it."

Karima shook her head sadly, her expression that of a parent who
has been disappointed over and over again.

Omar caught the look. His temper flared, but desperation
restrained him when she launched into her litany of reproaches.

"... and you promised me, Omar, you promised me the last time
that the money would not be thrown away on games of chance. You
told me it was to expand your business. But what do I hear two days
later? That you were betting hundreds of pounds on a single hand of
cards. And now, once again you have had 'business' reversals ..."

"Karima, this is different ..."

"It's always different with you."

Omar flushed with humiliation; his sister's scoldings diminished
and humiliated him, but what choice did he have? And when she
was finished, there was always the hope that she would rescue him
once more.

But this time was to be different. "A thousand pounds, Omar," she
said, "I will give you a thousand pounds and no more. No more—
ever—until you change your childish ways."

A thousand pounds! Not even a fraction of what he owed. His sister's stinginess, her superior tone were infuriating! "A thousand
pounds, Karima? What can I do with that? Are you telling me you
can't afford to help your only brother any more than that? You must
be a millionaire many times over. And you certainly don't spend
much—just look at this house! What do you expect to do with all
your money?"

The look she gave him was lethal. "My spending habits are none
of your concern, brother. You can thank Allah that only one of us
lives like a millionaire—else where would you run for help? Have
you forgotten I have a child? Do you think I exist only to pay your
debts? Have you considered that I might want to help Nadia from
time to time? At least I know she won't throw it away on hashish and
cards."

If he stayed another minute, he would strike her. And he could
not afford to do that. Bristling with fury, he took the pittance she
offered and left. What right did she have to dismiss him with such

contempt? She'd been little better than a whore and he had saved her life. He had arranged the marriage to Munir. He had been responsible for all her good fortune—and now she treated him like a dog.

Losing no time, Omar gave the thousand pounds to his creditors—for once resisting the temptation to try to raise more by testing his luck. This was merely a show of good faith, he explained, making light of the amount. Omar was reminded that the sands in his hourglass were quickly running out. He promised another payment soon.

In the weeks that followed he felt as if he were being dismembered, limb by limb. First he sold all the elaborate furniture that he had selected with such care. And then he sold his beautiful villa, to a Cypriot who sensed his desperation and practically stole the place. Karima could have done something then; she could have said: "Brother, don't give up your beautiful home that you have worked so hard for." But no, she just stood by and watched him lose everything.

His debt was paid with little to spare, but now he lived like a pauper. And when he tried to shame his sister, the bitch *laughed*. "A nice apartment in Stanley Bay is not exactly poverty, brother. And God willing, you will have more if you stay away from the cards. You have always been successful," she added in a softer tone. "Use your intelligence to make a new beginning. Find a nice woman and get married. Leave your old ways behind . . . you will be much happier, I'm sure of it."

That was easy for her to say. Yes, he had always made money in the past, but now Egypt was in turmoil. There had been arrests after Sadat's death—and more arrests—but these only fueled the gossip and speculation: Mubarak would not last long, the fundamentalists were planning to destabilize the country—and then launch a revolution, and so on and so on. Even if he hadn't lost so many key government contacts, businessmen were retrenching now, not expanding. Where would his commissions come from? And his "new beginning"?

"I wish you'd come with me, Nadia," Karima coaxed. "Spyros has booked a tour to promote my new album. I'll be traveling all over the

Middle East. It would be such fun if you could join me, at least for a little while. Have you ever been to Amman? The king is a good friend of mine . . . I'm sure we would be invited to the palace. And then I could show you Petra. It's an awe-inspiring place, Nadia. You'd have a wonderful time . . ."

Gaby had in fact seen the glorious rose city of Petra during one of Tarik's calls on a wealthy Jordanian businessman. But sightseeing really wasn't the point. She wanted to say yes to her mother; Karima never asked much—all she wanted to do was give. But this was a delicate juncture in Gaby's career: more and more she was being given the kind of assignments she had always yearned for. She was not due for any kind of vacation, and she felt it would be unwise to take any unscheduled time off.

". . . and then I'll be going to Damascus. It's a wonderful city—the mosque is truly exquisite—and the food is superb. I have so many friends there; I know they would love to meet you."

"You're tempting me, *Ummi,*" Gaby cut in reluctantly. "But really this is not a good time for me to take a holiday. There's so much to do here right now. But I'll make you a promise: by the time you finish your tour, I'll find a way to take a few days off. We could meet somewhere in Europe. I do want to see you, *Ummi,* truly I do. I've missed you," she added shyly. It was true. She missed her mother's presence, her all-encompassing love, especially when she went to the places they had shared together.

Karima laughed, though Gaby could tell she was genuinely touched. "With all that excitement you have in New York, you miss your mother?"

"I do."

"But what's wrong with all those New York men? Aren't they keeping you busy?"

Gaby smiled. She knew Karima had a wildly unrealistic notion of what her life was like: a fairy-tale concoction spun of magazine stories and television series. Though Karima's own life had been rather simple, she imagined that New York was her daughter's personal playground. "*Ya ummi,* you know that the hours I keep are crazy.

Most days I'd rather sleep than go anywhere. When do I have time for a social life?"

"*Allah!* That's terrible, Nadia. Is it all worth the sacrifice? Surely you'd like to have a home and a family of your own?"

There was a pause. The only real prospect for a home and family had been Ron. There were, of course, the daydreams, the fantasies of another man. But no, that was not what Karima meant. "Yes, I'd like to get married someday, but . . ." Quickly she shifted gear; this wasn't the time for a serious discussion. "What's wrong, *Ummi?*" she teased. "Are you so anxious to be a grandmother? Surely that wouldn't do your image any good."

Karima laughed long and hard. It was a lovely sound, clear and bell-like and filled with joy. "Ah, *ya* Nadia, I think you have become too much a New Yorker if you're talking about such ideas as 'image.' If Egypt likes my voice, they will still like it when I am fat and old and have a dozen grandchildren."

Now it was Gaby's turn to laugh. She could hardly imagine her-self—or any of the women in her position—keeping their jobs if they were fat and old. "All right, *Ummi,* let's make a date. Call me when your tour is winding down, and we'll arrange a nice visit some-where—I promise."

"*Inshallah.*"

"Over here, *effendi,* bring my friends another round." Omar's words were slurred, his gestures expansive, but he would have bristled at the suggestion that he was even a little drunk. This was how business was done, and he had been working hard at it for the past two hours, in one of Cairo's finest restaurants. He had provided his companions with a lavish dinner, and he had maintained a steady flow of Johnny Walker Black Label, a favorite with government functionaries whenever others were paying.

The bill for the evening would be high, but Omar thought of it as an investment in his future; the two men with him were minor bureaucrats with strong connections to the new regime—and especially to the ever-growing intelligence community. Omar was working hard to ingratiate himself with this pair. They were in a position to assist him with introductions to those who dispensed lucrative government contracts. Equally important, they could keep him informed about those who had fallen out of favor and those who were under suspicion. Omar had always known how to make use of information, but at a time when paranoia led everyone to suspect his neighbor of belonging to one illegal faction or other, the value of real intelligence multiplied tenfold. This evening, in addition to offering an excellent repast and eminently acceptable gifts—Cartier cigarette lighters for both men—Omar had provided them with the names of several fundamentalists suspected of terrorist activity.

"You are a real patriot, Omar," said Ramzi Sayyad, one of the few Copts in the new administration. As a member of an often persecuted Christian minority that had once enjoyed tremendous wealth and privilege in Egypt, Ramzi was particularly sensitive to the growing threat of fundamentalism. "I'm sure the new regime will find a way to reward your vigilance."

"I did nothing more than my duty," Omar said modestly. In truth, he had bought his information with a relatively small bribe. Whether or not the men he named were actually terrorists, he did not know, nor did he particularly care. Probably they were guilty, but if they weren't they could no doubt be persuaded to pass on the names of others who were.

"No," Ramzi insisted, "there are many, especially people of means and standing—" with a gesture he included Omar, who thought of himself as living in near-poverty—"who care only for their own enrichment. I salute you, sir, for having a care about Egypt's future."

Omar beamed.

"And your excellent sister," Ramzi continued, quickly dimming Omar's smile, "she, too, is a great patriot. I congratulate you on the award she received from President Mubarak for her continuing service to the country. The light from a thousand candles, he called her. And of course everyone remembers her heroism in wartime."

Omar struggled to maintain his smile. His sister again. He was fed up with her high-and-mightiness, fed up with kissing the asses of men far less worthy than himself, while Madam Karima Ahmad placed herself above it all. Quickly he swallowed the drink in front of him.

"Be careful, friend," Ramzi cautioned, "soon you won't be able to stand up."

"Don't worry about me, friend," he said, slurring his words even more. "I was just drinking to the health of my sister. No one knows better than I what a wonderful woman she is . . . the sun and the moon and the stars. And a great patriot. Yes, no one will ever get me to say anything else, not even if I should be tortured . . ."

"But why should anyone want you to say something else?" Ramzi inquired, suddenly more interested in Omar's ramblings.

Omar smiled drunkenly, lifting a finger to his lips in a gesture that was clownishly comical. "Hush, hush," he mock-whispered. "Some people like to gossip about their betters. But I say my sister makes her tours to sing and nothing else. What if she's planning a concert in Israel? Is that a reason to condemn her? Sadat went to Israel after all. What if she travels a great deal? Is that a reason to spread lies about her? To hint that she is engaged in . . . By God, I won't even say the word! And I swear I will kill any man who says that she uses her fame to help the enemy!" With that, he slumped over in his chair and began to snore.

His companions shot him a look of disgust and left him where he lay. But at a time when rumor and plots abounded, when the country's fate seemed once again in jeopardy, even a fool's ravings could not be ignored. Especially when they involved one so famous, so well-placed—and so potentially dangerous.

Three weeks later, on the morning of Karima's final engagement in Damascus, a chambermaid knocked on the door of the Presidential Suite of the Semiramis Hotel. And when there was no answer, she used her passkey to gain entry.

She carried her vacuum cleaner into the sitting-room and plugged it into the wall outlet. When she glanced into the bedroom, she saw that the bed was still occupied. Murmuring an apology, the maid was about to leave, when she saw what appeared to be broken glass on the floor. Gingerly she entered the room. The lady was lying on top of the bedcovers, her eyes wide open, her expression rigid and fixed. The maid had seen Death before, and now she knew she was seeing him again. *"Allah!"* she called out, then ran from the room. She continued to run until she reached the manager's office. "Dead," she blurted out, "the lady in the Presidential Suite is dead."

Confusion and consternation broke out immediately. Karima Ahmad dead in their hotel? But how could such a thing happen? And what was a mere manager to do?

The police were called. And, in due time, the secretary of President Assad was called as well. This was a delicate matter and it called for delicate handling.

The reports that came out of Damascus were vague, but the rumors were many, foremost among them the story that Karima had died of a drug overdose. Though Karima had been beloved, the rumor was, oddly enough, widely circulated and widely believed. These were difficult times after all, and so many entertainers had died in such a fashion.

Under Egyptian law two-thirds of Karima's fortune went to Omar, the rest to Gaby. Omar accepted his good fortune with great satisfaction and little regret. Once he had uttered the lies, they took on an aura of truth. And though he never again mentioned Karima's name among his colleagues, he did convince himself that if she was not a spy, she was at least deserving of the fate that Allah had sent her.

He wept copiously at her funeral, which was the largest Egypt had seen since Um Kalthum's—and then he made up his mind to buy for himself what Karima had so often advised, a new beginning.

6

Denial

Alexandria and Damascus
New York and Paris

"Come back to Paris with me, Gaby," Tarik pleaded.

"Or if you're ready to return to work, I'll fly to New York with you."

Gaby shook her head mutely.

"But why? Why must you stay here, in . . . her house? It must be so painful."

There was no reply. Gaby's gaze just drifted off to some distant horizon. Tarik was worried about his daughter. More than that, he was frightened. He had stayed behind in Paris during the nightmare days following Karima's death because Gaby had insisted on burying her mother without him. But he had flown to Alexandria immediately after the funeral, and now he was glad that he had come. Tarik understood bereavement—God knows he had endured it—but Gaby seemed so . . . so altered by her grief. It was almost as if she had departed her body and left behind an empty shell—and for all his medical skills, Tarik did not know what to do for her.

———————

Cruel and senseless and unbelievable. To lose one mother was heart-breaking, to lose two was beyond endurance. She could find no closure, no comfort, not even in Tarik's love.

"Why must you stay here?" he kept asking. "It must be so hard."

"Yes," Gaby finally replied. "It is hard. More than you know. But when I walk through this house, I can still smell her perfume. And sometimes I can even hear her voice. I'm afraid that if I leave this house, this city, I'll lose her completely."

Tarik thought for a moment. Yes, there was truth in what she said. His life had seemed so shrunken after Celine died that he had considered moving to a smaller apartment. But in the end he could not leave. Not while Celine's presence lingered, in the kitchen she loved so much, the bedroom they had shared, in the very air he breathed. At first this sense of her had sharpened his pain, heightened his feelings of loss. Now he took comfort from it, feeling as if she somehow watched over him. "I understand," he said to Gaby, "truly I do. But you won't lose Karima no matter where you are. She loved you too much, *ma petite*. She won't let you go."

Days passed, then weeks. Tarik had phoned the network on his daughter's behalf shortly after the funeral. She was ill, he told Gaby's producer, and would need a leave of absence.

How long? the producer asked, trying to appear properly sympathetic, to conceal the annoyance he felt.

Tarik could not say. But he would keep in touch. He wondered if Gaby would have a job when she was ready to return to New York.

As time passed, the Austens visited regularly, with Catherine bringing fragrant dishes from her kitchen; most remained untouched. Farid Hamza came, too; he seemed comfortable with Gaby's long silences, and the two would sit together on Karima's veranda in silent, mournful communion.

Even Omar stopped by several times. He brought flowers and boxes of Turkish delight. He was a changed man: serene, confident, expansive. "Stay here as long as you wish, my dearest niece," he told

Gaby. "It's true the house will have to be sold to settle the estate, but that can wait. And please know that you will always have a home in Alexandria as long as I live."

"Thank you, Uncle, you're very kind."

Gaby tried to question Omar about her mother. But his answers confused her. "Uncle, did you *ever* know my mother to drink alcohol?"

"Never!" he thundered. "My sister was not that kind of woman." Then, in a lower, sadder tone, "But only Allah knows what goes on when no one can see."

"They said she took pills, Uncle. But I've looked all through this house, and all I found were some aspirin. Do *you* believe she used sleeping-pills?"

"I will not believe it!" he pronounced. He paused. "Though of course these things can be hidden . . ."

Then his expression brightened. "But let us not speak of such sadness now. Let us remember my sister in better ways." He opened his crocodile briefcase and extracted a sheaf of papers, placing them on Gaby's lap. On the top sheet, which was made of a delicate parchment, was an engraved nightingale adorned in subtle shadings of gold and crimson. The text, in fine calligraphy, began: "The Karima Ahmad Foundation." And then: "Omar Ismail, Director."

"It's beautiful," Gaby said. "But what . . . ?"

"I have done this in your dear mother's honor. A charity to benefit Egypt's war orphans and widows."

"Oh, Uncle . . ." Gaby was moved beyond words.

Omar smiled benevolently. "I believe this would have made my sister very happy."

"I feel so ashamed," Gaby told her father. "All I can think of is my own grief. But my uncle has put his sorrow to work, helping families that have lost people they loved."

"Grief is nothing to be ashamed of," Tarik said briskly. "But if you're ready, let's think of something constructive you can do."

"I want to go to Damascus," she said, as if she had been considering this plan for some time. "I have to see the place where she died. I have to talk to the police. There must be something more than the official report."

"But Hamza has already gone over that ground, Gaby. If he couldn't find anything, how will you?"

She shook her head in that stubborn way he knew so well. "I'm going, Papa. I can't not go."

"Then of course I'll go with you." Tarik called Farid Hamza and told him of Gaby's decision.

Hamza accepted this news without comment. "Shall I accompany you?" he asked.

"Thank you, Farid. But I think Gaby wants to ask her own questions, conduct her own interview. Perhaps you could speak to your police contact? Explain why Gabrielle needs to do this . . ."

Farid promised he would make the call. In fact, he came to Karima's house to deliver personally the name of his contact. Tarik surmised that the old soldier was glad of any opportunity to be in Karima's home again.

"The person you should talk to is Antoon Sayyad," Hamza told Gaby. "He has assured me that he will show you everything he has."

"Thank you, Farid. You've been so good to me."

"It's nothing at all, dear Nadia. Nothing. I wish I had taken that wretched position with Intelligence when it was offered to me. Perhaps then I would know more, learn something that would give you comfort . . ."

"And you, Farid," she asked gently, "have you found anything to give you comfort?"

His eye misted with unshed tears. "No," he said hoarsely, his voice breaking. "Nothing."

Gaby insisted on going everywhere Karima had been: the concert hall, the restaurant where she had eaten, the suite where she had died. Speak to me, *Ummi,* she entreated silently, tell me why you were taken from me. But as much as she wanted to find Karima's presence in these places, all she felt was her own anger, her own pain.

Police Inspector Antoon Sayyad answered Gaby's questions with a gentle tact that Tarik appreciated. "As far as we know, Madam Ahmad was alone when she died. The maid found no evidence that there had been any visitors in her suite. Nor did any of the hotel staff see anyone on the penthouse floor."

"What about phone calls? Did you check to see who she might have called that . . . that last night?"

"There were no calls on her bill."

"But if she'd spoken to anyone in the hotel, that wouldn't show up on the bill."

"That's true, Miss Misry. We did, however, go over the hotel's register—to see if there were any guests who were connected to your mother in any way."

"And?"

"There was only one person: your mother's manager."

"Spyros?"

Inspector Sayyad nodded. "He told us that he was with your mother during the concert, but that he did not return to the hotel until four or five in the morning." He paused, reaching for delicacy. "We determined that he was, indeed, otherwise engaged. With some of his . . . gentlemen friends, if you take my meaning."

Gaby did.

"He told us your mother was in fine spirits that evening. Though we did wonder if perhaps she had been depressed about something, if there was some reason for her to . . ."

"No, never!" Gaby cut off the thought. "She and I talked often. She had no serious problems, nothing that would make her . . . We were planning to meet, and we were both looking forward to it. She wouldn't have . . ."

"It was a question that had to be asked," Sayyad said mildly.

"Then you should also be asking questions about the drugs mentioned in the police report. Seconal and Nembutal? Those are powerful narcotics. I've never, ever seen my mother with drugs of any kind."

"Pardon me, Miss Misry, but you did not live with your mother day in and day out. And these drugs were not the type that the filth of our society use," he continued, trying to be kind. "But your mother was a successful entertainer, much in demand. She worked hard and she had to keep long hours. Perhaps she asked a doctor for something to help her sleep. Perhaps, on that sad night, she was a bit groggy and took too many . . ."

"But there was no doctor's name on the empty bottle you found in her room!"

"That's true. But keep in mind that pills can be obtained through . . . other channels. Perhaps she did not want the gossips to know she used narcotics."

"What about the alcohol? My mother didn't drink. Ask anyone. She didn't like the taste of alcohol."

Antoon wouldn't meet her eyes. "If she were unaccustomed to alcohol . . . if she took some . . . let's say for medicinal purposes, to help her sleep—then she wouldn't know how dangerous it was to mix the two."

Yes, Gaby thought, that had been Tarik's theory. It sounded less . . . sordid than any other possibility. But Gaby still did not believe it. "What if someone else gave the pills to her?" she persisted. "Why do you discount that theory?"

Sayyad returned to old ground. "What you're talking about is murder, Miss Misry. Do you have reasons to believe that? Your mother's room was locked, and, as I told you, no one else was seen in the vicinity. Did your mother have enemies that you knew of?"

Gaby shook her head.

"Well then, I'm afraid my report must stand. I wish I could help you, Miss Misry, I do. I was a great admirer of your mother's, but . . ."

Gaby left Damascus empty-handed, drained. Hope had buoyed her for this trip, and now it was gone. Pills? Alcohol? The equation simply did not work. If Karima had used drugs, then Gaby had not known her at all. And if she had not, then the police report was not true.

"I can't accept this, Papa, I just can't."

Tarik was torn. What was best for his little girl? To persuade Gaby that there had been a terrible accident? Or to ignore the medical evidence and support her blind faith that there was more to Karima's story?

There was nothing for Gaby to do but return to New York and try as best she could to live her own life.

". . . and until next time, this is Gabrielle Misry."

No sooner had she unhooked her microphone than her producer, Jim Robbins, approached. "What's wrong with you, Gaby? That picture we ran wasn't the Philippines Labor Secretary, it was the Minister of Tourism . . . the information was right on your teleprompter! Couldn't you see the damn thing? Do you need contact lenses or something?"

Gaby shook her head. "Sorry."

"Yeah, well, 'sorry' covers one or two goofs, kid. But you've been racking them up like an amateur. And you read the copy like a zombie, for God's sake! Can't you put some life into your pieces?"

She had no defense, no snappy rejoinder. Jim was right. In the month she'd been back, her stories had been almost uniformly dull and lifeless. She had lost the fire and passion that had made the network hire her.

She was working mechanically, oblivious to the pitying glances around her—and to the fact that staffers had begun to distance themselves from her. Gaby had swerved off the career track, and no one wanted to be nearby when she crashed and burned.

She tried to pull herself together. She practiced yoga and meditation. She went to a spa in upstate New York that promoted "spiritual balance and physical harmony." Nothing helped. All these remedies called for acceptance. And that, Gaby would not, could not do.

Sensing that she would probably get fired, she resigned from the network. What she'd been doing was no longer journalism anyway, she rationalized. She had become simply an attractive talking head. She sublet her apartment and flew back to Paris. She was tired. She was beaten. She wanted to be a child again. To cry. To be held and comforted. To do nothing at all.

Time meant nothing. She slept badly, haunted by nightmares from her childhood: the fire, being torn from her parents, being lost in a sea of strangers. She cried out, she called for her mother, but no one came to help. She was alone. Sometimes Karima came into the dream, holding out her arms, but there was always a barrier—a fence, a wall of people—and Gaby could not reach her.

To avoid the dreams Gaby began to stay up all night, reading her way through her father's library, sleeping instead through the daylight hours, which somehow held no menace. In different circumstances Tarik might have prescribed sleeping-pills, but he could not do that now.

Seeing the dark hollows appear below her eyes, the way her clothes began to hang loosely on her ever-diminishing frame, he feared that her physical health, as well as her emotional well-being, was in danger. He coaxed Gaby to eat—if not well-balanced, nutritious meals, then tidbits of this and that. A small cup of consommé with fine noodles. A few salted crackers. Toasted bread and Coca-Cola. Flavored gelatin. Invalid food, but he was grateful when she took it.

He was relieved when she began to stir from her bed, to perform simple tasks around the house. Then he began to notice that she arranged the linen closet not once, but several times, that she had done the same with the bathroom medicine cabinets, and with the books in his study. Afraid to discourage her—God knows, it was better for her to move around than to spend all day in bed—Tarik tried to distract his daughter.

He called the Austens and Farid Hamza, explaining that Gaby was having difficulty dealing with her grief and that he wanted to revive her interest in the world outside her head. Could they help?

The Austens responded with more pictures of Charles, with lively stories about his boyhood. Hamza thought long and hard—and then he began writing to Gaby about his military career. "I apologize for boring you, my dear Nadia," he prefaced his first letter, "but it would mean very much to me if we could stay in touch. And as my life has been the military, I hope you will indulge an old man and write to me about what interests you."

Gaby was charmed. And she began a brisk correspondence, with him and the Austens. Heartened by what he saw as progress, Tarik tried to get Gaby to spend some time outdoors.

"But I'm so busy," she protested, holding up one of her letters.

"Not too busy to care for your health." Tarik was firm. He had seen patients develop all kinds of phobias after spending weeks and months indoors. "Farid and the Austens will not mind your getting a breath of fresh air now and then." And so, as if Gaby were a child, Tarik created little outings for her: a walk through the Tuileries Gardens, a stroll along the Seine, stopping now and then to browse through the books in the outdoor stalls.

He made reservations at the Tour D'Argent, thinking that Gaby might, if only for a little while, respond to the allure of sublime food in a beautiful setting. But she picked so listlessly at her masterfully prepared duck that the waiter inquired if something was wrong with the dish, if Mademoiselle would perhaps prefer something else. No, she said, she was simply not feeling well.

Tarik's patience came to an end. "Enough!" he said, "enough, Gaby. You're not the only one in this world who has suffered. When Celine was ill, I cursed the universe. I even wished for death. But at some point, one must rejoin the living. Karima would be deeply hurt to see you now. She wanted nothing more than your happiness. To see you like this, throwing away these precious moments of your young life—it would break her heart."

Gaby burst into tears. "You're right, Papa, you're absolutely right. I've been weak and useless and . . ."

Merde, he thought, that was brilliant. Just what the patient needed, a heaping dose of temper and some self-abuse. And in public, too.

He got up from the table and gathered Gaby into his arms, paying no attention to the worried looks from the *maître d'*. Quickly he paid the check and got her back home. Now what? he asked himself. I seem to have run out of ideas.

Fate intervened in the person of his assistant, Nelly Dutoit. Tarik had earned a great deal of money during his long and successful career; he had no need to work. But shortly after Celine's death he had begun to donate his services to a free clinic for poor foreign immigrants, many from the Middle East.

One day, Nelly told Tarik she needed a few weeks off. "My sister is expected to give birth very soon. She was very ill with her last child, and she will need someone to be with her. I would like to go." Tarik readily agreed, an idea beginning to form in his head. If Gaby could not respond to the life going on all around her, then perhaps she would respond to the suffering of others.

He went home early and told Gaby he had a small emergency at the clinic. After explaining Nelly's situation, he asked, "Could you possibly give me a few weeks of your time—until Nelly's family emergency passes?"

"But I don't know anything about medicine, Papa."

He smiled inwardly. She hadn't said no. "We leave that part to me, *ma petite*. But the people who come to us need many kinds of help. Often they speak little or no French. Often they have no friends, no resources. They have difficulty obtaining the *Carte de Séjour*. They have difficulty enrolling their children in school. They are afraid of the bureaucracy, especially if they come from a place where asking questions can be dangerous. What Nelly did was to act on their behalf, as a kind of . . . ombudsman. Surely you could do that for a few weeks?"

Gaby agreed. Without enthusiasm, but she did agree.

Mother of miracles, the first family that showed up at *La Policlinique Familiale* the following morning consisted of an abandoned mother and child. The husband and father of this sad group—one Mah-mmoud Habbash—had left for work one day and failed to return. His wife Nazli had gone to the café where he worked as a waiter, only to be told that he had never reported for his shift. And furthermore, the irate owner added, if Mahmoud was going to be this careless about his job, then perhaps it should be given to someone else.

No, Nazli protested, her husband was very conscientious about his work. Something terrible must have happened to him. The café owner shrugged; this was a matter for the police, not for him. Police! The young woman was terrified. She prayed for help, she prayed for her husband's return. To no avail. On the second day of Mahmoud's disappearance, a distraught Nazli plucked up her courage and went to the Préfecture to file a report. But the sergeant who took her complaint listened for only a minute or two before making it clear that Paris could do very well with one less terrorist. Fearful that she was about to be charged with some crime or other, Nazli had fled.

Now what was she to do? Her child was ill, she had no money to pay the rent on the single room they all shared. She was willing to work—cleaning houses, washing dishes, anything—but how could she find anything when she could scarcely speak this strange and dif-ficult language? And who would care for her child?

Gaby looked at the little girl, who might have been four or five, but whose sweet, heart-shaped face already wore an expression of resignation. "You're not feeling very well today?" Gaby asked in Arabic. The child smiled shyly at the sound of her native tongue. No, she was not well. Tarik made his examination, soothing the girl's fears with gentle expressions, assuring her that all would soon be well.

"She has a mild infection," he told Gaby in French. "The antibi-otic I'm giving her will clear that up quickly. But she seems to be malnourished . . . I suspect she has been for some time. Check Nelly's resource file and see if you can find them some assistance. Try the religious agencies as well as the municipal ones. And later, when you have time, perhaps you can file a police report yourself on the missing husband. Wait. Before you do that, let me give you the name of someone at the Ministry . . . an old friend. I think if he calls the Préfecture before you arrive, your complaint will be treated with some respect." Tarik sighed. "The mother will need some help getting a *Carte* so she can work. She'll need help finding a job, and a *jardin d'enfants* or an *école maternelle* for the child."

Gaby ushered mother and child into the small room that served as Nelly's office. She looked at the little girl. Another lost child, poor thing, almost alone in the strange and unwelcoming city where her father had thought to make a better life. She rummaged through Nelly's top drawer and found the cache of sweets that was kept there for the clinic's young patients. "Choose one," she coaxed the little girl. "No, choose two."

"Her name is Karima," the mother said.

Karima. Gaby almost burst into tears. But she swallowed hard and recovered her composure. "That's a beautiful name," she said softly. "Truly beautiful." She went to the cabinet that held her personal belongings. Surreptitiously, she opened her handbag and extracted all the cash she had. She returned to her desk and opened another drawer, pretending to remove the money from some "official" repository. She counted out the bills, placed them in an envelope and handed them to the young mother. "Here," she said. "This should take care of your rent and some groceries. Give me a description of your husband and I'll take it to the police station this afternoon. Come back tomorrow and we'll begin the paperwork for your *Carte de Séjour*. Then we'll see about finding you work and a school for your daughter."

The young woman looked dazed, as if she could not believe what she was hearing. She grabbed Gaby's hand and began to kiss it. "God's blessings on you, dear lady. May His Mercy shine on you all the days of your life."

Embarrassed, Gaby patted Nazli's arm. "It's nothing, really. This is what we do here at the clinic."

There were other families that day, all needy, many as sad as Karima and her mother. Gaby worked hard for all of them, making phone calls, badgering bureaucrats, filling out forms, even reaching into her own pocket—or rather Tarik's pocket, since she had no money left—for emergency funds. When Gaby went to her father for a small loan, he smiled and gave her the money without question. He, too, gave his patients money when the situation was desperate, and he was pleased to see that his daughter was at last engaging with real people instead of books and letters.

A week passed, then two. When Nelly called to ask if she might stay in Normandy a little longer—her sister still needed a great deal of help—Tarik readily agreed. "Take another month, dear Nelly. With pay, of course. My daughter will help me until you return."

One day, while Gaby was comforting a little boy who had broken his arm during a fall down a flight of stairs, the door to her office opened. A pair of green eyes met her own. An engaging grin, but tentative, almost apologetic. "*Bonjour,* Gaby. How have you been?"

"Sean! Sean McCourt! What are you doing here?"

"I came to see you."

The simple declaration was so unexpected that Gaby had no answer. "I . . . I have work to do," she finally said. "I don't have time to talk."

"Fine. I'll wait until you're finished." And with that, he left Gaby's office and parked himself in the clinic's reception area.

Tarik noticed him at once: tall, deeply tanned, rugged, with a face that invited a second look. "Can I help you?" Tarik asked.

"I'm waiting for Gaby."

"Ah. And who might you be? I ask because I'm Gaby's father."

Sean smiled and stuck out his hand. "Sean McCourt, sir. Gaby and I are old friends—" the exaggeration was conscious, but it was a small one. "I flew into Paris yesterday. Actually I've been trying to track you down . . . thought I'd find Gaby that way. Then lo and behold, the receptionist told me she was here, too."

"Yes. Gabrielle has been helping with the clinic's work."

Sean glanced at the people around him. "Looks like these folks need all the help they can get."

Tarik nodded. "More than we can give, but . . ."

Sean understood. It was the same the world over. There were never enough resources for the poor and disadvantaged, especially when they were immigrants. "You don't mind my waiting here for Gaby, do you?"

Tarik studied Sean, then said half-seriously, "I don't know you well enough to mind or not mind, Mr. McCourt."

"Sean, please. And I'm hoping we will get to know one another very well."

Tarik glanced at the closed door of Gaby's office, then back at Sean. "Ah," he said, with the hint of a smile, "that's not really up to me, is it?"

"...I wanted to stay in Egypt when your mother died, Gaby, to spend time with you. But I had an assignment in Italy—some bigwig had been kidnapped—and I had to fly right out. I'm sorry about that..." Sean leaned over the bistro table, trying to close the distance between them.

"You don't owe me any explanation, Sean. We hardly know each other. You made it clear that was the way you wanted it... rolling stone, no ties, no relationships—remember?"

"I remember," he sighed, toying with his sandwich, and wondering why it was that people always recalled so clearly the stupid things you said. "But things change, people change, Gaby. Otherwise what would be the point of living?"

"So how long will you be in Paris?"

"I'm not here on a job, Gaby. I told you, I came to see you." He took in the haunted look in her eyes, the dark circles, the too-prominent cheekbones and the thinness of her arms. "You haven't had an easy time of it, have you, since your mother died," he said gently.

The kindness of his tone, the concern in his expression brought tears to her eyes. "I know she's gone and nothing I do will bring her back. I can accept that. But the other...I just can't."

Sean nodded. "I understand how you feel. The story I heard... that would upset anyone."

Gaby's eyes squeezed shut. "Upset" didn't begin to describe what she was feeling.

"But you have to let go of it sometime, Gaby. You can't change the past, any of it, and hanging on just eats your life away."

She opened her eyes and looked intently at him. She had heard pain and experience in his voice, and that, more than his words, made her pay attention.

"You heard some of my family's story on the news program, I think . . ."

She nodded.

"There was more. My father—he *was* Sinn Fein—was killed by soldiers when Eamon and I were kids. That's probably why they took Eamon, who was guilty only of being Patrick McCourt's son. My mother, God bless her, was a rock. She raised us on her own, she put food in our bellies as best she could, and she made sure we knew right from wrong—even when she had to whack us a few times to get our attention."

"Is your mother still alive?" Gaby asked.

"Yes, thank God. It was my mother, you see, who finally pounded some sense into me."

"She whacked you a few times?" Gaby couldn't help but smile at the image of big, strapping Sean being "whacked" by his mother.

He smiled back. "I think she would have, if she thought it was necessary." Now he was serious again. "I think Ma always understood that deep down I was a lost soul. Wandering the world, searching for . . . something. Not a day went by that I didn't think of Da and Eamon . . . all the people I've loved and lost."

Gaby reached over and squeezed his hand.

"But lately I've been going home more often, to be with Ma . . . I think it hit me that she wasn't going to live forever, that I'd never forgive myself if I didn't make good use of the time she was here." He swallowed hard. "Anyway, Ma made me see that I owed it to Eamon and Da and all the people I loved whose lives were interrupted . . ." He trailed off for a moment.

Gaby waited for him to finish.

"That I owed it to them to live my life, fully and with passion. That anything less would be a sin against them and against God."

She was quiet for a long moment. "Your mother sounds like a remarkable woman."

"She is that." A pause. "I think you'd like her."

There was more to Sean's story than he had told, Gaby was sure of that. But she felt instinctively that he had shared with her more than he was in the habit of revealing. And so she, too, shared bits and pieces of her personal life: her childhood with Celine and Tarik, the revelation that neither of them was her biological parent, her reunion with Karima.

They talked for a long time, and it was nearly midnight when Sean took Gaby home. Tarik was waiting up, though it was his custom to retire about eleven.

"Well, I guess I'll say goodnight," Sean told father and daughter.

To Gaby's great surprise, Tarik said, "Won't you come in for a cognac, Mr. McCourt . . . Sean? Unless you're in a hurry . . . ?"

Sean was not in a hurry. He accepted the cognac, and soon he and Tarik were chatting amiably—the doctor describing his extensive travels, the photographer discussing his impressions of the wars he had covered.

In the end, it was Gaby who yawned and said, "You'll have to excuse me. I have a long day at work tomorrow."

Sean's courtship of Gaby was slow and unpressured. He understood that she was not ready for a full-blown love affair—and that she did not trust him not to disappear.

He wooed her with routine and predictability, stopping by the clinic at the end of each workday. Sometimes they would go out for a simple meal. At times Gaby would prepare a meal at home and share it with Tarik, who was ready to give his blessing to the relationship. But no one asked.

Sean was prepared to be patient. To keep himself in baguettes and *café au lait,* he picked up small local assignments. His expenses were minimal, since he was staying in an apartment borrowed from a pal, a photographer who was taking pictures in India for a lavish coffee-table book.

One beautiful autumn night, when the smell of fallen leaves and wood fires was in the air, Sean invited Gaby to his borrowed apartment.

"Are you planning to seduce me?" she asked.

"Are you planning to let me?"

She smiled.

They stopped at a charcuterie and bought a quiche, an endive salad and a bottle of wine. When they reached the apartment, a tiny studio in Montmartre, Gaby looked around approvingly. "Very neat," she said. "Did your mother teach you to keep house?"

"Yes," he said solemnly. "My mother taught me many domestic skills, all of which make me a very good catch." He set the table with a linen cloth and matching napkins. "I want you to know I bought these myself," he said, "in anticipation of your visit."

"You were very sure of yourself then."

He grinned sheepishly. "Let's say I was hopeful."

They made small talk while they ate their simple meal, but there was a tension in the atmosphere that made them suddenly awkward with one another. When they finished, Gaby rose to clear the table; Sean turned on the radio, tuning to a classical station. Then he came up behind her, circling her waist with his arms. He kissed her, lips gentle and undemanding. Running his hand up the small of her back, he stopped at her shoulders. They were so thin, so knotted with tension. Poor kid, he thought, a wave of tenderness suddenly supplanting desire. And now his "seduction" turned into something else. With the flat of his hand he massaged deep, firm circles across her shoulder-blades and up her neck.

She sighed. It had been such a long time since she'd been touched by a man. A long time since she'd felt so . . . good.

With a quick motion, he picked her up and carried her to the bed.

Settling her against a bank of pillows, he traced the outline of her face, her nose, the curve of her lips. "Beautiful," he murmured.

She laughed self-consciously. "Everyone says I'm too thin."

"Maybe a little," he agreed amiably, "but still definitely beautiful." He picked up her foot and began to massage it, moving from toe to toe. Then he pressed a knuckle into her arch, sending what felt like an electric current up her leg.

"Ouch! What are you doing?" she protested. "Is this some kinky sex ritual you learned during your travels?"

"Yeah, I learned it in Bangkok. Something you need more than you need a kinky sex ritual. Now just lean back and trust me." Gaby closed her eyes and relaxed into the pillows, letting the music wash over her. He massaged her legs, her hands, her arms and shoulders, digging his fingers into her acupressure points, awakening her senses, making her feel so . . . alive, yet so light and relaxed and . . . soon she floated into a deep, deep sleep.

Sean kissed her forehead, gently stroked her cheek. "I think I love you, Gabrielle Misry. And one way or another, I mean to make you happy."

Gaby didn't awaken until ten the next morning. She sat up suddenly. "What time is it? I'll be late for work!"

"Relax, darlin', it's Sunday. A day of rest."

She sank back into the pillows. She felt good, for the first time in a long time. "That was nice. Even better than seduction," she added mischievously.

"Oh, the seduction is still on, darlin' . . . I've just begun. To do it properly takes time and imagination . . ."

"I see," she said solemnly. "Well . . . thank you."

"If you really want to thank me, you'll let me spoil you today." He began by making breakfast: a hearty omelette with asparagus, a buttered chunk of baguette, a steaming mug of *café au lait*.

To her great surprise, Gaby was hungry. And the food was delicious. "And you cook, too."

"I told you, my mother made sure of that. She said it was not manly to depend on women for your daily bread."

"Your mother's a wise woman."

"You'll see how wise when you meet her."

She understood what he was saying. And for the first time, she glimpsed the possibility of true and enduring love.

Winter rode into Paris on a cold, wet wind. But to Gaby and Sean, in the first flush of passion and discovery, it was no less wonderful than sunshine and balmy breezes.

They did all the things that lovers do, feeling as if every moment, every trivial event they shared was new and unique in the history of mankind. They took long walks, visited the museums—the Louvre, the Rodin, the Picasso—only half-seeing the splendid works of art. They ate bowls of onion soup and drank rough red wine in tiny bistros. They rode the *bateaux mouches* like tourists, reveling in Paris by night, as if they had never seen it before.

Gaby kept waiting for him to disappear. It was not a conscious thing but rather a premonition—like Karima's enduring sense of foreboding. Soon she was spending more time in Sean's borrowed apartment than she was at home. She waited for Tarik to object or at least to notice. But her father seemed quite content with the situation. "Have you and Sean considered marriage yet?" he asked one day.

"There's no point in rushing something like that," she responded quickly.

"Ah." Tarik's expression was sympathetic. "He has that problem that Americans call fear of commitment?"

Gaby was annoyed. "It isn't that simple, Papa. Neither of us is ready for anything as serious as marriage. Don't you want me to be careful? To be sure?"

Tarik retreated, unconvinced that Gaby was telling him the whole truth.

The weekend in the country was Sean's idea. He had noticed how Gaby lingered over the paintings of Monet when they visited the Louvre. And when she admitted that she'd never been to Monet's home, Giverny, he decided to give her that gift. He rented a small cottage near the Epte River—the same river the artist had so often painted. He shopped, to excess, buying enough food for a family of six, then he picked Gaby up in a rented Renault.

"Where are we going?" she asked. "and why are you being so mysterious?"

"It's a surprise," he explained with exaggerated patience. "And the very nature of surprise incorporates an element of mystery."

They drove northwest, forty or so miles. The trip took about an hour and a half. When they reached Giverny, it was late afternoon. The air was cold, but sunlight filtered through the clouds, casting a subtle gold-white light on the bare fields, the trees, the houses. Gaby was delighted. "It's just the way it was in his paintings," she exclaimed. "Oh, Sean, you're wonderful to have thought of this."

The cottage was charming—simply furnished, yet eminently inviting. But it was cold. Sean started one fire in the fireplace and another in the old-fashioned wood stove in the kitchen. He set an enormous basket on the wooden table and opened it, releasing a pungent medley of aromas: there was good, rich coffee, freshly ground, country bread, some rough pâté, smoked trout, a chicken, fresh vegetables and a medley of charcuterie and cheeses. Gaby unpacked the bottles of wine—he had left that selection to her.

With the ease of a long-married couple, they put the seasoned chicken, along with some potatoes, in the oven to roast. After washing the salad greens and preparing a simple dressing, they put their coats back on and went outside for a walk.

"Looks like snow," Sean observed, pointing to the changing colors of the sky.

"Oh, good. Then maybe we can see the place where Monet painted *The Haystack in Winter*. Of course, there are no haystacks anymore, but the light will be the same, the atmosphere."

Sean nodded amiably. He didn't know much about art, but he

enjoyed Gaby's enthusiasm and he enjoyed looking at beautiful pictures.

They walked until Sean declared he would soon be frozen beyond any possibility of thawing. When they returned to the cottage, Gaby lit some candles while he cut the bread and prepared the meal for serving. Appetites sharpened by cold air and exercise, they ate until they could eat no more.

"Have you thought about going back to work at all?" Sean asked, as he sipped his wine.

"What a strange question! And what a time to ask it. Are you trying to get rid of me?" Gaby was only half-joking, for in spite of Sean's declarations of love she did not quite trust her newfound happiness. I'm like my mother, she thought, I search my joy for signs of sorrow ahead.

"Ah, Gaby, don't even joke about that," he said vehemently. "But I don't think you'll be happy just working at the clinic forever. Don't get me wrong, you're doing good things for people who need it. But you're a trained reporter. Why don't you try picking up some assignments from an outfit like CNN . . . that's more like real reporting. I think you'd like it."

"Maybe I will," she said slowly. But Sean could see that she wasn't yet ready to face the world outside Paris. Perhaps he could do something about that. He had learned that sadness didn't have to crowd out all possibility of happiness; he wanted to share that experience with Gaby.

The snow began to fall just before midnight. The bedroom in the cottage was chilly, so they took their pillows and their goosedown quilt into the living room. They warmed their hands in front of the fire, while icicles tinkled outside like wind chimes. The wind crooned softly as it dusted the snow against the windows, wrapping them in a thick and fluffy cotton blanket.

When Sean held out his arms she went to him without hesitation, pressing her lips to his, feeling the warmth of his body flow into hers. When his tongue pressed against her mouth, she yielded readily, tasting his sweetness as it mingled with hers.

And then he enveloped her, kissing her eyes, her nose, her shoulders. When he reached for the zipper on her trousers she helped him, slipping her clothes off and letting them fall to the floor. Her skin glowed warm and golden in the firelight; the touch of his skin against hers inflamed her. They sank down on the quilt in a tangle of limbs. Sean's touch was sure and certain; it was as if he had known her forever. His fingers sculpted her body, uncovering new sensations every time they came together. "I love you," he said huskily, his green eyes dark with desire.

"I love you," she echoed, touching his cheek. Her eyes were dreamy, half-closed as he kissed and caressed her. She moaned softly, her body shimmering with heat and desire as he entered her. Arching her back, she drew him in deeper and deeper, her nails digging into his flesh, as if she would consume him with her need.

In the half-light of dawn, she opened her eyes. The fire had burned away, leaving behind graying embers. The room was cold, and she huddled into Sean's body for warmth.

"Are you cold, sweetheart?" he asked, reaching for her.

"A little," she said, burrowing deeper into his chest. "Sean?"

"Yes?"

She hesitated. But she needed to know. "You told me once that you'd loved someone a long time ago. That it had caused you pain . . ."

"Yes."

"Can you tell me about it?"

He sighed. He'd known the time would come when Gaby would ask this question. And though it no longer caused him terrible pain to talk about Siobhan, the memory of her still made him sad. "It was a long time ago, Gaby. She was my first love. We'd grown up together, and to me she was always different from other girls. The others . . . we'd tease and torment them in school, chase them with snakes, pull their hair. Adolescent boys doing obnoxious things. But Siobhan . . . I was always bringing her little presents. A flower. A book . . . she loved to read."

"And did she feel the same way about you?" Gaby asked, a little jealous now of a memory.

He nodded. "When we were just thirteen, she told me, as solemn as could be, that she planned to marry me when she turned eighteen." He paused. "She didn't live to be eighteen."

"Oh, Sean, I'm so sorry . . ."

"Some eejit kid made a bomb. Thought he'd be a hero for the cause. Blew up his whole family—and two of the people who lived upstairs. Siobhan and her mother."

Silently Gaby took his hand and held it in hers.

He sighed. "Losing my father was hard. But losing her . . . I never wanted to go through that again."

Gaby understood.

"Until I met you."

Gaby closed her eyes. *Nasib,* she thought. I believe, *Ummi,* that I may have met my destiny.

"Gaby . . ."

Her eyes flew open.

"There's something I've been wanting to tell you. I don't want you to be upset . . ."

No, she thought, no. Whatever it is I don't want to hear it.

"I've been asked to go to Sri Lanka. I said yes." The words came out in a rush. "I wanted to stay here, to be with you, to make you understand that my intentions were serious. But I can't keep turning down assignments indefinitely, Gaby. People will just stop asking . . ."

No, no, no.

"Gaby, this isn't like before. It's a job, just one job. I'll call and I'll write—and I'll be back before you even have a chance to miss me."

She was silent.

"I promise you, on my life, that I'll be back. And if I get another job, I'll be back from that, too. Forever, Gaby, I promise you."

Though life had given her every reason not to, Gaby believed him.

Book Four

I

Redemption

Paris and Beyond, 1988

"Pack your bag, darlin." We're going to Cyprus!" Sean called out as he breezed into the apartment he and Gaby shared. It was just three rooms in the Rue du Four near St. Germain des Prés—a modest little place in the sixth *arrondissement*. Not very grand, but the years of love and living had made it into a home.

She laughed. "You remind me of my father," she said. "He would always come in like that, full of energy and ready to fly away. My mother teased him about making gypsies of us, but I know they both loved the trips and the adventure."

"Ah. So you're coming round to my way of thinking. About my work, I mean."

Gaby thought for a moment. "Not exactly. But I'll be happy to go with you to Cyprus." She did enjoy the occasional trips they shared; sometimes she was even able to pick up a freelance assignment of her own. But when Sean went off alone to some "hot" spot, there was always the fear, the worry that he might not return. Not because he didn't want to—they had gotten past that—but because a random bullet, a stray mortar shell had stolen him away from her.

A few days later they were stretched out on the deck of a small boat, drifting lazily in azure waters off Paphos. The sun was warm, the sky was clear, and there was not another living soul in sight. The quiet was broken only by the lapping of the waves. "And you get paid for this?" Gaby teased. "You should be paying someone for sending you here."

"It happens like this sometimes, love—a false alarm. The Turks have occupied the northern part of this island since 1974. There's been a war of words going on about it in the UN, in the newspapers, in whatever back rooms diplomacy gets carried on these days. But every so often there's an 'incident.' Some poor bastard gets himself shot trying to cross the barricades—the kind of thing that happens at the Berlin Wall—and then it looks like there might be big trouble. They call Sean McCourt and all the others like me to record it for posterity. But I'm glad it didn't happen this time, even if we do have to go home soon."

"I'm glad, too. But I'm also glad we came." The past few days had been idyllic. She and Sean had frolicked on the island's beautiful beaches, they had taken pictures near the rock where Aphrodite was said to have risen from the sea. And they had swum languidly in those waters in moonlight—because it was said that those who did so would remain forever young.

"This part of Cyprus is really unique," said Sean. "There are spots that are pretty much the same as they were during biblical times. St. Paul traveled here, you know," he added authoritatively. "He converted the island to Christianity."

"Thanks for the history lesson. Papa used to do that sometimes— give me little bits of information about the places we went. And now you and I . . ."

". . . and maybe one day our children," Sean said softly.

Gaby's expression was solemn. "I love you, Sean. But when I think about a family, I get this . . . this strange feeling. It's like I'm stuck in Alexandria and my life can't really get moving until . . . until I put my mother to rest. Really put her to rest."

He was quiet for a moment. Gaby hadn't talked about her mother in this way for a long time. But he knew that she hadn't given herself completely to their life together. He had seen it in the way she avoided any discussion of marriage and family. He dropped the subject. And brought it up again after they had their picnic lunch of cold roast chicken and salad and bread, washed down with crisp Cypriot white wine.

"I have an idea," he said.

"About what?" Gaby asked.

"What if you put together a tribute to Karima? An article, maybe even a book. Be a reporter, try to be objective. Even if you don't get all the answers, maybe you'll finally get the kind of closure you're looking for . . ."

Gaby considered this idea. Yes, she thought, yes. My mother spent years looking for me. It's only right that I spend some time trying to discover who she really was. She threw her arms around Sean and kissed him.

"I'll take that as a yes," he said. "Good. And I'll help. You've trailed after me more than once; this time I'll be your helper."

The Austens were thrilled to see Gaby, for whatever reason. And when she told them why she had come, they begged her and Sean to stay with them for a few days. Gaby agreed. Here was where it all began. Love and tragedy—and the fortune-teller's dire prediction.

"You're so thin, dear child," Catherine noted with grandmotherly concern. "Aren't you eating well?"

Sean grinned. "I keep telling her she needs to bulk up. But I think your granddaughter's secretly training to be a supermodel." In truth, Gaby had filled out considerably since that dark period following Karima's death. But she still had a kind of fragile waifish quality, due in part to the sadness that often shadowed her deep blue eyes.

Catherine went into the kitchen to confer with her cook. A short time later a servant appeared carrying a princely array of *mezze,* surrounded by pita bread still warm from the oven. Gaby nibbled a bit of cheese, a morsel of bread. "This reminds me of the day I met my mother for the first time," she said softly. "She told me then that food meant 'welcome' and 'I love you.' " She seemed on the verge of tears.

Catherine and Sean both rose from their chairs. He sat down again; a woman's touch was needed. "Your mother was right, Gabrielle dear. And you are loved here, as you were loved by your mother," Catherine said, stroking Gaby's hair. And when it seemed the sadness had passed she retired to the kitchen once more, returning with a steaming bowl of soupy greens. "Your mother used to make a fine *mouloukhiyya,*" she said, presenting the bowl to Gaby. "This is from her very own recipe, so you must try some. For her sake."

Gaby obliged with a few mouthfuls, and then, with Catherine's urging, she cleaned the bowl.

What a long road we've traveled, Henry thought, as he observed grandmother and granddaughter. A long way from the time when Catherine would scarcely tolerate Egyptian dishes. Anything Egyptian, for that matter. And how painful had been the lessons that had brought them this far.

"I can't eat another bite, really," Gaby declared, just as the maid appeared with a large glass bowl filled with a creamy-looking dessert.

"Oh, but you must," Catherine said. "Your father adored my trifle. And Karima came to like it, too . . . so you must have a taste, for both their sakes."

Gaby laughed at being coaxed to eat like a child, but she dug into the mound of sponge fingers, cream and fruit dessert that filled her plate. It was a kind of communion with a past she wanted to know and remember. To her great pleasure she found that she, too, liked her father's favorite pudding. Just as she liked being cocooned in her grandparents' affection.

"Bravo," said Henry with a twinkle in his blue eyes. "I see that the way to fatten you up is to serve you dishes with a bit of family history. And we certainly have plenty of that."

"Oh, yes," Gaby said enthusiastically, "that's what I'm really hungry for. Tell me everything you remember. Please."

"Well," Henry said, "on the subject of food, your parents had much in common. They loved to buy treats from the street vendors, especially during Ramadan. All the Muslim children on the plantation would eagerly wait for the sun to set and the cannons to fire. As soon as the lights around the minaret began to flicker, that was the signal that it was time for *iftar*, the breaking of the fast.

"Then the children—Karima and Charles in the lead—would rush off to the vendors to spend their Ramadan allowances on *foul* and *falafel* and *qataif* and *kanafa*. And after they'd stuffed themselves with as much food as their money would buy, they went out in search of more. His mother never knew," here Henry cast a mischievous glance in Catherine's direction, "but Charles often ran along with Karima as they went from house to house, knocking on doors and calling out '*Ramadan karim*' and begging for sweets. Your mother had a real sweet tooth," Henry added.

Gaby closed her eyes, picturing her parents as children, imagining their innocence, their simple pleasures. It was a poignant picture, especially since, for Karima, childhood had been so short.

As if reading her mind, Henry continued. "When Shams—your grandmother—died, the life seemed to go out of your mother's family for a time. But Karima pulled it all together. She left school and took over Shams's work here—and she kept house for Omar and your grandfather, Mustafa. It was a heavy burden for a young woman, little more than a child, really, but I never heard her complain."

"That's so sad," Gaby murmured, picturing again a child, now burdened with an adult's cares.

"It was. I stepped in and tried to help. I spoke to Mustafa, and at first he agreed to bring in his unmarried cousin to live with them. But Omar wouldn't hear of it. He felt it was Karima's duty to leave school and take care of the house. And Mustafa—the heart had gone out of him, poor man—he just didn't have the will to argue with his son. So Omar prevailed."

"But why? Why did Omar feel that way? What would have been so wrong with my mother staying in school?"

Henry thought for a while. "He was an odd duck, that Omar. Terribly broken up when his mother died—he was very devoted to her. It seemed, oh, perhaps I'm wrong, that he wanted everyone to suffer, as he was suffering."

"My poor mother," Gaby said softly. "To lose so much, so early."

Henry coughed into his napkin, then wiped his eyes. "But she kept her spirits up in spite of it all. Always singing her songs around the house. She *was* like a nightingale, indeed she was."

"And my father," Gaby interjected shyly, "he brought some happiness into her life, didn't he?"

Henry glanced at Catherine, who nodded, as if giving permission to recall their pain, their loss. "Yes," he said, "Charles's love for Karima was deep—and true—from the time they were children, I think. He never wanted to leave Egypt, he never wanted to go to England. He asked, he begged, to be enrolled in the American University of Beirut, which would have allowed him to come home often. But we insisted that only a fine English university would do."

"Because you wanted to keep them apart." It was not a question.

Henry flinched. "Yes," he said quietly. "We wanted to keep them apart. That mistake cost us our son. And our only grandchild."

Gaby got up and hugged her grandfather, as if to reassure him that she was no longer lost. She had heard some of the details of her mother's life, but during the first overwhelming wave of grief. As she listened now, the stories took on a shape and form, like a rich and intricate tapestry. And she felt as if she were just beginning to understand her mother's courage, her passion for music, her love of life. That understanding made her ashamed of her own weaknesses, her spells of self-pity. Karima had lost a mother—and overnight she took on her mother's responsibilities. I just turned into a big baby, Gaby reflected. But that's over, she resolved. No matter what she

found on this voyage of discovery, she was going to be strong, as
Karima always had been.

Omar insisted that an afternoon was insufficient; they must come for
the weekend.

He sent a chauffeured Bentley.

As they crossed the Abul Ela Bridge to the Gezira, the larger of
Cairo's two Nile islands, Sean eased back in the leather seat, poured
Gaby and himself champagne from a bottle in a silver ice bucket, and
said, "I didn't realize your uncle was an honest-to-God tycoon."

"No, I guess I didn't know that either. I did hear that he had
become a great success—and a great philanthropist, too. A regular
Lord Bountiful. Funny, my mother always seemed to worry about
him . . ."

"Seriously. You say your mother's family came from the *fellahin*?
Then Egypt must be the real land of opportunity. Can't understand
why my ma packed me off to the poor old USA instead of here."

"Don't forget she wanted you to become a cop," Gaby laughed.

"Of course. All the Irish in America are cops." This had been a
running joke between them: Mary Rose McCourt had told her emi-
grating son that if things did not go well for him, he should look up
a distant cousin who was a sergeant on the Chicago police force—
and who would put him on the force as well.

"Then you must be a terrible disappointment to her," Gaby teased.
This was another running joke. When Mary Rose had paid them a
brief visit the year before, Gaby had seen immediately that the
woman adored her elder son.

"Disappointment, you say! We Irish eat disappointment for
breakfast. And dinner, too, if there's enough to go around. Besides,
what about the disappointment you've inflicted on my poor
mother?"

"Me? What have I done?"

"Have you forgotten how distressed she was when she found out we had no marriage plans? I told her we were engaged so she'd come without an argument. And it didn't hurt that I sent her the ticket. But then you had to let the poor woman know that she would not be attending a wedding any time soon. No doubt she's lighting candles, even as we speak, for her poor fallen son. And the hussy who won't make an honest man of him."

Gaby laughed, then grew serious again. "Sean . . ."

"I know, I know, love. Case closed." He changed the subject. "So what does Gezira mean?"

"Island."

"Island. I hope they didn't stay up all night thinking of that one."

"Names are different here. No one calls it Cairo. It's always Masr."

"I thought *Masr* meant Egypt."

"It does."

"Ah. New York, New York."

The house was in Zamalek, an expansive and expensive neighborhood on the northern part of the island.

"Reminds me of the Austens' place," said Sean. "Only more so."

"My God, it is like it."

Before the Bentley had halted, Omar came bouncing out to greet them. For a moment Gaby might have mistaken him for an unusually enthusiastic servant—he bore so little resemblance to the sorrowful figure she remembered from the time of Karima's death. Sleek, exuberant, smiling, he obviously was thriving on the success he had attained.

"My beautiful niece! And Mr. McCourt, I presume? The photographer. A great honor to this undeserving house. A thousand welcomes."

The weekend soon developed into a floating party. Quite literally so on the first night: Omar had rented a small flotilla of feluccas for a lantern-lit outing on the Nile. The next day was nonstop feasting, music, games, gifts—for Gaby there were a dozen richly embroidered *galabiyya,* antique turquoise jewelry, and a beautifully crafted cartouche, a tiny gold oblong medallion, spelling out her name.

"You're too generous, Uncle," she protested. "I thank you with all my heart. But what I want most is to hear about my mother. I knew her for such a short time . . ."

"Of course, of course," said Omar, his dark eyes expressive with understanding. "Too short, dear niece, for all of us. Well, why not now? I think my other guests can survive without us for the moment."

He led her into his study. Hundreds of books. On the wall behind his desk a display of plaques and awards: acknowledgment of his charitable works.

"This is impressive," said Gaby.

Omar shrugged modestly. "Those whom God has given good fortune must do good for others, you know. But this will interest you more."

He flipped a switch. "Behind you."

She turned to see a huge oil-painting of Karima. "But . . . was this hers? I don't remember it from before, after the funeral."

"You are right. It was painted after my sister's death. I could have painted it from my heart," he said, touching his chest, "but alas, I lack the skill. It is from a photograph. I had a fine artist—the best in Egypt—copy the photo. And now she is here with me forever."

Surrounding the painting were photographs: Karima with President Nasser, with President Sadat, with Um Kalthum. And, off to one side, a small, sepia-toned image of two children: a beautiful girl of about ten, a boy just in his teens, his arm draped protectively around her shoulder, smiling at her as she looked gravely into the camera.

"That was your mother. On my birthday. She had just sung the most beautiful song in my honor. I was so proud of her. My father took our picture. I've treasured it ever since."

"You loved her very much."

"More than she ever knew. I only wanted what was best for her. After the Austens turned their backs on her—may God strike them with his vengeance—I made a very good marriage for Karima. I helped launch her career. I always tried to protect her, but sometimes, sometimes, she was so headstrong. She was an artist, a dreamer, she did not realize that her actions had consequences."

"I don't understand."

"Ah, my dear niece, not all of Egypt loved Karima, may God be merciful to her. She was too generous, too open with her affections. There were whispers, rumors. Especially about the Jews—that she was too close to them."

Gaby was startled. "What do you mean, Uncle? Are you saying . . . ?"

Omar put a finger to his lips. "No, no. I've said too much already."

"No, I have to ask: was this something that might have led some-one to . . . want her dead?"

Omar looked at her with compassion. "Niece, please understand. Your mother's death was a tragic accident. These other things—jealous rumors, nothing more, that her naïvete allowed to flourish. I'm sorry I mentioned them. Let us talk instead of the Karima that we both loved."

For an hour he reminisced: sentimental anecdotes of childhood, sister and brother together. It sounded as if they had been extraordi-narily close.

"Funny," Gaby told Sean later. "To hear my uncle talk, you'd think he and my mother had their own brother-sister Garden of Eden."

"That doesn't sound like any brothers and sisters I know."

Gaby had no brother or sister. "The Austens don't remember it that way either."

"Well, memory can play tricks. Most people, I think, tend to remember the good rather than the bad when someone close to them dies."

"Or maybe that's what he wants to pass on to me, this idealized picture of my mother's childhood. Maybe he didn't understand what I wanted."

"Maybe."

"I'd rather have had the truth, warts and all."

"You should be careful what you wish for. In my experience, the truth doesn't often please people."

She was quiet for a moment. "Yes," she said, "I think that's true."

Farid Hamza lived in Heliopolis. His house was light, open, and airy, as if he had tried to capture the best desert days and bring them indoors. The simple wood furnishings were almost monastically austere, the walls were plain white, no touch of ornament anywhere.

It was midmorning, not really mealtime, but after a snack of nuts and dates Farid brought out *shak-shouka,* serving it on a weathered table in the house's little shaded courtyard. It was a simple dish, something you could buy in streetside stands: chopped lamb in a tomato sauce cooked with an egg on top. Warm pita bread to accompany it.

"This is delicious!" said Gaby.

"You like it?"

"I'm going to steal your cook."

The old soldier actually blushed. "I made it myself. The bread as well."

"A man of infinite talents," said Gaby, enjoying this glimpse of Farid's feminine side.

He smiled, pleased, and then said, "My wife was very ill for many years. She could do nothing. We had servants, but sometimes I wanted to do something just for her. So I tormented the cook, following her around the kitchen, getting her to show me a few things. And I learned, at least a little. I still enjoy it."

"It shows," said Gaby. She let the subject rest for a moment, then said, "Was my mother a good cook?"

"After her mother was killed, Karima cooked all the meals, everything. From the time she was quite young." He smiled. "Yes, she was a very good cook, but sometimes, if her mind was preoccupied with other things—or if she started singing some new or difficult melody—the food would be forgotten. Whatever should be tender came out tough, and whatever should have texture came out mush. Dishes that should be cool grew warm, and those that should be hot grew cold." He laughed. "This happened more than once in the years I knew her."

Gaby laughed with him. Then: "What did she like? Besides singing."

"That's easy. Your mother loved her family above all. And she always honored her parents. The first thing she did when she became financially successful was to buy her father a comfortable home near the sea. And she even persuaded Henry Pasha to sell her his Packard, so that Mustafa could continue to drive the old car that he loved. And after his stroke—well, this you know—she brought him home with her and took very good care of him."

"Uncle Omar told me how generous she was."

Hamza's face clouded. "Omar knew her generosity very well," he muttered.

"You don't like my uncle very much."

The general thought it over. "'Like.' It's not that he's unlikable. He has a charming side. But there's nothing behind it. Whatever Karima did for him—and she did very much—it was like pouring water into a sieve. I don't know if she told you this, but after Munir died, she turned his business over to Omar. She believed it would give him the financial security he needed, so that he wouldn't be quite so dependent on her. 'A man needs his pride,' she told me. I agreed. But a man also needs to use the common sense God gives him. Unfortunately, Omar did not. Or perhaps God did not give him any. He bankrupted the business in less than two years—and created financial problems for your mother."

"What kind of problems?"

"Omar's creditors. They came to Karima, saying that she must pay his debts to preserve her family's honor."

"And did she?"

"She would have wiped herself out at that point—she had only just started to make money for herself then—but I stepped in and arranged a settlement of debts that was fair and just. A woman needs a man to handle her affairs, to protect her from being cheated."

Gaby tried not to smile. "I'm very grateful my mother had your friendship."

"As am I."

"But after your wife's death, you and my mother . . ." Hamza's pained expression made her wish she could take the words back.

"A marriage to your Karima would have meant great happiness to me. Great happiness. But you see, it was not meant to be. At first, of course, I was married, and your mother . . . well, she told me at the beginning. She said: 'Hamza, I have known love both as an all-consuming passion and as a dutiful devotion. Both ended in terrible grief. I cannot endure any of it again.'" He smiled ruefully. "At such times she could talk like one of her songs. I told her then that I would always respect her wishes. More than once I prayed to God that she would change her mind. And who knows? Perhaps with time she did—a little. But by then we were older, we were comfortable with the great friendship we had. The great love. Perhaps we both were afraid. Afraid that . . . that any major change might destroy it."

"I know you miss her terribly," said Gaby. "Tell me: is it any easier with time?"

"Easier? No. Different. Not easier."

"I hate to ask this, but I have to. In the years since my mother's death, have you had second thoughts about the . . . circumstances? Any suspicions?"

"Suspicions?" She saw that he was not thinking of the question, but of how to give her the answer he had long ago reached. "The circumstances, of course, I wondered about. I questioned. As you know, I have resources. I investigated. The men in Damascus—perhaps they were not the best, but they were not fools, and the evidence, as much as I still hate to admit it, was clear."

"An overdose of drugs, Hamza?"

He sighed. "Gaby, as long as I knew your mother, night was hard for her. Sleep was something she had to work for, fight for. So I was not surprised that they found pills. The alcohol . . . well, that did surprise me, but . . ."

"So you don't think . . ."

"No. I understand how you feel. But I have reconciled myself to what I believe to be the truth, however hard it might be."

One last try: "Was there ever anything you knew—anything you heard—about her and the Israelis?"

His face darkened. "In those days there were many stupid things said about Egyptians and Israelis. I wouldn't be surprised if there were fools who said such things about her. But not to me. Do you know," he added thoughtfully, "I have fought the Israelis in four wars, and I still don't hate them."

"But if . . ."

He put his hand on hers. "My dear Nadia, please don't torture yourself. Where you are going I have already been. The truth hurts, but it can never make us love her less."

"No."

"Can it?"

"No."

When she was leaving, Hamza stopped her. "I almost forgot. This story you're writing about your mother. I've made a list of people you should talk with." He opened a desk and brought it out. "Spyros Pappas, her agent—you know him—he will cry, he always cries. These, they are singers, musicians. These are neighbors, friends. And these . . . these are soldiers."

She went to see them all. Each of the people she interviewed gave her something: a shared moment with Karima, an anecdote, even a new insight into her mother's life.

Spyros did cry, as predicted. He cursed his many weaknesses and berated himself for having gone out "for a bit of fun" the night of Karima's death. "If I had been nearby, if I had invited her for a soothing cup of tea after the concert instead of thinking only of my own pleasures, perhaps she would have been able to sleep better. Perhaps there would have been no need for sedatives. I was a bad friend to her that day, my dear Nadia, a bad friend . . ." In the end, Gaby had to comfort Spyros to staunch the flow of tears. Self-recrimination then segued into adoration, as the Greek began to detail how brilliant a performer Karima had been and how good and loyal she had been to him. "Other managers would have killed to represent her," he said sadly. "But she would not leave. She said I had been there at the beginning of her career and I would be with her at the end." A fresh new wave of sobs threatened, and Gaby took her leave.

"It's strange," she reflected, when she and Sean were alone. "I know my mother had some problems with Spyros. Hamza told us as much. For one thing, he was stealing from her until Hamza put the fear of God into him. But now he's acting like they had a perfect relationship. Just the way my uncle did. Is *everyone* I talk to going to rewrite history, do you think?"

"I don't know, love. All we can do is keep asking questions."

And they did. The soldiers told of Karima's bravery, of her tenderness and kindness to men who sorely needed a human touch. Karima's former neighbors told stories of her generosity when they were in need. A long night sitting up with a young woman, recently bereaved. An offer of help, of money. Personal errands done for an elderly man who had no family. And so on. It was the same with Karima's musicians, who seemed to adore her without reservations. Like Spyros, many expressed regret that they had not somehow intervened during Karima's last night on earth.

But no one could tell her anything new about Karima's death.

Months later, in Paris, Gaby turned from her notes with tears of frustration in her eyes. "I can't bear it, Sean . . . that her story ends with an overdose in a hotel room. It's just so . . . brutal. That's not the story I want to tell our children. And it's not how I want my mother to be remembered! There has to be more. But I just don't know where to look."

Sean took her in his arms. "We'll find it, don't worry." He couldn't tell her that he believed Farid Hamza was right, that the Damascus police had already discovered as much as there would ever be. "We'll keep our eyes open," he said. "You never know when something will break. When someone will break. You just never know."

2

Storm

On 1 August 1990 Iraq invaded its neighbor Kuwait. It was over very quickly. Kuwait—tiny, extremely rich, and long accustomed to being protected by others—put up little or no resistance.

Within days American forces were pouring into Saudi Arabia in preparation for a massive counterstrike. Perhaps the reaction surprised Saddam Hussein, who had received assurances that America had no interest in Iraq's relations with its Arab neighbors. Or perhaps he had simply miscalculated. Certainly nothing was clear that August. The pieces were still being placed on the chessboard. Who would win—or whether there would be a game at all—was anyone's guess.

Sean checked into the Nile Hilton on August 15th. The Kuwait action had ended before he could even book a flight, but he had taken the Paris-to-Riyadh Concorde on the chance that Saddam might try to extend his invasion to Saudi. It soon became obvious that this would not happen.

Sean was in Saudi when the first Americans arrived. Many of the officers had been young infantry or artillery lieutenants in Vietnam. Now they were colonels and generals, middle-aged as he himself was. From them he learned that months of logistical buildup would precede any serious action. Few things made for more boring photographs than military supply. Nor did he want to go to Kuwait. The war there was over—for the moment at least. Besides, he had no particular liking for the place. He was still Irish enough to regard it as a puppet sultanate created by the Brits for their usual reasons. As far as he could tell, Saddam had as legitimate a historical claim to it as anyone. He did not, of course, voice this opinion in Saudi.

All right, what were the options? Well, there was Baghdad. But what was the point? The war was on hold there, too. Tel Aviv? At least the Israelis would have some interesting insights into the situation. But you couldn't photograph insights.

In the end Sean decided to hell with it, he was going home. But as long as he was in the neighborhood, why not spend a few days in Egypt and see what he could find out about Gaby's mother. It was crazy—a whim, less than the ghost of a chance, but why not?

At the Hilton he placed his photo gear in the hotel safe. He traveled light: three Nikon bodies, a half-dozen lenses, a hundred rolls of film in an X-ray-shielded bag, a couple of small strobe units with spare batteries. Two of the lenses were zooms—a 35–70mm and an 85–200mm—and he used them almost exclusively. They weren't as sharp as the fixed-lengths but far more versatile. On a battlefield you weren't doing art photography anyway.

His room had a Nile view overlooking the Gezira, with the park-like oasis of the Sporting Club. He luxuriated in the air-conditioning. August in Cairo. There was a time when he would have gone native—found a little two-bit hotel or a local who would offer hospitality—but he no longer worked that way. There was plenty of hardship at the front; no need to start early. He was getting old, he told himself. He had seen more than fifty wars.

He showered, put on his tropical-weight suit, and went downstairs to the hotel bar. In his experience, the bar of the Hilton in any foreign capital was a good place to start looking into dirty little secrets.

He was pleased to see that they stocked Old Bushmill's Special. Made in County Antrim. He ordered a double, no ice, and proceeded to, as they said in show business, work the room.

The first night he chatted with a dozen likely-looking middle-aged strangers who, unfortunately, all turned out to be engineers, sales reps, and other relatively normal types. An attractive woman in her late thirties who had something to do with banking told him that she liked the travel of her job but often found it lonely. In the old days . . . but he no longer worked that way, either.

By the time he called it a night he had accomplished little except to disappoint the banker and build a slightly fuzzy head for the following morning.

The second night Stuart Bassinger walked in.

Bassinger had been a spook in Vietnam. He'd had a cover, of course, something to do with the Civil Operations and Rural Development Support program—but he was a spook nonetheless. Sean had barely known him and had not much liked him. Which didn't matter. What mattered was that one fine day in the boonies Sean had pulled Stu Bassinger from a burning helicopter that some lucky VC had hit with a rocket-propelled grenade, on a landing zone that was not supposed to be hot but that had very quickly become very hot indeed. Stu owed him.

"Hiya, Stu."

"McCourt? McCourt, you son of a bitch! What the hell brings you here?"

"R and R. Been in the war zone, my lad."

Over a drink Sean described his sojourn in Riyadh. He didn't bother to ask what Stu was doing in this part of the world. It would only have meant listening to a long, elaborate cover story. Once a spook, always a spook.

Over a second drink the reminiscences came out—the bars on Tu Do Street, the taste of "33" beer, the incredible screw-ups and scams.

On the third round Sean got to the point. Any minute Bassinger would be showing pictures of his wife and kids.

"You know, Stu, the fact is I'm not just here for the pleasant summer breezes. There's this private situation I'm looking into. A death."

Bassinger turned instantly, professionally wary.

He relaxed just as quickly when Sean told him that the death was that of Karima Ahmad.

"The singer? Are you serious, McCourt?"

"I know it sounds crazy."

"Christ, why not check out the Elvis thing while you're at it."

Sean grinned sheepishly. "I know it sounds crazy, but as I said, there are private reasons. I'm really hoping to find someone who knows more than what was in the local papers."

Stu went spookish again. "Well, good luck, buddy. Wish I could help. But hey, I'm just a troubleshooter for Intercontinental Insurance. A glorified claims adjuster. It's why I'm here. We're exposed all to hell on some Kuwaiti oil wells."

Right, thought Sean. "I wasn't meaning you, Stu. But now that you mention it, in your business you must have some local contacts." He looked Bassinger in the eye. "Maybe an old Egypt hand or two."

Stu said nothing. He was obviously beginning to get the message now. Sean decided to make it loud and clear. "Someone who's been out here a while, knows the ropes. I'd take it as a great personal favor if you could put me onto someone like that."

Bassinger's eyes were distant. Sean knew what they were seeing. Some favors had to be repaid.

The sigh was a surrender. "Yeah, OK, McCourt. There's this guy, an old geezer, been here forever. American. Retired businessman. Don't remember what line of work he was in."

Right. Sean waited.

"You want," said Stu, "I could give him a call, set up a meeting. Hell, you wouldn't have to go far. He must be in here, the Hilton, two, three times a week."

Sean nodded. "That's great. I really appreciate it, Stu. What's his name?"

Stu gave him a look. "I think I'll let him tell you that."

"You McCourt?" The old man extended a deeply tanned hand. "Jake Farallon. Let's grab a table."

He was in his seventies. Plaid pants, Lacoste shirt. Except for a gray silk sports coat, he looked as if he should be golfing at some Florida retirement community. Sean wondered why he wasn't.

A waiter arrived. "The usual," said Farallon. "And whatever this gentleman wants."

"What's the usual?" asked Sean.

"Iced mint tea with a little firepower added."

"Make it two," Sean said to the waiter.

"Yes, sir." The man left.

Sean and Jake studied each other for a moment.

"I don't hear from our mutual acquaintance very often," said Jake. "He must not think your problem is very important, handing it off to me. I think he figures I'm some kind of dinosaur. Hell, maybe he's right."

"He said you know the territory better than anybody." It rarely hurt to embellish things in the direction of flattery.

Jake shrugged and glanced around the bar. The patrons were mainly Americans, a few young but most older. All exhibited the trappings of corporate success.

"I could be in Boca or Lauderdale, I guess," Jake said as if responding to Sean's earlier thought. "But when I go down there, visit some of my retired buddies, all they talk about is golf and who died. That, and how the world has gone to hell since the old days. To me, it's like a poker game. You fold your cards, sit out the hand, it's like being in limbo. You want to stay with the action. Here, though, interesting things happen. Sure I'm retired, semiretired—bits of business here and there I won't bore you with—but people still come to me with interesting questions. You, for example."

Jake broke off as the drinks arrived. He raised his glass. "Slawn-cha."

It was a moderately accurate pronunciation of the traditional Irish toast. "*Sláinte*," Sean replied. He sipped the drink. It was like a mint julep with a Middle Eastern twist. Not bad.

"Anyway," Jake took up where he had left off, "I never had a family and I never liked golf. And I guess I've lived here more than anywhere else. So here I am."

He leaned forward. "So tell me what it is that you want to know about the Nightingale."

Sean remembered that this had been Karima's nickname. "According to all the stories, she died of an accidental or suicidal overdose. I want to know if that's true or not. And if it isn't, I want to know who killed her. And why."

"You don't want much, do you?" For the first time, Farallon gave a hint of a smile. "Look, I know you must have done something big for our acquaintance, but just so you don't think I'm a careless kind of fellow, after I talked with our friend I got on the horn, shot the breeze with a few old contacts. They tell me you're very close, no offense, with Gabrielle Misry, and of course I know how she fits into this."

Sean was both impressed and a little angry that someone in Cairo could find this out with a few phone calls.

"So I figure you've probably got a legitimate interest here. Otherwise we wouldn't be having this conversation."

Sean nodded.

"On the other hand, you might be working some kind of game." The old man's eyes went surprisingly hard and cold. "I have to tell you that wouldn't be a good idea. Not a good idea at all."

"Gaby—Gabrielle—wants to know how her mother died. She thinks something's wrong with the official story. I want to know because she wants to know. That's the whole of it."

Farallon held his gaze for a moment, then nodded. "OK. We'll proceed on that basis. I've already made a few inquiries. I'm waiting for answers. Meanwhile I'll make another call or two. Why don't we meet here same time day after tomorrow?"

Sean hardly knew what to say. "I feel as though I'm putting you to a lot of trouble, Mr. Farallon."

"Jake. No trouble. If I'd been in the country at the time, I could probably tell you what you want to know right here and now. But as it happens, I was elsewhere." Farallon signaled the waiter. "One more thing," he said. "If this comes up any way but kosher, you don't know me from Adam."

Two days later they sat across the same table.

"It's one of those good news, bad news deals," said Jake.

"In what way?"

"Well, part of the good news, you wanna call it that, is that you may be right. Something feels fishy about this whole thing. The bad news is there's no handle on it. All I could get from my contacts in . . . back in the States was that for about half a minute some people were working with information that our gal might be hooked up with the Israelis. Turned out to be crap, but those were crazy times. If somebody believed it, it could have got her zinged all right."

"You said part of the good news. What's the other part?"

"Maybe nothing. I know this guy in Alex. An older guy. Sometimes I think he's getting senile. I spoke with him and he lets on that he might know something about this business. Only trouble is, he won't talk about it over the phone. This is an old-time Russki who goes back to Stalin. You know how they are."

Sean didn't know how they were, but he could guess. "You think it might be something?"

"Who knows? Like I said, this guy is getting way, way up there."

Coming from Jake, that was quite a statement. "So what should we do?" asked Sean.

"You feel like a train ride?"

Alexei Tartakov was certainly very old, but, like many old men from Soviet Georgia, he looked as if he could still mount a horse and come at you with a saber if the mood struck him. He lived in a pleasant little hillside house with a distant view of the sea. From time to time a very pretty young woman, Egyptian to all appearances, came in to check on his needs and those of his guests. Sean understood just enough Arabic to know that she called the old man "grandfather."

Alexei insisted on beginning the meeting with a large glass of vodka, downed Russian-style in a single gulp. "Just one for me these days," he apologized. Sean was glad to hear it; one like that was more than enough for him. To his surprise the two old men then set up a chessboard and began a game. It looked as if it was going to be a long afternoon. But by the fifteenth move Alexei was obviously winning and began to intersperse his play with comments to Sean.

"Junior here—" meaning Jake—"tells me you are investigating the death of the singer."

"Trying to learn what happened, yes."

Alexei slid a bishop slowly across the board. "Like Junior, I am no longer active. Retired, as you say. From the diplomatic corps."

At least, thought Sean with amusement, the old commie didn't claim to be yet another retired "businessman."

Jake tentatively moved a knight.

"Ah, you think this will save you," said Alexei and inched a pawn forward. To Sean: "What I have for you may be nothing. But who knows what information will be useful? Or when." He contemplated the board for a moment. "In my diplomatic duties I had many dealings with foreign citizens. For many reasons. I too heard a rumor about the singer and the Israelis. It was nothing, nonsense. She was just a singer. Check."

Sean glanced at the board. Jake was in deep trouble.

"About two years after her death, a man, a Syrian, came to my attention. This was on a totally different matter. I had a long conversation with him. Perhaps he became confused. He did not want to discuss the matter that interested me. He told me something else. Perhaps he thought it would please me. He said that he killed the singer Karima. He was proud of this, you see. He said she was an Israeli agent. He said he knew this as a fact."

"Did you believe him?" If Sean was understanding the Russian correctly, the Syrian might have confessed to anything.

"I believe he killed her. I believe he thought she was an Israeli asset—isn't that the word, Junior, that the American CIA uses? But she wasn't."

It made no sense. "Did he say how he killed her?"

"She was drugged, something undetectable that left her semiconscious, then fed pills and alcohol so that they would be in her system. For good measure she was given an injection—somewhere that didn't show—of the same narcotics. Someone on the hotel staff was part of this."

"Can you give me names?"

"Yes. I will do that. But I don't think you will find these people. I think they have gone away. Checkmate in three moves or give up the queen."

Jake surveyed the position for a long moment, then grudgingly tipped his king.

"You're saying it's a dead end?" Sean asked the Russian.

"He's not saying that at all," said Farallon. "You're missing a big question."

"What?"

"Why this fellow believed she was with the Israelis when she wasn't."

Alexei nodded.

"All right," said Sean. "Why did he?"

"He said that the leader of his group, the man who paid him for the job, told him. He said at first he didn't believe it—he liked the singer's music, you know. But he said that the man swore that he got his information from the singer's own brother."

"Omar?"

"If that is her brother."

Both old men were watching Sean, gauging his reaction.

"That's all?" he said.

"All I know," said Alexei. "As I said, I was concerned with another matter. This was unimportant to me."

"I see." Sean got to his feet. "I thank you both. I owe you both. But right now I need to catch a plane."

"Unbelievable," said Gaby, "this is really unbelievable." She, Tarik, and Sean sat huddled in the apartment like conspirators.

"It's far-fetched, true enough," Sean admitted. In Paris he was finding the stories of two old men in Egypt less compelling.

"I don't mean I don't believe it," said Gaby. "That's the horrible thing: I *do* believe it. Just something about him. Omar." She shuddered. "God, if he did it . . ."

"Her money might have been a motive, surely," said Sean. "But I thought Omar was well fixed on his own. And even if he weren't . . ."

"Let's say he did it," said Gaby grimly. "Let's assume he did it, all right? What can we *do*?"

"I don't know. What we have amounts to nothing. No court on earth would touch it."

"I could report it. As a news story, I mean."

"No you couldn't. Even if anyone would run it, you'd be laughed out of the business."

"We can tell Farid Hamza."

Sean nodded. "Yes. I'd thought of that. I think we should. But unless he can come up with something more, I don't know what even he can do."

"He can make life damned unpleasant for Omar Ismail!"

"There is certainly that."

Tarik had hardly spoken since Sean brought the news. Now he broke his silence. "There *is* one thing we can do. Forgive me, Gaby dear, it's not pleasant. But we can go to Egypt and get an order to exhume Karima's body. Even now a proper autopsy might very well find something."

"Oh, God, Papa, I don't know." She looked at Sean, then back at Tarik. "All right. Yes. Yes, of course."

The three conspirators settled in to make their plans.

———

"Go over it once more," said Omar.

"Very well," said the lawyer patiently. "There are two ways to defeat the petition. The first is to demonstrate that the woman Gabrielle Misry has no standing. And that appears to be true. According to you, and according to everything else I can gather, she cannot prove that she is your late sister's child, or related to her in any way whatsoever. There is only anecdotal evidence."

"I still like that option," said Omar. "Humiliate her as she's trying to humiliate me."

"But as I explained, that would be like inviting the press to a feast. They wouldn't leave the table till they were stuffed to the throat."

Omar knew that this was true.

"And of course, you yourself have made statements indicating that you regarded her as your niece. You brought her into your home, entertained her with many other guests present . . ."

"If I had known then . . ." Omar left the sentence unfinished.

"The other way is simpler," said the lawyer. "You refuse to permit an exhumation on religious grounds. In the absence of even the slightest evidence of a crime, no one can fault you, not even the press. Most people would admire your principles."

Omar gritted his teeth but had to admit that the man was right. "All right. Let's do it your way. Now what about the other problem?"

"What problem?"

"I told you. I think I'm being watched, followed. My phone might even be tapped. What can you do about it?"

The lawyer, a small, bespectacled man, looked uncomfortable. "Yes. You mentioned this. But you said you had no idea who might be doing it. Or why. And in fact you have no proof that anyone *is* doing it."

To hell with it, thought Omar. Maybe he *was* just imagining things. God knows he was under enough strain. "Just get rid of this petition," he growled. "Then we'll see about the other matter."

Gaby couldn't believe that it had ended so quickly.

The courtroom looked like a classroom, the judge a schoolmaster. Having seen videos of the trials of the Sadat assassins, Gaby had expected an imposing chamber with cages for the accused. The lawyer Tarik had hired pointed out that this was not a criminal proceeding.

The man had been pessimistic from the first—religious considerations carried great weight in these matters—and he turned out to be right.

There were brief statements from both attorneys, a few questions to Gaby, Tarik, and Omar. Then the magistrate dismissed the suit. The lawyer announced his intention to file an appeal, and the magistrate curtly acknowledged his statement. That was all.

Omar, who had been only a few feet away during the proceeding, stood and turned to Gaby with a sympathetic expression. "I'm very sorry to have had to oppose you in this, Nadia. I understand your concerns, although I know they are unfounded. But you must understand my feelings, too. You've been in the West a long time. Here . . . your mother . . . I simply couldn't allow it."

Gaby regarded him coldly. "I know your feelings for my mother. It's too bad she was so close to the Jews."

Omar was startled. Exactly *what* was the girl saying? Then he composed himself and looked to Tarik as if expecting a more reasonable attitude. "This is all a misunderstanding. Some day, *inshallah,* we will look back on it together and wonder how it happened."

Tarik said nothing, but as Omar turned to go, Gaby stopped him. "Do you really think that this is over?" she asked him. "That you can just walk away? I'm a reporter, Uncle. My job is finding out things. It's like a war, you know. It can take a long time. You can lose a lot of battles and still win in the end."

For just a moment there was a glint of anger in his eyes. Then his face showed sadness. "I'm truly sorry you feel this way, niece. I pray that one day you will accept your mother's death as it was—a tragedy, but one for which only she was to blame. God's peace be with you."

Neither Gaby nor Tarik replied.

————

Farid Hamza felt weary and detached. It was a pleasure, as always, to see Nadia—Gaby—again. But at this moment, filled as she was with fire and passion, she reminded him so much of Karima—and that was painful. Her obsession with discovering precisely how her mother died was also painful. At the time he had used every resource at his command and had found no reason to doubt the officials in Damascus. To go over it again returned him to those tortured weeks and months when the wound was fresh.

Yet here were Gaby and Tarik and McCourt, all expecting him to work a miracle, come up with a revelation.

"It's as I told you," he said. "Since your call, I've done everything I could think of—reviewed the records, my notes, even talked to my sources again. There's nothing—nothing new, and nothing in the old material."

"And nothing on Omar?" That was McCourt.

"Nothing." Farid debated whether to tell the whole truth, decided that there was no reason not to. "I didn't mention this before, but since your call I've had him under surveillance. Not officially—there are no grounds for that. Privately."

"And?"

"The man has some unappealing habits. But this, too, is nothing new."

"But if he told someone that my mother was an Israeli spy . . ."

Farid sighed. She wanted so badly to drive out the demons.

"He might well have said it. I'm prepared to believe he did. It would be like him—despicable. But beyond that, what? Other evil things were said about your mother—yes, even about one so greatly admired. It happens to all who are famous. Can we say that someone murdered her because of this?"

Gaby looked stubborn, Tarik thoughtful, McCourt merely attentive.

"Nadia, my child, please understand that if I had a shred of evidence that someone had harmed your mother, I would track him to the ends of the earth. But perhaps I am too close to this. I remember your mother telling me that sleep was not always easy for her. So how can I say with certainty that she never took pills?"

Gaby relented. "I'm not blaming you for anything, General Hamza. I know how you cared for her. It's just . . . we hoped to get proof from an autopsy. Now we've been blocked, and the chances don't look good. And I don't know what else to do."

"I'll do what I can. But my advice to you is to go home. There's no telling what will happen with this Iraq business. Travel might become difficult."

"Well, I can't do that," she said. "As I've told Sean and Papa, CNN wants me here until something breaks. Then, if there's fighting, they want me to cover that. For once Sean and I will be on the same story."

She smiled, saying this, but McCourt looked less enthusiastic. Like me, thought Farid, he has seen too much war.

"So you're stuck with me for a while," Gaby went on. "And as long as I'm here, I'm going to try to nail my dear uncle."

Farid could not help admiring her spirit, misguided though it might be. He told her what he would have told her mother: "As long as you are here, I am here for you."

When they had left him, he took a photo from his desk drawer. Karima a year or two after the Pyramids concert. He looked at it for a long time. "Your daughter loves you," he told the image. "As do I, my heart. As do I."

Omar paced in his library. When he had bought the house in Zamalek, a lovely neighborhood on the northern end of the Gezira, he had insisted on converting one large room into a library, complete with more than a thousand books. He paid others to select and purchase the books. He read newspapers closely—there was useful information to be gleaned from them—but he rarely opened any of the volumes on which he had spent so much. Why read about life when life was all around you? He had built the library for only one reason: it was the proper thing for a wealthy and influential man to have. Henry Austen had a library.

Wealth and influence. He had worked a lifetime. And now it was all in danger of unraveling. All because of that little bastard of Karima's. Why had she not died in that fire? Why did Allah have to torment him with her presence? And why could she not have accepted the story of the Syrian authorities, as everyone else had done?

The possibility of an autopsy had been worrisome. Who knew what those cretins might have done, what traces they might have left to be found? Well, that possibility still existed, but it seemed remote now. What truly worried Omar was the threat the little bastard had made in the courtroom. A reporter. A news story. Even without evidence, she could rain disgrace down on him with a few words. Make his very name a synonym for evil. She might do it at any moment.

What to do? On top of everything, money was becoming a problem again. A few bad investments—they had looked so promising, foolproof, really—and too much given to that damn charity. It wasn't the gambling, he hardly gambled at all, purely an occasional entertainment.

But money was only money. There was always more to be made. The real danger was Nadia. Gabrielle. His bastard niece. A few words from her—and then all the others, even his so-called friends, would be on him like wolves. Like lions. Especially the young ones. He had seen signs of it already. They were always waiting to bring down a man of his age, a man in power. To take his place. Like wolves. Like lions.

What in God's name to do?

It had to be providence. Just at the moment when he called upon God, a newspaper on the reading table caught his eye. A headline. *American Abducted in Lebanon, Terrorists Suspected.*

Of course. That was the answer. Abductions happened every day, or nearly so. Sometimes for political reasons, sometimes for ransom, sometimes for both.

What if his niece were to be abducted? Held for a large ransom? And then, when the money was paid, killed anyway?

It was a brilliant idea.

He couldn't paint her as a spy. That would not work a second time. No. He needed criminals. Mercenaries. It would cost money, but the ransom would more than cover the expense. Kill two birds with one stone.

Truly a brilliant idea.

He could set it in motion this very night. Renew some old friendships. He would do it.

And those shadowy figures that were following him? What about them? Not a problem. If necessary, he could vanish anytime in a hundred places in downtown Cairo. And he would avoid saying anything incriminating on the telephone.

There was a thrill to it, like the last time. Stronger, even.

Victory went to those who dared, Omar told himself. And he had always dared.

In the early morning the walk down the Nile Corniche from the Hilton to Television Tower was a pleasant one, and long enough to make good exercise. If there was time, Gaby wandered out onto the bridge, Kubri el Tahrir, and watched the timeless river. This morning she was in a hurry. Sean had bumped around in the dark preparing to go out and photograph the Pyramids at sunrise—something he claimed he had always wanted to do. Curling cozily in bed again, she had overslept.

Just above the bridge she passed Shepheard's Hotel. It wasn't the original Shepheard's, of course. That had been in another part of the city. It no longer existed. This was merely a reconstruction. A revival. Still, the name gave her an odd little quiver of—what? Fear? Memory? Foolish to let it affect her that way.

It was in front of Shepheard's that they took her. A street vendor approached with flowers. She smiled but waved him off. "No, lady, not to buy," he said. "A gift of this gentleman."

A short, smiling man with a close-cropped beard came toward her with more flowers. Not until both men were almost touching her did she see the weapons.

"Give you a lift?" said the second man in English. "Silence, please. Or we will kill you."

There was a car, a typical Cairene vehicle, a fifteen-year-old Ford. She was in it, pushed down on the floor, covered with a filthy blanket. Someone rested his feet on her thighs. Someone held a pistol barrel against her head through the blanket.

Merde. She had always wondered how Americans and Europeans allowed themselves to be kidnapped so easily in the Middle East. And here she was.

She tried to discern where they were going by street sounds, by the feeling of turns right and left. It was no good. Maybe in Paris, or even New York. Not in Cairo. Within two minutes she was totally disoriented.

Time. She could at least count that. A million and one made one second. A million and two. A million and three.

After some forty minutes the car stopped. The blanket was yanked away and she was lifted upright—long enough to glimpse a cotton field before a blindfold blacked it out. She was pulled quickly from the car and placed in the trunk.

The car started again. The trunk was fiercely hot. She feared that she might suffocate. She tried to keep time but lost count. Perhaps two hours passed before the car stopped.

When they took her from the trunk she smelled the ocean. Not close enough to hear, but there was salt in the air.

She was taken through a doorway, then another, then thrust onto a floor. Someone tied her hands behind her. She could feel the texture of the wall. Cinder block, she thought.

"One word and you die," said the voice that she recognized as that of the second man.

By now they would have missed her at the studio. They would try to reach her at the Hilton. Sean would be back. He would get the message. Papa—no, Papa had returned to Paris. Sean. Would there be a ransom demand? Or was it a terrorist action aimed at gaining not money but publicity?

Sean would contact the police. No he wouldn't. He would go to Farid Hamza. That was better.

They were looking for her right now, she told herself. Her job was to stay alive until they found her.

She sensed that the house she was in was quite small. She could hear the two men in the next room. They spoke a dialect she could barely decipher.

"Not bad," said the flower vendor.

"The job?" asked the second man.

"Yeah, the job. The woman too."

"Forget that till I tell you. Forty-eight hours, we can do whatever we want. Until, then, it's a job."

Obviously they didn't know that she spoke Arabic. Or maybe— much more frightening—they did.

She leaned against the cinder-block wall and waited.

The call came at nine o'clock that night.

Sean answered on the second ring.

The voice said, "This is the Islamic Jihad. Pass this message to the woman's father. One million American dollars in bills of one hundred and fifty. Thirty-six hours, no more. No contact with the police." Sean looked around. With him in the room at the Hilton were an inspector and a lieutenant of the Egyptian national police, two technicians from the Cairo police department, the director of Cairo's CNN bureau, and Farid Hamza. "Further instructions will follow. Obey them exactly if you wish to see the woman again."

There was an indefinable sound, then Gaby saying, "Here. I can't *see* it." Then she recited what sounded like a newspaper headline about Saddam Hussein. Then the connection was broken.

The inspector looked at the technicians. "Not enough," one said.

The other technician rewound and played the tape. He said something in Arabic. The first man translated. "He wasn't calling from where she is. That click? The play button on a tape recorder of some kind. A cheap one, not very good. You can hear that she's on tape."

"She sounds as if she is reading," said the lieutenant.

The CNN man, Rick Heflin, nodded. "It's Saddam's quote of the day. Came in about two o'clock this afternoon, we had it on the air a few minutes later."

"And someone wrote it for her to read. To show us she was—" the lieutenant glanced at Sean—"that she was unharmed as of this afternoon."

"The Jihad," said the inspector. He reminded Sean of the actor F. Murray Abraham. His name was in fact Ibrahim. "Always the Jihad."

The lieutenant nodded jadedly.

"You don't think it's them?" Sean asked Ibrahim.

"Who knows? If word were to get out—which will *not* happen," the inspector emphasized to everyone in the room, "there would be many messages, thirty, forty, all saying they did it. Once we even had one from America. Your Ku Klux Klan, I believe it's called."

Something was gnawing at Sean's subconscious, trying to get to the surface. "Play the tape again," he said. A moment later: "There. Right there. The first thing she says—'I can't see it.' Her eyesight is twenty-twenty. Maybe it's nothing, but if someone were holding a piece of paper too far away, I think she'd say 'I can't read it.'"

Everyone looked at him blankly.

"Run it again," said Sean. "There. The way she stresses *see*."

"Hell yes," said Rick Heflin suddenly. "The *sea*! She's near the sea."

"Ah," said Ibrahim. "Forgive me. It's not so easy in another language. You think this is possible?"

Sean realized that if he were wrong, he might be putting Gaby in even greater danger. "I think that's it," he said. "I'm sure of it."

"It's something," said the lieutenant. "We can checkpoint the coast roads."

"Do it," the inspector told him. "Make it look routine." The lieutenant went to one of the extra phones that the technicians had installed.

"What else?" Sean asked Ibrahim.

"Call her father. You say he's in Paris?"

"Yes. I have to tell you, he's going to want to pay them. So do I."

The inspector merely nodded.

Sean made the call. When he finished, he realized that it was one of the hardest things he had ever done.

"He'll be on the first flight," he told the inspector. "He's calling his banker now. Tonight."

The inspector nodded morosely.

"There are relatives here," said Sean. "You probably know the story. Grandparents. And an uncle. What about them?" He was suddenly aware of Farid Hamza's attention from across the room.

"Why not leave that till her father arrives," said the inspector. "For now, the fewer who know about this the better."

"Right."

A few minutes later, while the inspector was giving instructions about questioning street vendors, pedestrians, any other possible witnesses at the scene—assuming Gaby had been snatched on her way to work—Sean had a quiet word with Hamza.

"Are you thinking what I'm thinking?"

"Perhaps. As much as I dislike thinking it."

"That Omar might be behind this?"

"Last Thursday night, and again two nights later, he eluded the people I have following him and was not seen for hours. It might mean nothing, of course. He might have been gambling, whoring, his usual things."

"Or not," said Sean. "Should we tell the inspector?"

"No. Not yet. Police like these . . . they're not subtle. They'll either drag him in for interrogation or put twenty men on him. In either case, if he has anything to do with this, he'll cut everything off. And that, I fear, would not be very good for Gaby."

Sean nodded. That was his fear too.

The two men, a generation apart, looked at each other. One had lost the mother; the other was in danger of losing the daughter.

"So we let it ride," said Sean. "For now."

"Yes."

Tarik arrived late in the morning. He obviously had not slept. Inspector Ibrahim brought him quickly up to date. There had been no more calls. The investigators in the field had run across a little luck. A street vendor had witnessed the kidnapping. He sold flowers and was unhappy to see another flower vendor, a stranger, on his block. His description of the men and of their car was so general as to be useless—except for one thing: the car had a large rust spot on the trunk. The man remembered it not because rust was unusual, but because it was in the shape of a crescent moon.

"He didn't get the license number?" Sean asked, hoping against hope.

For the first time, the inspector looked amused. "He can't read, Mr. McCourt. He couldn't make change if it weren't for the pictures on the money. I've often thought that's how money came to have pictures on it."

The phone rang. Tarik looked for a moment like a trapped animal, then answered it.

This time the instructions were all about the money. To be placed in a numbered Swiss account. The account would be accessed and the money removed by wire. Twenty-four hours after this was safely done, Gaby would be released. No tricks. No police. Another brief tape of Gaby reading a headline, one from the morning paper. No helpful little aside this time.

For the rest of the day, as policemen came and went, Tarik was often on one of the extra lines with his banker. The million dollars would almost impoverish him. Sean offered to add what he could.

It wasn't much. There were few wealthy war correspondents.

Sean also called Jake Farallon. Maybe the old spy's contacts would be useful once again. But late in the day Jake called to say that he was having no luck.

"My people don't know anything," he reported. "And they say there are cops all over the place anyway. Might as well let them do their job."

"Thanks, Jake."

"I'll keep on it, but I'm not optimistic." Jake paused. "Of course, there are places where the police can't go, and I can't go, and even most of my people can't go."

"Like where?"

"Like where the refugees are. The Palestinians. Places like that."

After he hung up, Sean thought about what Farallon had said. There was someone. A man he hadn't seen in a long time. Sean had heard he was in Cairo. What was his name? Damn, he couldn't remember it for the life of him. For Gaby's life.

"I have to go out," he announced. Tarik looked at him questioningly, the inspector disapprovingly. "There's something I have to do," he told them. "Don't worry, Inspector, it's nothing that will get in your way. But it may take a while."

He took a cab to CNN and found Rick Heflin. "I need the best fax you can get of a photograph. It appeared in the *Times* and about a hundred other papers," he told Heflin. He gave him a description of the shot and the approximate date it had run. "I need it now."

An hour later he had it. He remembered the village, or what was left of it. Remembered the twelve-year-old boy kneeling over the woman's body in the middle of the dusty street. His mother. Remembered the boy's name now.

He took the fax with him.

He had been afraid a thousand times in war, but it was always in places like this that he was most afraid. Once in a housing project in Chicago. A little village in Afghanistan, no soldiers around, when someone had said the wrong thing. And here, a back alley in Cairo, conversation stopping as soon as people saw him. Men moving behind him. Closer. And now one blocking the way. Not even thinking of moving.

There was only one thing to do. Sean told him whom he had come to see. "Give him this." He handed the man the fax.

After an eternity of perhaps ten minutes, the man reappeared with two others. All let Sean see that they were armed. He followed them. There was a door—opened after a coded knock. Dark stairs. Three floors up, a teenager with a Kalashnikov in his hands and hate in his eyes. Another door. It opened.

Sean would not have recognized him. Thin, scarred, nearing thirty.

The man held the fax and glanced from it to Sean. "I remember you. Why have you come here?" He listened in silence while Sean told him.

When he had finished, the scarred man thought it over. He looked at the fax again. "I remember this day. There were some who wanted to kill you, but you said that if people saw what the bombs were doing, the bombings might stop. And they did—at my village. Not at others. Not then. But I remember." He said something in Arabic to the other men and disappeared down the dark stairs.

"Come," said the hard-eyed boy, gesturing with the Kalashnikov toward the door.

"What for?"

"He says give you tea."

The name meant nothing to Inspector Ibrahim, but a Cairo police sergeant in the room looked up sharply when he heard it.

"You know him, Sergeant?" the inspector asked.

"Yes sir." The sergeant used an Arabic word for garbage.

"Then you know what I want. Do it now and don't worry about the finer points. I'll authorize everything."

Two hours later they thought they had what they needed. The

man was a small-time career criminal. He had a little place near Port Sa'id, inherited from his father, a low-level civil servant who must have hoped for better in his son. People knew about it because he sometimes took friends there. It was only a couple of miles from the beach.

"They'll be there," said Ibrahim with more certainty than Sean could muster. "Two, maybe three of them. And her."

"What are you going to do?" asked Tarik.

The inspector looked from him to Sean and back. "Dr. Misry, Mr. McCourt, I don't want to frighten you, but I don't have a good feeling. This fellow is only the tool. Someone else is behind the kidnapping. Whether the boss succeeds in getting the money or not, I think he will have given orders for Gabrielle to be killed. I say we should go in and get her. Stun grenades, an assault team. We can have it set up by first light. I assure you we are professionals. We will take every measure for her safety."

"I . . . I don't know," said Tarik. "It sounds very dangerous."

"Not as dangerous as waiting. Not as dangerous as a hostage situation could become."

Tarik looked at Sean. Sean nodded slowly. "Yes," Tarik said. "Go in and get her."

The inspector turned toward the phone. Sean stopped him. "One thing: I go with them. Otherwise it's no go."

Ibrahim studied him for a moment. "Very well. But stay out of the way. I think you know this without my telling you."

Gaby knew that this was the morning on which she was to die.

She knew it by listening to the men talk to each other. They also talked about what they would do to her just before they killed her. It was clear by now that they had no idea she spoke their language.

She was hungry and dirty. She had been given only water and, the first morning, some bread. There was a bucket in which to relieve herself. By day the room was suffocatingly hot.

There were two possible plans, as far as she could see. The only virtue of either was that it was better than nothing. The first possibility was to fight. It would require very great luck. If, when they came to get her, she were suddenly to shout at them in Arabic and use the bucket as a weapon, she might surprise them enough to be able to get one of their guns.

The other possibility was to try to talk her way out. Again, her Arabic might work for her. Bargain. Her father was wealthy, would make them wealthy too. Threaten. She was a friend of Farid Hamza, who would hunt them down wherever they might try to run.

Better than nothing, but not by much. Which way?

She would have to make up her mind soon. In the crack under the door was a hint of morning light—the men had at least removed the blindfold. She heard one of them stir in the next room.

If she fought, it would be little more than suicide. But under the circumstances that had something to recommend it. On the other hand, if she talked, perhaps she could at least gain time. Somewhere out there people were looking for her. The police. Farid Hamza. Sean.

The thought of Sean was almost too hard to bear. The thought that she might never see him again.

There were grumbles from the other room, the sound of men rising from sleep. One man berated the other, who was supposed to have been on watch.

If only one came in, she would have a better chance for the gun. But then she would be trapped in the room.

The men were eating. Her stomach growled. Amazing that she could be hungry at a time like this. It was as if all her senses were heightened.

They were talking now, loudly. Dirty talk. They were working themselves up, she realized. Working themselves up to rape and kill her.

There was an odd scratching sound on the wall behind her. An animal?

The door rattled, opened. Both men, one behind the other. Both leering at her.

Time to decide.

They moved toward her.

There was a blinding flash and a blast that threw her back against the wall. Terrible pain in her ears. She tried to stand and couldn't. There were men everywhere. One looked like Sean.

She fainted.

"Ruptured eardrums," the doctor said. "Slight concussion. She'll be fine."

They were rolling her onto a gurney and to a waiting ambulance. Sean was holding her hand. "What are you doing here?" she asked weakly.

"Just happened to be in the neighborhood and thought I'd drop by," he said. The joke couldn't hide the concern in his eyes. Or the love.

Another man was there. Egyptian. Pitted face. Looked like that ugly actor. What was his name?

"Those two," said the man. "They're not the Jihad. They're nothing. They've already told us everything they know. My men will be picking up the go-between in Cairo right now."

"What about Omar?" asked Sean.

"A friend of yours has asked for the pleasure of calling on him."

None of it made sense to Gaby. She held Sean's hand and felt the warm sunlight. "It's over," she whispered, "it's finally over."

"What are you talking about, darlin'? The good part is just beginning."

In an hour Omar would contact the banker. If all went well, there would be a series of fund transfers, ending up with a cashier's check by late this afternoon. If something went wrong, he had a plane ticket and an emergency fund in South America. But the wait was nerve-racking.

A servant entered the study. "General Hamza to see you, sir."

Hamza. That was a surprise. On the other hand, they had to send someone to tell him that Gaby was dead, and Hamza was a friend of the family.

The old man stood in the doorway.

"General, what a pleasant surprise! To what do I owe the honor of your visit?"

"I think you know," said Hamza. There was no softness in his voice.

"I assure you I—" Omar saw that there were other men with the general. Men in uniform.

One of them stepped forward. "Omar Ismail, I arrest you for kidnapping and for conspiracy in attempted murder."

There were handcuffs, cruelly tight.

"But this is an outrage," said Omar. "I've done nothing."

Farid Hamza drew close to him. "You have done a great deal more than nothing. Which you will confess. And for which you will pay to the last day of your life. This I promise you."

Later that spring in Alexandria, the house where Gaby's mother had once worked was filled with the perfume of ten thousand flowers. The silver was polished to a high shine, the linen tablecloths gleamed white, the English china sparkled. The servants were turned out in new uniforms and the musicians played a haunting melody; it was called "Nadia's Song."

Upstairs, in the bedroom where her father had grown up, Gaby looked at herself in an old-fashioned mirror, adjusting the delicate cascade of white lace that framed her face.

There was a knock on the door. "Are you ready, Gaby dear?" Catherine Austen called out. "Everyone's waiting."

"Coming," Gaby said, executing a slow pirouette so she could see her white silk gown, front and back. She walked to the open window and looked out, gazing past Catherine's garden, past the bubbling fountain to a modest little house. She let her imagination fly away, as she had done so often these past few days. In her mind's eye she could see a beautiful dark-haired girl hanging laundry, the young man she loved reaching out to help her. How sad that their happiness had been so fleeting, so brief. But their love had given her life, and that, Gaby knew, her mother had never regretted. "I wish you could see me, *Ummi,*" she whispered. "I wish you could know that I really have found my *nasib.*"

She turned back to the mirror for a final look, smoothing out an imaginary wrinkle in her billowing skirt. And now it was time to leave. She had a wedding to go to.